PRAISE FOR *IF I STO*

"I devoured this debut by Colby Wilkens! The author writes with such authority and conviction that I really felt like she had lived in a haunted castle in Scotland, just like the characters. Every sentence felt like it was coming from a place of authenticity, which I loved. In addition, the spooky elements are genuinely spooky, the enemies to lovers genuinely enemies, and it all came together beautifully. I didn't realize I needed a romance book married to cozy horror, but now I'm wondering where this particular mash-up has been all my life. Can't wait to read the next!"

—Jessica Clare, *New York Times* bestselling author

"*If I Stopped Haunting You* skillfully balances creepiness, difficult conversations, and a lot of steam to deliver readers a satisfying debut and a well-earned Happily Ever After."

—Helena Greer, author of *Season of Love* and *For Never & Always*

"*If I Stopped Haunting You* is a complex deep dive into identity, history, and staying true to one's self that pulls no punches. With a toe-curling romance and bone-chilling ghosts lurking around every corner, this effortless blend of romance and horror is not to be missed." —Sonia Hartl, author of *Heartbreak for Hire* and *Rent to Be*

"Brimming with angst, heat, and heart, *If I Stopped Haunting You* is the unputdownable rivals-to-lovers romance I've been craving! Set in a haunted Scottish castle with atmosphere to die for, this is a cozy-season must-read. I fell hard for Penelope and Neil as they traversed their differences toward deeper understanding and love—with lots of steam along the way! Writing with thrilling boldness, sparkling wit, and profound care for queer and Indigenous representation, Colby Wilkens is a highly necessary and breathtakingly talented fresh voice in romance—meet your new auto-buy author."

—Courtney Kae, author of *In the Event of Love* and *In the Case of Heartbreak*

"Masterfully blends the delicious tension of a great rivals-to-lovers romance with the gothic vibes of a creepy haunted-house story. The heat between Penelope and Neil ignites as they untangle their complicated relationship and grow closer together, and the horror elements create some truly memorable moments of forced proximity. *If I Stopped Haunting You* hooked me from the first page, and I didn't want to put it down when it was over!"

—Jenny L. Howe, author of *On the Plus Side* and *The Make-Up Test*

"Wilkens's debut is the perfect mix of enemies to lovers, haunted castle, and steamy spice. Pen and Neil's slow burn is smoldering with the spooky atmosphere."

—Roselle Lim, author of *Natalie Tan's Book of Luck & Fortune* and *Sophie Go's Lonely Hearts Club*

"If you're in the mood for a steamy enemies-to-lovers romance but also a chilling haunted-house horror, GET YOU A BOOK THAT CAN DO BOTH! Colby Wilkens's debut, *If I Stopped Haunting You,* is so inventive and immersive—I couldn't tell if my shoulders were up by my ears because of the creeping dread of whatever was going on in that castle or because of the electric chemistry between Pen and Neil. I blazed through this book in one sitting because I just couldn't wait to find out what would happen next!"

—Alicia Thompson, *USA Today* bestselling author of *With Love, from Cold World*

If I
Stopped
Haunting
You

COLBY WILKENS

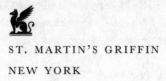

ST. MARTIN'S GRIFFIN

NEW YORK

First published in the United States by St. Martin's Griffin, an imprint of St. Martin's Publishing Group

IF I STOPPED HAUNTING YOU. Copyright © 2024 by Colby Wilkens. All rights reserved. Printed in the United States of America. For information, address St. Martin's Publishing Group, 120 Broadway, New York, NY 10271.

www.stmartins.com

Designed by Omar Chapa

The Library of Congress Cataloging-in-Publication Data is available upon request.

ISBN 978-1-250-29290-2 (trade paperback)
ISBN 978-1-250-29291-9 (ebook)

Our books may be purchased in bulk for promotional, educational, or business use. Please contact your local bookseller or the Macmillan Corporate and Premium Sales Department at 1-800-221-7945, extension 5442, or by email at MacmillanSpecialMarkets@macmillan.com.

First Edition: 2024

10 9 8 7 6 5 4 3 2 1

To Alexander. My love, my best friend, my travel partner, my everything.

Author's Note

If I Stopped Haunting You contains explicit sexual scenes, on-page drinking, mention of marijuana use, talk of death and pregnancy, foul language, mention of racism and the use of a racial slur relating to Indigenous people, and claustrophobic scenes. Please take care while reading.

Dedication from *Fight You* by Daniela Mitchel

To the two weirdos who inspired this book.
Never stop being weird.

Especially you, Stormy.

Prologue

PEN

FOUR MONTHS EARLIER

Pen wondered how drunk she must have been when she accepted this invitation, because it was a disaster in the making. Her sales had never been great, but she couldn't simply revitalize them with a Book Con appearance and some plastered-on smiles, not when *he* was in the room with her.

She sweated through the polyester of her blazer as she fiddled with the warped corner of an annotated copy of her book. The edges had since yellowed, and the flags denoting her favorite passages poked out from between pages that were bent and ripped. She'd thought it would make a nice giveaway, but the audience didn't even care that she was there.

All they cared about was *him*. She peered nervously down the table at the other participants in the Indigenous Fiction panel, at their smiling faces and stacks of books. Unlike her, the other woman on the panel wore beaded earrings that dangled and tangled in stray strands of her hair, and many of the men had long, thinning hair twisted back into slim braids. The only other author who stood out was Neil Storm.

While Storm's dark curls barely reached his ears, Pen's hair was long and thick, pulled into a messy bun at the back of her head. She wasn't proudly representing her heritage with beads or braids. She couldn't even slip out a Cherokee tribal identification card to prove her Nativeness. Pen didn't belong among them. But Storm? Storm belonged everywhere he went, and he knew it.

"Neil, this question is for you."

He leaned forward on his elbows, smiling. "Of course."

Pen had once fallen for that smile, for a grin that felt like it was just for her. But she knew better now.

"You've found your groove, so to speak," the moderator continued. "You have mastered dark, Indigenous modern horror that features men looking for their place in a world taken from them. I'm sure you hear this often, but what inspired you to write *For What Savages May Be*? Where did this idea come from?"

"Oh, here and there. I've always wanted to reclaim the cowboy stereotype, you know. Trent is a man searching for something, and it's not until he crosses the reservation line that he realizes what it is he's searching for."

"A whole lot of nothing," Pen muttered, too low for the audience to hear.

"Penelope Skinner," Neil drawled. "You've been awfully quiet today."

Her head snapped up in surprise. He was everything she hated about publishing, manifested in one smirking, attractive man. Damn him, did he have to be attractive? Neil Storm's gaze was steady, but his nostrils flared as he leaned toward his mic, dark curls falling into those emerald eyes.

"You haven't exactly been quiet about your distaste for my writing, though. If I recall from a certain *Writer's Digest* interview, you think my writing is 'pathetically palatable.' You use that word a lot, 'palatable.'"

Someone snickered in the audience, but she refused to look away from him.

She straightened in her seat, ignoring the curious glances from their fellow panel members. "I struggle to relate to your stories.

They feel . . ." She hesitated. His eyes were a captivating green, and it was difficult to focus.

"It's okay, you can say it."

"You set up Trent to be a wayward Native in search of a home, experiencing the horrors off the reservation, but instead you wrote a—"

"Let me guess, palatable?" Neil interrupted.

"—*tasteless* book that paints our people as the bad guys. You attempt to reclaim the word 'savage,' but only continue to promote its usage. We are not savages, we were never savages. That imagery is from a white lens. Why would you ever want to reclaim a word that has only done us harm?"

"Is that so?" he ground out.

Pen looked from his face to the table before him. *For What Savages May Be* was propped up, a critically acclaimed *New York Times* bestselling dark horror about what the world expects of modern Indigenous populations. But his main character, Trent—a play on the traditional white cowboy—was cocky, sexist, and racist, all wrapped up in a bow and quiver full of arrows. Neil Storm had played into every stereotype possible in a book he claimed shattered them all. He was a joke, a phony, but to the white book world, he was palatable.

Pen, on the other hand, was simply too much. Had always been too much. Too much prose, too much Nativeness, too much whiteness. *Too much.*

Grinding her teeth, she said, "Yes. Trent is supposed to be the hero, but you literally titled it *For What Savages May Be*. You don't care if we are painted as the hero or the villain."

"That's a serious accusation," the moderator warned.

"Great, because it's true."

"Why do you get to say that?" Neil demanded. "What entitles you to that opinion? We should be supporting one another, not tearing each other down."

"Maybe if you cared more about your people than your wallet."

He stared at her, and a long silence settled between them. Pen looked out to the audience, to the few faces she recognized in the crowded hall. Her friend Laszlo had flown out to Seattle on a whim to see both her and Storm in their panel in what he claimed was a "momentous occasion." He sat ramrod straight in the second row, shaking his head subtly, but before she could stop herself, her lips were moving.

"Get over your masochistic shit and write something with a soul for once."

Pen would never know why she'd opened her mouth, never understood what had overtaken her in that moment, but the Prince of Horror had crossed a line, and she'd followed right after him. Maybe she was a self-destructive time bomb, and her clock had finally reached zero.

Maybe she just wanted to see how he'd react.

Her mother had always warned her that she wore her heart on her sleeve. And the publishing world had warned her it was a business, not an art, but she'd ignored both. She'd always thought that if she could just get her stories into the world, into the hands of readers like her, everything would sort itself out.

But that wasn't how publishing worked.

Pen looked from Storm to the audience, her vision hazy as his fans started yelling at her. Someone was trying to quiet them down, and other panel members attempted to calm the crowd, to change the subject, but it was no use.

"Penelope—" Storm started.

Fuck. Why did she do this? She could feel it all slipping through her fingers—her career, her future, her *life*. Swallowing, she looked out over the audience, unfamiliar faces glaring back at her. She'd hurt the boy they loved—the Prince of Horror.

"I asked: What did you just say?" Neil demanded into his mic.

Pen licked her lips as the crowd fell silent, waiting, and her vision blurred with tears. Oh god, not here. "I said," she started, voice wavering, "write something with a soul."

They glared at one another.

He worked his jaw, eyes focused on her.

"Maybe we should take a quick break," the moderator offered.

But Pen had had enough. She was done pretending that she deserved a seat, that she was of their caliber.

That *he* deserved a seat.

This table was full of Indigenous authors who had paved their way, and what did Neil Storm or Penelope Skinner have to offer but a forgotten novel and some lousy, white-centered bullshit?

Pen pushed back from her seat, picking up the single copy of her only novel, *The Lies They Told Us*. She needed to leave the hall before she did anything else or *said* anything else. People yelled obscenities at her as she moved to leave. And then she heard it, muddled in with "bitch!" and "worthless!"

"Racist!"

She was racist? She almost laughed. They hadn't known; even on a panel for Indigenous authors, they hadn't known who she was. And by calling out Storm's hypocrisy, she was racist? With anger she hadn't felt in ages, she leaned forward and ripped her mic from the table.

"You know?" She threw up her arm, the book still clutched in her sweaty palm. She wanted to tell herself to stop, but she couldn't. "I'm sorry my characters are too Native for you, or," she said, narrowing her eyes on Neil Storm, "not Native enough. I'm sorry I'm only mixed, and I'm sorry that I look like a bagpiper and a scullery maid fucked in a castle."

Pen didn't know where she was going, and she should have put the mic down, but she only clutched it tighter and leaned away as one of the convention volunteers motioned for it. "Someday, I'm going to write the best fucking horror novel you've ever read, and the name Neil Storm will be forgotten forever."

He grabbed his mic, standing. "You think it's been easy for me?" She turned to leave, but his voice only rose. "You think I walked into this market and had it all handed to me? Sometimes, we have to give up titles and characters and entire books before we get what we want, before we can write what we want."

She turned on him. "Well, I wrote what I wanted."

"And look where that landed you."

Nostrils flaring and nerves buzzing, she dropped the mic on the table and turned to go. He wasn't wrong, fuck, he wasn't wrong, but she needed to go before it got any worse.

"And that, folks, is my competition," Neil said, returning to his chair with a heavy sigh.

She should have left.

Pen should have fled, but her book was still clutched in her hand, and there was no one to hold her back. Sliding her left foot behind her, she turned and chucked her book at the cocky bastard. She watched gleefully as it smacked into the side of his temple, and he flew out of his chair, yelling obscenities.

There was a twinge of guilt in her gut as she watched blood trickle down the side of his face, but Pen stamped it down as people rushed forward to help the Prince of Horror and she was dragged backward out of the room by convention security.

Alone. She was alone.

Chapter 1
PEN

PRESENT DAY

Pen's hand tightened on her phone as she fought the urge to text Laszlo. Again. Were ten texts in twenty minutes too much? Pen didn't know what was socially acceptable anymore, and the last thing she wanted to do was annoy the one person in the world who had stuck by her side these last four months.

Puffing out her cheeks, she slipped her hands into her pockets and squinted down the Royal Mile, regarding the thin crowd. Bundled in jackets, hats, and scarves, people wandered down the cobblestone street, meandering past wool shops and dark pubs, celebrating the last of the highs of New Year's. Despite the chill, Pen found herself smiling.

There were moments since she'd landed, small, freeze-frame instances where she imagined what it would be like to live here. She'd spent the last two days getting lost amid the brick and cobblestone, traipsing through Edinburgh's Old Town while munching on Scottish shortbread, her breath turning to fog in the air. Pen had hidden inside small cafes with fresh pots of tea as she watched the passing crowds through the glass. She'd buried her nose in antique books, curling onto worn leather sofas and nestling into warm, dark corners that smelled of spices and roaring fires. Edinburgh felt like magic. It was a place built of fantasy, with bronze water fountains, wilted gardens, and Gothic architecture all under the same roiling gray clouds. She was glad she'd come to Scotland a few days early. She'd had a chance to see and enjoy the city before she, Laszlo, and several other writers disappeared into the Highlands for their retreat. And now that she'd gotten to know this city, it felt like she was meant for this place.

"You made it!" Laszlo called, rushing through the crowd. The passersby parted for him, rolling their eyes as the tall, gangly American swerved between them. A lock of his blond hair slipped out from beneath his beanie, flopping into his eyes as he laughed and threw his arms around Pen. She couldn't help but smile as he picked her up and squeezed tight, making it nearly impossible to breathe.

"Laszlo," Pen wheezed, patting his back, "I can't breathe."

He set her down gently, hands on either shoulder to steady her as he leaned back to get a good look. She'd changed a lot in four months; even she knew that. Her skin had become paler, her cheeks gaunter. Her freckles stood out starkly against her pale skin, a spattering of galaxies across her face, disappearing down her neck. She looked as though she hadn't seen the sun in months. Which, truthfully, she couldn't remember the last time she basked in a warm ray of sunlight.

Though she hated to admit it, Pen had become a homebody. This was her first time out of Seattle since the Incident, her first time out of her apartment and away from her fluffy black cat, Apawllo. But if there was anyone to convince her to leave her little nest in a city of rain and hate and fly halfway across the world for a writing retreat, it was Laszlo.

When she'd disappeared from the world, she'd hardly spoken a word to her author friends, assuming that, like the rest of publishing, none of them wanted anything to do with her. Except for sweet, sweet Laszlo with his clear caramel eyes and sandy blond hair. Since Book Con, he'd texted and called, checking in on her.

He'd been the only one. And despite his close friendship with Neil Storm, she loved Laszlo like a brother. Not that it was easy being friends with someone who talked regularly with one's enemy, but timed rants, no-Storm zones, and the adoption of her cuddly companion, Apawllo, to help ease her loneliness had gone a long way in repairing her complicated friendship with Laszlo.

Just as Laszlo took a step back, a tall woman wrapped in a puffy blue jacket launched herself at him. Grinning like a fool, she wrapped her arms around him and squeezed, eliciting a wheeze from Laszlo.

"Pen," Laszlo choked, prying himself free with a laugh, "this is my sister, Louise. Louise, this is Penelope Skinner."

Louise smiled at Pen with soft brown eyes, her blond curls bouncing as she held out a pale, slender hand. Her nails were trimmed short, and several small scars crisscrossed her hands. "The famed Penelope Skinner! I liked your handiwork." She winked conspiratorially.

"My handiwork?" Pen asked with a raised brow at Laszlo.

"Hope you don't mind me joining," Louise said, ignoring them. "I don't get to see Lasz too often these days, and I'm visiting from London before I head back to the US for work."

Pen smiled warily, taking the offered hand. "Not at all. What do you do, if you don't mind my asking?"

"Archaeology. I'm working down in Georgia now with a colleague."

"And she wonders why I don't visit her," Laszlo muttered.

Louise shook her head. "There's some beauty there, brother. If you would just visit me for once instead of making me chase you across the planet—"

"No, thank you." Louise raised a brow, and Pen stifled laughter as Laszlo shot her a look. "So," he said, actively ignoring them and starting down the Royal Mile, "are you ready for a bit of a fun surprise?"

Pen narrowed her eyes. "A good surprise?"

"All surprises are good surprises," Louise countered.

Pen frowned at Laszlo, fight or flight taking shape in her gut like a stampede of butterflies. With a sigh, she hooked her arm through Laszlo's and followed him down the street.

Now that she was actually in Scotland, the writing retreat felt more and more like a mistake. There were a million reasons why going was a bad idea. While Pen had the money to take a few weeks off for the first time in four years thanks to her side (now full-time) hustle as a freelance editor under an anonymous name, she'd never traveled outside the US, her passport tucked away in a drawer.

Besides preferring the quiet of her small apartment and judgment-free cuddly companion who consistently looked at her with round, bottomless eyes like she knew the answer to everything, there was Storm to think about. She hadn't seen him since the Incident, and though Laszlo had insisted he wasn't coming on the retreat, he'd paused on the phone. A short pause, possibly caused by a mere tickle in his throat, but Pen felt a strange nagging at the back of her mind nonetheless.

Except this would be good for her. This retreat could fix whatever was broken in her head, in her heart. She hadn't finished a book since her debut, and with five years of blocked-up creativity, Pen had begun to wonder if she should give up. If she should stop trying to write. Her agent had dropped her, and she and her book had become public enemy number one. What was the point?

"You look like you're thinking really hard about something," Louise observed.

Pen winced. "That easy to tell?"

"You have one of those faces. I know this is kind of nosy, but if you don't mind me asking, why haven't you put out another book?"

"Sorry?"

"Lou," Laszlo warned.

"Laszlo told me not to say anything, but I read your book a few years back when I was visiting him. You have such beautiful, heartfelt writing . . . but you haven't put anything else out."

Because I can't.

"So, any plans?" Louise went on.

Pen wished she could tell Louise *yes*. She wished she could promise something else soon, but she couldn't. "It's kind of why I'm here," she admitted.

"In Scotland?"

Pen nodded as they came to a halt behind Laszlo. "I don't really do this."

"Traveling?"

"Going to retreats or buying last-minute airfare." Pen worried her lip, swiveling to the large cobblestone square. "I don't do things on a whim. But I'm hoping this will be good for me. Getting out of my apartment, seeing the world. Inspiration, you know? I just need a bit of inspiration, and I'm not finding that back home."

Pen didn't say that she'd also made a pact with herself. If she walked out of that castle with nothing, then it proved she wasn't meant to be a writer, and she'd finally give up for good. She deserved more than half-assed promises of a better future. She deserved to really try.

"Ta-da!" Laszlo sang, waving his arms at a sandwich board.

"*This* is your big surprise?" Pen asked, raising a brow.

"Oh, come on! Haunted tours are fun. I figured it would be good preparation for the castle."

"You don't really think the castle's haunted, do you, Laszlo? It's probably just a gimmick to pull in more tourists."

He shrugged. "Won't know until we go."

Pen frowned, but Louise smiled and nudged her. "I'm game if you are."

The black sandwich board was covered with bloody lettering

and a terribly photoshopped ghost that looked remarkably like a human draped in white sheets. It was kitschy, yet the longer she stared at it, the more she wanted to go. It was probably the most touristy thing she'd ever do in her life, and damn it, Laszlo was right.

"*Fine,*" Pen relented, the corner of her lips curling.

"Good, because I already bought tickets."

He hauled her and Louise toward a crowd of tourists beside a church. It was a gorgeous cathedral illuminated from the inside with candles. The soft, ethereal glow shone through beautifully crafted stained glass depicting religious scenes. Louise elbowed Laszlo when a balding, middle-aged man with a thick accent and a silky red cape appeared, checking their tickets. Laszlo held up his phone and nodded to their guide.

"Welcome to the City of Ghosts," he called in a great, rolling accent, turning to their group. His cape billowed out around him, the cheap, luminescent fabric catching the last of the day's faint sunshine peering in from between stormy clouds. With dramatic flourish and a coy smile, he waved his arms and bowed before walking her and their small group of tourists through a narrow alley, across a lit lobby for the tour company, and down a set of stairs into what appeared to be a tomb.

"What have you gotten us into?" Pen murmured.

"This trip is about inspiration," Laszlo insisted, "so take it all in while you can."

"It's perfect," Louise murmured, eyes round and excited.

Grumbling under her breath, Pen clutched her jacket close, the cold of the underground creeping in past her layers as the guide swept their group through the narrow rooms and farther under the city. The crypts were crumbling, stone lying in heaps at the base of faceless walls, and Pen shivered as a chill crept across the back of her neck.

"These vaults were built in the 1700s, expanding to well over a hundred separate chambers for storage. They even housed taverns and businesses at times. But because of the porousness of the rock, they were subject to flooding. And as the vaults were abandoned, another group began to take over the secret chambers under the city."

They meandered down through a narrow doorway and into a large, open room. This one was taller than the others, and Louise and Laszlo stretched out, lazy smiles gracing their lips, but the large space, left empty but for a single light, only made Pen shiver more.

"Are you scared?" Laszlo asked, catching her eye.

"No."

"Many claim to hear the heavy breathing of a man in this room or see a glowing orb of light lingering in the farthest corner." The guide rounded the group, bent low and creeping as his voice filled the room. Pen rolled her eyes but curled her hands into her jacket as he stepped between her and Laszlo. "Maybe they were just seeing things, hmm?" He raised a brow. "Or were they?"

Laughing, he urged them on, and Pen followed behind Laszlo and Louise as they leaned into each other. She didn't like this place. She captured Laszlo's hand with hers, and though he raised a brow, he didn't say anything as he squeezed her fingers. Louise followed the movement with a question in her eyes, but her brother only shook his head.

"While people without housing ventured here for a reprieve from the streets, the seedy underbelly of Edinburgh trickled down to these vaults. Illegal gambling dens, distilleries, and even the storing of illegally obtained corpses all took place here not long after the businesses fled. But the cold, damp conditions of these vaults led to many, sometimes gruesome, deaths."

Pressing a finger to his lips, he motioned them on. The group stopped in a small room, and he continued, "Perhaps the most beloved ghost of these vaults is the Watcher, or Mr. Boots if ye will." The group laughed, and Pen chuckled along with them, ignoring the creeping feeling of something on her left shoulder. The tour guide held up a finger, expression suddenly serious. "Many say he was a city guard, but all know him by the sound of his boots."

"Is he real?" someone called.

The guide shrugged. "There's only one way to know for sure." Silence filled the chamber, and Pen straightened, searching the group as they waited for some sound, some sign that this ridiculous tour wasn't all just a way to scam them out of their money.

And maybe she was imagining it, maybe it was someone else in the tour company, but she could have sworn she heard the sound of heavy boots on stone.

"And to this day," the man drawled in a slow, deliberate tone, "ye can hear the sounds of his boots on the stone."

He flicked off his lantern, plunging them into darkness. Pen froze in place, fingers tightening around Laszlo's. The underground rooms were pitch-black without his guiding lantern, making the nerves in her gut twist. The guide laughed, but before he could turn the light back on, someone squealed. Pen screamed and stumbled back into the wall, pulse thundering in her ears as she scrambled for purchase before righting herself.

"Are you okay?" Laszlo asked quietly.

"I'm fine," she lied.

As soon as the lights flooded the space, she tugged Laszlo out of the crypts, sucking in a sharp breath of cool, fresh air when they emerged on the street, Louise following quickly after. It was fully night now, dark except for string lights and old lampposts illuminating the streets.

"Pen, are you sure you're okay?"

She shivered as she tugged on the sleeves of her jacket. She was not okay. Not in the least. Pen didn't believe in the paranormal. She'd never had any reason to, but she was starting to doubt herself. That silly little tour was making her question everything. And she was meant to spend a week in a supposedly haunted castle?

"I need a drink." She sighed, meeting Laszlo's curious gaze. Louise waited awkwardly off to the side, lips puckered in thought as she scanned the darkened street, giving them some space.

Laszlo smiled. "Good thing we're in Scotland."

They meandered until they found a small pub on the Royal Mile and went down a set of stairs with "Live Music" posters plastered to the brick. Scottish punk music filled the place, loud and blaring, the words molding into one another. After motioning to the bartender, Pen ordered a whiskey, and Laszlo and Louise asked for ciders.

"It's good seeing you," Laszlo said to Pen as they found a corner booth in a small room off the main hall. "It feels like it's been years."

"Well, *I* haven't seen you in a year," Louise said, taking a long sip of cider.

"Hush, you," he chided.

Pen smiled warily. "Only since . . ." Since Book Con.

He'd been there, of course, to witness the beginning of her downfall. Laszlo had been with her through it all. Pen swirled the amber liquid in her glass as she watched her friend. His fingers flew across his phone, the screen casting a bluish light across his pale skin, throwing shadows over his eyes. She took a drink of her whiskey, reveling in the burn as it seared a path down her throat.

Louise looked at her phone with a frown before standing. "I need to take this really quick." Smiling, she slipped out of the booth with her cider in hand and disappeared around the corner, a quiet "Isi, are you okay?" melting into the sounds of the pub.

The pub smelled of booze and cigarette smoke, the table and floors sticky. Pen tried not to think about the way her sleeve had adhered to the table as she lifted her hand for another drink.

"So, what'd you think of the tour?" Laszlo asked, turning back to Pen.

"I don't know." She sighed as she swirled her glass from side to side, staring at her warped reflection. "Do you really believe in all that stuff?"

"Ghosts? Not really, but it's fun, isn't it? I love hearing local legends and myths. This city is full of them."

"I bet," she murmured, taking another sip.

Louise reappeared, a whiskey in hand this time. She slid onto the bench beside Pen, grinning sidelong. Her curls danced with her every movement, brushing the collar of her jacket as she turned to Pen.

"Sorry for interrupting your evening. I really enjoyed the tour, though!"

"You're not that sorry," Laszlo muttered.

"No, no I'm not." Louise shrugged, leaning back in her seat. "My brother is terrible at returning my texts or calls."

"Only because you text me daily."

"I'm your older sister," Louise protested. "I get worried."

"If I had a younger brother like Laszlo," Pen said, "I'd be worried too. He disappears without a trace *constantly*."

"See, she gets it, Lasz."

"Only because she doesn't have an older sister," Laszlo said.

"But if I *did*—" Pen started.

"Penelope Skinner," a familiar low alto interrupted with a drawl, "as I live and breathe."

Pen sucked in a sharp breath, the whiskey blazing down the wrong pipe and igniting in her nose as she glanced past Louise. Clamping one hand over her nose and mouth, Pen pounded a hand against her chest as she gaped up at a woman she hadn't seen in years. Not since her first retreat, to be exact. Pen looked from Laszlo to Daniela, eyes watering and cheeks heating as she sputtered.

"It's been a while," Pen wheezed as Daniela perched on the edge of the bench beside Laszlo. Daniela smiled coyly, dark eyes glittering dangerously as she took a drink of her cider, lips pursed in thought as she stared across the table at Pen.

Laszlo peered between the two women, worry coloring his round eyes. Wiping away the tears, Pen pried her glass from the table and drank down the rest of her whiskey, swallowing her questions. Because she had *a lot* of questions for her friend Laszlo. Like: *Why?* Just why? Why didn't he tell her? Why was he insistent on keeping so much of this retreat and everything surrounding it a secret? Was this week going to be filled with the ghosts of Pen's past?

Pen ran her finger around the rim of her glass, staring daggers at Laszlo. Pressing his lips into a flat line, he stood, climbed over Daniela, and wrestled Pen's glass from her fingers. Grunting, he dragged Louise out of the booth before slipping out of their dark little corner and back toward the bar without a word.

Leaving Pen and Daniela alone.

With nothing to toy with, Pen leaned back in her seat. She hadn't been near Daniela since the Boathouse Incident. Truly, well, not so much an incident as it was Daniela going down on her in a boat covered in cobwebs while the others smoked a blunt on the pier.

Daniela looked good, as always. Too good, if you asked her. Pen could see the hints of Daniela's Irish and Choctaw ancestry, a mix that was indescribable in its perfection. Her curls fell into place even as she brushed them back, her full lips coated in gloss, cleavage exposed beneath a deep V-neck sweater. When she lifted her glass to her lips and took a sip, Daniela's warm eyes never left hers.

She'd always been out of Pen's league, and Pen hadn't been surprised when Daniela never called her back. It was a one-off, a giddy mistake, a few minutes of connection, nothing more. Even still, Daniela's smile was full of mirth.

"Wait, Neil—"

Pen's head snapped toward the voice, dread climbing her throat as a person rounded the corner and stopped beside their booth. Behind her glasses, she wondered if she was mistaken. So, she pulled them off, wiped them down with a cloth from her bag, and checked again. Maybe she was drunk? But, no, she'd seen it correctly.

Stumbling back a step, hands limp at his sides, was none other than Neil Storm himself.

A torrent of emotions swirled through her at the sight of him with those shaggy black curls, that tilt of his lips, and that smooth, light brown skin. Anger, frustration, guilt, hate. But above it all (even the hate) was confusion. Because Laszlo had *assured* her Storm wouldn't be there.

Yet even now, she remembered, there had been a *pause*.

She sat frozen in place, mouth agape, eyes wide behind her dark-rimmed glasses. She felt betrayed. How could Laszlo tell her Storm wasn't coming when lo and behold, here he was, gaze turning to the man who'd conned them all? Laszlo looked from Pen to Storm, guilt scraping over his kind features.

"What did you do?" Pen and Storm demanded at the same time. Pen swiveled and glowered at him. As if sensing her stare, Storm's green eyes shifted to her, and she felt a jolt of warmth as he looked her over. What did he find when he surveyed her? Pen wished, not for the first time, that she could read his thoughts, get into that thick skull of his.

Louise peered around her brother before she leaned forward and grabbed her whiskey. She drank it down, shivering as she slammed the cup on the table. "Well, brother, it looks like you've gotten yourself into *another* mess. Did you learn nothing from the time you accidentally joined a vampiric cult?"

"That was a total accident and I still regret it to this day, but how can you even compare the two? They'll be fine. Neil and Pen are adults."

"I beg to differ," Pen said.

Louise patted Laszlo's shoulder and nodded to the others. "As much as I'd love to see this play out, I would really rather not."

She turned to Laszlo. "Text me sometime. Pen, it was nice to meet you." Shaking her head, she zipped up her coat and squeezed past Neil toward the exit.

Laszlo set down the whiskey and cider, holding up his hands in surrender. "I can explain."

Teeth grinding, Pen ducked her head and focused on the drop of amber liquid sliding down the outside of her glass. She snatched the whiskey and swallowed it in one gulp, gasping as she wiped her hand over her mouth. She didn't drink often, but oh, did she need that drink now. Betrayal sat at her side, its claws scraping down her arm as she tightened her hold on her empty glass.

"I'm getting another drink."

She slid out of the booth and shoved past Storm, heat building behind her eyes as she rounded the corner and leaned back against the wall. This was not how she expected their first meeting to go. What had she done in the last four months? Nothing, nothing at all. This retreat was supposed to be it, the place she finally found that *something* she'd been missing all these years. But she couldn't do that if Storm was here.

Damn it, why had she made that declaration at the panel? If she didn't pull a bestseller out of her ass, she'd remain the laughingstock of the book community forever.

Pen sniffed and closed her eyes. What a fool she'd been.

Chapter 2

NEIL

What the fuck was Penelope Skinner doing here? Neil eyed Laszlo sidelong, but his friend would not look at him.

"Laszlo," he started. Laszlo took a long swig of his cider as Daniela Mitchel leaned forward on the table, eyes blazing with curiosity. "I know you can hear me," Neil groaned.

"It's going to be good for you." Laszlo nodded, as if he were trying to convince himself. "This is what the two of you need."

"Laszlo."

"Just try for me. You can both be civil, can't you?"

Neil could try, but Penelope Skinner had never made it easy. Though he wanted to resist the urge, he couldn't stop his gaze from drifting around the corner. She leaned against the bar, head in her hands as the bartender filled her glass with whiskey. She looked . . . She looked like the life had been drained out of her.

Over the last few months, he'd stared at her picture for hours and rewatched the recording of their panel time and time again. He knew every shadow, every line, every facial expression. Although her physical appearance had changed, her demeanor had not.

"Well, this is juicy," Daniela drawled.

Neil ignored her, his attention focused solely on Penelope Skinner. She'd made him doubt *everything*. Made him doubt his success, his seat at the table. Penelope Skinner had made him doubt his own ability to write. Before the Incident, Neil had simply praised the conviction with which she held her ground. *No one* had ever called him out before, and then she had to do it on a panel in front of hundreds of people. Yet, in taking him down, she'd taken herself down too.

He grabbed Laszlo's arm and yanked him to the side. "Do you have any clue what she did to me, Lasz? I haven't been able to write a single fucking word in four months. *Four months.*"

"I know! I know and I'm sorry, but I didn't have a choice."

"What do you mean, you didn't have a choice?" Skinner hissed, rounding the corner. She held a fresh glass of whiskey, just less than a finger's worth of the amber liquid in the glass. Neil found himself suddenly distracted. He'd never taken her for a whiskey drinker.

Laszlo wouldn't meet either of their eyes, his attention turned to the floor, sandy hair a mussed mess as if he'd been running his fingers through it nervously. "It was a last-minute change," Laszlo started. "Okay," he amended, "that's also a lie."

"Laszlo," Neil ground out.

"I may have fibbed a bit! To both of you . . . But it was the only way."

"Why?" Skinner demanded. She set down her whiskey and pinched the bridge of her nose, her glasses fogging up. She pointed at Laszlo, her tone accusing. "Did you only invite me because *he* canceled?"

"Pen—"

"You did! You really chose him over me?"

"No, it's not that. I didn't think you'd want to come if he accepted, and he'd backed out last minute, so I called you. But after you bought your ticket, he called and said he'd changed his mind and wanted to come! And instead of being honest, I figured what better place to work out your problems with each other than in a *castle.* I haven't seen you since . . . and I hardly hear from you. But you said yes!" He threw up his arms and sighed. "He's my friend too, Pen. I can't be in the middle of you two forever."

"You invited her because *I* canceled?" Neil asked quietly.

That hurt. They'd known each other since sophomore year of college. They'd been dormmates, then friends. Neil was supposed to come first. He knew he shouldn't make Laszlo choose, but Neil should have come first.

Laszlo sighed, defeated. "Yes, okay. And after she accepted, you reached out and walked back your answer. Was I supposed to tell her she couldn't come?"

"Yes! Yes, that's exactly what you're supposed to do."

"Wow," Daniela cut in. "I feel like I'm on a reality TV show for spurned writers."

"Not helping, Dani," Laszlo admonished.

"I can't do this," Skinner said. She grabbed her whiskey and turned to go. Neil's nostrils flared as he watched her.

"How are you ever going to write again if you don't let this go?" Laszlo called. He turned to Neil, raising his voice over the pub's music. "You both need this, and you know it. You need this retreat more than you're willing to admit. What are you going to do without it, huh?" Skinner stopped, back still turned to them, and Laszlo continued, his voice softer. "You two could do so much good together in the book community if you got over this little rivalry."

"It's not a rivalry, Lasz," she said, jaw clenched as she whirled around to face them. "It ruined my career."

"*Your* career?" Neil laughed, taking a step toward her. "What about my career? What about what you did to me?" His hands curled into fists at his sides, and his stomach churned when she looked up at him, storm clouds brewing behind black-rimmed frames.

"To you?" Skinner slammed her whiskey on the table. The

amber liquid spilled over her hand, and she shook it off, fingers curling into a fist. He followed the movement warily and thought, almost jokingly, that if anyone were to punch him, it would be her. "You have always been able to float on by without a worry. You have a solid audience. You're a *man*. Everything for you is that much easier."

"Easy?" He took another step forward, towering over her. He wanted to grab her shoulders and shake some sense into her. "I'm a Native man in a white man's world. Nothing in my life has ever been fucking easy."

"You had me fooled."

Their chests rose in time with each other, and Neil wanted to laugh. Even their breaths were in sync. They would fall together and rise together, a tide and a moon connected by some invisible string of fate, whether or not they liked it.

Though they would deny it, they were more similar than either of them would be willing to admit. Stubborn and hell-bent on hating each other, Penelope Skinner and Neil Storm were too like-minded for their own good. He needed this retreat as much as she did. Neil knew that Skinner hadn't written a book in years, not since *The Lies They Told Us*. Writing retreats were often a terrific way to meet hard deadlines. And he hated to admit it, but without this retreat, without something to hold him accountable for his writing, Neil was ready to give up altogether.

And from the hard set of her jaw, if he wanted this retreat, he'd have to give in first.

"A temporary truce," he ground out. God, he hated the sound of those words.

"What?"

Neil cleared his throat and stepped back. "A temporary truce. Civility in the face of foolishness." He directed the last bit at Laszlo, glaring sidelong at his blushing friend.

"You make it sound so easy," Skinner muttered.

As if to prove his point, Neil held out a hand. He would be the first, that much he could do. "You and I have both paid for our portion of the castle. We're already in Scotland. And surely the castle is big enough that we never need to see one another. We'll sequester ourselves in our respective corners and hunker down to write." He paused, searching her face. His muscles uncoiled as she scowled at him. "Tell me you don't need this as much as I do."

Because he needed this. *Fuck,* did he need this. Without this retreat, without this week, without the structure, Neil was going to fail. Neil Storm did not fail. He was not used to failing, and he wasn't going to start now.

She pressed her lips into a flat line, resolve flitting over her features as her eyes flicked from his hand to his face before she turned to Laszlo. "Whatever happens," she started, grasping Neil's hand in her small, warm palm, "it's your fault."

Laszlo's shoulders slumped in relief. "I deserve that."

Neil frowned at their joined hands, confusion warring in him. Her fingers lingered for a moment longer, brushing the inside of his wrist as she pulled her hand back. The touch made Neil unpleasantly warm, and he snatched his hand away with a grimace, wiping it down his jeans like that would make him forget her phantom touch.

Skinner lifted her whiskey. "To not killing each other."

He could have sworn he heard Daniela say, "Please, do."

Skinner drank the small bit of whiskey, slamming the empty glass on the table with a gasp. After nodding to Laszlo, she turned and fled.

"I'm going to regret this." Neil sighed, pinching the bridge of his nose.

"I won't," Daniela called cheerfully.

Neil shot her a glare before he, too, slipped out of the pub and made his way back to his hotel, more sober than when his night had started.

* * *

The next morning, when Neil rolled up in the rental van to the bed-and-breakfast Skinner was staying in, a bitter part of him hoped she wouldn't show. He'd spent most of the night tossing and turning, dreaming of a small, angry woman who'd made him doubt his entire career. He'd hoped, when he pulled the van into park and rolled down his window, that maybe she'd decided to go home, give him the retreat. Be the bigger person.

Because he sure as hell wasn't going to be.

But of course, she was waiting for them outside.

Neil tightened his hands on the steering wheel as she glowered at him. When he swiveled to get a good look at her, he could see that a rather large part of her had hoped he wouldn't show up. *Touché, Skinner, touché.*

Laszlo hopped out of the car and helped load her bags, and when they were done, she climbed quietly into the back seat, her body carefully angled away from Daniela as Laszlo slid into the passenger seat and slapped a hand on the dash.

Neil jumped. "Is that necessary?"

"I hope you all don't mind," Laszlo said, ignoring him and turning to the others, "but we're going to make a pit stop first."

"Where?" Neil asked, changing the gear. The grin his question elicited from Laszlo was nothing short of terrifying.

"That's for me to know and you to find out."

Without meaning to, Neil caught Skinner's gaze in the rearview over the top of his sunglasses. Her lips were pursed, fist covering her mouth to keep from laughing. Her eyes were more blue than gray today, and they widened, her lips curling down. Something in Neil's stomach twisted when she didn't immediately look away, and he blinked in surprise, focusing on the road as he pulled away from the curb.

Neil suddenly had so many questions for the woman who'd

ruined everything, but his tongue felt heavy, and his stomach was a mess of knots. Was he nervous? He tightened his hold on the steering wheel until his hands were numb. Pressing his lips into a flat line, he ground his teeth, saying nothing for the rest of the drive.

God, this *fucking drive*. He would never admit as much aloud, but it was setting his nerves on edge, and he didn't know how much longer he could mask it, especially in her presence. Something about Penelope Skinner had him leaning forward, wanting to lay his soul bare, and it was *terrifying*.

Her attendance only made the treacherous journey that much more difficult, because as much as he wanted to focus on her, he needed to concentrate on the road. These Scottish roads were excruciatingly tight. His stomach dropped as he rounded each bend, fully expecting an oncoming car barreling down the narrow road toward them. He hated being afraid more than anything, and he'd be damned if anyone knew just how terrified the drive was making him. Skinner didn't need any more fuel to use against him.

When Neil had finally lost feeling in his fingertips, Laszlo motioned for him to pull over. Neil could feel his heart thundering in his chest, the painful *bud-ump* working its way through his fingers as he flexed his hands. He squinted through the windshield until he saw a pullout a ways down. The van slowed to a stop, and he changed gears, putting them into park.

"Here? You want me to pull over here?" Neil blinked against the midmorning light.

"Well," Laszlo said as he slid out of the car, not quite looking at Neil, "I'm not one hundred percent on this, but I think we might be lost."

Daniela unbuckled and climbed out after Laszlo.

"Of fucking course we are," Neil muttered.

He unbuckled before opening his door and hopped out of the van. His neck and lower back popped as he reached up and stretched, his body angry from fifteen years spent hunched over books and keyboards. Yawning, he rolled back his shoulders, enjoying the brisk morning breeze that sent a fresh wave of goose bumps across his skin.

Laszlo and Daniela stumbled off to the side of the main road, both of them motioning to an empty field out beyond the trees, visible through a break in the brush.

"Where are we?" Skinner asked, leaning out of her window.

"Are you talking to me?" Neil said, jabbing his thumb into his chest.

She rolled her eyes and pushed open her door, climbing out. She unfolded to an astonishingly short height. Standing side by side, he had the strange urge to rest an arm on her head.

"Laszlo and Daniela are a bit busy," Skinner said, pointing. "So, yeah, I'm talking to you."

Indeed, they were leaning over Laszlo's phone, talking in hushed whispers. Laszlo peered back at them once, turning around just as quickly, shoulders hunched.

"I honestly don't know where we are. Laszlo was navigating." Neil shrugged. Much as he liked Laszlo, the man could be a bit oblivious. Neil sighed and ran a hand through his hair, trying to calm himself. "Now that I think about it," he continued, "the last road trip I took with Laszlo was back in college, and it ended with us stranded at a motel in the middle of the desert with no gas. We probably shouldn't have let him navigate."

Skinner made a small sound but said nothing more. When Neil scowled at her, he found her smiling. Annoyed that he'd caught her, she scrunched up her nose and peered past him to the others. He tried not to stare at the way her braid swung down her back, exposing the expanse of her neck. Or the way one side of her sweater slipped down to reveal her shoulder and the light sprinkling of freckles across her pale skin.

Annoying as she might be, he couldn't deny that she was pretty.

And . . . white. She looked it, anyway. It was strange, the differences between multiracial and biracial. While her skin was pale, his was a smooth gold that only grew darker in the summer. He knew she got shit for it, for not being Native enough. No one said anything like that about Neil Storm. Despite the curly hair and the green eyes clearly inherited from his mother, he was always *enough*. He was enrolled. He had proof of his Nativeness, but she didn't.

There was never any nuance about these sorts of things. Getting enrolled in a tribe included paperwork, Dawes Rolls numbers, birth and death certificates, and an extensive list of living and dead family enrolled in the same tribe along with their enrollment numbers. Neil recalled the paperwork his dad did when he was younger, the dozens of times his dad was rejected before the application was finally accepted, well into Neil's teens. Neil felt a strange sense of pity for Skinner and all the crap she encountered, all because she couldn't present some card.

"Stop staring," she said. "You look like a creep."

Well, she was certainly more annoying than she was pretty. He'd focus on that.

Neil tried to calm his breathing. His vision was growing fuzzy at the edges, the beginnings of a headache drumming a beat at the back of his skull as Laszlo and Daniela wavered before him. Skinner sighed and crossed to the others, squeezing in between them before taking the phone from a confused Laszlo. She zoomed out with two fingers and glanced down the road, back the way they'd come.

"Laszlo, you took the wrong turn. It looks like we need to go back a ways before taking a right."

Neil moved behind her and peered over her shoulder, squinting at the phone. "How the hell did you figure that out?"

She motioned to the terrain view, her finger tracing along a thin trail. "Logic, which no one here seems to use."

Neil almost snorted.

Almost.

Skinner handed the phone back to Laszlo and disappeared to the front seat of the van, slamming the door shut behind her. Neil stood there, flabbergasted. Daniela rolled her eyes before climbing into the back, and with a shrug, Laszlo slid in beside her.

A week, Neil thought as he clambered into the van and buckled in. He'd agreed to spend a week with these people, trapped in a castle. The thought made him want to eject his passengers and drive back to Edinburgh alone. But he needed this, needed a week away from civilization to focus and reconnect with his story—well, his outline.

Okay, his paragraph-long summary of an *idea*.

Oh, god. What had he been thinking? He came on this retreat without a plan, without an outline or a map. Neil needed to draft a book, but he'd never taken the time to figure out what he'd do once they reached the castle.

He started the van and pulled out as Skinner ordered him back the way they'd come only minutes earlier.

As it turned out, Penelope Skinner had a knack for directions. She swiveled in her seat and met his stony expression with a knowing smile as he took the turn.

She was right.

He'd rather be dead before ever admitting it.

Chapter 3

PEN

Much to her dismay, navigating meant riding in the passenger seat. She grunted as she squirmed in her seat, her feet barely touching the floor, her toes skimming the mat. Storm laughed sharply before clearing his throat and covering his mouth with a fist. Pen eyed him sidelong.

"What?" she snapped.

He pressed his lips together, shaking his head. "Nothing."

Nostrils flaring, Pen narrowed her eyes, taking in his posture, the way he leaned forward, both hands on the wheel like a new driver. Holy shit, Neil Storm was *nervous*. Well, that was new.

She knew she shouldn't, but Pen found a bit of satisfaction in the knowledge. She watched him in her periphery, tilting her head as he ran a hand through his curls, fingers catching in knots.

When the light hit him just right (and really any other time), he looked remarkably handsome, and as much as she hated him, well, she would enjoy the view. As if sensing her stare, his green eyes slid to hers, face expressionless. She tried to ignore the way her nerves twisted, or the way she shuddered when she met his gaze through the tinted lenses, but something else lurked beneath the surface of his severe expression as his eyes lingered on her.

Pen frowned but returned her attention to her phone. When it seemed like they'd driven away from civilization completely, the area surrounded by a smattering of homes and farms, she motioned for Storm to pull over. Before them was a run-down castle, the building merely ruins. Its stone walls dripped with ivy, and the whole of the property was surrounded by a chain-link fence. As soon as they shifted into park, Daniela quickly exited the car, dragging a sleepy Laszlo with her, and together, they disappeared around the back of the castle, phones poised for photos.

Storm brushed away a few curls, tilting his head forward to show off the thin streak of silver skin that cut into his brow. The very sight had the pit in her stomach dropping.

Pen grumbled as she opened her door and stepped down, pulling on her jacket with a shiver. She'd hated that she'd fallen to throwing books, hated that he knew how to push her buttons, whether he meant to or not. But there was a part of her, a small one, that regretted stooping so low. Teeth clenched, she rounded the van and hurried past him.

"You know, you never apologized!" he called. Pen staggered to a stop, her back to him, heart thundering as she froze in place.

He continued, "Even after everything that happened, you never even reached out. I don't understand why you needed to make it all so public and leave me to clean up the mess. *Poof* and you were gone from the world."

She spun toward him. "Well, *you* could very well apologize for everything that happened. For writing Trent the way that you did, for all your books, for the hurtful stereotypes you include, catering to your white readers." She stepped forward, jabbing a finger into his chest. "You had the chance to do something great, and you blew it."

"So, you're still blaming me for all of it?"

"Of course I am! I looked up to you once, Storm. I looked up to you and you failed me." Pen hated how quickly the tears came, but she felt the heat grow behind her eyes and the disappointment sink in her stomach.

"Wait, are you crying?" he asked, hand inching up. She thought she saw something resembling guilt in his eyes, and the sight had her stumbling out of reach. What the hell was going on?

Pen wiped hastily at her eyes. "Do you ever stop to think about your decisions and how they affect other Native creators? Do you *ever* think about the repercussions of your choices?"

He said nothing for a long moment, and she couldn't tell if the words had any effect on him, his eyes hidden behind his sunglasses, the lenses darkening when he tilted his head just so. But then his blank expression quickly stretched. He smiled with something akin to admiration, leaning back.

"Penelope Skinner, you never cease to amaze me. You're always so brutally honest." He shrugged, his smile settling into something more natural. "I respect that."

She huffed, crossing her arms. "Why are you even here? What need do you have for a writer's retreat?"

There was something almost sheepish about the way Neil scoffed. He kicked the gravel with the toe of his boot. Had she . . . *offended* him?

"Every writer struggles."

She gasped, pressing a hand to her heart. "Neil Storm," she said with reverence, "are you struggling to write your next novel?" She was egging him on, but she couldn't help it. He was *the* Neil Storm, the man she'd sworn to tear down. And he was . . . *struggling*? With his writing? The end of the world had to be near, because Pen never thought she'd see the day.

He pulled off his sunglasses, eyes steady on her. They were brighter than she remembered, clearer, even as he drawled, "Says the woman who hasn't had a single book published in five years."

It was an echo of his words on the panel. She sank back on her heels, shoulders scrunching up as she opened and closed her mouth, floundering for a retort. It hurt because it was true. She was a failure, and they all knew it. Pen bit down into her lip hard.

What was she doing here, really? Why had she agreed to go half-way around the world to flounder before a group of successful authors? She should give up and commit to editing full-time. She should move back home with her mom and stop trying to be someone she wasn't.

Storm must have seen it in her eyes because he reached out, as if to console her. "I'm sorry," he started.

"What are you doing?" she snapped, taking a step back. Of all the people in the world, he was the last person she wanted to console her.

He worked his jaw. "I didn't mean to . . ." He puffed out his cheeks, an almost boyish action, and there was that pain in his eyes again as if she'd hurt him. "I didn't mean to be rude."

"That's all you are, Storm! Rude, uncaring, cold. Just like your books. Just like your characters, just like every fucking reader who decided that one skirmish was enough to cancel me and ruin my life."

"You did that yourself, Skinner! *You* threw the book. *You* said those words. And *you* ran away when the going got tough and you were too afraid to face what *you* did. Stop pretending like this was all my fault."

The words rang out in the silence between them, and as angry and frustrated as she was, she knew it was true. She threw up her hands, spinning toward the castle. God, this trip was already turning out to be a disaster, and they weren't even to the retreat yet. If this was the result of a day in the car together, what would happen after a week in a castle?

She stopped on the walkway, hands buried deep in the pockets of her jacket as she looked toward where Laszlo and Daniela had vanished around the side of the castle. Storm shoved past her with a huff, disappearing in the same direction.

Pen breathed in through her nose and out through her mouth, calming her erratic pulse. She was here for inspiration, not to fight with Storm. Problem was, he knew just how to egg her on, how to turn every little thing into a weapon against her. She needed to stop getting so riled up. The anger whooshed out of her as she stared at the castle, pausing to admire the ruins of what must have been a beautiful home. It was neither large nor small, a castle for a comfortable family, perhaps.

As she walked closer, she forgot about Storm and imagined what it must have been like to be the owner of a castle of any size, to be the sort of person to host parties and balls and banquets in large stone rooms with giant fireplaces. The more she looked, the more she could picture what it must have been like in the height of its time.

Pen rounded the corner of the castle, no Daniela or Laszlo to be seen. Large signs across the fence read NO TRESPASSING in bold, black font. A hole had been torn in the fence some time ago, the sharp edges filed away and rusted from exposure, the opening just large enough for an adult to fit through.

Storm stood before it, scratching the stubble lining his jaw as he peered beyond the fence. He half turned to Pen and, pressing his finger to his lips as if to say, "This is our little secret," slipped through the fence and vanished into the ruins.

"Are you fucking kidding me," she grumbled as she stepped up to the same spot.

She surveyed the area, noting several pipes poking out from the layer of dirt, as well as broken pieces of stone from the castle walls. Pen peeked over her shoulder at the heather-sprinkled hills, crumbling stone fences, and quaint homes. The castle was surrounded by farms. Certainly, the four of them weren't the first people to stumble upon the ruins, but from the look of the rust along the fence, they wouldn't be the first to ignore the signs either.

"This could be great fuel for a story," she said, hands gripping the fence. Or it could get them in trouble. Either way, how many times in her life would she have the chance to wander castle ruins?

With the smallest of smiles, Pen ducked through the opening in the fence.

It was truly like something out of a fairy tale; Pen had never seen anything like it. The floor was a forest of leaves and dirt and ivy and moss. The debris was velvety under her feet, and the castle had been blanketed with a thick layer of greenery. In fact, it looked so inviting that Pen thought momentarily of lying down and taking a nap in it. The outside had reached through the last remaining walls of the castle and scraped its nails across every surface, leaving behind drapes of ivy, living, breathing nature overtaking humanity once more. It was like a small, dystopian world, and already ideas and images were flashing through Pen's mind.

She was careful where she stepped, eyes trained on a path through the castle floor created by fellow rebels. Parts of the floor had caved completely, large gaps in the dirt exposing what must have once been a cellar of sorts, only darkness waiting for Pen when she peered down into it.

Brick and stone were piled in abandoned clumps, entire stairs missing as they led up to the tops of turrets. Pausing, Pen angled her head back, imagining what it must have been like. The wallpaper that might have been plastered to the walls, the fireplace that roared to life in the heart of the kitchens.

The castle would have been beautiful in an entirely different way. Still, it was beautiful as it was, in its fallen state. Lush and green despite the bit of graffiti and garbage abandoned in large rooms and empty halls. It was mystical.

She inhaled the fragrance of the ruins. It smelled of earth and dampness, a strange musky scent lingering around her. It was silent but for the light traipsing of the others in the distance, scouring through the ruins. The peace and quiet that it allotted were much needed after her little squabble with Neil Storm.

Pen paused in a large rectangular room, most of the walls

around her still standing. She ran her hands over the moss-covered stone, relishing its plushness. It was nice to get outside, to see a bit of the world for once. She'd been pushing back travel for so many reasons until they'd stacked and stacked and stacked. Who would take care of Apawllo while she was gone? What if she couldn't finish a deadline before vacation?

Penelope Skinner wasn't often a coward, but in this, she was. She liked being comfortable, liked the familiarity of her home and her couch, and coming here to Scotland felt like her own private challenge.

Scotland seemed to settle some ache in her shoulders, calm her breathing. It was a gentle country with rolling green fields flecked with purple heather and musical accents that lulled her to sleep. She'd found a strange sense of peace since she'd come here.

But of course, it hadn't lasted long.

Neil Storm had ruined it, as he did with all things. And as Pen wandered through an old doorway, she came to a stop, hands gripping the stone as she peered around the wall.

He was seated like a sculpture at the base of crumbling stairs, head in his hands, a swirl of emotions flitting over his face as he buried his fingers in his curls with a deep, guttural sigh. While his appearance had always been clean and pressed, he needed a haircut. Ever since the Incident, he'd let his curls grow, let them lengthen and knot, and Pen had the odd urge to run her fingers through the mess, to untangle it.

The thought made her stomach twist viciously, and she peered over her shoulder to go, but she found she didn't want to. Swallowing, she froze, her emotions warring. If she left, he'd either see or hear her. But if she announced her presence instead, he'd probably claim she was following him.

There were simply no good solutions here.

Finally, Pen turned, ready to flee back through the large room, but the image of Storm grabbed hold of her. He tore at his hair, teeth gritted, pain breaking across his features. She didn't want to feel it, didn't even want to think it, but Pen found herself pitying him. She knew, in some way, that she was to blame for this feeling. Whether or not he'd deserved to be put in his place, Penelope Skinner suddenly wished he'd be the person she knew he could be.

Be the young, excited author he'd been once upon a time.

The one she'd looked up to.

The one who'd been her hero.

But that Neil Storm was gone, and this echo of that boy she'd once admired was left in his place. And it was all her fault.

Chapter 4

NEIL

Neil sighed as his fingers tangled in his hair. How did she know just how to infuriate him? Neil was terrible in social situations, and her presence only seemed to make it worse for inexplicable reasons. He ran his hand over his forehead, feeling the whisper-thin scar beneath his fingers.

He hated to admit it, but all these years, Neil had unknowingly made publishing that much more difficult for her, and the thought made his hands clench into fists even now. It should have been fun, angering Penelope Skinner, but there was an itch at the back of his mind. She'd had the guts to speak the truth on that fateful day, and he'd had the nerve to say those things because he was too damn scared of the truth.

Damn it, Skinner was right. He was the Native author people could stomach, the one who wrote books the woke white feminists in the world could relate to. No one had ever questioned his right to be in that seat. Neil was Native American, and that's all that ever mattered—until Penelope Skinner opened her mouth. She came in with her hard truths, and no one had listened because she was a one-hit wonder, and Neil Storm was a household name.

But Neil had listened. Even though he'd tried to block out her voice, he'd heard every word she said. He had worked so hard to get here, but Penelope Skinner had been right about one thing, whether or not she'd said it outright: Neil Storm was a coward.

Neil breathed in the musk and mud and dampness of the castle. It smelled ancient. He pictured the old, torn wallpaper covering stone, tapestries hanging above fireplaces, large leather chairs, and long, food-adorned tables in cool stone rooms. When he closed his eyes, he painted lavish scenes of parties with nobles dressed in rich clothes. He imagined Scottish lairds and bards before the hearth, singing in Scottish Gaelic. *What a place it must have been,* he marveled.

Exhaling, he opened his eyes. It had always been easy for him to imagine, to pretend. It's why he was an author; it was second nature for him. But his creative well had run dry, and he was tired of the same stories he'd been writing for years, the very ones that publishing was expecting of him.

The ones Penelope Skinner hated so much.

Where had his tenaciousness gone in the years since his debut? What happened to that energy, to *that* Neil Storm?

A twig snapped from somewhere to his left, and Neil straightened in surprise, swiveling to get a better look. He didn't know what he expected, but Penelope Skinner stood, her expression twisted into a grimace as if she'd been caught. She was half-hidden behind a stone wall, hands buried in moss as she swayed in place, trying to decide whether to stay or to go.

"Sorry. I didn't see you. I was just going."

She turned to leave, but Neil stood, smoothing down his fleece. He pictured her crying, the disappointment creasing her brow, and the lines around her mouth as she'd frowned. They had their differences, but Neil hated knowing he made her cry.

"No, it's fine. I'll go."

Neither of them said anything. Neil watched her quietly, her eyes not quite meeting his. She folded and unfolded her arms, jaw clenched. Her glasses were askew, wisps of dark hair falling free of her braid, and altogether, Neil could admit there was something almost *sweet* about the woman.

In an "I'll-throw-a-book-at-you-when-I'm-mad" kind of way.

Damn, that look. Neil cleared his throat and motioned to the little piles of rocks surrounding them. "We could also just sit here quietly?" he offered instead.

She stared at him, her expression blank but for the scrunching of her nose in thought. Finally, she nodded curtly, finding her own pile of stone. They sat in silence for a few minutes, crouched in the heart of the ruins, not quite looking at one another. Although he resisted at first, Neil watched her in his periphery. Her nostrils flared as her hands fiddled absently with the zipper on her jacket. She angled her head back to get a good look at the turrets of the castle and the trees that bowed inside the stone limits.

God, things couldn't change between them. What had he been thinking? He wasn't certain there was anything he could do to combat this level of animosity. So, without another word, Neil stood and spun on his heel toward the entrance.

"Where are you going?" she called loudly, tripping after him.

"Shhhh," he hissed, rushing toward her and clamping a hand over her mouth. He froze, lips parting in surprise as he stared down at her. At large gray eyes above his hand, at the feel of his palm against her smooth skin. He shook his head and pulled his hand free. "Jesus, Skinner, we're not supposed to be in here."

Right then, a deep Scottish voice bellowed, "Yer no supposed to be there!" Neil shot her a look as if to say *I told you so*.

Skinner's eyes widened. "Where's Daniela and Laszlo?"

He shook his head and straightened. Clenching his teeth, he clasped her hand and pulled her after him in the opposite direction of the tear in the fence.

"No clue."

She wanted to protest, he could feel it in the way she fought his touch, but finally, she followed, quickening her short stride to match his.

He had no way of knowing if they'd get in trouble for wandering in some old ruins. From the looks of the place, Neil could only assume they didn't want people meandering around here for safety reasons. With the floors caving in and the earth so soft around the stone, it was no wonder.

"How are we supposed to get out?" Skinner panted as they stopped beside a strip of the fence. Her glasses fogged up, beads of sweat trickling down her forehead from running. More hair had come loose from her braid, dark wisps floating around her face and clinging to the sweat.

Damn her, she was distracting him. He motioned to the fence before them.

"Climb."

They stared down at their clasped hands before she slipped hers free, wiping her palm on her pants before grabbing hold of the fence and trying to haul herself up. Neil snorted and moved to climb after her. She slipped, almost kicking him in the face, and he yanked back just in time, Skinner nearly falling from the sudden movement. Neil tried not to laugh, his face heating as he pressed a fist to his lips. Grunting, she struggled to pull herself up, but she only looked like a beached dolphin, flapping over the top of the metal fence.

"Use your upper body strength!" he said, voice cracking with humor.

"I don't have any," she admitted, locked in place. Her face was beet red, her glasses tipping dangerously down her nose as she floundered.

"I apologize in advance," he warned as he stepped up to the fence. Neil had no choice but to shove Skinner's butt up and over. "Just throw your leg over," he instructed, using a shoulder and a hand to push. It felt strange, touching her again. Not wrong, just . . . strange. In a million years, he never could have imagined this scenario.

"I can't," she gasped.

Squeezing his eyes shut, Neil used the last of his strength to shove, one hand gripping her inner thigh, the touch eliciting a strange sound from her throat before she fell over and landed in a bush with a squeak. Neil decided it was best not to interpret the sound. Muscles aching, he pulled himself up and over with ease, landing beside her. He straightened his clothes, untangling twigs from his hair. He glared down at her as she stood, brushing off her pants.

"Thanks a lot." Her tone was a double-edged blade.

"She can be thankful," he said a little too cheerfully. He was trying so hard not to think of the way his fingers had skimmed her inner thigh, but his eyes betrayed him.

Skinner was curvy. Neil had never noticed before. She generally dressed in loose sweaters and skirts and dresses, comfortable fabric that did nothing to accentuate . . . well, anything, but her tight jeans were hugging curves he didn't know she had. Before he knew it, his eyes raked down her, skating across freckles, down to a full chest and fuller thighs. Neil straightened, meeting stormy gray eyes.

"What?" she snapped, cheeks reddening.

"Nothing."

His hand flexed, fingers straining to touch her again.

She rolled her eyes and brushed off her jacket angrily. And like that, the sight of her frustration pulled Neil back to the surface. Suddenly, everything was right in the world: Skinner with her condescending tone, and Neil with his annoyance rolling off in waves.

Skinner's cheeks were flushed, her eyes anywhere but on him. "What now?" she asked, craning her neck to peer down the way. She pushed her glasses up and tugged a branch from her braid.

"Where are ye?" the man called out, closer now.

Neil looked to Skinner. Right when he thought he'd avoided trouble, he found himself back in the thick of it. Would she hate him after this? What was he thinking—she already hated him. He might as well throw more fuel on the fire.

"Just trust me," he said, one hand going to her waist.

"What are you doing?" she asked, eyes wide as she backed up. If looks could kill.

"I'm not going to eat you."

"It certainly feels like it," she snapped as he bent down. She followed him with her eyes, her head angling back as he stepped closer. From his place, he could smell the coconut of her shampoo, the mint of her lip balm.

They were a hair's breadth from one another, their lips inches apart, noses brushing. His grip on her tightened as he stared down at her, and her eyes met his. He thought, for one wild moment, to kiss her. They were already so close; it would be so easy. It was the drunk giddiness, the strange electricity their banter brought out in him. Nothing more.

Right?

But there was that spark of an almost kiss, the heat in the moment before. Her lips parted, and his eyes followed the movement. God, she really was beautiful. They could hate each other all they wanted, but he couldn't deny the sliver of *something*. Neil swallowed hard, his hand trailing up to cup her cheek and slide into her braid. He itched to unravel it, to tug her head back and take her mouth with his.

If he could, Neil would stay in that instant for a fraction longer. He heard a groan from behind them, low and annoyed. For a moment, he thought it was himself. But when it sounded again, he knew instantly it wasn't. Neil pulled back slowly, fingers sliding over her waist and away, unable to meet Skinner's glower as he turned and blinked at the older man.

"Off with ye," he grumbled with a wave of his hand. Straightening and stepping back, Neil turned down the road, steps long and quick. Skinner ran to keep up with him, her short legs no match for his.

Damn it, he needed a moment to compose himself. His heart was beating a frantic rhythm against his ribs and other . . . *parts* of him were in all sorts of disarray. What the hell was wrong with him?

"Storm," she hissed.

"Skinner," he mimicked.

But he wouldn't look at her.

He couldn't look at her.

"What was the point of doing that? He found us, what, *cuddling*?"

Neil didn't have an answer because why in the fuck had his first instinct been to pull her close? He didn't know why, and it was sending him spiraling.

Daniela and Laszlo were waiting for them beside the car, waving them over frantically as they rounded the castle. "Come on!" Daniela called out, cackling. "What took you two forever?"

"Nothing," they responded in unison.

Skinner slid into the front seat with ease, buckling in and crossing her arms over her chest before pulling out her phone again. As Neil crossed to the car, Laszlo touched his elbow, raising a brow. "What happened in those ruins?" his friend asked quietly, honey-brown eyes flicking to the woman in the front seat.

"Nothing." Maybe, if he kept telling himself it was nothing, it would stay that way.

"If you say so."

Neil climbed into the car and buckled in, hands tightening around the steering wheel. What had he been thinking, touching her like that? More so, why was he still thinking about the feeling of her so close to him? He ground his teeth together, eyes squeezed shut.

"Are we going?" Laszlo asked.

Jaw working, Neil opened his eyes and started the van before pulling out, the castle ruins disappearing behind them as they wove down the long, narrow road. The four of them were silent as they hurried through the coming darkness to their final destination, soft Scottish music filling the void.

Part of Neil wished he'd let Laszlo drive. The Highlands was more beautiful than he could have ever imagined, and he wanted nothing more than to pull over and look. The days were shorter here, the oranges of sunset cast over the rolling landscapes. Though the Scottish roads were winding, and the light drizzle turned to snow as night fell, there was something almost magnetic about the sights.

They zigzagged across the Highlands before dipping east toward the Cairngorms National Park. According to their map, this strange, looping path was the quickest way to get to the castle. The drive wasn't long, but it felt longer in the darkness, with few cars traveling into the Highlands as night descended.

Cities disappeared until towns sprang up in their place, and soon there were only farmlands and signs pointing to a zoo, reindeer, trails, and various campsites and inns. The national park was thick with trees, the temperatures dropping as the elevation rose. Neil cranked up the heat as they all shivered from the pressing cold, but it was no use when the snow began to fall. Long, strange patches of open ground and farmland popped up as they drove farther into the park, lit only by their headlights and the white snow. The area was all but deserted.

It wasn't until the sun had dipped down completely and the road grew slick with snow that, according to their GPS, they had arrived.

The road to the castle was nearly impossible to make out, the fresh snow a thick layer of powder, building up along the embankment. The road snaked down a tunnel of darkened trees, with nothing and no one out in sight. Neil slowed, the van's small, worn wheels struggling over the frozen ground.

"Everyone left a copy of their itinerary and the castle's address with someone, right?" Laszlo asked, eyes glued to the road, hands clamped around the back of Neil's seat as they went around another curve.

"Is it really only the four of us here?" Skinner asked shakily.

"Everyone else couldn't make it."

"Couldn't or wouldn't?" she said.

Neil peeked up at her. She blinked, expression blank and carefully guarded before dipping her chin.

"I feel like we're about to get murdered," Daniela whispered, hands pressed to the glass.

That about summed it up. They were veering into a tunnel in a country they weren't familiar with to spend a week at a castle that claimed to be haunted.

What could possibly go wrong?

Chapter 5

PEN

If Scotland was already a fantastical place, the snow only enhanced it, casting a curtain of mystery over the landscape. The van lurched down the path, the snow steep on all sides. When Storm finally parked the van in the round drive with a bit of difficulty, Pen unbuckled, pulled on her jacket, and slid from her seat, landing in the snow with a *crunch*. She couldn't stand another moment in that small space with him.

Despite doing absolutely everything in her power to think of literally anything else, Pen had spent the better part of the two-hour drive from the ruins trying not to think about the way Neil Storm had pulled her close.

Or the way he'd held her hand when he tugged her along after him.

Or the way he'd cupped her cheek and leaned in.

Or the way he smelled (of vanilla and coffee and something musky she couldn't quite place—not that she'd thought about it). (She *definitely* hadn't thought about it, and it *definitely* hadn't flooded her senses, making the bag of chips she bought when they refueled taste stale on her tongue.)

Pen could still imagine the press of his fingers on the inside of her thigh, the pressure building between her legs as he lifted her up and over the fence, and his muffled laughter when she flailed miserably. And he hadn't meant to, it had been an accident, but a finger had slid up even farther, applying the smallest of force against the crotch of her jeans.

And she'd liked it.

Fuck.

She breathed sharply, letting the air cool her down. She was blushing hard, heat rising from her neck and flooding her cheeks, and she felt the strange, sudden urge to bury her face in the snow. She couldn't get him out of her goddamn thoughts.

Get it together, she urged herself. It was Neil Storm, for crying out loud. The man she'd reportedly hated for the last few years.

Fuck.

"Did you say something?" Storm asked, frowning over the hood of the van.

"Nope!"

Had she said something? For fuck's sake, she was unhinged.

Gritting her teeth, she tried to ignore him as she pivoted to survey the purple sky. Pen could feel Storm's eyes on her, tracking her movements. When he closed the door and angled away from her, she found her eyes drifting back to him. She considered his tousled hair and his loose sweater. Storm was hot in that probably-works-in-a-library sort of way. She didn't know why she had a thing for the soft, nerdy look, but Neil Storm had it and more, and the longer she looked at him, the more vulgar her thoughts turned.

Because she was imagining his hand there, slipping onto that soft spot on her full thighs, squeezing gently, fingers traveling up to toy with her—

Oh, god, what was wrong with her?

She dug her nails into her thigh, trying to calm herself as the others began gathering their things. Pen could hear Laszlo and Daniela moving in the back seat, their voices muffled before they opened the doors and came out into the cold night. There was a sudden change in the air, a tingling down her spine as she glanced about them.

They were well and truly alone in this place.

Blinking, snow melting on her lashes, Pen turned and surveyed the property. She wasn't sure what she'd expected. She'd never been to a castle before coming to Scotland. Oh, she'd seen them in film and travel guides with people like Rick Steves. And every time she heard the word "castle," she imagined tall turrets, gardens, and large, wooden doors.

This castle was none of that. While it wasn't entirely small, it wasn't huge either. Larger than the last, this one rose out of the ground, towering over the trees and blotting out the purple clouds in the sky. After a day spent looking at ruins, it was a breath of fresh air.

And for a castle in Scotland, it was in great shape. The snow illuminated it at night. Stone stacked up in two small turrets on either side of the rectangular base. It was two stories in height, windows littering the front and the towers.

The garden, however, was a different story. It was overgrown, dried, and withered to the left and right of the castle. The trees had snaked their fingers over it, leaving little room for the sky and natural light to make the stone building known. Powdery snow was sprinkled over the lot of it, covering the castle in a bit of mystery. Stone stairs led up to its entrance, where a set of small wooden doors were opened inward, casting a soft glow over the steps. A figure waited impatiently on the upper landing, back hunched and hands fiddling with a large ring of keys.

"Let's go!" Daniela said. She dropped her bags beside Laszlo and made a run for it, pausing on the first landing to catch her breath before weakly jogging the rest of the way and stopping beside the figure.

"Who's that?" Pen asked, turning to Laszlo.

"The groundskeeper."

"She seems exciting," Storm cut in, leaning around Pen. He was so close that his hand brushed her thigh, and Pen flinched away, trying to put some distance between them.

"Would you give me some space," she gasped.

"I'm not exactly trying to cuddle you, Skinner."

"Could have fooled me."

"Well, it's cold," Laszlo said, motioning to the castle. "Unless you two would rather stay out here and bicker in the snow all night?"

Pen shook her head and rounded toward the back of the van for her things. Laszlo waved to them as he hauled his and Daniela's bags up the steep steps. Pen stopped short as Storm motioned to her large patchwork duffel bag in the trunk, his suitcase already on the ground by his feet.

"This yours?"

"Yes?"

He looked from the bag to her. "No offense, but it's hideous."

She sucked on her teeth, swallowing her retort. *You can do this, Pen. Play. Nice. For Laszlo. Only for Laszlo.*

"It's made of recycled material." She couldn't help the bit of pride that seeped into her tone.

He ogled it. "I can tell." Storm raised a brow, and she wanted to pinch it between her fingers. "Penelope Skinner, saving one tree at a time with her . . . bag." She opened her mouth to retort, but he lifted her bag, weighing it. "It's heavy."

Pen nodded, puffing out her cheeks. *Calm. Cool.* "Ugh, yeah, but I can—"

"I've got it." He threw the thing across his shoulders, large and bulky and nearly bursting at the seams, before closing the trunk and grabbing his bag.

"You really don't need to," she called after him, struggling to jog across the gravel drive. She nearly slammed into him as he spun toward her, the bag held out to her. He waited a beat, shaking it. When she didn't take it, he sighed.

"No, I really don't. I could let you take it up if you're so hell-bent on doing everything yourself. It's all yours."

Pen stared at it for a moment, dreading the thought of carrying it upstairs. She reached out as if to take it, but he snatched it back with another long, blush-inducing sigh.

"Sometimes, Skinner, people just want to help." He turned and hurried up the steps, disappearing past the groundskeeper without so much as a hello.

Why. The question bouncing around her head was: *Why?* She thought back to her conversation with Laszlo, to that pause after she'd asked if Storm was going. Why hadn't she seen this coming? Why hadn't she foretold this, the most dreadful of scenarios?

Out of breath, Pen stopped on the stairs. Snow flitted down around her and she shivered, pulling her jacket close. She wanted to tear her bag away from him. She wanted to grind his face into the snow and demand to know why he was being nice. The Neil Storm she knew didn't carry her bag or help her get out of trouble.

The Neil Storm she knew didn't cup her face gently and almost kiss her.

Damn it, now she was thinking about the castle ruins again. Pen tugged violently on the end of her braid as she stalked up the snowy steps toward the castle. She wanted to demand why everything he did contradicted the Neil Storm she knew. He shouldn't be sitting with her in the car in companionable silence. He shouldn't be carrying her bag, and he certainly shouldn't be touching her the way he had.

"Ye look like ye want to punch something," the groundskeeper called out from the top step. Pen paused on the steps, scrutinizing the woman.

She wasn't much older than them, in her early forties with graying blond hair and watchful, dark eyes. Her frame was hidden under a large, heavy coat, a knit scarf wrapped tightly around her neck like a protective charm. Hands worn from years of hard work fiddled absently with a giant key ring at her belt.

Feeling a bit like a toddler, Pen stomped her way up the last few steps, stopping before the woman. "Or someone," she responded, glaring through the door.

"Fanny." The woman offered Pen a hand. "I'll be giving yer group a tour of the grounds."

Pen perked up, eyes crinkling as she smiled. "We get a full tour? I thought we'd just get a key in one of those little boxes."

"Ye thought I'd leave the key in a wee box, did ye?" Pen shrugged sheepishly, and Fanny laughed. "Americans. Yer used to normal doors." She brandished a large skeleton key. "Cannae exactly fit this into one of those wee boxes."

"No, you can't," Pen agreed with a chuckle.

Fanny gestured to Pen, and she slipped through the doors, pausing on the entry rug beside Laszlo to take it all in. She had seen Edinburgh Castle, a village within its walls, full of museums and exhibitions. From the outset, it was tall and striking, towering on a landscape of sharp, jagged rock that overlooked Old Town.

But this castle? This castle felt like people had lived here, like it held the homely touches of a family, of a refuge in the Highlands passed down from generation to generation. It was a place caught in a time capsule. The walls were clothed in tapestries, and some of the colors had drained from the garments. The floors, though stone, were covered in rugs of rich colors, some new, others worn down by feet.

The castle might not have been large, but it was still a castle, and that, in and of itself, was some type of magic. The corridors were narrow, with strange doors set into stone walls. Pen's eyes dragged over the details, taking note of anything and everything she saw. *This* was a place that could inspire. *This* was a castle where she could write.

Her friend had chosen well.

"A few rules 'fore we start," Fanny called, drawing their attention. "When I leave this castle, I willnae be coming back during the week. Only reach out if ye have a true emergency. The nearest hospital is three hours away, and we wouldnae want ye to bleed out or anything rash."

"That's reassuring," Daniela said.

"Why won't you be coming back?" Pen asked.

Fanny turned to her, expression masked. "We ask ye not to smoke, party, or move anything in the castle during yer stay."

"What about orgies?" Daniela asked, deadpanning.

Fanny looked between their group with narrowed eyes and pursed lips. She opened and closed her mouth several times before she cleared her throat and said, "Cannae believe I have to say this, but no orgies either."

"Well, that's no fun."

Pen scanned the open room. Before she knew it, she was spinning toward Storm, pulled to him like a magnet. She was startled to find his eyes already on her. Blinking, he turned away, lips pressed into a thin line as he looked around at the foyer like nothing was at all strange between them.

Fanny led Pen and the others through the vestibule with hooks for their coats to their left, the floor covered by a plush rug with a family crest. A large stag was embellished with bits of gold thread that caught the dim lighting and was surrounded by laurels, and Pen stared down at it until Laszlo closed the door behind them, blocking it from view. Pen returned her attention to the groundskeeper.

"This castle was built in the late eighteenth century. It has only had five owners in that time, which we know is a wee bit unusual. There was something of seventy-five years left to dust and ghosts after the family was unable to produce any more heirs. My grandfather was hired on by the owners of the castle in the mid-twentieth century, and we have been its caretakers ever since."

"Ghosts, you say?" Daniela asked.

"Ghosts," Fanny agreed. "If yer here, I'm assuming ye read the description on the website? It's why we keep the cost so low. Just enough for upkeep and the like."

That's not worrying, Pen thought, wiping her sweaty palms on her pants.

They stopped just inside the foyer before a large painting of a woman. It was hung beside a staircase that led up to a landing that overlooked the foyer before splitting off to separate wings of the castle.

Pen kept her distance from the oil painting, eyes locked on the woman's face. Although she knew little about art, Pen guessed it dated back to the early to mid-nineteenth century. The woman was dressed in black, stays pressing her breasts up to spill over the swooping collar of her empire-waisted Regency gown. Her skin was white, so translucent it was stark against the black of her hair. Her eyes were gray, and no matter where Pen seemed to stand in the foyer, it felt as if they followed her every movement.

"Creepy, isn't it?" Daniela asked, leaning close.

"Creepy," Pen agreed quietly.

"Who was she?" Laszlo asked.

"We dinnae ken, but many visitors have claimed to see her ghost lurking in the hall at night or looking out over the grounds from the abandoned wing. Some say she is searching for a boy she killed. Many say his screams can be heard when the clock strikes three."

Also not worrying, Pen thought.

"Have you seen her?" Laszlo asked.

"The woman in black?" Fanny shook her head. "Nay, not the woman in black."

Pen noticed Fanny didn't specify further, and the thought of even more ghosts made her shiver. She wanted to look away from the painting, but she was drawn to the woman captured on canvas. There was a small, jagged tear in the canvas across the top, splitting the charcoal paint like a wound on skin. It was uneven and imperfect, almost as though something or someone had scraped their sharpened nails across it.

"Don't you have records?" Storm asked from Laszlo's other side.

"No. They were all lost from a leak in the roof. Many of the books in the study were replaced in the eighties because of it. The castle has since been repaired, but too late for the records, I'm afraid."

Pen frowned, forcing herself to focus on the groundskeeper.

"There are different versions of the legend," Fanny continued. "Locals stopped coming here in the nineties after an incident involving a local youth, but my pa used to tell me of the weeping maiden trapped here. He said she was a young noble lady who'd died alone and heartbroken, having murdered a boy. Her family shunned her, and she was left to waste away in her room, looking out wistfully over the grounds for someone to take her away."

Storm cleared his throat. "Well, that's depressing."

Fanny laughed, winking. "Our legends are milder than others. Ye should take one of those haunted tours in Edinburgh. It's nay dubbed the City of Ghosts for no reason."

Pen shuddered as she pictured the dark crypts under the city, the soft, echoing sound of heavy boots. There was a part of Pen that was beginning to think staying in this castle was a bad idea, and not because Storm was here. If she was that scared down in the vaults beneath Edinburgh, how could she spend an entire week in a supposedly haunted castle?

Stepping to the left of the staircase, Fanny tapped a wall, making Pen jump to attention. "This here is the cellar. I dinnae suggest going down there unless ye have a death wish."

"What's wrong with the cellar?" Pen regretted having asked it immediately.

"There's said to be an angry spirit down there. Mostly sticks to the shadows, ye ken. A wee little thing. My pa said it was the maiden's brother, protecting her and ridding this place of any wrongdoers or some sort." She patted the wall fondly. "Should be fine if ye keep out, though. Ghosts willnae hurt ye unless ye give them a reason to."

Pen and Laszlo shared a look of horror.

"Anywho!" Fanny motioned them to the stairs, ignoring their dubious expressions. "Much of the castle is easy to navigate," she promised, crossing to the staircase, "but let me show ye the upstairs level where the bedrooms are."

Pen fought another shiver. Something about this place and that painting felt off. She met the woman's gray eyes before reluctantly tearing her gaze from the painting and hurrying up the plush steps after the group.

It seemed much of the castle had been renovated over the years. Wooden steps and banisters had been put in place, dating back no more than a hundred years, Fanny told them as they trailed behind her. While much of the décor was faded, there were copies of paintings hung in golden frames that caught the light, and the wallpaper was newer, only peeling in small, dark corners.

There was a peculiar, almost earthy scent lingering in the halls, growing stronger the higher they climbed. No matter how much Pen tried to focus on it, she couldn't quite place the scent. As they ascended the staircase, she ran her fingers over the smooth wood of the banister, taking in the small details, the gathering dust, the paintings and curtains leached of color. If Pen didn't know they were in a haunted castle, she would have assumed as much from the décor alone.

Fanny led Pen and the others up to the second landing, and though she was speaking, Pen could not focus on the groundskeeper's words. She kept imagining the portrait below, a woman with a knowing, unwavering stare. She had expected paintings and

statues and strange old props set about the castle. After all, they'd
wanted the haunted experience, hadn't they?

But that painting of the woman . . . Even the thought of it sent
a shudder through her.

It felt *alive*.

"This is the east wing, where ye'll be staying. And that"—
Fanny gestured to their right, eyes wary—"is the west wing. The
west wing and any locked doors or passageways throughout the
castle are strictly off-limits."

Pen peered down the darkened hallway. "What's wrong with
the west wing?" Pen asked.

Fanny paused. Pen swore she saw something there, a twitch
of her lips, a furrow of her brow, something close to fear reflected
in her tired eyes, but it was gone just as soon. Clearing her throat,
Fanny turned toward the east wing, toward the light.

"Unless ye want to be sleeping with the ghosts, I'd suggest
following me."

Pen decided she did *not* want to sleep with the ghosts.

Chapter 6
PEN

Glancing over her shoulder every few seconds, Pen moved on reluctantly, a strange coil of dread tightening in her gut. There was almost a feeling of being pulled, a string tied tight around her center, yanking her toward the darkness. It took everything in Pen not to immediately follow the urge and tiptoe over that invisible line.

As if sensing Pen's reluctance, Storm paused and turned back to her. "You okay, Skinner?"

She stared past him, taking in the darkened corridor, a contrast to the lit hall of the east wing. Was she imagining this feeling? Were they all oblivious to it? It was the same sort of foreboding she'd felt on the tour in Edinburgh, the same sickening trepidation.

"Are you?" Pen asked. "Does none of this bother you?"

He looked over her head as if he was drawn there, and Pen followed his fixation down to the space where the darkness somehow soaked up the light that seeped in from the east wing. A sponge, hungry for the slithering shadows.

"I don't know how much I believe in these things," Storm said, his voice low and velvety smooth. It seemed to dip down Pen's front, pooling between her legs. She clamped her thighs together, disbelieving.

What the fuck is wrong with you, woman? she chided. *It's Storm.*

He cleared his throat and refocused on Pen. "Hard to believe in something I haven't seen for myself, you know?" Shrugging, he turned and rejoined the group.

Narrowing her eyes, Pen swiveled toward the east wing and quickened her pace. If the legends were to be believed, the woman in the portrait wandered that hall, and Pen was not in the mood to find out if the legends were real. She felt sick as she followed Storm back toward the light, but for now, she was more than happy to turn away from the west wing and whatever lurked in the dark.

The hall leading to the bedrooms was lined with oil paintings, small LEDs illuminating the name plaques beneath them. Pen scanned the neat lettering as Fanny motioned them on. On Greek-like pedestals, marble busts sat, with matching plaques that had been dusted and cleaned regularly based on the light lemony scent lingering in the air.

Pen ran her fingers over the maroon wallpaper, the color contrasted with an inlaid silver pattern of little laurels like the tapestry rug in the foyer. She felt as though she were walking into a vampiric lair, alluding to something horrific waiting for her at the end of the hall. She peered into rooms as they passed them, fireplaces and canopied beds lying in wait.

One by one, Fanny opened doors and showed them in, and one by one, their group dwindled. Daniela filed into a room first, closing the door with a *click*, and Laszlo disappeared with a grateful sigh soon after. When they reached the end of the hall, it was just Pen, Storm, and Fanny.

Fanny opened the door to her right and nodded to Storm. "This will be yers," she said as Storm unceremoniously dropped Pen's bag at her feet and disappeared into his room with a grunt. "And this is yers," she said, opening the one to their left.

It was a cozy room, much like the others. A tall oak-post bed sat a few feet from the door, an antique trunk at the foot. A fireplace was nestled into the farthest wall, and before it was a pair of brown leather chairs draped with blankets.

On the wall next to the door was a massive, towering wardrobe. Two large windows overlooked the garden on the wall across, which was sloped like a rotunda, with a padded bench beneath. It was cold, the stone walls doing little to trap the heat without the fireplace going.

Pen deposited her backpack beside the bed and dragged her duffel in from the hall. "They really went all out here, didn't they?" She smoothed her hands over the blankets on the bed, fine and thick for the cold nights ahead. She wanted to wrap one around her shoulders, cover her face, and pretend like she was at home, burying her face in Apawllo's soft belly. Pen needed some sense of comfort to ground her.

Fanny fiddled with the doorknob. "Most of the rooms look like this. The previous owners wanted it to feel authentic."

She met Pen's eyes for a moment, and Pen thought she would say something more, but the groundskeeper stayed silent.

"You hate it here, don't you?" Pen ventured.

"If I truly hated it, I wouldnae be here now, would I? Do ye have any questions for me 'fore I go?"

"If we need anything, how do we get ahold of you?"

Pen fought a shiver at the look of pity in her eyes. "Ye dinnae get ahold of me unless it's an emergency."

Pen opened her mouth to respond, but Fanny closed the door without another word. Fanny didn't seem to want to spend another second in this castle, and Pen was beginning to think that even if they had an emergency, Fanny wouldn't be rushing to help them. Rocking back on her heels, Pen glanced around the space and to the bed, the exhaustion of the day hitting her all at once. Her bickering with Storm had worn on her, and she could feel the beginnings of a headache thrumming away at her skull.

Alone, Pen sighed and flung herself backward on her bed,

staring up at the canopy. What a mess she'd gotten herself into. She'd known it would be difficult at the retreat. She hadn't been around this many people who knew her intimately in months, but Neil Storm . . . Well, he'd done a number on her.

Reaching for a pillow, she pulled it to her face and screamed into it. Pen screamed from anger, frustration, guilt, and embarrassment. Why could nothing in her life go according to plan? Between Neil Storm showing up and the dawning self-made deadline she'd set, Pen would bet she'd come out of the retreat worse for wear.

She should have given Storm this. The minute he showed up at the pub, she should have backed off. Pen really needed to start thinking things through before she made rash decisions.

Like blowing her savings on a spur-of-the-moment writing retreat.

A long, terrible *squeak* cut through the silence. Frowning, Pen tossed the pillow aside, leaning up on her elbows as she surveyed the room.

"Hello?" she called.

No one answered. She frowned as she searched the room. She was alone.

Licking her lips, Pen stood. People always said that strange sounds were houses settling, but what about stone castles? Besides, in the world of horror, it was always something *more*. A ghost, memories of something sinister lingering in tainted walls, a monster, perhaps. As a horror author, Pen of all people knew not to creep toward the noise, but she couldn't help it. Curiosity had won her over.

Pen crossed the room, fingers dancing over the fireplace, kicking up dust. She coughed, waving her hands in the air to clear away the cloud. She paused at the edge of the fireplace, her eyes bouncing around the room. Then she heard it again: that long, dreadful *squeak*. A foot on the stairs, a hand pushing a door, a terrible, monstrous thing teetering on an edge.

Whatever it was, it stilled once more, the room falling silent. She felt the faintest of drafts, cold air slithering across her skin, and Pen wrapped an arm around her middle as she stepped toward the wall. She tested the edges of the tapestry hanging there, a banner of a stag in crimson reds and forest greens. Behind it, cool air hit her fingers, a soft, chilling caress. Lifting the tapestry aside, she came face-to-face with a dark corridor. The door had been opened wide, and stone steps led up and down, dissolving into darkness.

"What on earth?" she said, leaning in.

Frowning, she slid her phone from her pocket and turned on the flashlight, moving the light up and down. This was breaking horror movie protocol number one: Never go into a dark space alone. And yet, she felt that incessant tether again. Puffing out her cheeks and slightly regretting the decision, she began her descent.

The passageway was cold and barren, only narrow stone walls and steep steps guiding her to somewhere else in the castle. Her footsteps echoed in the stairwell, and though someone like Laszlo might have needed to duck in the slender passage, she did not. Her fingers skimmed over the stone until they landed on something wooden. Pen blinked, shining the light on a short wooden door.

"Hello?" she whispered, pressing her ear up against its smooth surface. She saw nothing through the sliver of light bleeding through the side, but she heard footsteps pass her.

"Rent out a haunted castle," someone said, "what could go wrong? These damn Americans . . ."

"Fanny?" Pen exclaimed as she tugged open the door and burst out into a wide hall.

Fanny screamed, turning to slam a wineglass into the wall. White wine and blood dribbled down her hand as she held out the broken stem toward Pen.

Pen's heart raced, sporadic beats playing in her chest. She pocketed her phone and held up her hands, taking a step toward the groundskeeper. Fanny moved back, eyes wide with horror as she brandished the shattered glass like a weapon. Pen flinched, sweat sliding down her spine.

"Oh my god, Fanny, it's just me."

Breathing shakily, Pen hurried forward, gently prying the stem from Fanny's grip. Grabbing her wrist, Pen urged her down the hall, stumbling in the direction Fanny pointed. Finally, in the kitchen, she ran cool water over the cuts before pressing paper towels to Fanny's pale skin. Blood oozed through wide gashes, dark and crimson seeping through and staining the white towels red.

"Where in the bloody hell did ye come from?" Fanny asked, grimacing as Pen applied more pressure.

Pen stood, wiping her hands down her dark jeans. "I found a secret passageway in my room." Fanny made a noncommittal sound, as if "secret passageway" was entirely normal. "I thought you left."

"Wanted a bevvy from the cellar," Fanny murmured. She held a bottle in her other hand, her fingers wrapped around the neck of it, choking it.

"First aid?"

"Under the sink."

Clearing her throat, Pen bent and searched through the stuff under the sink. Finally, she found a first aid kit, discolored and nearly empty, with decades-old supplies.

"What happened?" Pen asked, looking up at her through a mess of bangs. "I know I surprised you, there, but you went into major fight-or-flight mode." She used a few drops of alcohol to clean the wound before affixing gauze and wrapping it around Fanny's hand.

Fanny swallowed and peered over her shoulder. "I thought I heard . . ." She trailed off, breathing deep. She clenched her jaw, blinking away what might have been tears. "It was nothing."

Pen wrapped her hand around Fanny's, imploring. "It wasn't nothing, Fanny. It's okay to admit—"

"It. Was. Nothing." Fanny tore her hands from Pen and stood. She pushed off the table and hurried out of the room, breaking into a jog as she rounded the corner.

"Okay, then," Pen muttered under her breath.

She stood on wobbly legs, closing the first aid kit before rubbing a hand over her eyes as the clatter of Fanny's jingling keys quieted and the front door slammed shut. Pen pressed a hand to her chest. First the secret door, then the groundskeeper. Although she wanted to, Pen wasn't sure she could keep chalking it up to coincidences. Already, the castle was doing things to them, and she couldn't tell if the stories were getting to her or if there really was something more to this place. Either way, she didn't like it.

Grabbing some paper towels, Pen cleaned up the mess in the hallway, stooping to pick up the small glass fragments from the floor. She wiped down the wall and soaked up as much of the wine as she could from the rug before retreating to the kitchen to drop it all in the bin beneath the sink. Leaning forward, she gripped the edge of the counter and breathed deep, squeezing her eyes shut.

"Looks like you could use a drink," Storm murmured.

Pen jumped in surprise, eyes flying open. She turned toward him with a sigh, and she was startled to find she'd *wanted* him to appear. She could play nice, but it didn't mean she needed to smile or put on a fake mask in front of him; Pen could glower and grumble all she wanted. She studied him, carefully considering all six feet of him. He leaned languidly against the entryway, legs stretched out before him and crossed at the ankles.

Face-to-face, she felt an entirely different emotion overcome her, warm and unwelcome. She tried not to think about that moment at the ruins, or the way he'd carried her bag (after insulting it) without even asking.

Or the way his fingers had slipped so easily into her braid as his thumb brushed her cheek. He'd held her face like she was the most precious and fragile thing in the world, and the more Pen thought about it, the more her pulse began to ratchet up.

But he was still Neil Storm. He was still the man who fought with her, who made her hands curl into fists, who set every part of her aflame. People didn't just change.

"Why do you say that?" she ventured, crossing her arms.

He smiled, a dimple forming to the left of his mouth. And, oh, how she wanted to press her finger into it and force it to disappear. How had she never noticed that before? Such a small thing with massive consequences.

"I saw a liquor cabinet in the study."

Pen puckered her lips. Why would she ever willingly spend time alone with him? On the other hand, she couldn't deny that she was going to need something strong to get through a week in this castle with these people and whatever the hell else was residing inside these walls. She narrowed her eyes, the man unflinching before her.

"Lead the way."

As he turned on his heel, Pen ran a hand over the back of her neck, her hair standing on end. She had the uncomfortable sense that they were being watched. Peeking over her shoulder toward the secret door in the hall, she sped up, her shoes clicking in time with Storm's.

The last thing she wanted right now was to be left alone. Even if it meant being alone with *him*.

Chapter 7

NEIL

In their awkward, heavy silence, Neil led her through the castle. She followed him down the long corridor, past the front foyer, and to the study. Neil had stumbled upon the room after Fanny left them in the east wing and he'd unpacked his things. He'd wandered curiously through the long, wide halls until he'd come upon the oak doors. It was as if his soul knew just what he needed.

He'd always had a knack for finding books in people's homes. Neil was the kind of person at parties who wandered bookshelves, judging people on their selections, thumbing through collections as the others mingled about with wine and cocktails dangling from their fingers. He couldn't help it: He was always more at home among stories than people.

Neil pushed open the double doors and motioned for Skinner. She tiptoed inside, lips parting as she took it in. She looked like a child in a candy shop. Tall walls had been gutted and filled with bookshelves, the cases crowded with a library an author could only dream of owning. He'd scanned the titles earlier, fingers brushing over leather-bound novels and encyclopedias dating back centuries.

The study was a place he'd always imagined for himself, a silent, leering friend that took up the better part of a home, dark and lit only by towering windows and firelight. But here in this strange study, the books had hardly been touched, only the chairs and couch well worn.

Of course, there was also the liquor cabinet.

Whoever owned the castle prior had a refined taste in alcohol, or so he guessed through the thick layers of dust coating both the doors and the bottles. The glasses and bottles were exquisite, the collection like something that belonged to a wealthy lord or other. The bottles were sealed shut with wax seals and cork, handwritten labels hidden beneath layers of dust that Neil couldn't quite read. Some of the liquor was decades old, possibly more from the look of them, and Neil could picture the owner in a fine evening jacket, balancing a small glass full of the finest brandy before a large fire.

"Why are you being so nice?" Skinner asked as she pulled a book out from one of the shelves and leafed through its contents, purposefully not looking at him.

Neil shrugged as he leaned over one of the chairs, brow raised. "I'm not being nice, you just looked like you could use a drink and I could use a second set of eyes on this liquor cabinet."

She slid the book back onto the shelf and turned to him, interest piqued. "Right. Liquor cabinet."

He nodded behind him. "I haven't been able to unlock it. You're smart," he started.

Skinner gasped, hand flying to her mouth. "Did the Prince of Horror just *compliment* me?"

"I hate that name." He hadn't meant to say it aloud, but she'd heard it all the same.

Her mouth opened in surprise, and she stared up at him. "I-I'm sorry," she apologized, voice small. "I didn't realize it was a . . . Well, if you don't mind my asking, why don't you like it?"

Neil frowned down at her. No one had ever asked him before.

"I'm not royalty. I know I've done . . . *well*, but it doesn't warrant some imaginary crown. It feels like an inside joke. People use it snidely; no one ever means anything good when they use it, especially not to my face."

Fuck, was he oversharing?

"That's . . . tough."

Jaw working, Neil motioned to the liquor cabinet. "I don't need your pity; I need help getting this thing open so I can have a fucking drink."

With a coy smile, she rounded the couch toward him. The sudden approach with a glint in her gray-blue eyes made his heart thud. She was looking at him like he was a delicacy, like he imagined he'd looked back at the ruins.

"*That,* I can do."

Together, Neil and Skinner searched through desk drawers and small hiding places before Neil produced a large ring of keys. Standing before the liquor cabinet, they tried key after key on the medieval-looking ring to no avail, metal clinking as they abandoned one key for another. When that didn't work, his strange companion produced a hairpin from her hair, short, loose strands falling away in its absence.

Neil tried not to notice the way the hair framed her face, making her gray eyes larger. Or the light scent of her coconut shampoo as her braid continued to unravel. For entirely unknown and confusing reasons, he wanted to reach out and run his fingers through it, let the dark hair slide through them.

"Fuck," she cursed as the hairpin broke.

Clearing his throat, Neil straightened. "There's another way to go about this."

"I'm listening."

Neil took a stumbling step toward the entrance. After a moment of hesitation, Skinner followed him back to the kitchen. Under the sink, he riffled around in a toolbox before unearthing a rusted screwdriver.

"Ah," she said with a nod.

Neil's only response was a brilliant smile.

With painstaking slowness, Skinner pulled out the screws as Neil held up the doors to the liquor cabinet. Their hands played a game, careful to avoid one another as they bent close, nearly forehead to forehead, the silence of the castle surrounding them and spilling into the narrow space separating them. When she leaned close, he arched away, and vice versa. And when the last screw had been twisted free, Neil set aside the doors, and they peered into the open liquor cabinet. The bottles were in a variety of shapes and sizes, most of their labels coated in a healthy layer of dust. Neil reached forward and pulled out a green bottle, wiping a hand over the label to reveal—

"Whiskey," they said in unison as if sighing.

Neil raised a brow, appraising her. How could he possibly forget the way she'd downed that whiskey the night before? "I keep forgetting you're a whiskey drinker."

She smirked, reaching for two glasses. "People like to make assumptions about me." She motioned for the bottle and unstopped it, the sound reverberating in the quiet room. Neil watched in fascination as she wiped the insides of the glasses with a napkin before pouring in two fingers' worth of the amber liquid.

"Most people," she continued, closing and setting aside the bottle, "assume I don't even drink. My dad always warned me about firewater. There's that stereotype about Natives and alcoholism. There have been so many studies over the years, but the one thing I've taken from them is it has nothing to do with genetics. The higher rate of alcoholism in Natives has more to do with contributing factors, things like economic disadvantage, generational trauma, cultural loss, lack of treatment options. My dad loves beer, but he refuses to drink whiskey because he believes he'll become addicted. I've simply limited most of my alcohol consumption to more social environments."

"You've thought about this a lot, haven't you?"

"Every single time I drink." She laughed, and Neil was alarmed to find it was a soft sound. "I can hear my dad's voice nagging me at the back of my mind every time I take a sip. When I'm home, I tend to stick to beer, but even then, it's just sad to sit alone and drink."

Skinner held a glass out to him, and he took it, his fingers grazing hers. Neil yanked back with a grimace, whiskey sloshing over them both.

"Sorry," he muttered, setting aside his glass and reaching for a napkin.

"Don't worry 'bout it."

She swatted away the offered napkin. A drop of the amber liquid splashed on the back of her hand, and Neil watched, captivated, as she brought it to her lips and licked it clean. Her tongue snaked out from between bow-shaped lips, trailing a slick path toward her wrist, and the sight of it, the imagery of all the other vulgar things her tongue could do instead, made his cock hard.

Neil had a boner.

For Penelope Skinner.

What in the actual fuck?

He blinked in surprise, something unwelcome flitting about in his thoughts as he stared down at her. He found himself remembering the ruins, the way she felt under him, against him. The way he'd wanted to capture her mouth with his.

Skinner's lips parted, eyes going wide as if she could read his thoughts.

"Would you stop staring at me?" she said, taking a step away, face heating.

The rush of cool air from her absence seemed to knock some sense into him. "Sorry." He laughed awkwardly as he wiped the rim of the bottle with another napkin, angling his body away to hide the bulge in his pants. "Who would've thought we'd end up here four months later."

"Who. Would've. Thought."

Her tone was sharp. *Too* sharp. Neil frowned at her. "I'm sorry, did I say something wrong?"

"Who. Would've. Thought," she repeated. "Do you have *any* clue what you did to me?"

"To *you*? What about what you did to me?"

"To you? To me!"

Neil pinched the bridge of his nose, the whiskey fumes flooding his senses and making his eyes water. "I'm sorry, but what did I ever do to you?"

Skinner blanched. "What. Did. You. Ever. Do. To. Me."

"Stop talking like that. And don't look at me like that," he started.

"Like what?" She stepped forward, eyes narrowed on him. "You ruined *everything*."

"Me?" Neil scoffed. "*You* were the one who threw the book! *You* made that choice."

"And you? Have you ever stopped to think about the repercussions of your decisions on other Native authors? I had to work ten times harder than you. One, because I can't just prove how Native I am, but also because you keep writing these harmful stereotypes. You can't reclaim the word 'savage.' You can't claim your characters are changing the world when they themselves are problematic! Misogynistic, racist—what did you think you were doing when you wrote Trent?" Skinner shoved her hand into his chest, making Neil stumble back a step. "For every two-dimensional character, for every racist slur, for every white influencer you cater to in one of your books, me and every other Native author are working to undo that damage and take back the space you're taking up."

"Maybe I didn't want it! Maybe it wasn't me!"

"What?"

They stared at each other for a long, heated moment. Neil could feel his pulse in his fingertips as his chest rose and fell with each breath.

He'd just admitted his biggest worry. That he never wanted this, any of this. He wanted to write. He wanted people to read his books. Neil Storm had wanted so many things, the *usual* things, but he never meant for any of it to get this far. He never meant to lose sight of his goals and aspirations.

He never meant to hurt her.

"Excuse me?" she panted when he said nothing more.

"Maybe I didn't want it," he repeated. "Maybe I made a lot of bad decisions when I was younger, and now I don't know what to do or where to go. I don't have as much power as you think I do, Skinner."

Skinner opened her mouth to respond, brow furrowed in confusion.

"Thought we heard bickering," Daniela drawled.

Heart in his throat, Neil took a staggering step away from Skinner as if she'd burned him, turning in surprise to where Laszlo and Daniela had appeared in the entry to the study. Laszlo's lips twisted into a frown as he took in the scene.

"Cough it up," Daniela said, motioning to Laszlo.

Laszlo produced a small bill, slapping it into Daniela's palm as he mouthed, *Sorry.*

"You *bet* on us?" Skinner spat.

"It's not that big of a deal," Daniela said with a shrug, sauntering into the study. "You two are just predictable."

"Are not," they said in unison.

Neil and Skinner turned toward each other, his fury reflected in her expression.

"Case in point," Daniela slurred. Her eyes flew to the liquor cabinet, hands clasping together. "Oh, you managed to unlock it!" She headed toward it, Neil and Skinner's bickering already forgotten. Neil stepped back as he motioned to the doors behind Skinner.

"By all means."

"Looks more like they removed the doors," Laszlo said with a pointed look.

Neil swept his arm to the cabinet, holding up his glass. "Yes, yes we did. It's not cheating, and it clearly isn't being used. We opened a bottle of whiskey, but there's plenty there."

Daniela lifted and sniffed the bottle, grimacing. "I don't know how you two can stomach it." She coughed, holding the bottle out of reach.

Skinner shook her head as she pried the bottle from Daniela's grasp.

"You get used to it."

Chapter 8

NEIL

Giddy excitement crept into Neil's bloodstream at her words, flooding him with warmth. *You get used to it.* As if *he* were someone to get used to.

He shook himself, snuffing out a smile as his fingers tightened around his glass as the others surrounded the cabinet and Skinner. Neil pivoted and crossed to the fireplace, taking a swig of his whiskey as he strode away from them, as far as he could possibly go in this large room.

Distance, he needed distance from her.

The whiskey was strong, the harsh fumes racing down his throat and lighting his insides. Coughing, he pounded a fist against his chest, eyes watering as he set aside the glass, knelt, and reached for some firewood.

Neil could do this. Neil could focus on something else, keep his hands and his mind preoccupied for a few minutes. Working with his hands always seemed to calm him; he wasn't meant to sit still for long. Even when he wrote, he did it in twenty-minute intervals, too antsy to stay seated for any longer.

His fingers tore off strips of newspaper as he began to carefully place the wood in the center, building a cone-shaped master-piece. As he bent over the woodpile, Neil jumped at a soft sound coming from the back of the study, a faint *crash* somewhere in the darkness. He straightened and squinted over his shoulder, straining to see, but everyone was still by the liquor cabinet, the rest of the massive room empty.

Strange, he thought. Frowning, Neil turned to the fireplace.

The groundskeeper had left some supplies for them by the fireplace, and his hands worked of their own accord, muscle memory kicking in. He finished stacking the firewood and filling in the bottom of his formation with kindling and newspaper before lighting a match to it.

"How do you know how to do that?" Skinner asked from behind him.

Neil whipped his head around in surprise, exhaling when he met her stormy eyes. Grabbing his glass, he stood and wiped his hands on his pants, taking another sip of the fiery drink. He smelled the smoke and saw the firelight from his periphery as he stared down at her.

"Cub Scouts . . . and my older brother. My dad taught us how when we built a sweat lodge in the backyard." The memory of the smoke and the heat seemed to soothe something in him, loosening his shoulders. When was the last time he took part in a sweat? When was the last time he visited his family?

She nodded slowly, rocking back on her heels. She'd relaxed since earlier, her shoulders had slackened, and her eyes had softened. Swallowing, she held out the bottle of whiskey.

"A peace offering."

"Peace?" Neil asked with a raised brow.

Skinner shrugged. "Or an apology. For yelling at you and the like."

"And the like," he said, taking the bottle and filling his glass. He noticed how she carefully avoided any mention of the Incident or the rest of their past. Two could play at that game. "You have an odd way of apologizing."

"I'm not very good at it," she admitted.

Clearly.

"I can tell."

His voice came out harsher than he'd meant to, like gravel was caught in his throat. God, what was wrong with him? Even when he meant to be kind to her, anger seeped into his voice, poisoned his words. He didn't know if he could make it a week under these conditions, with her and Laszlo and Daniela and this godforsaken castle in the snow. Would he and Skinner be spending the entire time bickering about things that couldn't change? Could *they* change, or was it simply too late for either of them?

"So," Daniela started, plopping into a leather chair. Her sugary voice sliced through the uncomfortable silence. "Do we think this place is actually haunted?"

Neil forced his eyes from Skinner, focusing on the others as they made their way toward the couches and chairs. They congregated near the warmth like cats, lingering on the rug, scrutinizing the furniture like the leather held secrets.

Laszlo shrugged, cradling his drink close. "Haunted? I dunno about that. I don't really believe in ghosts, but I've gotta say, this place is *weird*. And the groundskeeper?" He shivered. "Abandoned us to the ghost's mercy. What did she say?"

Daniela snorted, her voice a poor mimic of the groundskeeper, "Yer on yer own."

"Love that for us," Laszlo said.

"Thought you didn't believe in ghosts?" Neil countered.

Laszlo shrugged but said nothing, taking a long drink instead. Neil took the moment to search the room again. He eyed the bookshelves and the shadows dancing on the walls, breathed in the thick smoke, the hint of dust and forgetfulness lingering in the corners. How many people rented out a castle? Rather, how many people rented out a *haunted* castle? Few, he supposed.

"Reminds me a bit of that creepy show," Neil began, his free hand sliding into his back pocket. "The one with the family who tries to fix up the manor?"

"*The Haunting of Hill House,*" Skinner offered.

Neil spun toward her, tilting his head in thanks. She pressed her lips into a flat line to keep from smiling before bringing her glass to her lips and sipping.

"That one gave me nightmares for weeks," Laszlo drawled as he shuddered and settled on the arm of the couch. "I don't really *do* spooky."

Everyone turned toward him, mixed expressions of shock, confusion, and accusation on their faces.

"This was *your* idea!" Neil yelled. "You set this up!"

"You *write* thrillers," Skinner said slowly.

"Not horror," Laszlo corrected. "I don't write horror."

"Laszlo." Daniela laughed, throwing back her head. "Why the fuck are we here?"

"You went on that haunted tour with me!" Skinner yelled, tone accusatory, with a hint of laughter curling the ends of each word. "I was the one who was scared!"

"Are you kidding?" Laszlo shook his head. "I was shitting myself the entire time, Pen. I don't do basements or crypts."

They all burst into laughter. As if this week couldn't get any more ridiculous, the person who'd set up the retreat, the person who'd tricked Neil and Skinner into coming here at the same time, was terrified of this place. And, looking around at their surroundings, at the dim lighting, the dust-covered books, the cobwebs lingering in the corners, and feeling the overall sense of dread, Neil couldn't blame his friend.

"We'll try to keep you out of the basement," Daniela said, sinking farther into the large armchair.

Skinner surveyed Neil before turning to join the others. Laszlo and Skinner settled onto the couch. She leaned into his side, stretching out her legs along the leather. Neil tried to train his eyes away, attention going to the table or the bottles, or literally anything else in the dark room. But his concentration strayed to her and away again, and he forced his feet past the couch, his free hand curling into a fist, eyes going to the bookshelves that surrounded them, titles and spines lit by the glow of the fire.

Daniela cleared her throat, and Neil's gaze slid to her over his shoulder. "Why don't we play a game?" she suggested, tossing her legs over the arm of her plush leather chair.

Neil rolled his eyes, running his fingers along the book spines on the nearest shelf. They were soft and worn under his fingers, the spines broken, the letters fading. Some were newer, crisper, but this shelf was well loved.

"We're not children, Daniela," he muttered.

"And we're not all as boring and serious as you, Neil."

He opened his mouth to reply but paused, attention going to something at his feet. He stooped and lifted a thin red book from the floor, his eyes not quite focusing on the pages in the dim lighting as he skimmed through it one-handed, whiskey still dangling in his left hand. He didn't catch any of the words, just saw glimpses of handwritten journal entries. Frowning, he slipped it onto one of the shelves. *Must have fallen*, he thought.

"What kind of game?" Skinner asked from the couch. He could hear the suspicion dripping from her words, the waver in them. Was she scared? Did she believe in ghosts and all the strange, otherworldly things they wrote about in their novels?

Neil turned to the others, brow furrowed. Daniela sat up, swinging her legs over the chair before standing. "How many times will we have the opportunity to play truth or dare in a haunted *castle*?"

Neil swallowed his sigh, taking a sip of his whiskey. It burned a path down his throat, settling into the embers of his stomach, warming him from the inside out.

"Don't be ridiculous, Daniela," he chided.

Daniela leaned forward on her elbows, drink swinging precariously from her fingers. "What, does Neil Storm believe in ghosts?"

His nostrils flared. He'd forgotten how annoying she could be. "No."

She smiled, all teeth. "Then what are you afraid of, Prince of Horror?"

Neil's glower met Skinner's over the couch. She knew now how much he hated the nickname, but he'd be damned if he let Daniela get to him.

"Fine!" He threw up his hands and moved toward the light before settling in the other chair. He swirled his drink and surveyed their small group. Although he didn't know them all well, he much preferred Laszlo's calm energy to Skinner's fiery temper and Daniela's sharp tongue.

"I saw the groundskeeper run out of here like her life depended on it," Daniela said, turning to Skinner. "She muttered something about secret doors and you?"

Skinner frowned as she fidgeted with her glass. "Yeah, we . . . it was nothing." She waved her hand dismissively. "Just a misunderstanding."

But it hadn't been nothing. Fanny had looked sincerely distraught as she jogged past Neil and out the front door with the jingle of her keys trailing in her wake.

"Well, I'd much rather be down here with you three than in my room alone. Besides, being alone kind of defeats the purpose of a writer's retreat," Daniela said, puckering her lips.

Neil decided it was best not to point out that truth or dare defeated the purpose of a writer's retreat.

Daniela smiled knowingly as she took a long drink of the clear liquid in her glass. Neil watched warily as she settled on the edge of her seat and leaned forward with a devilish grin. They were playing with fire, agreeing to Daniela's games. She was nothing but trouble, and after having heard some of the rumors, Neil knew the aftermath of Daniela's potential meddling.

When Laszlo had told him Daniela would be at the castle, it was nearly enough to deter him from going. But he'd thought there would be more people as a buffer. Of course, there was everything with Penelope Skinner, though that was a whole other mess. He'd work through whatever *that* was another time. Though Neil did wonder: If he'd known Skinner was coming, would he have come? She'd been haunting him for years, a shadowy figure in his rearview that wouldn't go away no matter what he did. Perhaps he'd come to confront his own ghosts, to understand why Skinner had felt the need to tear him down so publicly.

Alas, he'd never know.

"Penelope, dear," Daniela started, leering at the smaller woman on the couch, "you should go first, seeing as you're the youngest."

"I'm twenty-nine."

"Still the youngest."

Skinner's eyes flickered around the room, careful to avoid Neil. Leaning forward on her knees, she tucked a stray strand of hair behind her ear. "Truth," she chose after a long beat.

"Boring," Daniela drawled. She sighed before her eyes flicked to Neil and back to Skinner. Neil watched them curiously, something passing silently between the two women. "Why did you throw the book at Neil?"

"Yeah, I should have expected this." Skinner sighed. She rolled her neck back, toying with the loose strands of dark waves that had fallen free of her braid.

Suddenly, he didn't know what to do with himself.

"It's easier for men in the publishing industry. You make mistakes, you say the wrong thing, and most of the time, you don't get canceled." She gestured to him, sharp and meaningful. "And there you were, sitting up there on your little throne, leaning toward your mic, telling me I'd never be as good as you. Even if I was right—"

"You're not right," he said automatically.

She smiled, and Neil's gut twisted.

"Aren't I?" she asked after a beat. "You have so much power in your position. You know what this industry does to voices like ours, and when I called you out, what was your first instinct?" She leaned forward, and Neil found himself frozen under her scrutiny. "You and I could have spent this entire time working together to strengthen our positions in this genre, but you never cared. And there you were, sitting with your glowing stack of books before you, and all I had was a measly copy of my one and only, and I just . . ."

She mimicked throwing it and he flinched, extending his fingers on instinct to smooth over the small scar above his brow.

Silence settled between them, and Neil reached for his whiskey, taking a long, eye-watering drink.

"You're not wrong," he admitted. "Maybe I could have tried harder, said no more often when editors and my agent wanted to change things. Hell, I probably should have left my publisher years ago, but I also wonder if they're right, you know? If my other ideas, if my stories just aren't good enough, and they're the only ones who will publish me. I know what I *could* be doing, but I already tried it. Nobody wants that. Nobody will buy it."

"What do you mean?" Skinner asked, frowning.

Neil held up his glass, laughing. His mind was foggy, the whiskey finally hitting him and clouding his thoughts. He barreled on, ignoring Laszlo's look of concern. "Oh, I *tried* to write the stories you claim you want to protect. I *tried* to be the hero you wanted me to be, but there's only so much a Native man can do in a country that's been built on the genocide of his people."

The room fell into silence. Neil had always been good at ending conversations. Laszlo cleared his throat and squirmed as his and Daniela's gazes met.

"Fuck the colonizers!" Daniela yelled, throwing back her head and holding her glass high.

Neil met Skinner's wide eyes over his glass. "Fuck the colonizers," he whispered, taking a drink.

"Fuck the colonizers," Skinner echoed.

"Can I say that?" Laszlo asked.

Skinner's lips puckered in thought as she turned to Daniela. Neil shrugged and gestured to Laszlo.

"He is our token white friend," Daniela said.

Skinner laughed. "Eh, why not?"

And as they all raised their glasses and drank, something seemed to settle in the room. When Neil glanced up and met Skinner's cloudy gaze, he thought, *Maybe we'll be okay. Maybe we'll move on.*

Then she tilted her head, something else in those gray depths. "Neil Storm."

Neil tried to focus on her words, but he'd severely underestimated the whiskey. He licked his lips, eyes narrowing on her. He made a soft sound at the back of his throat, urging her to continue.

Her eyes glinted. "Truth or dare."

He tapped the rim of his glass, eyes never leaving hers. "Dare." His voice came out gravelly, a smile curling the corners of his lips. And then Penelope Skinner smiled, and it was too much like Daniela's, all harsh lines and cruel gleams. Neil's stomach dropped. God, she was terrifying.

"No, truth," he amended, sitting up.

"No take-backsies," Daniela singsonged.

Neil ground his teeth, eyes blazing as he glared at her. "What are we, in kindergarten?"

"I dare you to go down into the cellar."

They all froze, turning to Skinner.

"That's a bit far, Pen," Laszlo chided.

Neil laughed, unmoved. "That's it? You want me to go down to the cellar."

She shrugged. "Neil Storm doesn't seem to think it's too far." Skinner waved to the castle around them, cheeks flushed as her eyes met Neil's. "Besides, if the castle isn't haunted, where's the harm in it?"

"Really," he slurred, standing, "I don't mind. It's just a cellar. What can go wrong?"

"Said every doomed character in a horror novel ever," Laszlo said.

They all stood and followed Neil down the hall toward the front foyer. They walked past more creepy paintings, eerily re-alistic stone busts, and tattered tapestries hidden in corners he hadn't yet noticed, feet trampling over worn-down carpets before circling around the backside of the staircase with the portrait of the woman in black.

His attention snapped to her as the others moved past, and he thought, for a moment, that she *smiled*. Fuck, no more whiskey for him tonight. He quickened his pace, rounding the corner to join the others. There was a strange sense of unease flitting about him as he hurried down the hall, a sense of being watched from the darkness, and Neil was *not* a fan.

Skinner licked her lips anxiously and waved her hand at the door. "Well, this is it."

It was a simple door, although difficult to see if you didn't already know it was there. Made of the same wood of the stairs, it blended into the side boards, only a small brass handle making it clear there was anything hidden beneath the staircase.

Neil searched the others' expressions, noting their concern. Everyone, that is, except for Skinner. Her eyes were lit up, her bottom lip clamped between her teeth. She looked almost *excited*. Eager to see him go down. Eager to see him hurt.

He thought of the stories these people would tell, about how Neil Storm had chickened out at the last second on a haunted writing retreat, how he'd run away screaming from this door. How much pleasure would she get out of seeing him back down yet again? Swallowing, he stared at the brass handle before wrapping his fingers around it, the metal cool against his skin.

"Here goes nothing," he whispered before pulling it open.

Chapter 9

PEN

"Wait!"

Pen reached forward and covered his hand with hers. His pinky wrapped around hers as if out of instinct. She stared down at their joined hands, remembering the moment in the ruins, being crushed against the fence . . . Why did she keep thinking of that? Why the fuck was she so goddamn hung up on a fake almost kiss when Storm felt as little for her as she felt for him: a whole lot of *nothing*.

She glanced from their hands to his face, cheeks heating as she failed to banish the thoughts. God, she was a terrible liar. If he saw it, if he *asked*, she wasn't so sure she could lie to his face.

"You really don't need to do this," she said as she tugged her hand free.

Neil Storm looked down at her, emerald eyes serious, pupils dilated. He was buzzed, cheeks colored pink, weight shifting awkwardly as he tried to straighten. He seemed unsteady, because who in their right mind would say, *Why, yes, I will indeed go into the cellar of this haunted castle!*

Pen recalled Fanny's earlier warnings, something about death or peril lingering at the back of her mind. God, this was foolish. She was being petty, and it wasn't worth risking someone else's life if there was indeed some dark spirit waiting in the shadows of this cellar to kill them all.

He frowned down at her and this close, her hip brushing his, her fingers inches from tangling with his, she thought again of earlier, the heat of him so close, his breath on her lips as he leaned forward and pressed her into the fence. Pen had the sudden, strange urge to drag him down to her level.

"Yes," he said, pulling back and shaking out his hand as if it hurt. "I do."

"I'll go with you." Pen clamped her mouth shut with wide eyes. Damn it, she was being foolish.

His eyes snapped to hers, then to the cellar door, already partially ajar. Darkness lay beyond, and the longer she stared at it, the sicker she felt. He looked at her questioningly, waiting for her to back out.

"Let's just go back to the study," Laszlo urged, tugging on Pen's arm.

His eyes flicked between Neil and Pen, widening a fraction as if telling her, *Please don't do this again.* But this wasn't the same. This wasn't another convention, and Pen was a hell of a lot more focused and calmer than when she was on that panel.

"I'm going down there," Neil said, taking a step toward the stairs. He looked pointedly at Pen. "You dared me, and I agreed to it, so let's just get this over with, okay? No need to make a big scene."

"I'm not making a scene. But if you're going down there, so am I," Pen insisted, shaking off Laszlo's hand.

Laszlo looked between them. "You two deserve each other," he muttered under his breath.

Pen tried not to think about the nervous flutter in her belly at the thought.

Daniela nodded in agreement, and they shuffled away a few steps, wary of the cellar and whatever lay beyond. They could laugh and joke about the castle being haunted all day, but when it came down to it, none of them were willing to risk it. Because there was a sense of something else here. Franny had been shaken, scared, even, and Pen was suddenly certain that there had to be some truth to the local lore.

"You do know basements and cellars are like two of the *most* common haunting grounds, right?" Laszlo asked, shrinking away.

"I'd choose a haunted attic over a basement any day," Daniela said.

Storm pulled the door open the rest of the way, and nothing but darkness and cool air greeted them. Pen shivered, wrapping her arms around her middle as she stared past the doorframe.

All to prove a point. That's all this was. Storm wanted to prove he could do it, and Pen wanted to prove . . . prove what? That she wasn't trying to send him to his death? That she wasn't a total asshole? This was a fucking mistake. Could she truly not back down from Storm because of her pride?

He slid his hand into the open air before them, searching the walls on each side of the door. The sleeve of his fleece inched up, and Pen thought she saw a bit of black ink poking out from beneath it. She wanted to reach out and roll up his sleeve, to see what he kept hidden beneath it.

"There's no light," he mumbled, searching for an invisible string.

Pen pulled out her phone, switching on the flashlight feature. "Thank god for technology." Although, as she shone it into the darkness, she wasn't entirely certain it was enough. It cast a faint, white glow a few feet before her, but it was nothing to battle the depths of the cellar. Storm nodded and did the same, taking the first step down.

Swallowing, Pen followed.

It grew colder as they descended. Though Pen could hardly see past his tall frame, she moved her phone from left to right, sweeping the light over covered furniture and racks of wine along the farthest wall. It looked like any cellar one might expect beneath a castle. Creaking wooden steps, a concrete floor, shelves, wine racks, and abandoned and broken furniture. At its peak, the cellar might have been used to store food and wine, but now, it was a place for abandoned things. Lost things.

Like wandering spirits trapped in this world.

"Can you see anything?" she whispered, leaning close.

Storm shivered, waving her away. "Don't do that."

Pen eyed him sidelong, smiling. "Did I *scare you?*"

"No," he snapped.

She opened her mouth to retort, but her eyes landed on something lurking in the shadows of the cellar. It twitched. Pen paused on the step, her heart racing as she leaned down and peered into the dark. Something round caught the light of her phone, gleaming like an eye from the shadows of the cellar. She blinked and found the shape of a person, the wisp of a shadow.

Too human. It was *too human.*

Oh no, oh no, it was the spirit, the one that Fanny had warned them about. The protector. It was going to kill them, if spirits could indeed kill people.

Pen's breath caught as the thing moved, writhing as those glowing orbs shimmered. And then she smelled it, thick and heavy, the dampness and musk of growing mold. She shivered and gagged, that same dread from the secret passageway raising goose bumps along her arms and the nape of her neck.

"Ohmygodohmygodohmygod it's the ghost!" she chanted as she leaned close to Storm. One of her hands gripped his shoulder, her nails digging in past fabric to his flesh. "Storm, it's going to kill us, holy shit, we're going to die." Her heartbeat was erratic as she raised a shaky hand and pointed at the thing in the dark.

"What?" he said as he turned toward her.

"It's a ghost, there's a *fucking ghost,*" she cried out. "We don't mean your castle any harm, brother protector ghost!" she called.

"It's just a silly game, a very foolish mistake we won't be making again! Please, don't kill us."

He followed her finger and stooped over the railing of the cellar stairs, flashlight bright against the darkness. The beam scanned the cellar, and Pen followed the line of light across the floor eagerly.

But there was nothing. There was no monster, no shadow, no pair of glowing eyes watching them. Pen's lips trembled. Had she imagined it, that thing gleaming in the dark? She moved to shine her own phone to prove him wrong, but her hand was empty. She groaned, covering her face.

"Skinner, calm down," he admonished, reaching for her. His fingers skated over her wrist. "There's nothing here."

"I dropped my phone," she groaned again. She didn't want to peel back her hands, to see that thing again, the whisper of a human lurking in the darkened corners of the cellar. It was a mistake coming down here. What had she been thinking? Rumors and myths and legends existed because they relied on truths. And what's to say ghosts weren't real just because she wrote stories about them?

Slowly, he tugged her hands away with soft, warm fingers, and the tenderness of the action, of his touch, made her pulse flutter. Storm's features were cast in shadow as she blinked down at him, tracing his strong nose and bright eyes with new clarity.

"Skinner, there's nothing there." His voice was whisper-soft, a contrast to his sharp words earlier.

Something was changing between them, their pasts morphing into a present she'd never stopped to imagine, and although Pen wanted to ask what it was, she could think of nothing but the eyes in the dark. She was certain she'd seen something. She didn't know what it was, but there had been *something*.

Hadn't there?

Light leaked in from behind them, casting a bright glow down the stairs and into the cellar. Now Pen could see a string dangling from the bottom of the stairs, dancing in the air almost playfully a few steps down. Storm followed her gaze and reached out and tugged on it, his other hand still grasping Pen's as light flooded the room.

"Are you okay?" Daniela called down, her curl-framed face appearing in the doorway.

"We'll be up in a minute!" Storm said.

They turned in unison and scanned the cellar. Other than the wine and furniture and closed, labeled boxes, there was nothing else—*no one* else. Concern was written across his features, in the lines around his eyes and mouth, and her heart skipped a beat.

Imagining things, Pen was imagining things. Neil Storm could not possibly be *concerned* for her. Swallowing down her confusion, Pen tugged her hand free, swiveled back to the top of the stairs and jogged up.

"Are you okay?" Laszlo asked as she pushed her way past them. "We heard the scream . . ."

"I'm fine."

Storm appeared a moment later with two bottles of champagne tucked under his arm and her phone in his hand. Why had he gotten it for her? She stared at him as he closed the door with his hip, shutting in whatever she'd seen. He held her phone out, and she took it, their fingers brushing and sending a shock of electricity up her arm.

She snatched her hand away, anxiety peaking. Ignoring her, Storm passed the champagne bottles to Daniela, and they followed Laszlo back toward the study. Pen lingered behind, fighting a shiver as she tightened her hand around her phone.

"Hey," Storm started, reaching out as if to touch her, comfort her. "Are you okay?"

It was a loaded question. There were the stairs, the door that led to the cellar and the thing that lurked below. Had she imagined it? Or had it truly been there, waiting in the dark for someone to find it? Fanny seemed to know more about this castle than she was letting on, and Pen was beginning to believe that there was a lot more to the stories Fanny had told.

"I swear," she said, leaning close. "I saw something down there. The protector ghost Fanny spoke of. *Something.* I wasn't imagining it."

"Maybe you did see something."

Pen wrinkled her nose, watching him closely, searching those green eyes that had become shockingly familiar in just a day. "You don't believe me, do you?"

He sighed, running his fingers through his curls. "No?" He shrugged. "I don't know. I'd like to believe you. Maybe I just didn't see it. Maybe, if there was something down there, it didn't want to be seen by anyone other than you."

Pen shuddered and wrapped her arms around her middle. "Yeah, I don't like the sound of that."

"I can imagine."

They stopped just outside the study. Inside, Daniela had slid back into her empty chair, and Laszlo huddled next to the fire for warmth, the couch empty. Pen glared at it, aware of the heat of Storm beside her, and she imagined, almost strangely, what it would be like to sit next to him, thighs squished together, their bodies aligned. Touching. It was oddly comforting knowing he was beside her even now. And perhaps he was right. Perhaps, if it had indeed been a ghost down in the cellar, it had only wanted Pen to see it.

"Maybe you're right." She smiled weakly, meeting his eyes. "I've always had an affinity for lost things."

He watched her silently. Daniela and Laszlo laughed as they settled into their cushy seats beside the dwindling fire and passed the bottles back and forth, bubbly golden liquid spilling over their flutes. But Pen couldn't stay here any longer. She couldn't drink champagne and laugh and smile as if she weren't comforted by Storm's presence, as if the electricity between them wasn't transforming into something that scared her. As if she hadn't seen the thing in the cellar.

Mind buzzing, she turned to go.

"Pen," Laszlo started, standing.

"I'm just tired. I was up pretty early." Pen faked a yawn, covering her mouth with her hand as she avoided their gazes. "See you all in the morning."

They murmured their goodnights, and she turned down the hall, hurrying toward the stairs leading up to the second floor. The goose bumps wouldn't go away. There was something so very wrong with this castle, and perhaps they never should have come here.

"Skinner, wait."

She paused in the hall, peering over her shoulder to catch Storm as he stepped over the discarded bottles. His hair was disheveled, cheeks flushed. His fleece was unzipped, the sleeves rolled up to expose his forearms and more of the tattoo that peeked out from beneath. It looked to be a feather, the black ink fading out, stippled.

"What are you doing?" she asked, flicking her eyes away from the ink.

He shrugged. "Tired too."

She was exhausted. Pen didn't want to argue anymore tonight, and she especially didn't want to walk through this place on her own. Chewing on her lip, she nodded.

Storm followed closely behind, and she felt that odd comfort in his presence again. The castle felt peculiar on her own, too dark, too quiet. Storm was saying something as she gripped the banister to steady herself, but she couldn't hear him, a ringing in her ears as she ascended the stairs.

She paused on the landing, angling to the right. What had Fanny said about the west wing?

It was strictly off-limits.

Still, she felt herself pulled to it. Ignoring the call of her name, Pen stepped closer, squinting down the dark hallway. Well, she was just full of reckless ideas today. She shivered as she took another step forward. The eerie setting and the dark, looming hall reminded her of a passage from *The Lies They Told Us*.

"And in that hall, dark and long and harrowing, did I step toward the unknown. The Sounds crept toward me," Pen whispered, taking one step and then another into the shadows stretching out before her. The wood screamed beneath her feet, protesting each step as if she did not belong there in the dark. She took a deep breath and continued forward. *"And when I saw it, I knew."*

A door creaked open at the end of the corridor, and Pen froze, eyes wide as it swung outward. There was absolutely no way in hell it was air or a loose lock. That door had opened on purpose. It waited, unmoving, as if it had opened just for her. Pen swallowed hard, her throat dry as she took another step toward it. Her heart thundered, adrenaline pumping through her as a hand snaked around it, gripping the edge of the peeling wood of the door.

She knew she should go, flee from this place, but a strange feeling urged her forward, led her to wonder what might be luring her into the darkness.

"Skinner!" Storm called.

Pen jumped in surprise, whipping her head around to see him stopped at the landing, eyes wide. He felt so far away. In her haze, Pen had wandered farther down the hall than she'd thought. Breathing shakily, she turned back to the door, to the flicker of movement she'd seen moments earlier. Was it the woman in black? Was she looking for her next victim?

But the door was closed, the west wing empty but for the two of them.

"That's not possible," she said, searching the shadows.

"What's not possible?" he asked, slipping his hand into hers and pulling her back to the light.

Pen opened her mouth, but what was there to tell? Maybe she *was* imagining things.

"Nothing," she said. "It was nothing."

She let him lead her toward the east wing, enjoying the warmth of his touch far more than she was willing to admit, but she half turned, considering the door. Pen swore she'd seen a flicker of movement, a shadow, or a silhouette in the darkened corners of the abandoned corridor, but when she blinked, it was gone.

Storm pulled her silently down the hall, past the art and statue busts, until they stopped between their rooms. Pen struggled to focus on him, a breath settling between her ribs.

"Did you really see nothing?" she asked quietly, crossing her arms over her chest.

He shook his head, brows pinched together. "I'm sorry." He laughed awkwardly. "Not that I *wanted* to see something, just sorry that you're the only one who's . . ."

"The only one seeing ghosts or imagining things? Yeah, lucky me."

Pen smiled weakly as she toed the plush carpet. She'd seen things twice in one night. A coincidence, for now. But maybe the legends Fanny spoke of were truer than she'd let on.

Clearing her throat, Pen opened her door. Leaning against the doorframe, she summoned a smirk, the merriment not quite reaching her eyes.

"Goodnight, Storm. I hope you dream about flying books and angry writers."

He chuckled, taking a step back. "Just the one."

Pressing her lips into a thin line to keep from truly smiling, she closed the door between them. Her bag still rested inside the door, the mismatched colors a strange contrast to the décor. The top had been unzipped, but Pen couldn't recall opening it. She nudged it with her foot, stepping farther into the room.

It was cold at night, the darkness beyond the window lit only by the white of the snow sprinkled over the grounds. The sky had that strange, purplish glow to it; more snow in the forecast, Pen suspected.

She wanted to fling open the window and breathe that familiar scent in, to dispel the thick odor of murky dampness that she couldn't seem to shake from the cellar, but her chattering teeth and freezing hands convinced her otherwise.

Pen changed into her pajamas, her hands shaking, stumbling as she slipped off her clothes and into something warm. With her feet clad in a pair of thick wool socks and a hoodie thrown over a loose shirt, she pulled back the covers of her bed. She paused as she climbed in, her gaze going to the tapestry and the hidden door behind it.

Swallowing, she crossed the room and tugged on the handle, making sure it was closed. She locked it to be certain. Although Pen did not know what lay in wait in the castle, she was not willing to take any more chances.

Chapter 10

NEIL

There was something off about Skinner. Her usual snarky comments were gone, seemingly drained away since the cellar. Had she really seen something? The groundskeeper had spoken briefly of the spirit that guarded the cellar, but he'd thought nothing of it. Neil didn't believe in ghosts, and he found it difficult to believe there really was something in this castle.

But her reaction had been so . . . *visceral*.

Neil paused in the hall between their doors. As if out of instinct, he took a step toward hers, his footsteps silenced by the rug. He took another and reached out a hand to graze her door before settling his palm against it. He'd stay outside her door if he thought it would do any good, but she was safe in her room, they were safe in this castle, and nothing was going to get them.

With a small shrug, he turned and retreated into his room, closing the door tightly behind him. He wasn't tired, not mentally. Physically, his muscles ached and the space between his eyes throbbed, but it was simply too early to sleep. Kneeling before the fireplace, he built a small fire in his room, the warmth of the lapping flames spreading through the room and filling all the crevices until he stopped shivering.

Castles, he decided, were cold, harsh places.

Try as he might, he kept picturing the look of terror on Skinner's face down in that cellar. She didn't look like she was lying; she'd been visibly shaken.

Sighing, he crossed to his suitcase and threw open the lid. Neil changed into sweats and a T-shirt before plopping into the chair beside the hearth. He ran his fingers over the worn leather armrest as he propped his laptop on his legs and stared blankly at the screen.

As much as he hated to admit it, he hadn't been lying when he told Skinner that he was struggling, that he should have pushed back all those times with his editor and publisher, that he could have made choices that sent him on another path. But he'd chosen this one. Neil had made a lot of terrible decisions over the years, and those were only the tip of the iceberg. The instigators, so to speak.

Chewing on his thumbnail, he pulled open *that* document. Neil hadn't dared to look at it in ages, but he couldn't stop himself from scanning it once more. After he'd sent it to Tabitha and she'd sent her editorial letter in return, he'd made some changes. It was the process, and Neil had trusted the process. He rewrote a better part of the novel, and by the time he'd made it through revision after revision with his editor, it had been transformed into the published version of *For What Savages May Be*.

The original storyline of *For What Savages May Be* followed a young woman on a reservation looking for her sister's killer. He'd thought it was heart-wrenchingly perfect, and Neil had never been prouder of one of his books. A Southern gothic in its original state, it was everything he'd ever dreamed of. He'd used experiences from his own family, did research on the reservation, and even visited it. He studied the conditions of the Choctaw Nation, read about his ancestors, and spoke to a few Elders, and when he was good and ready, he'd drafted up an outline and sent off his manuscript.

"It's hard to stomach," his editor had said in an email. "We want you to tone it down."

Hard. To. Stomach.

What the hell did that even mean? Were people not willing to read horror about Missing and Murdered Indigenous People? Was it too *real* for them? But he was hellbent on writing this story. He didn't have to write the book, but Neil had known the minute he'd started drafting that there was no turning back.

So, he'd changed it. He'd followed his editor's suggestions to a T before sending it back, but it had only been shredded further. And Skinner was right; it was a sellout book. It held none of the heart of the original work. The main character was transformed into a man, the missing sister into a long-lost mystery in cowboy country. It was full of gore and stereotypes, scared women and villainous men, and Neil hadn't known how to turn it around.

The new version, his publisher's vision, was a classic horror in every regard. And that was the problem. There was nothing new, nothing original within its pages, nothing groundbreaking, and Penelope Skinner, who'd put her heart and soul into *The Lies They Told Us,* had every right to be angry. And not once during the entire process did he say no.

Angry, betrayed, confused, and heartbroken, he had erased everything he put down on the page with a vengeance, because none of it was good. Skinner had pulled the plug on his confidence, and he'd never doubted his storytelling more.

Fuck, here he was complaining about Skinner standing up for something he knew was wrong. Hadn't she just wanted him to listen? Hadn't she wanted him to hear her out, to understand where she was coming from?

Neil went to close the document but paused, and before he could second-guess himself, he reached into the small pocket of his messenger bag for a spare thumb drive, copying and pasting the file there with a hopeful smile.

After quickly scribbling on the thumb drive with a Sharpie, he went to his door. Pressing an ear to the wood, he turned the handle, the hinges squealing as he pulled it open. Neil peered past the lit lamps and glowing pedestals of the east wing. Everything was still and silent in the night, the dim lighting making it eerier. Laszlo and Daniela must have gone to sleep sometime since he'd slipped into his room. No sound could be heard but his own breathing.

Neil shivered as he crossed the hall to Skinner's room. This place creeped him out, and although he hadn't seen whatever Skinner was screaming about in the cellar at the top of her lungs, he was almost willing to admit there might be more to their world if it would just give him proof. Neil was open to being wrong if a ghost would pop out and yell, "Boo!" He'd never encountered the paranormal, never had any reason to believe there was something more out there, but it didn't mean there wasn't.

Reaching out, he slipped the thumb drive with "Sorry" written across it beneath her door. Maybe this would ease some of the tension between him and Skinner, bridge the gap after the pain they'd caused each other. If she only knew what he had given up to be here . . .

There was a creak in the hall. Neil jumped in surprise, nearly falling face-first into Skinner's door. He pivoted on his heel to scan the wing.

"Hello?" he called.

This was ridiculous. There was nothing else in this castle save for him and the other writers. So, then, why was he scared? Why did he want to pack up and leap out his window, feeling safer in the expansive woods than in this place? With a ragged exhale, Neil took another step down the hall, hesitating, his hands outstretched.

Then he smelled it. Rot and decay. It flooded his senses all at once, and Neil banged back into the door, his other hand going to the wall to steady him as he covered his nose and mouth.

"Oh god," he gagged, the whiskey in his stomach threatening to bubble up.

Neil wedged himself as far back as he could and searched the hall, his eyes tracing over framed paintings and busts and sconces. The lights flickered as something white swept into a room down the hall, and Neil froze. Oh, there was *something* all right, but he was *not* sticking around to see who or what it really was.

He turned and yanked open the door behind him, slamming it closed with a gasp. He leaned against the wood and squeezed his eyes shut, trembling hands gripping either side of the doorframe as his heart slammed against his ribs.

"Get out!" someone screeched.

Neil snapped his head back, his skull cracking against the door. Before he could get out a word, he was bombarded with a flurry of pillows, and he held up his hands in defense as Penelope Skinner cried out furiously.

"Skinner, it's me!" he yelled. He caught a pillow and tossed it to the side. "Stop, it's *me*."

The barrage of soft ammunition stopped. Wincing, Neil squinted against the dimness as Skinner pulled on her glasses, eyes wide. Her hair was mussed from sleep, her cheeks warm and flushed. Her braid had come undone in the time since he'd seen her last, dark hair spilling into her eyes as she looked up at him, brow furrowed. He was suddenly mesmerized, taking her in. Damn it, why couldn't he bring himself to say anything?

"Are you just going to stand there?"

"I'll be going," he said, turning to the door.

His hand stilled on the doorknob, his nails scraping against metal. He knew he needed to turn it, but he couldn't convince himself to, not when *something* was somewhere out in the hall. Probably waiting for him. Neil leaned his forehead against the door, fingers shaking and heart pounding.

"Storm?" He heard the creak of the bed, followed by the quiet padding of footsteps. Warm hands covered his, prying his fingers from the doorknob one by one.

"Storm," she repeated, calmer, "what happened?"

"There was . . ." He frowned as he focused on their joined hands. Hers were so warm as she held his. Gentle. *Kind.* "I saw a . . ." But what had he seen? What had he smelled?

He was an author, and for the first time in a long time, words were failing him.

Penelope Skinner looked at him as if she understood. And he supposed she did. She'd seen something too. Dropping her hands from his, she stepped back. "Why don't we . . ." Her voice trailed off as her eyes caught on something at their feet. "What's this?" she asked, stooping to grab it.

Reality slammed back into him. "Wait, Skinner, that's not—" He bent to reach for it as she straightened, her elbow slamming into his gut. Sputtering, Neil stumbled back a step, coughing. "You're so violent," he wheezed, plopping onto her bed.

She ignored him, turning it over in her fingers. "Sorry," she read. "What is this?"

He couldn't get the words out. Cowardly, damn it, he was so fucking cowardly. Clearing his throat, Neil held out his hand. "It's nothing. I'll take that back, please."

Skinner raised a brow. "It's not nothing," she argued, rounding the bed. "I'd recognize your sloppy handwriting anywhere."

"It's not *sloppy.*"

She pulled out her laptop and switched it on, the thumb drive poised for the USB slot. How could Neil have been so foolish? He'd had a moment of courage. Now, he didn't want anyone to read it, least of all Penelope Skinner. She'd just find more excuses to hate him for giving up this version. For letting go of this story.

Coward.

"What is this?" she asked, staring daggers at him as the computer started up. Skinner grinned when he didn't reply. "Did you make me a cute PowerPoint presentation about how I'm the superior writer?"

He said nothing in response, frozen as he watched her type in her password and click on the pop-up, taking her to the thumb drive's files. Frowning, she clicked on the single file.

Within moments, his words filled the screen, thousands of words he'd been so proud of nearly five years ago. Though his book had been a raging success, this was the version he'd wanted printed. Words only his agent, editor, and two beta readers had read. Skinner's shoulders drooped as her eyes flicked over the screen.

Neil stood and crossed the room. Jaw clenched, he reached out and closed her laptop, not quite meeting her gaze.

"What is this, Storm?"

He ran a hand over his chin, his fingers scratching across thin stubble. "I thought, maybe if you saw the original . . . If you understood what I was trying to do in *From What Savages May Be* . . . If you just . . ."

If she just what? Neil trailed off, face red-hot, skin itchy and irritated. Skinner was looking at him peculiarly, emotions flitting across her features too fast for him to take in. She stood and gestured to her laptop.

"In a single page, I can already see what you've given up. Why? Why would you let them butcher your work like this?"

"Because I didn't know what to do!" Neil grimaced, reaching up to prod the bump forming on the back of his skull. "In publishing, there's only ever one response when you're BIPOC, and it's 'yes.' If I said no, I wouldn't be where I am. They wanted to publish my book, just not *that* version."

"But look what you gave up! Look what you did to get here."

"And I'm embarrassed, okay?" Neil pointed sharply at Skinner. "We can't all be as brave as you. You don't care about what people think of you."

"Of course I do!" She stepped forward and shoved a hand against his chest, baring her teeth as she glared up at him like a ferocious kitten. "Because I spoke my mind, I gave up *everything*. I risked my career to be honest, and now . . ."

Her chin wobbled, and Neil was unsure what to do.

"I'm sorry," he said weakly. And he was. He was sorry for all of it. He had been for a long time, but he'd never said it to her. Her nostrils flared as she looked from him to her door.

"Please just go."

Neil's stomach twisted. She'd made him doubt himself, made him question every decision he'd ever made in his career, but he had not come to her room (had not even meant to come here) to make her cry in the middle of the night.

Swallowing, Neil turned and strode to the door. He left without another word, pausing to lean against the wood after pulling the door shut behind him. He puffed out his cheeks and shook his head.

Maybe she was angry, maybe she hadn't been as sympathetic as he'd hoped, but at least she knew the truth. At least she knew what he'd done in order to scrape his way to the top.

Neil pushed off to return to his room but paused, glancing down the hall. There was no sign of whatever had lurked before, no rotting stench lingering to send him spiraling into another panic attack. And though Neil couldn't be certain how much time had passed since he saw the flash of white disappearing into one of the rooms, he decided he didn't want to know what it was.

He returned silently to the warmth of his room. The fire had dimmed since he'd left, but the space was warm, the glow of the fire enough to light his way to the bed.

"Just to be safe," he said, locking the door behind him. He jiggled the handle for good measure, satisfied when it didn't budge.

Maybe there was something out there, maybe there wasn't, but Neil wasn't willing to take *any* chances.

Excerpt from *For What Savages May Be*
by Neil Storm

Trent Barker was a strange man. He'd spent the better part of his life on the reservation, waiting for his chance at an escape. He'd dreamed of what it meant to see the real world, to join it and experience the things that lay beyond that border.

And now that it was time for him to leave, he couldn't bear to. So much had happened to him, so many terrible and wonderful things.

But they'd all shaped him into the man that he was, the person he'd become.

Trent stood on the border of the land he called home, looking out over the empty space beyond. He sucked in a breath, closed his eyes, and leaped.

Chapter 11

PEN

Pen lurched upright as someone banged their fists against her door. Her cheeks were flushed, her underwear sticky, and Pen was alarmed to realize she'd been rudely woken from an incredibly *hot* dream.

As she stretched and yawned, arching her back with a shiver, she was certain she could still feel the leather of books digging into her back and the dragging of nails down her thigh as long fingers dug into bare skin and her leg was lifted aside for easy access, fingers squeezing almost painfully. The person in the dream had hefted her up against one of the bookcases in the study, pressing her into the shelves as books fell around them, clattering to the floor. Their bodies had clashed against one another, heartbeat against ragged heartbeat.

Pen could practically taste the burn of whiskey down her throat as someone kissed her deep, tongue dipping and tangling with hers, their teeth scraping her bottom lip. But already the dream's clarity was fading, and Pen couldn't make out the face of the man who'd devoured her.

Much to her dismay.

"Wake up! We have places to be, things to do!" Laszlo called.

The sound of her friend's voice pushed her thoughts of the dream away. For now. She'd have to revisit it later. For . . . reasons.

A piece of paper was slipped under Pen's door, and she pulled on her glasses before stumbling out of bed, hitting the floor face-first as she twisted in her sheets, legs tangled together. Grumbling, she reached out and snatched it up, squinting. Pen struggled out of the blankets and stood, pulling open her door and nearly mowing down Laszlo in the process.

"What's this?" Pen demanded, holding it up.

Laszlo raised a brow and looked from the paper to Pen. "It's an itinerary."

She blanched. "It's a writing retreat, not a boot camp, Laszlo."

Laszlo opened his mouth to respond, but Storm's door opened across the way, and both Pen and Laszlo turned to survey him. He was freshly showered, water dripping down his curls and soaking his shirt. And something about the sight of him in that button-up, the water making the forest-green fabric cling to his chest, made her mouth go dry.

"You look like shit," Laszlo observed.

"Thank you," Storm said. "I didn't sleep much last night."

There was a question in Storm's heated stare. She thought of last night, the way he'd looked at her like she could fix it all. And then she recalled her dream and the faceless man grinding into her, kissing her, and she shuddered, hand wrinkling the itinerary in her palms.

"Did *anyone* sleep last night?" Laszlo muttered, turning to go. "I'll see you two downstairs in the kitchen by nine!"

Pen watched her friend go, a small smile curling her lips. She'd follow Lazlo's schedule, sure, but Pen had forgotten how *strict* he was. Though if there was a time in her life when she needed it most, it was now.

"Is he for real?" Storm asked, holding up an identical itin-erary. She squirmed as he glanced up from the itinerary to sur-vey her. His eyes dipped down to her chest, and he blushed. She followed his gaze and quickly wrapped her arms around herself.

Damn it, she should have put on a bra. She could poke an eye out with one of her nipples.

"I'm going to shower . . ." she said, trailing off as she took a step backward into her room.

He frowned. "Um, enjoy?"

Without meaning to, Pen recalled the remnants of her dream, a hand clawing her thighs hungrily, and heat gathered once more between her legs as he stared blankly at her. She slammed her door shut and leaned her forehead against it. *Um, enjoy?* Who told you to enjoy a shower? And what the hell was *wrong* with her? A week was too long in this damned castle. If she was this irrational after a single night, how would she be after a week?

She undressed, peeling away her sticky underwear before stepping into the shower. She relished the hot water beading over her neck and shoulders. Her whole body was stiff, her muscles tight and exhausted. She hadn't slept much, and though she would never admit it to his face, Pen had spent four hours of her night reading through most of Storm's manuscript.

It was good. Fuck, it was more than good.

It deserved to be published.

Screw whoever had told him otherwise. *For What Savages May Be* had been pulled from the bones of whatever its parent had been. And Pen finally understood why he was the way he was, why he'd struggled to say no, to step out of his little safety box.

She almost pitied him.

Though Pen had finally fallen asleep, she had drifted in and out of wakefulness, remembering the glowing eyes down in the cellar. And the way Storm had looked at her when she opened the document on the flash drive.

How she managed to fit a sex dream into the mix was any-one's guess.

On shaky legs, Pen straightened and lathered her hair with shampoo. Head thrown back as she rinsed, she heard the loud squeal of a door opening and felt a gush of cold air through the bathroom.

Pen paused, shuddering as she peeled open one eye. "Hello?" Nothing.

Nerves buzzing, she rinsed out the last of the shampoo before shutting off the water. She peered around the shower curtain; her room was empty. "Hello?" she called again as she climbed out of the shower and wrapped a towel around herself.

The cold draft hit her, and she shivered, water dripping from her hair and down her front, soaking her towel. She stopped before the fireplace, the tapestry to its left sticking out strangely. Lifting it, she found the secret door ajar. She tugged it closed, turning the lock once again and pushing against it. The door held.

"Weird."

But weird didn't even begin to describe it.

Jumping at every creak of the floorboard, at every miniscule sound, Pen dried her hair, braiding it before slipping on jeans and another sweater. She grabbed her laptop and hurried out of her room.

She wanted to spend as little time alone in this castle as humanly possible.

"You're late!" Laszlo called as she rounded the corner into the kitchen.

Daniela was nursing a steaming mug of coffee, and dark purple bags were stark beneath her eyes. She muttered something under her breath as Pen walked past her chair.

Storm stood at the counter, pouring himself a cup of coffee, then sipping it with a sigh. He cradled it in his large hands, eyes closed. So, Neil Storm liked his coffee black. It didn't surprise Pen in the least. He seemed like the kind of man to prefer the bitter stuff as a necessity to begin his mornings. He wasn't the kind of person to *relish* things.

Because tea was soft and calming. Tea was familiar, warm,

and knowing. She knew what tea tasted like, and coffee was always unreliable.

Like Storm.

She watched him quietly as he took another long drink of the black liquid. He did not savor the taste and made no expression to indicate if the coffee offered him any sense of pleasure.

Pleasure. Why had that word come to mind when she looked at him? She squeezed her thighs together, butterflies flitting in her stomach. For fuck's sake, what was wrong with her?

"There's tea in the cupboard," Laszlo said, motioning to the one above the stove. "And the water is boiled and waiting for you."

Pen smiled warmly and crossed to the cupboard. "Thank you."

"We take our caffeine seriously," Laszlo said with a curt nod.

Snorting, Pen turned and pulled down the box of tea and a mug. It was a morning ritual, pouring in the water, mixing in a splash of milk, and stirring in a small spoonful of sugar before steeping two tea bags. Although everyone else here was drinking coffee, and it seemed to be the mascot for writers, Pen would never be swayed.

Steaming mug in hand, she settled into the seat across from Storm. He didn't look up, although he seemed aware of her presence. She leaned forward and blew on her tea as she watched him.

"That coffee is as black as your soul," she said, taking a scalding sip.

He raised a brow and gulped down a mouthful of coffee, eyes never leaving hers even as he swallowed. Pen watched the way his throat bobbed, her eyes flicking from the scrape of stubble along his jaw and down his neck before she returned her attention to his eyes. He smacked his lips, making a satisfied sound in his throat as he stared quietly on. She could feel that sound buzzing a pathway all the way down to her toes, and she blushed as she glared down at her tea, lips clamping together to keep from talking.

She was all sorts of flustered today.

"So, have you seen anything yet?" Daniela asked, leaning in. "Well, besides that fake shit in the cellar yesterday."

Fake shit? Pen thought. Did no one believe her? She recalled Storm's words the night before, the way he'd guided her up the stairs, away from the darkness and back to her room, the strange, comfortable energy humming between them as they'd stopped in the space between their doors.

"I saw what I saw," Pen insisted.

"Haven't seen anything," Laszlo said, ignoring her.

They all turned to Storm, who simply shrugged. Pen eyed him. She'd seen the way he'd flung himself into her room, the way he couldn't bring himself to open her door and go back to his. Had he seen the woman in black? Was there something he wasn't telling them?

"Okay!" Laszlo called, breaking the awkward silence. "We have a lot of work to do, so why don't we get started with writing sprints?"

Pen turned to survey Daniela and Storm. Laszlo's brows pinched together as he took them in. Everyone looked ragged, exhausted. Not fit for writing.

"This is precisely why I told you all to take it easy last night."

"Sorry we're not all *grannies*," Daniela sneered.

"I just didn't sleep well. New places," Storm said with a shrug.

Daniela snorted and set aside her coffee. "I fell asleep by the fire. Finally made my way up to bed around five."

That explains a lot, Pen thought, taking a sip of her tea. She could have sworn she'd heard someone stumble up the stairs earlier. Not that she'd wanted to look. Pen had decided curiosity was her enemy in this castle.

Laszlo picked up his itinerary and read down the list. "Well, we're supposed to be doing word sprints next, but no pressure." He surveyed their group. "Maybe I can move around the schedule and change what's up next instead?" He looked pointedly across the table at Daniela. "If that works better for you."

"Anything that doesn't require me to think," Daniela said into her cup.

"That shouldn't be too hard," Laszlo whispered.

"I'm sorry, did you just sass me?"

"I think I did." Laszlo motioned farther down the paper, ignoring them. "We'll swap tomorrow morning's exercise with this afternoon's reading, then."

Storm lifted his coffee, cradling the blue mug in his hands. Pen's vision narrowed on his soft brown fingers, and flashes of this morning's dream came to mind unbidden, making her flush. She squirmed in her seat, the buzz between her legs almost painful.

"Pen, are you okay?" Laszlo asked, reaching out for her.

She nodded as she turned to her friend. "Yeah, I'm fine."

Raising a brow, he called out, "Okay, ten-minute interval word sprints."

Opening her laptop, Pen met Storm's scrutiny over her screen. "What?" she asked, fingers hesitating over the keys.

"Nothing."

She took a long drink of tea, ignoring his pointed stare as Laszlo tapped the button on his phone. "Go!"

Dread coiled in Pen's stomach, but she reached out, put her fingers to the keys, and tried her damnedest.

Alas, her damnedest was *not* good enough. In the first interval, Pen wrote:

I like cheese. Cheese comes in all kinds of forms. We like cheese very much. Do you like cheese? Mice like cheese. Cheese likes cheese.

Cheese wins all.

Why she'd suddenly become obsessed with cheese was anyone's guess. She held down the backspace button and deleted the entire selection before she could stop herself.

In the second interval, Pen caught Storm watching her, his expression inscrutable.

He is a storm, and I wish he would just go hide in a corner so I can stop looking at his pretty face.

Pretty faces, corners, stormy men. There was one person crowding her thoughts, and Pen would never willingly admit that he was taking up every inch of space in her mind. She held down the backspace button again, teeth grinding. Pen caught him smirking over his coffee, and she turned to glower at him.

"What are you laughing at?"

"Nothing."

She wished writing didn't make her so damn angry, but it did. Maybe that was her problem, the anger that she used to fuel her craft. Clearly, whatever she was doing was not working. Maybe she needed happiness and comfort. Something soft and warm instead of cold and stony.

"Why don't you sit this one out?" Laszlo offered, tapping the back of her hand.

"Love you, Laszlo, but I've got this."

Daniela shot Laszlo a look over Pen's head, but Pen ignored it. She could do this. She could write *something.* Anything.

Her eyes met Storm's once more, and his brows pinched together in . . . what was that, concern? Damn it, now she really needed to succeed. She couldn't let him see her fail. Her career was riding on this. Half her savings had been spent on the airfare to get here, and Pen wasn't willing to give in and fail just yet.

She was so sick of the pity, of the way everyone avoided her. Pen would prove them all wrong.

She had so much worth fighting for.

Chapter 12

NEIL

Neil watched Skinner over his laptop. Her tongue stuck out of the corner of her lips; her brows pinched together, eyes narrowed as she tapped away. It was almost *violent*, the way she wrote. She attacked her keyboard with an energy that was frightening, a kitten pouncing on a toy mouse.

"Pen," Laszlo called. Skinner didn't look up. "Earth to Penelope Skinner? Okay, I'm starting the next one." Laszlo clicked the timer on his phone and motioned for them to begin.

Neil returned his attention to his screen, the sensor flashing in time with his heartbeat. This again. He needed to *write*, put something, anything down. Last night, he hadn't managed to write a single word, and writing retreats were for writing, weren't they? Neil stared at his laptop as the rest of the table began typing, and his eyes flicked over them. Their fingers moved confidently over the keys in a rhythmic *tap-tap-tap*.

Even Daniela, who'd complained loudly about not wanting to think, was writing, her eyes zeroed in on the words across her screen. But not Neil. There was nothing in that little head of his.

"Done!" Laszlo said, pulling him from his thoughts.

Neil's heart was in his throat as the others stretched and yawned, shaking out their fingers as if in those ten minutes of writing they'd written an entire fucking book. Fuck, this was not looking good for

Neil. Blinking, he focused on his screen. He didn't know what he'd expected, but it was blank, still blank. How in the hell had he managed not to write a single word? His focus drifted back to Skinner, and suddenly he knew why he was so goddamn distracted. Her—she was doing this to him.

Laszlo restarted the timer before standing and crossing to the counter, refilling his coffee. Daniela followed suit, searching through the fridge and cabinets for snacks and breakfast. Despite his growling stomach, Neil didn't get up. Neither did Skinner.

Taking a sip of his now lukewarm coffee, Neil found himself drawn to her like a magnet. She was still seated before her laptop, hands stretched out over the keyboard, mouth parted slightly, just enough to make him trail its bow shape. Swallowing, he searched her expression for any hint of what she was feeling. There were words on her computer, he could see them reflected in her glasses, but there weren't many.

He watched, mystified, as she reached over her keyboard and deleted them. They disappeared one by one until her document went blank.

Sighing, she slumped in her seat, curling in on herself.

"Why'd you delete them?" he asked.

Her head shot up, gray eyes meeting his. "What?" She flipped her braid over her shoulder, exposing her neck and making the words stick in his throat.

"The words," he croaked. He cleared his throat and waved a hand at her computer. "You deleted the words."

She scrunched up her nose, and leaning forward, folded her arms on the table and rested her head on them. Her voice was muffled as she said, "They weren't good."

"But they're still words," Neil argued. He didn't understand. He never edited as he wrote, instead preferring to write as much as possible in one go and tear the draft apart later. First drafts were never good, that was the point. Write the book and fill in the flesh of the story later.

She sat up, sighing again. Skinner sighed often, soft exhales marking her annoyance, her exhaustion. Strangely, he found he rather liked the sound.

Skinner shook her head. "Most of the time, I try not to erase anything until the second draft. Sometimes, I can move the words to another spot entirely, and reuse them in different contexts. But those words," she said, pointing to the screen, "they were terrible. Sometimes, it's best not to write at all than to write terribly."

He narrowed his eyes, leaning forward. "Do you have any hobbies?"

"Not really, just reading."

"Okay," he drawled, tapping the table, and thinking. "If I played, say, the piano—"

"You would play the piano."

"What's that supposed to mean?"

"Nothing," she snorted, waving her hand at him. "Continue."

"If I played *piano*, and I only practiced when I felt like it, do you think I would get better?" She opened her mouth to respond, but he held up a hand, leaning closer. "If we only practice things when we are good, we'll never get *good*. You have to dig through the nasty before you can get to the good."

Skinner watched him for a long moment, and Neil squirmed under her scrutiny.

"You're oddly good at pep talks."

Neil smiled, the comment oddly warming. "I know. It's because I practiced."

"You're not good at being humble."

He frowned. "I know you think I'm some big shot or something, but I promise, it's never been easy. I'm not this confident guy you've made me out to be. I'm constantly second guessing myself, watching everything I do to see when I'll fail because I know I will."

Skinner stared blankly up at him, her expression inscrutable. He squirmed under her attention, and she said nothing as the others rejoined them, mugs refilled, snacks piled in their arms. Neil wished she'd sigh again. But Skinner didn't look at him as Laszlo tapped the timer on his phone.

"Begin!" he called.

This time, Neil tried.

Though his speech had been gallant, and he'd meant what he'd said, sometimes there were no good words. Neil could be inspired, and still, nothing he wrote was worth the breath. He deleted and retyped the same sentence in six different variations:

She ran through the halls. Ran through the halls she did. And so, she ran. Through the halls. She galloped through the halls. She ran fast through the halls. She ran through the halls.

Neil glared at his screen. He was neither Yoda nor a horse, and he was certain both the first and the last iteration were the same. He'd tried, *oh,* he'd tried. Neil had thought if he switched the words around, if he found the correct path of the action, it would suddenly be okay. The story would flow from him like some unstopped dam of creativity, but that's not how these things worked.

In the end, there was still no plot, no characters, just a vague action and a vague girl running (or galloping) through the halls. He had no story, no sense of a plot. Neil was, once again, lost.

Failed, he'd failed again.

Laszlo's phone beeped, the round of ten minutes up.

"You can't be serious," Neil whispered.

Laszlo clapped him on the shoulder as he stood and stretched, walking away to join Daniela at the counter.

And again, only Neil and Skinner remained seated. He didn't want to meet her eyes, for her to know he'd failed so miserably, but he couldn't help the magnetic pull. His attention was locked on her.

"How'd you fare?" he asked, grimacing.

She scratched her scalp with both hands, mussing her hair. "Terrible, it was terrible." She narrowed her eyes, angling her chair toward him. "And you? How did the great, magnificent Neil Storm fare?"

He winced in turn. He did not deserve the title of "magnificent." He probably never did. It was likely the self-pity, the doubt, but there was nothing magnificent about him in the least, especially not now.

"I've been better."

She made a soft sound, her eyes not quite meeting his.

Neil thought back to his words in the ruins. What had he told her? He'd said something along the lines of "every writer struggles," insinuating that *he* was struggling. And to make it worse, last night he'd laid it all out for her, been the most open he'd ever been with . . . anyone. And what had she done? She'd turned him away. Grinding his teeth, Neil leaned forward conspiratorially.

"Can I ask you something?" he asked, voice low.

Skinner narrowed her eyes but inched closer. She was so close, in fact, that he could smell her, that fresh, sweet scent of her shampoo lingering in the space between them. Neil couldn't help but remember how she'd felt, how she had moved under him, *against* him as he'd bent toward her and cupped her face at the ruins. His hand gripped the edge of the table tightly as he fought the urge to touch her.

"What?" she asked.

She pulled out a nondescript tube of lip balm and rolled it over her lips, puckering them as she pocketed it.

He blinked, his thoughts trailing off as he stared across the table at her. "What?" he repeated numbly.

Skinner laughed weakly. "Um, you said you were going to ask me something?"

Neil frowned. He had said that, hadn't he? Whatever it was, it must not have been too important, because he suddenly found himself captivated by her lips. And her hair. And her eyes, which glared across the table at him as he floundered.

"Are we done?" she asked, standing and closing her laptop.

"Yeah," Daniela said, stretching. "I could do with a break."

"Be back here in an hour for the next exercise!" Everyone stopped and turned to Laszlo. "Fine," he relented. "Three hours!" he called as Skinner fled and Daniela sauntered off.

Neil didn't leave, his nails tapping against the table as he stared across at the empty chair where she'd been sitting. His emotions swirled, dipping and tumbling. Emotions were annoying. This whole thing was so goddamn annoying.

Laszlo touched his shoulder gently, making him jump. His tall friend pulled back and smiled down at Neil. "Are you okay, Neil?"

He shivered and closed his laptop. "Yeah, yeah, I'm fine. Probably just need to walk around a bit." He smiled up at him as he pushed back his chair to stand, but it rocked backward, sending him sprawling across the floor.

Neil struggled to sit up, shoving aside the chair with a string of obscenities. Laughing, Laszlo held out a hand for him, and he took it, cheeks flaming. Neil glared up at Laszlo, at the phone in his friend's hand.

"Did you take a picture?" he asked, suspicious. "Did you just take a picture of me?"

Laszlo shrugged, pocketing his phone. "Maybe I took a video. Who knows."

"*You* know, Laszlo. Please delete it."

"I don't have a clue what you're referring to."

"Not a word to anyone," Neil said, moving past Laszlo. "I better not see that picture . . . or video circulating anywhere."

"I make no promises, Neil Storm! We all need a bit of good blackmail from time to time."

Neil grumbled to himself as he turned down the hall and strode away. Fuck, he felt so lost. Maybe he just needed some time to himself. Yeah, that ought to do the trick. He needed to get his emotions under control and stop thinking about Penelope Skinner.

The others had dispersed throughout the castle, and Neil followed in their tracks, meandering lazily down the long hall. He wandered past creepy paintings and eerily watchful busts, pausing in the foyer to regard the painting of the woman in black. She looked almost regal up there, chin tilted just so, every hair in place. Her gray-blue eyes seemed to follow him as he took two steps to his right.

"Holy shit," he cursed, tilting his head this way and that. There was something uncanny in her narrowed glare. Had it been her in the hall? The more Neil thought about it, the more he believed there was merit to Fanny's words about a woman lost in this castle for all time. Neil shuddered and pivoted down the hall and into the study, shaking off the feeling as he took in the room. It looked different in the light of day, less morose with the sun blaring in through the tall windows.

As Neil crossed to the large desk, he heard what sounded like a whisper along his neck and the shell of his ear. His head whipped around, eyes scanning the room and the hall beyond, but there was no one.

"Hello?"

Nothing. Of course, it was nothing. He was alone in here.

His lips pressed into a thin line, Neil hurried toward the bookcases in the back. Toward the light—if he could get toward the light of the large windows, everything would be fine because ghosts in this castle seemed to prefer the night. Ghosts didn't like daytime, right? They liked darkness and shadows. Things just didn't go bump in the day.

Refocusing, his fingers danced across the spines, eyes scanning over the titles and authors. Fanny was right, these books were almost all newer. Neil could see the line where the shelves and the books had been repaired or replaced by crisper tomes.

But as he scanned, he heard it again, that soft whisper across his skin, so loud it was as if someone gasped it in his ear: *Archie.* Neil jumped as a red book landed on the ground behind him.

Almost like it had been thrown.

Or pushed.

Or worse, *pulled.*

Glancing around, Neil stooped and lifted it carefully from the floor, holding it delicately in his hands as he turned it over. It was brick red, the leather cover and spine seemingly empty of its title or author. Frowning, he flipped through the pages, recognizing the neat handwriting.

"This is the same journal," he murmured, standing. The same one that had fallen at his feet last night. The one he'd put back before truth or dare, as if it were nothing.

He turned through the pages, eyes going wide as he stopped on an entry, his finger shakily tracing the name "Archie."

And then he heard it again, clearer this time: *Archie.*

A feminine voice, raspy and aching.

Neil's phone buzzed. He slammed the book shut and tossed it behind him in surprise. Heart beating frantically, he pulled out his phone, eyes narrowed at the name across his screen. He could ignore it, pretend he didn't have service in this abandoned corner of Scotland, but she was known to call and call until he answered. His agent did not give up so easily.

Puffing out his cheeks, he settled on the arm of the couch and swiped the screen up. "Hey, Tabitha."

"How's my favorite client?" she asked, voice extra perky.

"You say that to all your clients."

A pause. "Yeah, you got me there. Listen," she said, speeding up, "you know how I am with phone calls."

"Hate 'em," they said in unison.

Tabitha laughed. "I just wanted to check in and see how you are." A pause. Neil rolled his eyes, focusing on the red book he'd tossed on the floor. "You aren't answering my emails," Tabitha chided. "I haven't heard from you in months, Neil. I wouldn't call if I weren't worried."

"Tabitha," he said, leaning back, "I'm fine."

Another pause.

"We both know that's not true."

He sighed, tugging on his curls. "Just because I haven't written anything new doesn't mean I'm struggling." He waved his hand in the air. "I have a TV show in the works, for crying out loud. Everything is on track."

"But no new work."

"I just turned in my copyedits for *On the Backs of My Ancestors,*" Neil hissed.

"Yes," she drawled, "a book you sold as an option three years ago."

There it was: the truth. No books. His creativity had been sponged from a floor covered in the guts of his stories, and he was hungry for scraps. For anything, really. He was starved for creativity.

"Neil," she said softly.

"Tabitha, I've got this figured out."

A third pause.

"I heard Penelope Skinner is there."

"How on earth—" Gritting his teeth, he lowered his voice, glancing toward the hall. "How do you know that?" he demanded.

"Eh, just have an inkling—"

"Tabitha."

"Daniela Mitchel, okay!" She sighed into the phone. "She's been posting nonstop since you arrived. I spotted Skinner in the background. Including," she said, voice raised, "photos of your trip *to* the castle."

Neil squeezed his eyes shut, running a hand over his face. *Of course* Daniela had posted about it. He'd seen her a few times with her phone, snapping selfies, typing furiously across the small screen.

He just hadn't known she'd included him and Skinner.

"Tabitha," he started.

"Neil," she snapped on the other end of the line. It was coming; it always was. He braced himself. "This could be good! No one has seen you two together since Book Con—"

"Listen," he started, switching his phone to his other ear as he crossed to the journal and snatched it off the floor. "I'm working on something, and it's going great. I just need to get together a proposal; a synopsis and a few chapters."

He hoped it would turn out great, hell, he hoped it would turn out at all. At this rate, he had maybe two sentences to work off of and it involved a girl running through a fucking hall.

"You are? What are you working on?"

Neil searched the room, scanning the bookshelves. "A period piece."

"You know how they feel about period pieces. I thought we talked about this. You said you were going to work on that gruesome horror you told me about instead. The one with the antlers?"

Neil worked his jaw, eyes skimming over the room once more, taking in the upholstery, and the décor. "I'm thinking gothic, so around early to mid-nineteenth century."

"Thinking about? Neil, have you or have you not started it?"

"Tabitha." He dropped the book on the desk and pinched the bridge of his nose, tamping down his anger. "We already talked about this. I'm writing the gothic."

"They don't want a period piece from you, Neil. We already tried."

"Then let's workshop it! My sales are stellar. We could go to another publisher, someone open to something new."

Even he knew it was futile. After the Incident, he'd approached Tabitha with a book he loved that he'd shelved previously. When they were happy with it, they'd prepped the proposal, then sent it to his publisher. It didn't take long for them to send back the dreaded "no." His ideas were too niche, or not original enough in an already crowded market. Not to mention, Neil Storm was a *brand*.

But what if his brand wasn't working for him? Neil had once turned down a path full of untold stories, Native characters, and hard truths, and publishing had steered him down another. He wished he'd seen the signs. And now, he was tired of catering to everyone else, of feeling like his books no longer deserved their spots on shelves when people like Penelope Skinner were writing from their hearts.

If he didn't get his shit together fast, it would be his first time in six years uncontracted. It made him feel like a failure. His newest book, *On the Backs of My Ancestors,* was set to release in nine months. After the last rejection, Neil was beginning to wonder how much more he had in him at this pace. Authors used to take their time and space out their releases, but if an author wanted to stay relevant in the modern era, a book a year had become the new minimum, and he just didn't have it in him.

"You have a contract, Neil. And you have a reputation at this publisher. Do you really want to burn that bridge?"

He sighed, tilting back his head. "I've gotta go, Tabitha."

"Neil—" she began, tone serious.

"I'll check in with you after the retreat," he promised before swiping down the screen and ending the call. He pocketed his phone and turned to go, then paused. Skinner stood a foot away, her eyes going from the book on the desk to him.

How much had she heard?

"Skinner," he said, tone resigned.

She crossed to the desk and picked up the journal, ignoring him.

"You know," she said, "my eyes kept going to this on the shelf."

Neil stepped closer, drawn to it.

Drawn to *her*.

"There's something about it, right?" he asked quietly.

She nodded as he stopped before her. Skinner leaned against the desk, the red journal in her hands, messy braid spilling over her shoulder. She didn't look up at Neil until he was a few inches away, his hand reaching for it.

His thumb brushed over the back of her hand as he took the journal. Suddenly, this close, he wanted to ask her about the night before. Neil wanted to know about the manuscript. He wanted to ask if she'd even read it, or if his apology was worthless at this point.

But every question, every word seemed to fail him as she stared up at him, expression carefully blank. His eyes were glued to her lips once more, to the freckle just to the left of them, so clearly the first thing he could think to blurt was, "Were you writing about cheese earlier?"

She stared at him, taken aback. "I'm sorry, what?"

What the hell, Neil? he thought. He wanted to hit himself in the head and tape his mouth closed before he said anything else absurd. But he couldn't seem to stop himself.

Neil cleared his throat, empty hand sliding into his front pocket. "I could see your screen reflected in your glasses." *Creepy*, he warned himself, *that's kind of creepy, Neil.* He shrugged, thoughts scrambling even as he continued, "I thought I saw cheese."

Blushing, she snatched the journal from his hand and slipped it under her arm, storming across the study.

"Fucking cheese," she cursed as she disappeared down the hall.

Neil went to the nearest bookcase and knocked his head into the shelf, eyes squeezed tight. He'd had the chance of a lifetime to say the things and do the things, but all the things had gone right out the window when the time came.

He had never been good at *things*.

Not that he'd had a lot of time to *think* about any of those things, seeing as how twelve hours ago he and Penelope Skinner had been rivals—no, not rivals, *enemies*, and oh, how twelve hours could change everything. The things he was beginning to feel for her were new and confusing, but Neil could not deny the fact that those very feelings were there, waiting for their chance to shine.

If only he could speak like a normal person.

"Yeah, because cheese is *really sexy*," he muttered, covering his face.

What an embarrassment.

Chapter 13

PEN

Cheese. Of all the things he could have asked her about, he'd asked about *cheese*.

Pen quickened her steps through the castle, ignoring the *bud-ump* of her heart against her ribs as she pictured the look on his face when he'd leaned close, or the way his thumb had brushed over her hand, lingering a moment too long and sending a wave of electricity down to her belly.

Knowing him, he'd probably meant nothing by it. Which only made her reaction even worse.

It was the castle ruins all over again. He was suave and confident, but not one second of that had mattered to him. Fuck, why had she ever opened up to him? Why had she ever been willing to listen to him, to understand why he'd done every-thing he'd done? Finally, after four months of avoiding him and their mixed-up past, she'd stepped forward to face it, only to flounder.

Damn it, why was she so shaken? She tightened her hold on the journal, her pulse in her fingertips. This was so unlike her. Pe-nelope Skinner was the kind of woman who stood her ground, who threw things at people, who never backed down from a fight, but Neil Storm, with his absurd questions about cheese, had left her tongue-tied.

Cheese. All because she'd written a ridiculous passage about ridiculous cheese because of her incessant writer's block.

Ridiculous, she thought as she ground her teeth and jogged up the stairs to the second floor before plopping down a few steps from the top. She smoothed her hands over the journal as she leaned her head against the banister and sighed.

No one had ever flustered her so. Pen shouldn't let him get to her, but she couldn't help it, and that scared her more than anything. Why she let him of all people fluster her was anyone's guess.

Forgetting Neil Storm for a moment, she returned her attention to the journal. Her eyes had gone to it on the shelf, and she'd followed a strange tether to it all the way down the hall and to the study. It felt like the night before, when she'd stumbled into the west wing and toward the door. When she'd seen the hand. The more she thought about it, the more she believed she wasn't imagining things.

And whatever she'd seen in that hall had tugged her toward the study, where she'd found Storm holding the journal in his hands like it had all the answers.

And now she needed to know for sure if it did.

She turned it over, fingers dancing over the worn, red leather. There was no author, no name imprinted on the spine or the cover. But for some minor cracking along the leather, the front and back of the journal were blank. It was slim, perhaps no thicker than her pinky, and yet felt oddly heavy in her hands.

"That's weird," she mumbled.

After glancing around, Pen peeled back the cover. It had that musky library scent, the paper yellowed with age, crispy and crinkling beneath her fingers. She smoothed her hand down the opening page, but found it was blank. Scrunching up her nose, she flipped through the pages until black ink caught her eye. She leafed through the entries, pages of handwriting filling it, blots of black ink splattered in places where the author had been careless with their quill. The entries were dated in the top right of every page, the furthest going back to the early nineteenth century. The handwriting was neat, the letters long and swooping across the aged paper in knowing strokes.

> *December 13th, 1814*
>
> *A new boy has arrived. He's the son of the groundskeeper. He will not look at me, but I can look upon him. I see him through my window as he trims the flowers in the garden. I watch him from the landing as he empties and fills the vases in the foyer.*
>
> *Mother says I am playing dangerous games, watching a boy I have no right to, but I am bored, and there is something that draws me to him.*
>
> *Father has not been home in several weeks, and Mother is forlorn as always.*
>
> *I am glad that at least I am entertained.*

Pen pulled the book down to her lap, something in her mind trying desperately to click. The passage . . . reminded her of something, but she couldn't quite put her finger on it.

Swallowing, she flipped a few more pages, stopping on a short passage.

> *January 22nd, 1815*
>
> *It has taken me ages to learn his name, but he finally dared speak to me. I approached him at night as he crept toward the front door. I reached for his hand, but he will not let me touch him.*
>
> *He gifted me with something else, though.*
>
> *His name is Archibald.*
>
> *I have dubbed him Archie for short.*

Pen leaned forward, her eyes drawn to the name. The *A* was looped, large and bold, standing out among the other letters like the owner of this journal had scribbled it down almost reverently. She ran a shaking finger over it. "Archie," she whispered.

The hairs on her neck stood on end as the name echoed back at her in a raspy voice.

Archie.

Pen slammed the book closed, her eyes going wide. "Hello?" she called, looking around. She thought back to Fanny's warning, to the west wing and the door and the thing in the cellar. Perhaps it was all connected.

"Is it you?"

But to no one's surprise, there was no answer. Pen glanced toward the west wing. Dark and ominous, it waited for her, calling to her. Hands wrapped tightly around the journal, Pen thought of the night before.

Maybe, if she just walked toward the door . . . If she moved a few feet closer . . .

"Pen!"

She jumped in surprise and pressed a hand to her chest. Heart thundering, she peered over the banister. Daniela waved up at her, seemingly innocent and unaware of what she'd been about to do.

"What?" she asked sharply, setting aside the journal.

Daniela smiled, and it reminded Pen of that night out by the boathouse.

"I've been calling your name for a while!" Daniela tilted her head, something mischievous glinting in her warm brown eyes. "Wanna play a game?"

"What kind of game?"

Daniela winked. "Something a little different today."

Pen needed a change of pace. She laughed and stood, stooping to grab the journal. Daniela beckoned to her, but Pen paused, squinting back up to the west wing. She had questions, and she knew without a doubt that hall had the answers, but for now, she wanted anything but to be alone. Being alone led to questions. Questions about this castle.

Questions about Neil Storm.

"If it's not your usual kind of game, what kind of game is it?" she asked, hurrying down the stairs.

Daniela withdrew a hand from behind her back and launched something at Pen. It was cold, wet, and icy, and Pen gasped in surprise, staring down at the snowball she'd thrown. It soaked through her sweater and braid, and she wiped it away with a shudder, the remnants splattering on the rug.

Reluctantly, she set the journal on a table in the hall, shaking her head. "Oh, oh, you are going to *regret* that."

"Not in the castle!" Laszlo called. "And we're due to start the next activity shortly!"

Snorting, Pen threw on her shoes and coat and followed Daniela out into the snow, where Storm was waiting.

He stood alone in the yard, already covered in snow. Pen blushed, thinking of those seconds in the library, the embers burning in his eyes. How long had she sat on those stairs? It had felt like mere minutes.

Her eyes traced over him as he wound up an arm and threw a snowball, hitting Daniela square on the cheek.

"Cheap shot!" she yelled, wiping it away.

Storm paused, an imperfectly round snowball in his hand. He turned to Pen, emerald eyes stark against the snowy backdrop. Hesitantly, he held it out.

"If I want anyone on my team, it's you. We all know how good of an arm you have."

Her stomach dipped as he smiled.

"No fair!" Daniela called. "We all know she's got great aim!"

Smiling, Pen reached for the snowball, her fingers brushing his palm.

"You've chosen well, padawan."

Laszlo appeared at the top of the stairs, his nose and cheeks red from the cold as he buttoned up his jacket. "There is no way in hell I'm staying in that castle on my own!" he said, hurrying down the steps.

Laughing, Pen launched the snowball at Laszlo, and her friend shrieked as bits of snow tumbled down the back of his shirt.

"No fair! I'm your ally!" he yelled, shivering as he stooped to pack some snow.

"No one is your ally when it comes to snowball fights!"

Pen reached down to pack another snowball, gasping as something cold slammed into her ass. She straightened, glancing over her shoulder and brushing snow from her pants.

"Who did that?" she demanded, eyeing them.

Daniela shook her head, motioning to Storm. "Don't look at me."

Laszlo and Daniela quieted as Pen turned to Storm.

"It seemed only fair after everything," he started. He dropped the snowballs in his hands as she stalked toward him in the snow. Pen smiled as she stopped before him. "You gave me a scar. A snowball seems only fair, right?"

Quietly, Pen bent at the waist and packed another snowball, ignoring him.

"Why don't we just call it a blank slate?" Storm asked, holding his hands out in surrender. His voice was shaky, eyes wide as he watched her.

Pen straightened and patted the snowball proudly. It was large, nearly the size of her head, and Storm gulped as he stared at it. Smiling, she tossed it at his chest. When it splattered against his front, his brow furrowed.

"Truce?" she asked, tilting her head.

He frowned as she took another step toward him. Storm

shifted back, hands between them as if he could ward her off. "Why does this feel like a trap?"

"It's not."

"I don't believe you."

Crying out, she launched herself at him. They fell back in the snow, and she laughed as she straddled him and held her arms up in victory. Sputtering, Storm squirmed beneath her, and one of his hands wrapped around her thigh, squeezing as he struggled up in the snow.

With sharp, undeniable certainty, she knew the dream had been about him. It had been *his* hand that squeezed her thigh, his mouth against hers as he'd pressed her back into a bookcase. Pen had woken this morning from a sex dream about Neil Storm, and there was no way to unknow it.

She froze as Daniela whistled and Laszlo coughed somewhere behind them. Hands planted on Storm's chest, Pen looked down at him, at his lopsided smile and snow-soaked curls. She couldn't look away. Impossibly, and against all odds, Pen had the terrifying urge to sink down and kiss him.

Face heating, Pen was reminded of the library, of the way he'd surrounded her, taking up what little space there was between them. And despite the cold of the snow, he was so warm beneath her. *Beneath her.*

Oh god, she was *straddling* him.

Suddenly, she wanted to tell him about the night before, about his book. How, despite everything telling her it was a terrible idea, she was having strange thoughts and feelings, and she wanted to act on them.

Like kissing.

She *really* wanted to kiss him.

"Why don't we all head in and dry off before we start the next activity?" Laszlo called from up the steps.

Clearing her throat, Pen struggled off Storm, his hand sliding leisurely from her thigh. His nails scraped over her leg, trailing a path of fire all the way to her knee as she stood and offered a hand to him. His hand was cold in hers, his fingers red from the snow as he stood and breathed warmth into them.

Her gaze locked on his lips, her thoughts heading in a direction that frightened her.

"Better head in," she mumbled, turning to go as she brushed off her pants, hiding the blush creeping up her neck and into her cheeks.

"Skinner?"

She paused, heart in her throat. "Yeah?"

He hesitated. "Nothing."

Blinking, she let out a deep sigh and jogged up the steps to the castle. In the foyer, she kicked off her boots and tossed her soaked jacket onto one of the hooks, clasping her fingers for warmth. She was already up the stairs and crossing to her bedroom when she heard the front doors open.

Puffing out her cheeks, Pen leaned back against her door and closed her eyes. No one could have predicted this in a million years. They were enemies or had been enemies. But talking to him, bickering with him, and finally, understanding Neil Storm had opened something in her closed-off heart.

Pen pressed her hands to her chest, shivering as the cold set in. She yanked off her sweater and slipped off her pants, tossing them carelessly to the side as she banged her head against the door.

Fuck, she hated to admit it, but Penelope Skinner *liked* him.

As more than enemies.

As more than friends.

As more than anything she'd ever allowed him to be.

Pen sank to the floor, head in her hands as she tried and failed desperately to banish her thoughts.

"I'm so screwed," she groaned.

Chapter 14

NEIL

Neil towel-dried his hair, pushing the curls away from his face. He tugged on a fresh shirt and then his fleece, shivering from the cold as he pulled the zipper all the way up.

As he smoothed his hands down his front, Neil couldn't help but think of her straddling him in the snow, of the way his hand had reached for her thigh automatically, wanting to pull her closer, of the way her braid had swung down as she bent forward, laughing and pumping her fists in victory.

He was spiraling so fast. He didn't know how he was supposed to pretend she had no effect on him when, clearly, he could speak of nothing but cheese around her.

Cheese.

"I'm never going to live that down," he groaned, crossing to his door.

Neil opened it just as she appeared on the threshold of her room, hair freshly braided, cheeks blazing. They stared at each other for a long, heated moment before they looked away.

"Hi," she said, not quite meeting his eyes.

Neil motioned to the hall as he closed his door, an invitation to join him. They walked silently down the hall toward the stairs, falling into step with each other. His hand brushed her hip, and she lurched away as if he'd burned her.

"Sorry," they said at the same time.

She smiled. It was so small, so gentle, Neil hardly recognized her. His heart pounded, and he was terrified she could hear it, the thunder of his pulse as he stared down at her.

"About earlier," they said in unison.

"Reading my mind?" she accused, laughing.

Were they *flirting*? Hot damn, maybe Neil had the moves after all. Forget cheese, forget every flounder until now, they would start *here*.

"I just wanted to apologize about earlier," he said carefully.

She stopped in the hall and ran her fingers over one of the busts. His mouth went dry as he watched her, her finger swirling over the smooth stone. Neil couldn't help it; suddenly, he was picturing her hand on *him*, over him, *touching* him.

"What for?" she asked, not looking at him.

He sidled up next to her, surveying the marble, wishing desperately that he were in its place.

"I can be . . . awkward, I guess. I don't do well around people."

"I noticed."

Neil chuckled, rubbing a hand over the back of his neck. "What gave me away?"

"When you asked about cheese."

They both burst into laughter, and Neil watched her, hand on his gut. It felt . . . nice, to laugh with her. To joke, even if it was at his expense. But the laughter died when she stopped on the stairs, her eyes drawn to the west wing across the way.

"Have you wondered what's down there?" she asked.

He followed her fixation to the darkened hall. The mere sight of it made him shudder. There was something *off* about the west wing, and though part of him knew it was the groundskeeper's warning, Neil couldn't help but think whatever thing he'd seen the night before, the eyes Skinner had seen in the cellar, the whispers in the castle, and the strange sense of being watched, all linked back to this spot in the castle.

It was rumored that the woman in black crept through the abandoned hall, and Neil wasn't so certain it was just a rumor.

Skinner took a step toward the west wing, and Neil reached for her out of instinct. He gripped her shoulder, fingers gently squeezing. "Hey, hey, we shouldn't go down there." He tried to keep his tone light, but a warning slinked into the cracks.

She turned to stare up at him, her gray eyes wide. His touch seemed to pull her out of whatever trance she was in because her blush only deepened as she shrugged out of his grip. Neil tried to hide his disappointment as she moved farther away from him, her hands worrying at a loose thread on her sweater.

"Sorry," she said, turning back toward the west wing. "I don't know what it is about that place, but I just feel so *drawn* to it, you know?"

As much as he hated to admit it, he did know. Neil felt it too. He'd felt it when he'd picked up the journal from the study's floor. And he'd felt it when he'd opened his door the night before and smelled something that made his stomach gurgle even now at the recollection.

He glanced sidelong at Skinner. Neil knew all too well what being drawn to something felt like, but only bad things could come out of a place so dark, so abandoned. When he searched the darkness, his gut twisted, and his hair stood on end. He didn't want to see the woman in black, if the portrait in the foyer was any sign of who she was. It was creepy and scary, and Neil was regretting coming to a haunted castle.

He cleared his throat and motioned to the stairs as the voices of the others grew louder below them. "Come on, Laszlo will kill us if we're any later than we already are."

She nodded and turned slowly, peering back at the west wing over her shoulder as they descended the staircase.

"You're late!" Daniela decreed as they turned into the kitchen.

Neil shook his head as Skinner pushed past him to the table and took a seat. "We got lost," he lied.

"Sure, you did."

Laszlo clapped, drawing their attention. "Okay! This time we're doing a partner activity. I was going to do it tomorrow morning, but you all seem to need a bit more stimulation today."

"Sure do," Daniela whispered to Neil.

"So, we pair up?" Neil asked, ignoring her pointed stare.

"Yes, we'll randomly select partners and rooms. The idea is to sit and write the first thing that comes to mind in these places. Take it in," Laszlo said, eyes flicking around them. "This castle holds a lot of inspiration. Look at the walls, at the floor, and just write whatever pops into your head, okay?" He clapped his hands again and motioned to the table. "I've already mapped out the creepiest rooms in the castle, so we'll draw from those."

Neil leaned toward the rough sketch Laszlo had laid out across the table. There were rooms he didn't know were there, secret doors and passageways in places he was frankly uncomfortable knowing even existed.

"Now that I think about it, this sounds like a terrible idea," Laszlo said, turning to Skinner.

Neil watched as the two leaned in toward each other conspiratorially. His stomach twisted at the sight. He wanted her to trust him like that. To smile without pulling back, to laugh freely.

"Laszlo, I will never understand why you decided renting out a haunted Scottish castle was a good idea," Skinner said.

"Frankly, neither will I."

"What about that one novel you wrote with the . . . thing that had the ghost doing . . . the thing? Wasn't that kind of scary?"

Laszlo squinted at her. "My gothic thriller?"

She shook her head, leaning forward. She tapped her finger against the wood of the table, scraping her nail in the grooves, and

Neil thought of her straddling him, her hands splayed across his chest as she laughed.

"No, no it was . . ." She scrunched up her nose, thinking. "The one with the underground tunnels? And the vampire."

"Oh, *The Drawn and the Closed.*"

"Yes!" Skinner laughed and clapped. "That's the one."

"Is that a sex dungeon?" Daniela whispered from behind Neil, pointing to the map.

"What?" he asked, momentarily distracted.

Daniela smirked. "I was testing you. You're spending an awfully long time studying this map, Stormy."

"Please don't use that nickname."

"But it's my favorite!" Daniela slung an arm over his shoulder. "You know, we're from the same tribe, Stormy. We're practically cousins. Aw," she said when he tried to pull away, "why so gloomy?"

"Please don't with the weather puns." He shrugged her off and refocused on Skinner and Laszlo.

"Are you telling me you wrote that despite being scared of ghost stories and haunted places?" Skinner asked Laszlo, tilting her head.

Laszlo waved his hand. "I've been on dozens of underground tours. Something about those made it easier to write, you know? But that cellar? *No, thank you.*"

"What kind of underwear do you wear, Storm?" Daniela continued.

"Don't do it," he begged.

"Thunderwear," Daniela and Neil said in unison.

Daniela pouted. "It's no fun when you do it."

"Precisely why I do it. You don't think I haven't heard them all already?"

Laszlo straightened and waved his hands at the group, holding up a cup. "Okay, okay, calm down. I'm drawing the first pair . . ."

Neil clamped down on his bottom lip as Laszlo reached in and lifted out two names. "I'm with Daniela."

Daniela's face was carefully blank. "And the room?" she asked.

Laszlo reached into a second cup. "The study."

Sighing in relief, Laszlo leaned across the table to high-five Daniela, but she maneuvered out of the way. "Woo-hoo," she deadpanned, standing.

"I guess that means we know who the other pair is," Laszlo said, looking between Neil and Skinner.

Neil could see what Skinner was thinking from the way her hands tightened around the edge of the table. But he couldn't help it; he felt *elated*. Finally, alone with her. No more running away, no more interruptions.

Just the two of them.

"I think it's fine," Laszlo said. "Assuming you two can spend an hour in a room together."

"Sure," he said too quickly. *Fuck, don't sound too excited.*

Skinner turned to him. He tried to school his expression and force his lips into a flat, uncaring line.

"I guess." Skinner sighed, looking away quickly, but Neil could have sworn he saw the beginnings of a smile curling her lips.

"Okay," Laszlo said, glancing between them. "Only the room left, then."

"Can you please hurry up?" Skinner asked. Neil watched her carefully. She'd tried to mask the fear in her tone, but it was there, in the tightening of her lips, in the furrowed brow, and the waver in her voice.

Laszlo held up the small piece of paper in his hand, eyes widening. "I can choose another."

"It's the cellar, isn't it?" Skinner groaned.

"Um, no."

"It's worse?" Neil asked quietly. His stomach swirled viciously.

Laszlo slid the piece of paper across the table toward them and pointed to a place on the map, and Skinner sat up, craning her neck to read.

Neil's stomach dropped, the nerves in his body buzzing.

"You have to be fucking kidding me."

"I have the worst luck," Skinner whispered.

Excerpt from *The Drawn and the Closed*
by Laszlo Morgenstern

Beneath the streets, a shadow waited. It lurked in the darkness like a phantom, half of its face hidden from view. It did not live there, nor in the theater above, but somewhere in between.

As in life, it lived in death: one foot on either side of the line.

Its throat ached with thirst, its teeth sharp and waiting for a person to wander above, alone and forgotten; for someone to fall into its trap. It was a lonely life, waiting and waiting, but, in time, it was always worth it.

And on this night, it did not have to wait long. A man wandered down the tunnels from the theater, slipping through the trapdoor beneath the stage.

The shadow watched him behind the curtain of darkness, waiting, waiting. But when he bent to bite the man, to suck him dry of his life force, the man met its eyes and said: "I've been looking for you."

Chapter 15

NEIL

Neil fiddled awkwardly with his laptop as Skinner swept her arm at her room. It was a mess. The small pile of pillows and socks she'd used for artillery when he'd barged into her room the night before still littered the floor. She hadn't stopped to make her bed; the blankets twisted in a tangled disarray. And was that underwear by the ensuite?

"You're already quite familiar with my room," she joked. She followed his apt attention to the underwear. She rushed over and threw them into the bathroom, slamming the door shut with an awkward laugh.

Coughing to hide a smile, Neil turned to her, holding up a hand in surrender. "About last night—" he started, remembering the way she'd gently removed his hands from the door and the way she'd stared back at him curiously from her laptop, then hungrily started reading the words he'd written all those years ago.

"I'm sorry," she said, spinning toward him. "I'm sorry for blowing up at you. I want you to do better is all."

Neil blanched. "Did you just apologize?"

"I read your manuscript."

Oh no, he couldn't look at her. His eyes went to his feet. She thought it was terrible; it was the worst thing she'd ever read. His gaze flicked back up at her, and she swallowed as she fiddled with the fraying hem of her sweater.

"I stayed up reading it."

He deflated and looked away as his hands slipped into his pockets. "Oh."

"No!" She crossed to him, taking his hand in hers. His pulse sped as her fingers swept over the soft skin on the inside of his wrist, brushing the edge of his tattoo. "Thank you, for being willing to extend an olive branch. You didn't have to, but I'm glad you did." She tilted her head, glancing up at him from beneath her bangs, and Neil tried to ignore the way his heart was thrumming at her touch. "I'm glad you trusted me enough to be honest. Especially when I've never given you a reason to."

"And I'm sorry, for not standing up for the things I wanted."

Skinner laughed as she patted his hand, dropping it and stepping back. Neil felt her absence at once, and he flexed his fingers, wanting to reach out for her.

"That's a big apology, but having read it, I see what you've given up. So . . . do me one favor?"

Those were not words he ever expected to come out of her mouth. Neil frowned as she walked toward a tapestry hanging on the wall.

"What?" he asked.

"Do better? Stop catering to your publisher and write the books you want to write? Write *your* books."

Swallowing, he nodded. "I can try." And he would. Neil would do his best to earn his place.

She smiled. He watched as she pocketed her phone and slipped her laptop under her arm before crossing the room and holding aside the tapestry to reveal a secret door.

"That's all I ask."

He cleared his throat. "While we're on the topic, can you do something for me?"

She frowned. "What?"

"Believe that you're enough. You don't need to be enrolled, you don't need to look Native to be Native. You're Native, and so long as you know, that's enough. There will always be someone who says otherwise, but they're buying into a system created by colonizers. *You're* enough, Penelope Skinner."

Skinner tilted her head, eyes shining. "Thank you. I didn't realize until now, but I've been waiting for someone to tell me that for a while." She cleared her throat and turned back to the tapestry.

"Happy to be of service." He rocked back on his heels, desperately wanting to keep her talking. "Do you have any recommendations on how I should move forward from this?"

He had a few ideas.

Like kissing her and . . . kissing her.

Kissing her would solve so many problems.

"From this?"

"How I can do better? As an author."

Scrunching up her nose, Skinner shrugged. "It's a heavy topic. Are you sure you want to have this conversation while we're trapped together for an hour?"

Trapped. Damn it all, had he completely misread the situation? He wasn't exactly hiding his intentions, and he'd thought she understood what was growing between them. *Fuck.* After everything, after all the amends, did she still hate him?

"You're probably right."

"Here, hold this for me." She handed him her laptop, and he tucked it next to his, adjusting his grip. "Laszlo said it should be up this stairwell."

"Do all rooms have secret doors?" he asked, drawing closer.

She smiled as she slid away the lock and pushed open the door to reveal a winding stairwell. Cool air hit them, and Neil coughed, the damp, dusty air filling his lungs. This castle needed a deep cleaning.

And maybe a good smudge with white sage.

"I'm not sure," she marveled, ducking her head into the dark and brandishing her phone, "but there's only one way to find out."

Teeth gritted, Neil followed Skinner and her dim light up and to the right. A chill met them, and the hairs on his neck stood on end, that terrifying feeling of being watched making goose bumps rise along his skin.

He jumped in surprise at the featherlight touch of something on his shoulder, a skim of ghostly fingers that reminded him too much of the touch he'd felt in the study, but there was nothing and no one there. Shivering, Neil pushed on, forcing his eyes forward.

The passageway was so narrow that he had to duck, but she was the perfect height. Neil watched, amused, as she guided them up the winding stone stairwell, her head not quite reaching the ceiling. He pressed a hand to the cold stone for balance as he squinted up at her, taking in the wisps of hair freed from her braid, the way her sweater slipped down her narrow shoulders.

Beyond the damp smell of the passageway, there it was again, that light, sweet scent of coconut shampoo drifting around her. Neil shivered, his nails scraping against the stone. Fuck, what was it about that smell that made his mouth go dry and his hand itch to reach for her?

"I think this is it?" she said, turning to him.

Surprised, he stumbled back a step, his foot slipping over stone, and she reached out and caught him, her fingers warm against his wrist as he righted himself on the narrow stairs.

"Thanks," he breathed as she let go and led them forward.

The door was much the same as the one in her room. It opened into the stairwell, and the plain wood was nicked and scratched as if something—or someone—had wanted in.

Or out.

The bolts squealed as she pulled it open and climbed into

the room, and Neil scrambled after her, the light from her phone fading around him. She made a small, disgruntled sound as she moved aside as she took her laptop from his hand, and he ducked through the entry.

They were in one of the castle's narrow turrets, the walls tall and the ceiling flat. This part of the castle seemed untouched by time, frozen in a strange state of disuse. Moss was growing in between the stone, and Neil ran his hand over it, sinking his fingers into the soft vegetation. That explained the smell. It reminded him of the castle ruins, that dampened earth scent that lingered everywhere he went.

Neil spun around, considering the rest of the space. The circular room had been recently swept, blankets and pillows laid out in the center on the floor, surrounded by candles and a box of matches.

He frowned, eyes flicking over the space. It looked more like a romantic—albeit *haunted*—picnic than a writing exercise, but when Neil turned to say as much to Skinner, he stopped, lips parting as he took her in.

The room was lined in small, narrow windows, the light from the snow seeping into the space, giving it an almost ethereal glow. Skinner leaned against the wall, laptop dangling from her fingers as she stared out at the surrounding landscape, the corner of her lips twitching into the faintest of smiles.

With a soft exhale, she leaned back on her heels. "This weather is *snow* laughing matter."

Neil groaned. "That's a terrible joke."

Skinner pointed to him. "But you called it a joke."

"A mistake."

She snorted, crossing her arms as she peered out the window. She was lit up, a silver glow over her pale skin. And when she turned to him, mouth open to say something else, she stopped and frowned. Her gray eyes were striking in the light.

"What?" she asked, straightening.

Neil shook his head and looked away toward the center of the room. "It's nothing."

They settled on the mound of blankets and pillows. Neil was careful not to touch her, leaving just enough room between them. Grumbling, Skinner readjusted herself, her knee brushing his as she sat cross-legged.

"Sorry."

"Don't worry about it," he said, even as his eyes locked on the place where they touched.

Clearing his throat, he opened his laptop to a new blank document. Damn it, how many blank documents had he started and stopped over the last four months? Neil poised his hands over the keyboard, lips pressed into a thin line.

"Maybe we could start by talking?" Skinner asked, her eyes flicking to his screen.

He turned to her in surprise. *She* wanted to talk to *him*? He'd take whatever he could get.

"I mean, if you think it'll work?"

She shrugged as she logged in to her laptop and scanned the turret, craning her neck back. Neil was immediately drawn to her throat, to the spot on her shoulder where it met her collarbone.

He wanted to press the little divot in her collar.

To kiss it.

To trail a finger between her freckles and connect the dots.

What's wrong with you? he thought, turning away from her.

"We could start by describing the room?"

Neil frowned. "Oh, okay."

Skinner laughed. "What did you think we would talk about?"

"Nothing."

Fuck, he was being a jerk. What the hell was wrong with him? Working his jaw, he followed her lead, taking in the cracked stone, the pale light seeping in through the windows. Closing his eyes, he inhaled that damp scent.

"This place is a dump," she said.

Neil sputtered and pressed a fist to his mouth. "That's a very eloquent description."

"It's really not." Skinner leaned back into the pillows, surveying the ceiling. A long crack split its length, reaching from one end of the room to the other. She sighed. "I can't stop thinking about last night."

Neil blinked in surprise. "Me neither."

"Every time I close my eyes—"

"All I can think about," he started, heart leaping into his throat.

"Are those eyes," she said as he blurted, "Is you."

Skinner leaned up on her elbows, frowning. "Sorry, what did you say?"

"Ugh, blue," Neil corrected.

Did I just say that out loud?

"Blue?"

He motioned weakly to the windows. This was the cheese line all over again.

"Blue light. It's kind of creepy."

Skinner's frown deepened, impossibly, but she said nothing. She sat up, returning her attention to the laptop. "Maybe we should write?"

"That's a good idea," he agreed quietly.

But he took a moment longer to watch her, to take her in as she worked. He liked watching her write. She was so serious, so determined.

Swallowing, he concentrated on his computer and tried desperately not to focus on her closeness. Instead, Neil thought of the night before, to the thing he'd seen disappearing into one of the rooms, and that wretched scent of rot and death that lingered in the hall. He thought of the featherlight touch in the stairwell, the whisper in the study. Of the portrait of a woman who likely haunted this castle. His fingers hesitated over the keys for only a second longer before he began to type.

He heard a creak on the stairs.

Neil licked his lips, eyes going to the splinters in the wood, the scratches on the door.

"That's shit," he muttered, returning his attention to the screen before holding down the backspace button. He tried again.

She heard a creak on the stairs.

"Still terrible."

"It can't be that bad," Skinner said, swiveling toward him.

Neil held his hands over his screen. "Please don't look."

"Then maybe stop talking out loud." Shaking her head, she bent over her laptop, brow pinched as she typed.

He ran a hand over his face, then held down the backspace key. Neil could usually see the story, click into the voice, and find the characters like plucking action figures from a shelf. But there was nothing. He'd lost something since Book Con, and he was struggling to get it back.

There was a creak on the stairs, he began. Running his tongue over his teeth, Neil continued. *It was a soft sound, something you wouldn't hear unless you were listening for it.*

He smiled to himself. Maybe he wasn't lost.

But Viola heard it. After all, she'd been listening to the night.

They jumped in surprise as the door to the turret slammed shut. Her fingers reached automatically for his, squeezing tight. Neil turned to Skinner with wide eyes. She glanced from their joined hands to him before pulling hers away with a blush.

"Did you do that?" he asked.

She scoffed and scrambled to stand, starting toward the door. "Do you think I'm clairvoyant or something? Of fucking course I didn't." Skinner yanked on the handle, teeth gritted as she leaned back with all her weight. "It won't open!"

"Is there another ghost that Fanny failed to mention? Because I don't recall anything about these turrets on the tour."

"I hope not," she said.

Neil stood and crossed to the door. He reached around her and wrapped his sweaty palms around the doorknob, yanking. The wood groaned as he planted his feet and pulled with everything he had, but it simply would not budge.

Was it the thing Skinner claimed she'd seen in the cellar, the protector? Was it whatever had lurked in the hall last night, the woman in black?

Or what had brushed against him in the stairwell?

Neil shivered as he tightened his hands on the doorknob, thinking.

"What do we do?" she asked, turning to him.

Skinner looked up at him like he knew the answers, but there weren't a lot of options, stranded in this turret. Neil peered around the room, anxiety spiking. The windows were too small, and the only way out of this place was barred by something he was too scared to even say aloud.

"Maybe if we put all of our weight into it, it'll budge? I know I'm kind of short—"

"Kind of?"

She glared. "Do you have any ideas, Storm? Because I don't recall you mentioning any sort of solution."

Neil surveyed the stone floors, searching for some hidden trapdoor. This castle had so many hiding places, so many strange little nooks, but it was clear this turret was empty, and there was no sense in grasping for an alternative.

"We could . . ." He trailed off as his eyes met hers.

They could, what? Whatever he was about to say died on his

lips. Hands planted on either side of her, Neil surrounded Skinner. The scent of her shampoo found him, flooding his senses as his eyes caught on the shine of her lips before sliding away.

The locked door, the night before, the last four months—the words for everything left him as he stared down at her. He thought of their moment at the ruins, the way his hand had fit into the notch at her waist so perfectly.

This scene was almost identical to the one in the study, but Neil knew now. He knew that last night, something had changed between them, and he couldn't hide it anymore.

He took her in, the slope of her shoulders, the way her sweater simply wouldn't stay up, the spattering of freckles over her pale skin.

The way her lips parted as she met his heated gaze.

He could have been thinking about any number of things, like whatever lay beyond the door, but the only thing on Neil Storm's mind was kissing Penelope Skinner.

Chapter 16

PEN

She could smell him from here, that sweet, rich scent of coffee, the slightest of musk lingering on his clothes. She'd tried desperately to forget that scent, but it was impossible. Clearing her throat, Pen turned to the door, her hands tightening around the doorknob. They needed to get out of here.

"Maybe if we work together," she offered, not daring to look at him.

What was *happening*? Pen was about to have a full-on existential meltdown.

You know what's happening.

And damn it, she *wanted* it to happen. She'd shoved him down to the snow and *straddled* him. She'd nearly let him kiss her in the study. There was something between them, now that the air had been cleared and their pasts could stay their pasts, but the part of her that kind of wanted a future, too, desperately wanted *this*.

He took a step closer, the heat of him along her back. Pen's nerves buzzed with his nearness. She tried to focus on the fear of being trapped, on the thing that had shut them in, on the anger she'd felt for him just last night, but he reached around her, a finger skimming the back of her hand before wrapping around hers.

Without even realizing it, she was leaning back, melting into him, breath coming faster. What in the actual *fuck* was happening?

Pen didn't have words to describe this tightness in her chest, but she knew what that slickness between her legs was, the ache building as he pressed closer.

And she could not ignore that.

Twenty-four hours ago, she would have never imagined talking to this man, let alone having an honest conversation, but in the time since they'd met up in Edinburgh, she and Storm had laid bare all the nastiness between them. After reading his manuscript, she'd finally understood where he was coming from, why he'd made every decision.

Though it didn't fix everything he'd done, Pen was willing to forgive him for his past mistakes if he was willing to forgive her for hers.

But *this* had not been on the agenda.

Not this morning, at least.

"What are you doing, Storm?"

She knew he knew very well that she was aware of what he was doing, but *fuck*, Pen was going to self-combust. She was hot all over, and everywhere he touched, everywhere they aligned was on fire.

He bent close until his nose skimmed her jaw, the hard angles of him pressing against her side. His breath blew across her skin, and she wanted to turn in to his warmth, capture his mouth with hers.

"I thought about kissing you at the ruins," he whispered.

"You did?" Her voice was small, too small, and Pen wished she could swallow the words.

Her hold on the door loosened, and she pressed back into him fully, relishing the feel of him against her, the scent that flooded her senses. When she'd woken this morning with her muscles clamped tight and the place between her thighs slick with want, she'd been thinking of him, and he certainly was having the same effect on her here.

"I didn't understand it until you and I talked," he said, his fingers trailing from her hand up to her arm, "until we were honest with each other, but I'm starting to wonder if there was always something else here, waiting."

"Storm," she said breathlessly, squeezing her eyes shut.

"Yes, Skinner?" he asked, lips brushing against her cheek. His thumb swept across her waist, and damn it, she was ready to give in, to turn in his arms.

But last night she'd hated him still. No, she'd *loathed* him. Penelope Skinner had loathed Neil Storm, so why did she want to turn and kiss him? She wanted him to wrap his hands around her waist like he had the day before and press her into the door. She wanted to reach down and feel his length against her, wrap her legs around him and drag him close and pull him *in*. She wanted to run her hands through his wild hair, wanted him to undo her braid and tug her sweater over her head, and just—

The latch to the door popped open, and Pen breathed out. Face flushed, she ducked her head and slipped out from the circle of his arms before reaching for her laptop. Her hands shook as she closed the lid and wrapped her fingers around it. Ignoring the look of hurt on his face, she hurried toward the door.

"Penelope!" he called as she thrust open the door and he stumbled back.

Pen took the stairs two at a time. She didn't trust herself right now. She'd wanted to kiss him.

Neil Storm.

Penelope Skinner had wanted to kiss Neil Storm.

She screamed as she flung the door to the passageway shut and locked it, tossing her laptop to her bed. How? *How?* She came here to take control of her career, to fucking *write*, not to, well, *fuck* around.

"Penelope, please?"

Why was he using her first name? He wasn't allowed to say

her name like that. He wasn't allowed to make her feel things for him.

Storm knocked on the door, and she swung toward it, heart in her throat. Waiting.

"Please, we need to talk." His voice was thick with emotion, low and sultry, and goddamn it, just the sound of his voice was making her horny.

"No, we *really* don't."

"Penelope."

Damn it, since when did he call her by her first name?

Hands planted on her hips, Pen paced. This wasn't possible. There was no alternate reality where she wanted Neil Storm to kiss her. Sighing, she turned and slammed her hands against the tapestry. She could imagine him on the other side, cramped in the narrow stairwell, hands on either side of the door as he leaned close and waited for her to give him a chance.

So close, they were so close. The only thing that separated them were these two inches of wood.

Pen shook her head. "I can't do this."

Between him and the strange things she'd seen and heard, Penelope Skinner had outstayed her welcome in this castle.

Pressing her lips into a flat line, she crossed the room and shoved her things into her bag. She didn't belong here with these people. She never had. And Storm trying to kiss her, the closure she felt when they'd both apologized for their fault in that dreadful panel, was enough to convince her that she was done writing.

Which was fine. She'd go home, move in with her mom and Apawllo as the disappointment she was always meant to be. She would continue her editing work, making other people's stories beautiful and polished while she abandoned her own. She'd live a semi-comfortable life and stay in the shadows, away from whatever new mess she and Storm had nearly started.

"Penelope, please!"

She jumped in surprise, her array of plain, albeit practical black underwear flying in the air.

"You have to be fucking kidding me," she spat, picking them up one by one and shoving them into the bag.

"Penelope, *please.*"

She spun toward the tapestry and the door that was hidden behind it, guilt churning in her gut. But Pen was done. She was so done letting her emotions rule her.

Pen grabbed her backpack and bag and ran from her room.

She was good at hiding; she always had been. She'd wiped all her social media accounts and avoided the world since she'd ruined her career. Whether or not it was for a good reason, she could have approached it a million different ways.

But she'd chosen violence.

"Pen?" Laszlo called out as she thundered down the stairs. "Pen, what's going on?"

Ignoring him, she crossed to the front door and tugged her boots on in the entry.

"Penelope!" Storm called from near the kitchen.

Damn it, she thought, *he must have realized the stairs led down to another secret door on the first floor.*

Pen cursed under her breath, pulling her jacket from one of the hooks. Her fingers shook as she buttoned it up, racing against the sound of Storm's approaching steps.

"Penelope, please!" Pen turned toward Storm as he stopped in the hall, hands on his knees. "Please," he wheezed, holding up a hand.

Shaking her head, Pen made to leave, but Storm reached out, his hand wrapping around her wrist, long fingers engulfing it. His grip was not tight, but the feel of his warm fingers was . . . it was . . .

She decided she didn't want to think about what it was. Because if she did, they'd be heading in an entirely different direction. Her eyes met his before flicking to his hand. A beat. Then two. Finally, he let go, swinging around to block her path with an arm instead.

"Storm," she hissed. "Let me go."

"Where?" He shook his head, chest rising and falling rapidly. "Where are you going? You said it yourself: We're snowed in."

"I'll figure something out. I always do, but I can't be around you right now."

"Because you wanted to kiss me."

"Did not."

"No?" He leaned close, and Pen felt the zing down her stomach, the sharp, almost painful throb between her legs as he stepped closer. "I have been trying to deny my feelings, Penelope, but I can't any longer. This feud, this thing between us, has been over since we agreed to step foot in this castle. Can't you see that we could be more?"

Honesty was too damn hot, and he was too damn hot, and god, she was sweating in her jacket now. Face heating, Pen made to move past him.

"I know you felt it too, Penelope!" He straightened, brow creased with concern as he reached for one of her hands. "Come on, let's talk."

"I've had enough of talking!" Pen shook her head and swung under his arm, but Neil dove forward and blocked the door with outstretched arms.

She froze, taking him in. There was something in the movement, in the way his shirt had been rolled up to expose a soft brown forearm with a tattoo of a quill that she'd never fully seen that had her blood singing. She said nothing, eyes glued to his arm, tracing black ink.

"But we can't keep pretending—" he started.

"I will go on pretending as long as I want." She blinked, breaking from the trance, and surged forward until she stood in front of him. "You can keep trying, and we can pretend that you haven't spent a better part of the time since I met you being too good for everyone, but there's nothing *here*."

"But just now—" he argued.

"Just now, what?"

"Earlier in the study," he started.

"Nothing."

"And the snow?"

She leaned up on her tiptoes, ignoring him. "We made our apologies. We are working to be better. What more can you possibly want from me?"

"I want—"

"Is everything okay here?" Laszlo asked, appearing around the corner.

Pen sighed in relief. "Laszlo."

"We were just talking," Neil said, dropping his arms.

Pen turned to stare at Neil. At the mess of his hair, the bags beneath his eyes, the wary way he glanced between them. With anyone else, she would talk, and she would listen. But not with him.

Not anymore. She didn't trust herself alone with him. So far, being alone with Neil Storm had done more harm than good.

With a sharp inhale, Pen stared up at Neil. She could feel it still, that same strange buzzing energy between them. It was too like that unexpected moment at the ruins, too like those lingering touches in the turret. And silly little Pen wanted it. God, she wanted him to touch her, she wanted him to—

Breathing hard, Pen whirled around to Laszlo. Her friend raised a brow, lips puckered in thought, eyes asking a question she refused to answer. Pen shook her head, teeth grinding.

"Pen, why don't you put the bags down?" Laszlo asked, reaching out toward her. "He's right; we're snowed in. There's more than a foot of snow on the ground, and there is no way in hell that van is getting out of here."

"See, even Laszlo agrees," Storm said.

"Shut up if you know what's good for you, Neil," Laszlo groaned.

"Actually," she said, raising her voice, and tossing aside the bags carelessly, "I was only going for a walk."

They stared at her.

"In the snow?" Neil asked slowly, not stepping away.

"Yeah, what he said," Laszlo echoed, taking two steps toward her.

"I need some fresh air."

"Please go!" Daniela called from down the hall. "Some of us still have a hangover."

"Just you!" Laszlo bellowed. Sighing, he rolled his eyes before pulling on his boots and jacket and following Pen outside as she threw open the double doors and hurried down the steps to the driveway.

"Okay, it's fucking cold," she admitted, wrapping her arms around her middle. Her teeth chattered as she and Laszlo wandered out into the snow, the fresh powder crunching and compacting beneath her boots.

The cool air was a reprieve, her cheeks flaming, her *everything* flaming. Her hatred was dissolving into an entirely different kind of heat, and Pen didn't know what to do about it.

Well, she did, but kissing Neil Storm needed to be the last thing on her mind.

"So," Laszlo drawled, tilting his head at her. "You and Neil, eh?"

She scrunched up her nose. "There's no 'me and Neil,'" she said. She squinted up at the sky. "It's weird, though. I assumed he was an asshole, this guy that didn't care about anyone but himself, and yet . . ."

"Not an asshole?" Laszlo offered after a beat of silence.

"Not really, although he seems a bit rusty on human contact

and all that. But just when I think we're getting along, he does something weird."

"Like get all cozy with you?" She shot him a bewildered look, and Laszlo laughed. "What? Everyone sees it. And by everyone, I mean Daniela and me. Hate is a strong emotion, and so is—"

"Don't you dare finish that sentence."

Laszlo shrugged, grinning. "Listen, I know you both really well. And I know it's been rocky between you, but isn't it also good that your relationship is changing? You two have had this animosity toward each other for so long. What's wrong with change?"

She shivered, the thought sending a trail of familiar fingers down her spine as she turned to the castle. Her attention went to the east tower, to the place where all pretenses, all walls had crumbled down to her feet. Flirting was fun when there was no end game, but a kiss . . . the honesty.

Pen couldn't handle that.

Laszlo raised a brow, steering them back down the drive. "Don't tell me you haven't thought about it? I mean, come on, the guy's hot."

"He's not hot." Why was she lying?

"Mm-hmm, like anyone would believe you." He tapped his chin. "If I recall, you told me at a conference a few years back that 'Neil Storm has no right looking that good in a tweed jacket.'"

"I feel differently now," she said, ducking her head.

"You love tweed jackets."

"But I hate them on *him*."

"Liar. He just gets better with age. He's like a good whiskey. I should know, I kissed him once."

Pen blanched. "You *what*?"

Laszlo rolled his eyes. "It was ages ago, back when we first met and I hadn't decided how I felt about him, and he hadn't decided how he felt about me, yet, but that's beside the point. I might not be his type, and he's certainly not mine, but you two?" He whistled.

"Whatever you say, Lasz," she said, waving her hand in dismissal. "I don't have a type."

"You don't have a type? Oh, my dear, sweet Penelope." He laughed, stopping in the snow to face her. She sighed, her shoulders slouching as she met his eyes. "In all seriousness, how long has it been since you've dated someone, Pen?"

She kicked the snow.

"Two months."

"Are you still lying to me?"

She flung her head back as she groaned. "Fine," she relented. "Seven."

"Years?"

"Months!" She laughed, smacking him on the arm. "Months."

Laszlo shrugged, motioning to the castle behind them as he rubbed absently at his arm.

"Look—and hear me out," he said, holding up his hands as if in surrender. "You may have *hated* Neil. He's not always the most transparent or straightforward person, but have you ever thought, maybe, that there was more to it? I mean, why did you start hating him in the first place?"

Pen puffed out her cheeks. "It started when he personalized a book to 'Penny' instead of Penelope."

"See!" Laszlo threw up his arms, turning away. He paced, shaking his head. "Isn't that childish? And because of *that*, you turned him into some rival. You made it your life's goal to take him *down*."

"Lasz, you don't understand. Maybe that's what made me look at him closer, but it's not just that. That moment only instigated my doubt. He had this standing in the book community. He had everything I wanted, and he wasted that power. He should have stood his ground and workshopped it to other publishers if he was so worried about losing power over his books. He took advantage of—"

"His advantages?" Laszlo raised a brow. "I love you, Pen, I truly do, but people change. And until you get to know someone like Neil, you'll never understand why they do the things they do."

"Laszlo, no offense, but you're white. You don't get it."

"I know I'm white. I know I have my own advantages, especially in a space like publishing, but shouldn't that make you understand why *he* did the things he did? Don't you see it? I've been friends with Neil for well over a decade, and I've seen what these choices have done to him. Maybe he's a sellout, letting his publisher walk all over him, but he had reason to, and you know it. Was he supposed to say no to the only publisher who offered?"

"I . . . didn't know that."

"No one does. They don't talk about what it took for him to get to where he is, Pen. They only talk about his successes. He simply hasn't corrected them."

Pen paused and looked up at her friend. Neil had never been her enemy. She'd turned him into a vessel to direct her anger, because of what? Because her book didn't do well? Because she couldn't figure her shit out? There were already so few Indigenous authors, particularly in horror. What had she been doing turning one of them into her enemy for something he felt powerless about?

"I guess I should have seen it. I just wanted someone to blame for my own problems, for my lack of success. Is that petty?"

"Maybe."

Pen sighed and nudged Laszlo's side. "How did I go all these years and not see it?"

"Because the publishing industry wants you to fight. They want there to be one of you, and you two were scrabbling for that spot, for a place on the shelf. Your names are literally 'Storm' and

'Skinner.' You had to battle for a spot on the same exact shelf, Pen."

"Wait, what?"

He made a strange, alarmed sound. "Alphabetically, you two are literally next to each other on a shelf. Wait, are you telling me you never thought about that?"

"No, and now I can't believe I never saw it."

Laszlo laughed. "Oh, my dear, sweet Pen, do you know how many times I went to a bookstore to mimic your books yelling at each other?"

"Please tell me someone has video evidence of this."

"No such evidence." He waggled his brows. "Also, can I once again point out that he's hot, and there's clearly something going on between you two? Feelings change, circumstances change, and maybe this is what you two have been waiting for. Why not take a chance?"

Pen shoved her hands in her pockets and swiveled toward the castle. She spotted Storm's face in one of the windows of the study, looking down at her. Laszlo laughed.

"Look at him, Pen. I don't know how you managed to do it, but in a single day, you went from hating each other to *this*."

"That's the problem. I don't know what *this* is."

Laszlo shrugged before hooking his arm through hers. "You won't know until you find out."

They walked for a moment, and Pen reached out to run her frozen fingers over a crystalized branch. "Why do you put up with me?" she asked.

Laszlo chuckled, the sound deep in his chest. "Pen, you are the strangest person I've ever had the honor to call a friend. And through my sage advice—"

"Someone's humble," she mumbled.

"I have saved you from a multitude of terrible decisions. And just the knowledge that you never went through with any one of the fifty-seven different ways you could have murdered Neil Storm is enough to leave me satisfied."

Pen straightened her glasses, clearing her throat as her face heated. "I still think the library idea would have worked."

"Neil Storm is probably immortal. He would have survived three bookcases falling on him."

"Would have been worth a shot," she muttered.

"I'm glad you don't show this side of you to the public. It's terrifying."

"Good, it's always been a lifelong dream of mine to terrify someone twice my height."

Laughing quietly, they meandered down the drive. Though Pen was cold, and her socks were soaked through with melted snow, she was glad they'd gone out. She'd desperately needed to clear her mind and breathe some crisp, cool air.

And get away from Neil. She knew where he'd been going, where they'd been going, what he was going to say, and try as she might, she wasn't ready to confront the part of her that had enjoyed the close press of him.

In twenty-four hours, her vision of Neil Storm had been turned upside down. Before, she'd wanted to strangle him, tear apart his books, and prove him wrong, but now . . . well, she wanted to kiss him. She'd wanted him to pick her up and crush her against that locked door at the top of the turret. She wanted to feel his hands on her hips, she wanted him to kiss her between her legs.

She wanted to feel him everywhere.

Whatever the outcome of the weeklong retreat, her view of the man who'd fueled her hate for the last few years had been changed completely. All it had taken was some honesty, a little heart-to-heart, and the willingness to listen.

Pen stopped at the bottom of the stairs leading up to the castle's entrance.

Laszlo touched her arm gently. "Are you going to be okay?"

"Yeah, I just need a few minutes out here to myself."

He frowned. "Don't stay out here too long! It's freezing." Shivering as if to prove his point, Laszlo hurried up the stairs and back into the castle, leaving her alone with her thoughts.

And they were dangerous thoughts.

Sighing, she crossed to the garden and settled on a frozen stone bench. She admired the wilted flowers and abandoned plants as she brought her knees to her chest, teeth chattering from the cold.

She saw a flicker of movement across the yard, and when she glanced up, she spotted Fanny among the trees. The groundskeeper was bundled in a large jacket and boots. Fear creased her face, and Pen angled her head back to see what had captured the groundskeeper's attention, but there was nothing. When she turned back, Fanny was already gone.

Pen was too scared to go inside because she was afraid of all the things she'd seen, and even if she wasn't, the idea of facing the man who'd played such a huge part in her own downfall was enough to make her hesitate. She knew Neil Storm could, if she let him, change her life in other ways. Perhaps for the better. But Pen feared change, feared allowing someone in past her formidable walls.

And it scared her to want something—or *someone*—so much.

Chapter 17

NEIL

Neil's thoughts were an absolute mess. He *wanted* her, wanted her in a way that shouldn't have been possible. Because it was Penelope Skinner, the woman who'd thrown a book at him, the woman who'd made him doubt himself.

But oh, did he want her. He could think of nothing else. Not the thing he'd seen last night, not the creeping sense of ghosts in the castle, and not the twenty-odd words on his laptop. Nothing but *her*.

With a groan, Neil leaned against the windowsill, his eyes going to the space beyond. It felt strange, knowing his feelings for this woman had changed so completely in so brief a time. Maybe it was simply who they were, maybe it was being trapped in this space for a week and being forced to confront their pasts. Whatever it was, Penelope's animosity had unraveled into something *new*. And he couldn't shake the feeling that it had always been there, hiding under the surface.

"You're pining," Daniela grumbled as she settled beside him on the window seat.

Neil looked up in surprise. He'd forgotten Laszlo had abandoned Daniela to go out in the snow with Penelope. Ignoring her, he refocused on the grounds, scanning the tree line for Penelope, but she was nowhere to be seen. The front door opened and closed, and Laszlo called, "It's just me! Leave her alone, Neil. She needs some time."

Daniela smirked, and Neil leaned back in the window seat.

From their spot in the study, Neil had seen Penelope and Laszlo wandering around the castle grounds, down the tunnel of trees that had deposited them here the night before. In the light of day, the grounds were more expansive than he'd originally thought, smaller buildings detached from the castle scattered across the land and hidden in the tree line. A church, maybe, and the groundskeeper's home with smoke billowing out of its chimney.

Still, no mention of the castle's owners. Neil had wondered, not for the first time, whom it belonged to, if anyone.

Neil tilted his head at Daniela. Her curls were twice the volume they'd been the day before, red and blond streaks catching the light refracting through the window. Dark bags were nestled under her eyes, her lips were dry, and alcohol seeped from her pores. "If we're throwing things out into the open, cuz," he started, leaning closer, "you look like shit."

"Take that back," she growled.

Neil squinted at her. "Only if we exchange a bit of information."

Balancing her coffee on her knee, Daniela tapped her chin, contemplating. "What's in it for me?" she asked slowly. She was watchful, lips pursed in thought.

"I don't know. I'm sure we can work something out."

"What do you want?"

"I want to know why she's so scared of change."

Daniela raised a brow and pointed at the window. "You already have the answer to it."

"What do you mean?"

She leaned forward and jabbed a finger into his chest. "You, you dipshit. It was always *you*."

"That's not helpful."

"Oh, it is." Her lips split into a playful grin. "You owe me something."

"No, we didn't exchange anything—"

"Write a blurb for my next book."

"What's your next book?" he asked skeptically.

Daniela smiled, all teeth and narrowed eyes. "Where's the fun in that?"

Neil turned his attention back to the window, unable to spot Penelope among the snow. "Fine," he grunted after a minute, relenting.

Daniela slapped him on the shoulder before taking up her coffee once more. "Now that's a good deal." She jabbed her thumb at herself. "Well, for me. Not so much for you."

He frowned. He could smell a trap. "What's your next book, Daniela?"

She raised her brows suggestively. "I'm hoping to debut an adult romance with speculative fiction elements—"

"You've got to be joking," he said, standing.

Daniela stood. "It's a little different than my usual tales, but I've got a great pitch for my agent."

"You haven't even written it yet?"

"No!" she exclaimed, laughing. "I just came up with it. Like, literally minutes ago." She shrugged. "I was going to take a bit of a break from writing—"

"Then why are you even here?"

"Buuuuut," she drawled, batting her eyes, "I can't say no to the perfect story that's fallen into my lap."

Neil pinched the bridge of his nose. "Please, don't."

"Picture it," she whispered, wrapping an arm around his shoulders. He shrugged her off, but she only wrapped her arm around him tighter. "A grumpy, brooding writer who, for the first time in his career, can't write." She waved her arm before them, painting a scene. "A beautiful, sweet young writer who is trying to find her place in publishing after a terrible fiasco. Their friends ditch them at the last moment, leaving them in a castle all on their own. A snowstorm arrives, trapping them inside with no cell service"—she winked—"you know, a traditional forced proximity romance—"

"This is forced proximity," he muttered, wrestling free of her grip.

"And there is only enough firewood to heat one room the entire time—"

"Enough!" Neil snapped, pushing her away.

Daniela's coffee spilled, splattering the rug beneath their feet. "You're no fun," she mumbled, shaking out her hands.

Neil turned to go.

"Where are you going?" she called as he stomped off.

"Out!" he said with a wave of his hand.

Neil needed some fresh air to clear his mind. Trapped in this stuffy castle, he was thinking about things. Romantic things, work things.

Spooky things.

Daniela might have thought it funny, but the forced proximity of the castle was getting to him.

After pulling on his jacket and boots, he opened the front door. He remembered the snowball fight earlier, the way she'd laughed and smiled. God, he couldn't get her out of his mind.

Pausing at the base of the stairs, he squinted into the distance, past the light snowfall dribbling down and catching in his curls. Penelope was nowhere to be seen, her and Laszlo's footsteps already being buried beneath a fresh layer of snow. Neil wrinkled his nose and shoved his hands into his pockets, fishing for the keys to the van. Maybe he could leave. He'd already caused enough damage as it was. Neil could forget about this week. He'd figure something out in the long haul, but he could not let his feelings

get in the way of writing, feelings that were apparently not recip-
rocated.

He stopped beside the van. Snow had piled high, covering
it, and he wiped away nearly a foot of powder on the windshield
before struggling to open the door. Grunting, he finally pulled
it free, sliding into the driver's seat and breathing warmth into
his fingers. As he closed the door and turned the key, the battery
clicked.

And clicked.

"You've got to be kidding me," he murmured, slapping the
steering wheel. There was no leaving this place.

Muttering a string of obscenities, Neil climbed out of the van,
pocketed the keys, slammed the door, and stalked around the side
of the castle. In the light of day, the castle looked grim. Its walls
dripped with dead ivy, the stone blackened in places as if a fire had
torched it at one time or another.

Neil stepped up to the stone and pressed his hand against a
blackened spot, his fingers coming away ashy.

"Strange," he said, bending to scoop up a handful of snow to
clear away the grime. He followed the side of the castle, with no
one in sight. The air was brisk, that odd, lingering scent of freshly
fallen snow filling his senses.

He'd grown more accustomed to snowfall since moving to
New York, but even still, there was nothing quite like fresh snowfall in the mountains. It was cold, so Neil kept his hands tucked
into his coat, his jeans doing little to combat the below-freezing
temperatures.

He followed the castle up toward its back, fighting through
the snow at a slight incline, pausing as he squinted against the
brightness. Something broke the surface, tilting up out of the
white powder at a strange angle. Still alone, he trudged through
the snow, cold creeping in through the top of his boots.

Neil stopped a foot away from the thing protruding from the

ground. He brushed his hands over it, exposing the top of a tomb-stone.

"Of course there's a grave out here," he said, leaning closer. Stooping, he swept his fingers over the stone to clear away the last of the snow and dirt, hissing as his fingertips grew numb from the cold. "Nearly there."

When he was done, he sat back on his heels, surveying his work. Lips barely moving, he read aloud: "Archibald Skinner, Fourth Duke of Skinner Castle."

Skinner. Like Penelope Skinner.

It was either a strange coincidence or Laszlo hadn't felt the need to tell Penelope it could very well be a place deeply rooted in her family history.

"No," he said, nearly falling over.

It wasn't only the last name. Hadn't he heard that name whispered in the study? Neil straightened, brushing off his pants as he turned to the castle.

There were simply too many coincidences.

Shivering, he folded his arms across his chest and hurried around the back of the castle. He paused at a side entrance, his eyes going to a flicker of movement in one of the upper windows. By the time he craned his neck, there was nothing there.

Fuck this, Neil thought.

The side door opened into a hallway. Old coats and muddied boots were lined up along the entrance. They looked like they belonged to the groundskeeper, but they were covered in a thin layer of dust as if she'd abandoned them. Neil stomped his boots on the entry rug, brushing off the last of the snow with his aching fingers.

"Where did you come from?" Laszlo asked, peering in from around the corner. "I thought you were a ghost or something."

If only you knew.

Neil shivered, undoing his coat and kicking off his boots. "I went for a short walk in the snow. Found the side entrance," he said, nodding to the door as he tugged off his scarf and hung it over his coat. "Where's Penelope?" he asked, eyes wide and searching as he craned his neck to look around the corner.

"She's inside."

"That's good."

Laszlo nodded slowly, chewing on his lip.

"What?"

"Nothing, just—"

"The Wi-Fi is down and we are doomed!" Daniela yelled from the other room.

Laszlo pressed his lips together before turning and disappearing down the hall. Neil followed him. The mudroom was around the corner from the kitchen, and as he stopped just inside the large room, he found Penelope and Daniela seated at the long table, phones, computers, and tablets out. Annoyance, frustration, and exhaustion were written across their features.

Penelope sat hunched forward, expression pained as she turned away from him, studying the itinerary before her like it was the most interesting thing in the room.

"I mean, aren't we here to write?" Neil offered as he leaned against the counter. His knee bounced nervously as his gaze clung to Penelope. He needed to tell her about the grave.

Daniela scoffed. "I have a process, Stormy—"

"That's not my name," he interjected, annoyed.

"And it includes," Daniela continued, ignoring him, "opening my computer, staring at my screen for about an hour, giving up, closing my computer, opening it again, checking my phone for twenty minutes to an hour, closing my computer, and eventually giving up altogether before moving to the couch and watching something."

"How do you get anything done?" Penelope asked, leaning forward.

"At some point or another, I actually write. But I go through spouts of writing where I do five thousand to ten thousand words in one hit and then nothing for a week straight."

"You baffle me." Laszlo laughed, shaking his head.

Clearing her throat, Penelope pushed her chair out and stood. "I'm going to wander a bit," she told Laszlo quietly. She ignored Neil's pointed stare as she moved past him and down the hall to the study.

"Don't do it, Neil," Laszlo said.

Neil looked from his friend to the hall, but he shook his head and hurried after Penelope. He reached out and caught her wrist, tugging her gently to a stop.

"What?"

"I know you and I have had problems in the past. And I don't need to know about . . . how you feel, or anything. I realize we are . . . working through things. . . ." He sighed and reached up to tug on his curls. "If you'll let me show you, I found something I think you'd like to see."

"What kind of thing?" she asked skeptically.

"Just trust me. Grab your jacket and boots and meet me in the mudroom past the kitchen."

Neil jogged down the hall, buttoning up his jacket and slipping on his boots. Penelope appeared a moment later, bundled up to her neck, eyes narrowed as he motioned to the door.

"Just . . . trust me," he said again, holding out a hand.

She frowned and stared down at it like the answers to the universe would spring out of his palm. With a sigh, she took it. Neil coughed to hide a smile.

Penelope trailed after him in the snow, shivering against the piercing cold. He peered at her every few seconds, stopping to let her catch up.

"What are we doing out here?" she huffed, sniffing.

His hands wanted to pull her into his side, but he resisted the urge.

"I was wandering out here earlier when I saw something sticking out of the snow." They came to a stop before the tombstone, and Neil motioned to it, waiting for her reaction.

Expression carefully blank, she stooped before the tombstone and ran her fingers over the name. *Her* name.

"Okay," she said. "It's probably not my family, but that is a really weird and incredibly uncomfortable coincidence. Especially after . . ."

After the eyes in the cellar. The smell in the hall. The white thing disappearing into a room. The touch of something on Neil's back.

The door slamming shut in the tower.

It was simply too much for a coincidence, and though Neil had walked into this castle unbelieving, everything tied back to the legends Fanny had spoken of, and he hated to admit that there had to be some truth to it all. Twice was a coincidence, but half a dozen odd things?

He turned to the castle, squinting against the glare of the snow. And that's when he saw it, or rather *her*, a figure standing before a window in the west wing. The very abandoned, very dark, and very creepy west wing that people claimed housed the ghostly woman who haunted the castle.

He motioned to Penelope, and she stood, her eyes unblinking as she peered at the woman in the window.

But she was not simply a woman. She was a ghost.

Dressed like someone from the early nineteenth century, her pale breasts were pushed up by stays, her chest and waist accentuated by a white empire-waisted dress. Half of her hair was secured in an updo, and the rest of her dark waves flowed in rivulets down her back as if someone had pulled the pins free. Neil could only see the left side of her body, and her pale, downcast eyes were watching them as if waiting.

But Neil knew at once who she was.

It was the woman in the portrait, the face captured in oil paint and tight, precise brushstrokes. It was the ghost they'd been warned of, the woman who haunted Skinner Castle. But she was not a woman in black, she was a woman in white. Somehow, that was even more terrifying.

Penelope took a hesitant step back in the snow, her hands tightening around Neil's arm. Earlier, by the warmth of a fire or the privacy of the tower, he might have relished the way she was gripping his arm, but now it held the tightness of worry and fear.

Neil and Penelope watched in horror as the woman snapped fully toward them, and though they'd been unable to see it before, there was no mistaking the stark contrast of her right side and the rot along her body.

It tore at her clothes and skin, and though they were far away, Neil was certain he could see bone piercing out from between skin, the draping, discolored flesh that hung from her in shambles.

"The eyes in the cellar," Penelope said slowly. "The thing in the hall. The smell."

"The voice in the study."

Penelope's eyes widened. "The journal."

"It was her," they whispered.

It had always been her.

Chapter 18

PEN

Neil stared down at Pen in horror.

She felt tears prick her eyes, the fear nearly swallowing her whole as snow fell around them. It was that creeping feeling again, that shiver of a finger tracing her spine that she recognized from their little visit to the cellar, when that thing had looked at her with wide, glowing eyes.

This woman was the lurking thing in the hall, the voice in the study, the thing opening and closing doors. All along, it had been this ghost, this woman, the one Fanny had whispered of as she'd gestured up to the oil painting in the foyer.

But why? Why was she haunting this castle? Had she killed someone? Was she looking for her next victim, and was Pen it?

Pen turned to the tombstone, tracing the name. *Archibald Skinner.* Why did that sound so familiar? She closed her eyes, desperately picking through her memories.

The journal. It couldn't be a coincidence.

"What did you hear in the study?" she asked, nudging Neil roughly.

"Someone whispered 'Archie,' who I'm assuming has *something* to do with this grave, but I'm not sure. Why?"

"The journal."

"The red one?"

Pen nodded. "I was reading through it earlier. There's a passage that mentioned—"

She glanced over her shoulder and up to the window, but there was no one, simply darkness beyond the panes. Pen tapped Neil's hand, and he turned, lips parting.

"She was just there," he said.

Pen shuddered and tightened her hands on him. "I know."

The woman wouldn't be going far. That feeling of being watched, the prickling at the back of her neck; Pen hadn't been imagining it. They'd probably been watched the whole time. In the shower, when the secret door had opened, at night, when she'd tossed and turned.

Laszlo and Daniela weren't experiencing anything, but there was no doubt now. They'd all wanted a haunted castle, a cute little getaway to write their cute little stories and live their cute little lives, but they'd truly found a haunted castle. The irony of a bunch of horror, thriller, and paranormal authors staying in this place was not lost on her.

Pen laughed. It felt good to laugh, to let all the disbelief seep into her voice. She let go of Neil and bent at the waist, slapping her knee as she shook her head.

"Are you okay?" Neil asked, worry written across his features.

"It's haunted!" she screamed between laughs. "It's actually haunted!" She crumpled further, her abs aching, tears leaking from her eyes as she laughed. It hurt, laughing so much, but she simply couldn't stop. Didn't he find it funny too?

"Let's go inside," he said, tugging her away from the graveyard.

She stopped, laughter dying on her lips. Pen reached up and wiped at her eyes before she motioned sharply to the castle, disbelieving. "So . . . what? We can go where the ghosts are?"

"You want to stay out here in the snow? What's to say ghosts can't come out into the yard? We don't know how these things work, Penelope."

As much as she hated to admit it, he had a point. They didn't know anything about ghosts because ghosts weren't meant to be real. But clearly, they'd been wrong.

Pen shivered. Ghosts were real, and they were stuck in a haunted castle in the Scottish Highlands with no internet in the middle of a snowstorm. It was their worst nightmare come to life.

But they'd brought it on themselves. All for a writer's retreat.

"What are our chances of making it out alive?" she asked, turning to Neil.

"So long as the ghost can't hurt us, I think we'll be okay. If the snow stops."

"And if the snow doesn't stop?"

His nostrils flared, jaw clenching as he struggled for an answer. She watched him for a moment, eyes going to the light stubble along his chin, the patch along his jaw where it didn't grow, the bob of his throat as he swallowed.

And that was answer enough.

They were trapped for now, and potentially for the near future. Trapped within a haunted castle, trapped together with their friends.

Trapped.

She had come to the castle for a new start, but it felt like the beginning of the end. She'd come for a story, for a way out of the pit she'd dug for herself, and she'd been handed more than she bargained for.

"All right."

His eyes snapped to her. "All right, what?"

"Let's go inside. At least it's warm there."

Silently, hand in hand, they trudged back to the castle. Knowing and seeing the thing in the window, the *person* in the window, made Pen want to stay outside, to linger until her limbs were too numb to withstand it any longer. But she didn't want to be alone, and she was cold, and at least she had Neil by her side.

She stopped outside the side door, chest heaving, breathing sporadically as all the what-ifs flitted through her mind. What if they didn't make it out? What if this was it? Neil turned to look at her, lips curving down. He took her hand, squeezing gently. Pen felt her pulse stutter under his touch.

"Hey," he said, stepping forward and cupping her face in his hands. "We're going to be okay."

"How can you know that?"

"It's us. And you're the most stubborn person I know."

Smiling, he reached around her and opened the door, motioning for her to go ahead of him. Her stomach twisted violently as she untied her boots and stepped out of them. Her socks were soaked through from the melted snow, but she was too cold to notice.

"You know what my father would say?" Neil asked as he slipped off his boots and unbuttoned his coat.

"What?"

He brushed curls from his eyes in a sweet, almost boyish way as he smiled down at her. "He'd have warned me to light sage before ever entering this castle. Smudge the shit out of it, he'd say."

If Pen closed her eyes, she could imagine it, that thick, familiar scent. It reminded her achingly of home. Her family had smudged enough when they'd moved homes over the years, ridding the places of any negative energy. So much so that her apartment and her things still had the softest hints of white sage even after all these years.

"Mine would have done the same."

Neil pulled off his jacket and hung it on one of the hooks, turning to her. Pen stood frozen, fingers wrapped tightly around her coat.

"Penelope."

Her head snapped up. God, she loved the sound of her name on his lips. "Yes?"

He gently pried her fingers from her coat. He smiled down at her, that dimple forming on his cheek. Pen met his eyes through her curtain of bangs, and there was something new there, a strange sense of understanding between them. They were more similar than they could have ever imagined.

They stared at each other. One beat, then another. When she didn't pull away, Neil nudged closer as he pushed her jacket down, and Pen thought about fleeing as he tossed it to the side.

Her heart was in her throat, and she hadn't felt like this about anyone in . . . well, ever. She'd been so scared of facing her past that now, standing in front of it, she wondered what it would feel like to *finally* face it.

"Penelope," he said again.

"Neil."

"Hmm."

"What?"

He leaned an arm against the wall behind her, and she caught sight of the black ink of his tattoo. "I like it when you say my name," he whispered.

Pen's heart was beating frantically as she slid her hand up his chest and neck to tangle in his hair.

"I love it when you say mine."

Neil leaned in ever closer, blocking everything else from view. He was so close and so warm, and she was impatient to touch him.

"I'm sorry about earlier," she apologized.

"Why?"

She tilted her head away, but he coaxed her back with a finger under her chin as she said, "I worried if I stopped hating you, things would change; *I* would change. But everywhere I went, you were there, haunting me, reminding me of every time I've ever been wrong, of every time I've ever failed."

Neil tucked a stray hair behind her ear, skimming her jaw and making her shiver as he whispered, "Hating me doesn't have to be your whole identity."

"I'm starting to think I don't hate you." He bent close as if to kiss her, but she pressed a finger to his lips. "But if you ever call me Penny," she warned.

He gently nudged her hand away as he laughed and said, "Never."

Then he was sliding a hand around her waist and bending closer, that rich, sweet smell of him invading her senses. Though she might have said no and pulled away a day earlier, she let Neil Storm in.

But Pen could be courageous and confident too. She stood on her tiptoes, curled her hands into his hair, and captured his mouth with hers.

Yesterday felt like a lifetime ago, and after all these hours trapped together, playing a game of cat and mouse, she and Neil were finally kissing.

And it was *good*. He tasted like snow, and as his tongue dipped in past her parted lips, Pen felt like she was outside once more, the snow falling in flurries around him, melting in his curls. Except he was warm, and his lips were warm, and there was nothing *soft* about this kiss.

Pen leaned back until she was completely flush against the wall, and he pushed in closer, his presence in this narrow space intoxicating. Her fingers tightened in his hair as his other hand snaked down to her hip.

It was a mirror of her dream, his mouth on hers, his hands digging into her hip and thigh, only this time her back was to stone, and he tasted like coffee, not whiskey. His hands were rougher, his grip stronger than in the dream, and damn if she wasn't already slick between her legs. Her dream had literally become reality, and Pen was growing lost in the taste and feel of him.

She broke the kiss, gasping for breath and arching back as Neil bent to trail his lips down her neck. He pressed kiss after kiss into her skin, sending a fresh wave of heat straight to her center. Her nails scraped through his hair, clawing at his scalp even as his thumb dug into the groove of her hip, tightening impossibly. He slipped down to the soft divot between shoulder and neck, sliding aside her sweater and bra strap. His fingers skated across her skin, leaving a trail of fire in their wake as his light stubble scraped over her shoulder and down to her collar. She whimpered as his teeth raked over the bone.

"A collar girl?" he whispered.

Pen squeezed her eyes shut, her fingers tightening in his curls. "Apparently."

He smiled against her and lingered for a moment longer, his tongue dipping out to draw lazy circles in the spot. He scraped his teeth deliciously over the bone, and Pen moaned as he clamped down on her collarbone and bit her, her body rocking against his in response.

His tongue painted a swirl of patterns over her shoulder, savoring every inch of exposed skin, and dear god, she didn't know how much more she could handle before she tore off his clothes.

Hot breath fanned over her skin, and she felt like she was on fire everywhere he touched her. Her body sank into his as she pulled him back to her lips, eager for another kiss. Neil moaned as his hand slid down her arm, thumb brushing the underside of her bra before stopping at her thigh and squeezing. Every caress made her come alive, thawing her from the outside in. Water dripped down the side of her cheek where one of Neil's damp curls clung to her skin. The sensation of the cold water against her flushed face made her body rock against his, yearning, craving. As if he could read her mind, Neil's hand edged under the hem of her sweater, his fingers dancing over warm, exposed skin as he parted her legs with a knee.

Pen made a soft sound in the back of her throat as she opened her mouth wider to him, wanting more than he could possibly give her. *This* was what she'd been avoiding? Pen wished she'd given in to the desire sooner. In the study, the snow, the turret, hell, even in the front entry. She'd been putting off the inevitable for far too long. Neil's other hand traveled down the wall to cup her ass, nails digging into flesh as her teeth scraped against his lips.

"I have been thinking about this all day," he panted.

"I'd be lying if I said I hadn't."

Neil groaned as her hips rose to grind against him. He felt so good, so unbelievably good. And where her mind was normally filled with noise, the only thoughts flitting about were of him. Of how he knew just where to touch her, how incredibly turned on she was, and how the pressure from the bulge of his cock had her itching to drag him upstairs.

Together, they were perfectly imperfect, and she wouldn't change a fucking thing.

He scooped her up, and she wrapped her legs around him, finally blissfully at the same height. And *closer.* That hard length of his was against the heat between her thighs, and as she moved against him, she could feel his cock nudging between her legs, searching. How the hell had they gone from hate to *this* so soon? It should have been impossible, but Pen wanted nothing more than to undress him.

She wanted him inside her.

"I've been wondering something all day," he started, hips grinding against hers.

"What?"

"How long these two would keep it up in a hallway knowing full well there are other people in the castle."

Neil and Pen froze.

"Please tell me I imagined Laszlo's voice just now?" she whispered.

"You didn't," Laszlo said blandly.

Pen opened her eyes and turned her head toward the hall. Laszlo and Daniela crowded the entrance to the mudroom. Did they have no decency? Pen glanced down at Neil and at the way her sweater had slipped even farther down her shoulder to expose the tops of her breasts. At the way her legs were locked around Neil's hips.

"How long have you been there?" she croaked.

Neil straightened and gently set her down, turning his back on the group. Pen followed his gaze down, an exquisitely clear outline of his cock protruding from his jeans.

Laszlo cleared his throat, and Pen turned to the others, fixing her sweater.

Daniela held out a bill to Laszlo, who took it while meeting Pen's scowl.

Sorry, he mouthed.

"No, you're not."

"Did he bet on us again?" Neil asked, leaning toward her.

"It would appear so."

"I bet *for* you!"

"I bet that you were having sex," Daniela confessed.

"Are you going to say hi, Neil?" Laszlo called, grinning.

Neil shook his head with a look of mortification. "You know very well I can't."

"Can't or won't?"

"Both!"

Laszlo pulled out his phone, and Neil eyed him warily. "What are you doing?"

"Texting Louise. She'll want to hear this. Damn, she was right."

Snickering, Laszlo turned to go, and Pen motioned to Daniela, who wore a wide grin.

When the hall was clear, Pen spun toward Neil, arms crossed over her chest. "They're gone."

"Thank god." Neil adjusted his pants with a grimace. "This thing won't go away."

Her eyes trailed down his body, hovering on the outline of his cock. "I'd offer to help with that, but they kind of killed the mood."

"Tell me about it."

"We also have some important things to do, certain *things* to see about."

Neil smirked. "Nothing turns me on more than solving mysteries and stopping ghosts."

She grasped his hand in hers. "Good."

They paused, hands clasped together, cheeks blazing as they stared at one another.

"That was good, right?" he ventured.

"No, Neil, it was absolute shit. *Yes,* okay, it was good."

"How good?"

She narrowed her eyes. "Don't push it."

"Noted."

She paused. "But just for the record, I was tested recently, and I'm clear."

"And just for the record," he said with a smile, "as am I."

"Good."

"Good," he echoed.

If it was the end of everything, the least they could do was enjoy it.

Together.

Next time, preferably without pants.

Chapter 19

NEIL

Neil should have been focusing on the journal, or the study, or literally anything else, but he couldn't. Penelope Skinner was like a fucking goddess, and now that he'd kissed her and touched her, he wanted to do nothing else.

"We're trying to save the world," she'd joked when he ran a hand along her side and kissed the delicate skin behind her ear.

"We could die at any moment," he agreed as she straddled his lap and ran her hands through his hair.

She let him kiss her for a long, dizzying moment, but when she pulled away and slid off his lap with bee-stung lips, mussed hair, and glazed eyes, she stumbled back a step and drew an invisible line in the air as he stood as if to follow her.

"Five-foot rule," she ordered.

"Penelope."

"We have important things to do."

"I know, but don't you just love procrastinating?"

He stepped forward and pressed her back against a bookcase, ignoring when several books were jostled free and landed at their feet.

"May I?" he murmured, tilting up her chin.

She paused for a beat before nodding, and he bent to kiss her, relishing the way she moaned into him. He broke the kiss before he gently spun her around until her ass ground against his front. He smoothed one of his hands down her arm before tangling their fingers together and lifting it to the shelves, holding her in place. His other hand trailed over her front, skimming over her breast and down her stomach until his fingers found the groove in her full hips, tracing small circles. From the way she arched into him, she wanted more.

"Neil," she groaned. "We've got important things to do."

"It would be so easy," he said against her neck, nibbling between words. "Don't you want to?"

"Of course, I do. But what if the ghost is watching?"

"Let her watch."

"Neil."

"Okay, forget the ghost for a second. We don't have to have *sex*. There are other things I could do," he went on. His hand tightened around hers, squeezing above them as she pressed against him, shifting her hips. "I want to make you come."

She paused for a dreadfully long moment. "Better make it quick."

"I plan to take my time."

His fingers slipped under her sweater, teasing the space between her jeans. He toyed with her button before popping it free, his hand inching down and under the band of her underwear. He was torturing her, her breath coming quicker, her body poised and waiting as his fingers skated down her front and to the heat between her legs. She jerked against him as his middle finger slid along her clit, and he groaned.

"You're so wet."

"Neil," she panted as his finger began circling.

A second finger joined the first, applying more pressure along her folds. She was so wet and so warm, and the realization that it was because of him made Neil grit his teeth, the circles over her clit turning tight and fast. Penelope threw back her head against his chest, her scent flooding his senses. She reached down and covered his hand with hers, gently guiding him slightly to the right, pressing the heel of his hand against her, and the reaction was almost visceral. It was incredibly hot to know what she wanted, how she wanted it, and he leaned forward and ran his teeth down the shell of her ear, groaning as her nails dug into the back of his hand.

"Neil," she repeated, voice low and sexy. He would never tire of hearing her say his name.

She bucked under him, gasping as he spread her legs. Her hand slid out from between her legs, and she reached up to cup his neck, tugging him down for a messy kiss as he slipped in one finger, then another. Her lips parted under him, her breath hitching as he increased the pressure of his heel.

"Faster," she gasped.

More books tumbled around them, but he didn't care, not as she settled against him, her hips gyrating as he pumped his fingers in and out of her, picking up speed. Her nails dug into his thigh, and she buried her face in her sweater, gasping silently as she shook. He slowed his fingers before stopping altogether, panting as time seemed to slow.

"That was probably the best orgasm I've had in a really long time," she admitted, leaning against him.

"You certainly helped."

"I prefer to show people what I like rather than wait for them to figure it out."

His cock was rock hard, but Neil didn't care. He slid his hand free, and she turned to watch as he sucked on his fingers, relishing the sweet and salty taste. "You taste even better than I could have imagined."

"Would you stop that?" she said, laughing as she pressed her hands to her flaming face.

"Are you embarrassed?"

"No, well, yes, but not because of . . . it's not that . . ." She sighed. "It was great, okay? Fuck, it was fantastic. Thank you? Do people say thank you for sex?" She ducked her head and stepped away, face red as she straightened her clothes. "But I'm reinstating the five-foot rule so we can return to important ghost things," she rasped, buttoning up her pants.

"Fair enough," he said, adjusting himself and grinning like a fool.

So, he trailed after her, four feet and ten inches between them, because five feet was simply too far.

"If the boy is Archie, then who is the woman?" Penelope called. "Is she a murderess? Did she perish alone? Why is she still here and haunting the west wing?"

"I don't know."

He followed her around the study like a dog, stopping to inspect in the corners. The more they hunted for truths, the more flaws Neil noticed in the castle's structures—the cracks and crevices that had grown, hidden behind books and plants and tapestries. He could see the traces of water damage even more clearly.

There was a bit of mold flourishing in a corner behind a couch, a long, snaking crack that had been filled in more than once behind a line of children's fiction from the thirties. The castle was falling apart, that much was clear. The instances were small, difficult to find among the things filling the castle, but they were there, hidden like little secrets.

Journal open in her hands, Penelope wandered along the bookshelves, searching the titles. "Are you looking?" she called.

Neil nodded, intent on her curves. "Yup."

"Are you sure about that?"

He met her blank stare.

"I'm looking at you. You didn't really specify."

She smiled as she nudged him toward one of the shelves. "Listen, as much as I loved making out with you and . . . *other* things, there's this woman in an old dress dripping in rot just *waiting* to do something really bad, so maybe get a move on?"

"Good point," he said. Gripping the rung of the ladder, he climbed up a few steps, scanning shelves Pen would have considered out of reach. "But I'm happy to hear that you *loved* making out with me, and *other* things."

"If you tell anyone I said that, you're dead."

"We might very well be anyway if we don't find whatever it is you're looking for."

She slammed the journal shut. "That's not funny."

"I mean, it kind of is."

Shaking her head, Penelope flipped through the journal, her expression twisting with anger. "It's not in here! No matter where I look, the woman's name isn't there. What are we missing?"

Sighing, she dropped onto the couch, hunching down until the only things Neil could see were her feet.

"We'll find it," he said with a chuckle as he climbed down the ladder.

"Will we?" she groaned. Her voice was muffled as she cried out, "I can't write a book, and now I can't even solve this mystery! I feel like if I can't even do this, then what's the point anymore?"

One of the drawers to the liquor cabinet shot out, making Penelope and Neil jump. She sat up as he crossed slowly toward it.

"Um, I think the ghost lady wants us to see something in here?" Neil pointed shakily. He stepped forward, goose bumps rising along his arms as he neared it. His fingers grazed the handle.

"Wait!" He jumped at the sound of Penelope's voice as she sidled up next to him, the journal pressed to her chest. "You don't think this is a trap, do you? Maybe she did kill someone. Maybe this is how she lures her victims."

He stared at her. The woman they saw in the window clearly liked to toy with them, but was she malicious?

"Do you *really* think a drawer in the liquor cabinet is a trap?"

"You never know."

"This thing was locked for a while. That could mean absolutely nothing, or—"

"Or it could mean it was holding something valuable." She motioned to the drawer. "Okay, proceed."

Neil snorted and stooped to lift the drawer from the cabinet, carefully setting it on the floor. Penelope knelt beside him, her arm brushing his, sending a shiver down his spine.

"Is it the ghost?" she asked, voice low as she peered warily over his shoulder. "Oh god, does that mean she saw us? Against the bookshelf?" Penelope covered her face, mortified. "I just got finger-banged and a ghost watched. I'm going to hell. Hell, where there is no finger-banging or books."

Neil smirked. "We're going to hell together. And she's been dead, what, a hundred fifty years? I'm sure she's seen plenty in this library. Besides, it wasn't the ghost, it's you. Always you."

She blushed but said nothing, focused on the drawer.

Neil's fingers combed over spoons and wine openers, checking in the narrow gaps between items.

"Anything yet?"

"You are so impatient." Neil squinted as he bent closer. "Hold on," he said. He pulled out a few utensils before his finger caught on a groove in the wood. "No way."

He dumped the contents of the drawer unceremoniously onto the carpet before flattening his large hand against the compartment in the back. He lifted the lid away, exposing a small bundle wrapped in a scrap of white fabric.

"What do you think it is?" she asked.

Frowning, he pulled on the black ribbon tying it together, then peeled away the fabric. There, nestled into the compartment, was a stack of letters bound together with a length of string. Folded and closed, with wax seals still intact, they'd been hidden here in this drawer of the liquor cabinet, waiting for someone to find them.

Or for a *ghost* to help someone find them.

Neil lifted the letters and turned them in his hands.

"Lovers?" he asked, glancing up at Penelope.

She shrugged. "It's possible. Fanny did say there were rumors and legends, so maybe they got it wrong. Maybe the ghost in the cellar is the soldier and not her brother? Her lover who died at war? Who else would write so many letters back and forth?" She motioned for them. "If I may?"

After taking the letters from Neil, Penelope stood and crossed to the desk. Setting aside the journal, she untied the string and dumped the letters across the oak surface. Neil followed, stopping at her side as their eyes scanned the name and address.

"That's this castle," he said, reaching for one of them.

Penelope ran a finger over the wax seal and held it up for him to see. It was a deep red, imprinted with a symbol much like the stag tapestries they'd seen throughout the castle.

"The woman," they said in unison. A noble lady's wax seal.

The letters belonged to the family that owned the castle, which only meant one thing: The journal and the letters were from the woman. So, who was Archie?

"Look at this one," Penelope said, handing him a letter. "Dated May 1815."

Dearest Archie,

My father has taken to locking me in my room. He will not let me leave. I eat in here, I bathe in here, and I sleep in here, all without you. When you held my hand and promised to be with me always, I believed you.

I do not know what to do without you.

I feel it growing inside of me, and there is nothing I can do to stop it.

Love,

Georgina

"Georgina," Neil said, testing it out. "That's her name, isn't it?" He shivered, a prickling sense of being watched sending him hurtling toward the edge. "Okay, I'll take that as a yes."

Penelope looked up questioningly at him. "Are you communicating with the ghost?"

Neil shuddered at the thought. "If that involves cold touches and me being creeped out and shivering in response, then yes?"

"But on the envelope, she's written 'Georgina Walsh.'"

"Walsh . . . Skinner?" Neil shook his head. "Something isn't adding up."

Their eyes went to the hall. The hall that led to the staircase, and from there to the west wing. Neil knew the answers were waiting there. He had sensed it since their first night in the castle, ever since the groundskeeper had told them not to go. Whatever happened in this castle more than two hundred years ago happened somewhere down that hall, in the room where they'd seen the woman standing.

There were a lot of letters left to read, a lot of the story still missing, but Neil's stomach gurgled. Penelope grinned up at him.

"Let's get some food," she urged, nudging him toward the kitchen.

She held out a hand, and Neil took it, desperately trying to ignore the soft caress of another hand along his shoulder as they retreated to the kitchen.

Chapter 20

PEN

Laszlo stared daggers at them as they slipped quietly into the kitchen. It smelled heavenly, thyme and butter lingering in the air and making Pen's mouth water. He was pouring a pint of beer at the counter, and Pen surged forward and snatched it from him, taking a long drink.

"You missed the afternoon session."

"We've been busy," Pen gasped as she handed it back to Laszlo and wiped her hand over her mouth.

"Bet you have." Laszlo snorted, refilling his pint.

"Can I have one of those?" Neil asked, leaning in past Pen.

"If it means you don't steal mine," Laszlo said, narrowing his eyes at a retreating Pen. "We have one more exercise today. Unless you two have other *things* you need to get to?"

Pen and Neil looked at one another. She thought of the grave, of the woman in the window, of the red journal and the stack of letters. Chewing a bite of sausage, she shook her head.

"No, no, we're free."

"How thoughtful."

"What is it?" Neil asked, popping a potato into his mouth.

"More partner work. You pair off and describe each of the five senses in whichever place you've been assigned." Laszlo raised a brow. "Should we get new partners, or stick with the ones we drew earlier?"

Pen coughed, remembering the way she'd been wrapped around Neil in the mudroom when the others had found them. The way he'd touched her in the study, whispered obscene things against her skin as his fingers slid beneath her jeans.

"I think we should stick with the ones we already drew," Pen said, motioning to Neil. He nodded vigorously, the corners of his lips curling, that dimple popping in his cheek.

"Wow, you two really dove headfirst into this partnership," Daniela muttered.

"At least they're not bickering," Laszlo warned. "No offense."

"No offense taken," Pen said.

Pen and Neil sat at the end of the table. She shoveled a spoonful of potatoes into her mouth, chewing quickly. It felt wrong to be keeping quiet about the woman in white, but would it do more harm than good to claim that there was a ghost? No one had believed her when she'd screamed in the cellar; what would convince them otherwise but solid proof?

Though neither of them had any clue what they were dealing with here, it was probably best not to raise the alarm until they had some concrete answers.

"What is with you two?" Laszlo asked, leaning toward Neil.

"Nothing," he said, not quite meeting his eyes.

Pen reached for Neil's pint of beer, taking another long pull. She burped, covering her mouth with her hand. Her stomach gurgled dangerously, the beer in her threatening to make a fast escape. She was too nervous, too anxious about the things she and Neil were going in search of, but if not them, then who?

"Hey," she ventured, "have you two seen anything yet?"

"No," Daniela said. "Was hoping to spot the lady in black,

you know? What's the point in renting out a haunted castle if it's not haunted by a murderous lady in black?"

Laszlo grunted, his expression twisted as if to say, *I'm actually quite thankful this castle isn't haunted.*

Pen met Neil's gaze, and he shook his head. She took another long pull of beer. The alcohol warmed her, making her cheeks flush as she silently shoveled more food into her mouth.

"While we're eating, we should talk about the rooms you were all sent to earlier," Laszlo announced. "What did you see?"

Daniela snorted. "We saw nothing in the study. We did find this cool old book about sex dungeons."

"It was eye-opening," he agreed.

"That wasn't the only thing that opened," Daniela joked, sputtering into her beer.

They turned to Pen and Neil. They knew about Pen's scream in the cellar, about the things she *claimed* she'd seen down there. This was her and Neil's chance to finally tell them the *truth*. Pen opened her mouth to respond, but Neil squeezed her knee, stopping her from spilling anything about the woman in white.

"It was creepy and cold," he said with a nod, "but we didn't really notice anything out of the ordinary."

Their ordinary, anyway.

He wasn't lying, per se, but he wasn't telling the whole truth either. Neil tapped her knee in a tune she couldn't quite pick out, and his bright eyes seemed to say, *You know it's better this way.*

And she did, but it didn't make it any easier.

Pen turned to the others, smiling weakly as she forked in another bite past her lips. "Just creepy," she agreed around the mouthful. The food turned to ash on her tongue, and she reached for Neil's beer, forcing it down.

She shivered, thinking of that creeping feeling in the stairwell. The darkness had been pressed to their backs, desperately reaching for them past the circle of light. And as they sat, examining the room, pretending like things between them hadn't changed, the door had been slammed shut and locked by some unseen force.

The woman from the window, presumably.

"Well, could you tell us a bit more about the next partner exercise?" Neil asked, turning back to Laszlo.

"This one is a bit more catered to the horror or paranormal writers here, but each pair will be sent to a specific part of the castle to describe it aloud to each other using your five senses." Holding up a finger for each one, he counted, "Sight, sound, smell, taste, and touch. What do you see? What do you hear? Taste and smell, and," he said with a smile, "if you're daring enough, what do you *feel*?"

"Not that kind of feeling," Daniela murmured.

Pen smacked her on the arm. "Will you stop it, please? It's embarrassing enough that you walked in on us, I don't need you rubbing salt in the wound."

"Ouch," Neil muttered. "Didn't know I was a *wound*."

"You're not a wound. That's not what I meant."

"I mean," Laszlo piped up, "you did use that metaphor."

She ran her hands down her face, groaning.

Laszlo and Daniela had strolled in casually and watched as Pen wrapped herself around Neil like a koala and practically *writhed* against him. Pen and Neil would never live it down, but her especially. And now she was saying all the wrong things. Couldn't she be normal for once?

"Okay, so, same pairings," Laszlo said, changing topics as Neil glared down at the table. "Do you want me to draw places, or do you want to choose?"

"Maybe we could choose? The study has nothing," Daniela drawled.

Neil turned to Pen, his expression carefully blank. Pen pressed her lips together, clearing her throat. It wasn't the place; it was the people. Whoever Georgina was, she did not want to communicate with this lot. For whatever reason, she had chosen Pen and Neil.

"I guess we could try the tower," Laszlo said. "I mean, Pen and Neil didn't see anything up there, but it could be different for us."

Daniela nodded as she drank the last of the beer. "Yeah, that's a good idea."

Pen swiveled to Neil. They knew where they needed to go; there was only one place in this castle with the answers.

"We'll head upstairs, check out the east wing," Neil lied.

"But not the west wing," Laszlo reminded as he and Daniela stood to go.

Pen wrung her hands as Neil stood. "Are you sure this is a good idea?" she hissed, following him out.

They abandoned their laptops and turned to the left, down the hall to the staircase. Pen paused on the bottom stair, glancing from the chandelier hanging in the foyer to the sconces and finally, to the portrait of the woman.

Georgina.

The tear she'd seen in it when they'd first arrived was even worse, the upper right of the canvas shredded. Georgina's eyes seemed even fiercer, and there was now a line between her brows like she was growing angry. It was weird to see a legend, a story passed down and whispered in the dark as children nuzzled in for bed, come to life. But Georgina was real, and here they were, planning to seek her out.

"We've got some Dorian Gray–level shit going on here," Pen murmured.

"I don't like that," Neil said.

"Me neither."

He grunted in confirmation but said nothing more. Pen pulled him to a stop next to her, searching his expression. "I'm sorry about earlier. I didn't mean what I said."

He raised a brow. "Which part? That I'm a wound, or that you're embarrassed to be seen with me?"

"Neil."

Neil sighed and pushed his sleeves up, exposing the tattoo on his right forearm. Her eyes were drawn to it, pulled to the soft brown skin etched with ink.

"I know you didn't mean it. I know this . . . us, is new. We can take it slow, but maybe, for future reference, don't refer to me or whatever we are as a wound?"

Pen smiled. "I can do that."

They resumed walking up the staircase, their arms brushing as she slowed on their ascent. Pen felt that strange tether at her core, the urge to go to the west wing and the ghost that lurked in its shadows. The owner of the hand, no doubt.

"It's a terrible idea," he said slowly, reaching for her hand, "but it's the only one we've got."

She rocked from foot to foot, teeth grinding as her attention was pulled up the banister to the landing, and then to the churning shadows that led to the west wing.

"I never imagined myself running toward ghosts," she admitted.

"You'd be surprised how much a person can change."

Pen looked up at him, her hand tightening in his. "I can't believe I'm about to say this to you of all people, but I'm happy that you're the one here with me."

"That might be the nicest thing you've ever said to me."

"Well, let's get this ghost show on the road, shall we?"

Neil's features softened. "Remember, I'm here with you. And if you want to leave, if you want to get out of there, just tell me, and we're gone."

"Okay, but promise me, if we make it through this," she said with a blush and a wave of her hand to the castle and their surroundings, "we'll finish where we left off earlier?"

Stepping forward, Neil cupped her face with one hand, brushing his thumb over her cheek, sliding it down until it lingered on the corner of her mouth. "That's a promise I can keep."

Chapter 21

NEIL

They ascended the last of the stairs, her fingers wrapped around his and squeezing tightly. He hoped they could find their answers without coming face-to-face with the woman in white, but he had the sinking doubt that it wouldn't be so easy. If there was one thing Neil had learned since they'd arrived in the castle, it was that this ghost didn't care about the time of day.

She appeared when she wanted to appear, day or night, and there was nothing to protect Neil and Penelope from her. He just hoped that they were on the right path, and she was some forlorn lover rather than a murderous ghost. If ghosts could indeed kill.

"I really wish I'd brought white sage," Penelope said as they stopped on the last stair before the landing.

"If I'm being honest, I thought about bringing some, too, but I didn't want to be the superstitious person in the group."

Penelope let out a laugh. "Well, whether or not you brought sage, you were right to think about it because this castle is definitely haunted."

"Yeah, I was unfortunately right in assuming the haunted castle we'd rented was haunted." Neil tilted his head at her, and asked, "Do you want to make this fun?"

"This is the *least* fun situation. We're running toward a *ghost*."

"But if I could make it fun?"

"How do you mean?"

Stepping onto the landing, Neil tugged her after him and toward the west wing. His stomach was a mess of nerves as he glanced over his shoulder, zeroing in on the cobwebs in the corners, and the torn and stained wallpaper. They stopped before the threshold leading down the hellish hall. The hall that belonged to the woman in white.

Letting go of Penelope's hands, Neil reached out and brushed her bangs from her eyes, adjusting her glasses. There was something so mundane about the action, so *comfortable,* he was startled to realize he'd love the opportunity to do it a hundred more times.

"Laszlo wants us to use our senses to describe this place, right?" She nodded. "And you've been struggling with your writing?" She hesitated, so he barreled on, "Then let's kill two birds with one stone."

Penelope shook her head and made to leave. His hands gripped her shoulders, steering her forward.

"Neil, this is a terrible idea. I'm beginning to doubt this. There must be another way."

"Stop thinking of this as an idea, or something we must do. It's inspiration."

"Inspiration? More like *nightmares.* This is—"

Turning her toward him, he leaned down, searching those pale eyes. "Do you write horror?"

She stared blankly back. Her mouth opened and closed, eyes narrowing. "Well, yes—"

"Then where are we?" he demanded, motioning to the space.

"In a hall?"

"More specifically?"

"I feel like I'm back in school," she muttered, swiveling toward the west wing. "We're in a hall in a castle," she said, several emotions flitting over her features.

"A *haunted* castle," Neil corrected as he motioned to the space around them, letting go of her shoulders. "We came on this retreat for two reasons, right?" He held up a finger. "First, to get away from the world and focus on writing. And second, to get inspired by our surroundings."

He thought of the woman in the window, of the way half her body was decaying, the raspy tone of her voice when she'd whispered to him in the study. He fought a shiver, keeping his eyes trained on Penelope. He could do this—*they* could do this.

For the sake of writing.

And the people downstairs.

"I know it's scary—literally scary, but you need to get out of your comfort zone. The best stories have a bit of truth behind them, and what's better for a horror writer than to find themselves in some danger?"

Penelope rocked on her heels, her whole body tensing in front of him. "Can we please just get this show on the road?"

Biting back a smile, Neil rolled up his sleeves and took a step away, gently nudging her forward.

"What do you see?" he asked, eyes locked on the space ahead. He wrapped his hands loosely around her shoulders from behind, and she flinched before settling beneath the weight of them.

"I see . . ." She trailed off, her head moving slightly as she took it all in. She breathed in deeply before releasing a shuddering exhale. "Blackened walls, as if a fire reached its way through this side of the castle and swallowed it whole."

"Keep going."

She cleared her throat, and he waited. Standing there like this, she fit into the grooves of him. He couldn't help but think of the kiss in the mudroom, of the path her hips made in the study when his hands had traced her every curve before dipping down between her legs, the sounds that she'd made as they ground against one another.

"Is this turning you on?" she asked.

Neil coughed, reaching down to adjust himself. "Just continue."

"This side of the house has been abandoned," she went on in a whisper. "The wallpaper has been torn from the walls, leaving behind dust and residue. The sconces are falling off." As she said this, the light in the dark space seemed to dim even further. "It is so dark that I can hardly see," she said a little quicker. "The cracks in the walls seem to grow, stretching farther and farther, a maw opening wide."

He felt a slight pang of jealousy at Penelope's ability to paint an image. How she wasn't a bestselling author was anyone's guess.

"Now close your eyes," he urged in her ear.

"No, thank you."

"Only for a moment." He cupped his hands in front of her face. Neil waited for a beat and then asked, "What do you hear?" He shivered at the thought, eyes flicking around the space. There was nothing and no one; just the two of them.

For now.

"Nothing," she said. "I hear nothing."

"Come on, what else?"

"Everything is too still, too quiet. I could hear a pin drop, a squeak of the floorboard." She tilted her head ever so slightly, a lock of hair falling from behind her ear where she'd tucked it. "The silence of a graveyard."

No wonder she wrote horror; she was fucking terrifying. Neil shuddered. "Good." He cleared his throat, the dread coiling in his gut as he asked, "And what do you smell?"

She breathed in deeply, letting the air out with a sigh. "Dust and mold, and a bit of smoke as if the fire has lingered here long after." She smelled the air, tilting her head up slightly like a cat. "And . . . and decay?" She stopped suddenly, her voice shaky. "It smells like death, like something died here, is still here."

No. He knew the scent she spoke of and could imagine it from the night before. But that meant—

There was a long, dreadful screech. Penelope flinched in his arms, a hand flying up to tighten around his wrist.

"What was that?" she asked, her voice wavering.

She was right. The castle—the wing—was too still, and they could hear the slightest noise. Neil watched in horror as a door down the hall swung slowly outward. The squeak of a step across the floorboards sounded, then another.

And the smell hit him, that sickeningly sweet stench of rot. It was the same one, the same dreadful scent that had filled his senses and blotted out everything else around him, even the comforting, fruity scent of Penelope's hair.

"Neil," she whispered, "is it her?" And he wanted to bask in the sound of his name on her lips, but there was no time for that.

The woman in white stood before them, ragged dress trailing behind her. Her image flashed between whole and rotten, who she must have once been to who she now was. Neil's hands tightened around Penelope protectively, and slowly he began to ease backward.

"Neil!" Penelope screeched, clawing at his hands.

"Don't look," he urged her. "Please, Penelope, don't look." If he could do anything, he'd protect her from this.

The woman's mouth opened wide, a maw full of sharpened, blackened teeth, jaw unhinging, just as Penelope had described the cracks in the walls. It was a nightmare made manifest. Everything in Neil seized up as he tightened his hold on Penelope.

"Don't look," he repeated, more to himself than to Penelope as he pulled them away from her.

"Archie," the woman croaked.

He stumbled, too in awe to notice as Penelope wriggled free of his grasp. She floundered into him with a high-pitched scream, and they fell, landing with an *oomph* as the woman surged forward.

"Neil!" Penelope cried. She flung herself off him and half dragged, half yanked him backward.

Neil stared up at the woman in horror, his heart pounding in his chest, his eyes wide as he and Penelope scrambled back the way they'd come. His father had taught him that spirits lingered in places, settling like memories of pasts and futures, reflections of experiences tied to the place of their death. But ghosts were entirely different things—different beings. They were fun things to write about, strange, otherworldly beings to craft tales out of, but never in his wildest dreams did he believe he'd see one, let alone meet one.

"Holyfuckingshit," he cursed as the ghost descended on them.

Penelope struggled to stand, her breath shaky and hands clambering for purchase.

"Archie," the woman moaned, her image flickering in and out.

And then he was being yanked away, his shoulder popping as Penelope apparently used all her strength to propel him down the hall and toward the landing.

Neil gasped as he sat back on his heels, hugging his arm as he turned to Penelope. God, he'd been so foolish to think they could just waltz into the hall and pluck the answers out of one of these rooms like the fucking lottery.

"What is she doing?" Penelope asked, nudging Neil.

With a long, shuddering sigh, the woman in white turned and glided into the room she'd come from, the door slamming shut behind her. The sound rattled the hall, one of the sconces along the wall bouncing from the impact, casting warped shadows until all fell still.

Penelope sank to her knees, hands limp in her lap as she stared past Neil. "If I have writer's block after this, I can really only blame myself."

Neil chuckled, unable to stop the laughter bubbling up in him. She joined in only moments later, her laughter short and sharp until she was throwing back her head and cackling uncontrollably.

"Your plan kind of failed," she said as he held out a hand to her.

"I know." Neil scratched at his neck as he peered down the west wing toward the ghost's door. Damn it, how were they going to get the answers they needed when this woman was guarding that room? This castle was a ticking time bomb, and Neil couldn't be certain how much longer they had in this place before things escalated. If they could even escalate.

"Neil?"

Her hand was soft and warm in his, and he turned slowly toward her, his brow pinched. Smiling, she reached up and smoothed her thumb over it. Adrenaline was still pumping through him. His heart was beating a frantic rhythm.

"What are we supposed to do?" he asked quietly.

"You know, we're obviously at some sort of impasse. Maybe, while we're thinking *really* hard about next steps and how to save ourselves and our friends from a potentially dangerous ghost, we could do . . . *other* things."

Neil smiled down at her. "Are you coming on to me, Penelope Skinner?"

Penelope dropped his hands and leaned up on her tiptoes to loop her arms around his neck. "Maybe."

His hands went automatically to her hips, his eyes soaking in her every curve as if to memorize them. Neil groaned as his hands ran down her side, scraping over her jeans before he gripped her ass and squeezed.

"We could die."

"We could," she agreed with a sigh as his thumb brushed the notch of her waist.

"And instead of figuring out how to stop the ghost . . ."

She nodded solemnly. "I would like to fuck."

Neil straightened and cleared his throat. "Well, when you put it like that—"

"Hard to resist?"

He laughed. *"Impossible."*

With one hand wrapping around her wrists, he nuzzled into her and backed them up until her back was flush with the wall.

"What is with you and walls?" she breathed.

"They're sturdy," he said as he pinned her wrists above her head, "and reliable," he whispered against her collarbone, "and let me focus on other things."

His lips skated across her jaw, down her neck, breathing in that heady, sweet scent of hers.

"You smell like summer," he said against the hollow curve of her collarbone. His tongue traced her pulse, and she squirmed beneath him, breath hot on his ear as he tasted her. God, he was already so fucking hard. "You taste like sugar."

"Are you using the five senses to turn me on?" she gasped.

Ignoring her, he pressed his ear to her breast, her heart thrumming against her chest. He tapped his fingers against her wrist in time with her heartbeat. "You sound like a drumbeat." He pulled back to look at her. Stormy eyes were wide above a thin, straight nose. Her bow-shaped lips were parted as she looked up at him.

"You look fucking magnificent."

"And touch?" she asked.

Grinning, he ran a hand up her side. His fingers skimmed over her breast, toying with the collar of her sweater before he bent and kissed her bare shoulder.

"You are so soft," he whispered against her skin. "And your body is driving me *wild*."

Dizzy with her closeness, Neil let his hand slide back down, his thumb brushing the underside of her bra, toying with the wire. She moved into him, with him, her chest rising and falling as his hand cupped her breast.

Neil's thumb brushed over her nipple through her bra, but there was still too much fabric between them. He wanted to drag his hands slowly over her skin, stoop down between her thighs and taste her, *really* taste her.

When he pulled back and met those gray eyes, she seemed to read his thoughts.

"Maybe we should move to the bedroom?" she asked. "Wouldn't want to be interrupted again."

"Now *that* I can agree with," he said into her hair as he hoisted her up and carried her down the hall, the ghost and the castle and the years of animosity between them forgotten as their bodies searched for each other.

Chapter 22
PEN

Her mouth opened wide for him, tongue seeking his as his hips dug into her. They crashed into her door and her hands rummaged for the doorknob.

"Hold on," she said, breaking away, laughing as his nose skimmed along her jaw. She twisted the knob, and they fell into her room, stumbling toward the bed.

His hand snuck around and grasped her ass, fingers inching ever closer to the heat between her legs, and Pen bit down on his earlobe, breathing hard as her arms tightened around him. Everything in her wanted to tear away his clothes, to straddle him as she'd done in the snow, and the memory of how he felt beneath her, how he'd hardened against her even then, made Pen blush.

Neil kicked the door shut behind them and carried her to the bed, laying her down. He tasted like beer and cinnamon, a strange, intoxicating mix that had her pressing her hips in closer, searching, wanting. Her hands glided over his shoulders and tangled in his hair, and Neil moaned into her as her nails scraped down his scalp.

And finally, alone in this room, it could be just him and her, two writers lost somewhere among the mess of this place.

His hand slid to her waist, thumb brushing the underside of her bra once more, digging in under the wire to lift it from her skin. She arched into him, gasping as his fingers skated across her breast, and she erased the small gap between them until her body was flush with his, her movements hungrier, her kisses sloppier.

Perfectly imperfect. She didn't understand why they'd hated each other before. She was angry at the world, sure, but she'd projected it on him. Wouldn't she have done the same in his position? Five years ago, wouldn't she have taken whatever publishing deal was offered to her, even if it meant changing everything?

He slipped one hand under her thigh and pulled her leg up and around him, the length of him pressing flush with her, and Pen refocused on him, on the *feel* of him. She clamped down on his bottom lip, dragging it between her teeth as she leaned back on the bed. He made a low sound that vibrated against her chest, and Pen scrabbled greedily at him, hands roaming over his shoulders and neck, diving into his hair.

"You feel so good," she said against his lips.

"Did you ever imagine this?" he asked, pulling back to look at her.

"Never in a million years."

And that, in its own strange way, was a kind of magic.

Neil kissed along her jaw, and she tilted her head, letting him in, hips crashing into his. He bit her there, in that special little place he'd found in the study, letting his teeth graze the soft skin behind her ear and down her neck, and her pulse spasmed beneath him, playing a melody against his mouth.

Pen wanted him, damn, she wanted him. Against all odds, against the things she'd felt for him a day ago, a week ago, a month ago, she wanted nothing and no one more than him. Screw the ghost, screw this castle and all the people who'd failed her over the years. He was here, and that's all that mattered. Pen slid out from under him and scrambled on top, her fingers splayed over his chest as she settled on his lap.

His fingers slipped into the belt loop of her jeans, tugging her hips closer, and she ground against him, making a frenzied sound as his fingers inched ever closer to her zipper. Pen could feel his hard-on through his jeans, feel what she—this close and this horny for him—did, and she rode his length, relishing the way he gasped her name against her ear. God, she was turned on. She could get off from this alone.

"Wait." He pulled away, his lust-glazed eyes struggling to focus on her. Their chests rose and fell together, hot breath mingling in the small space between them. "Fuck," he cursed. "You don't think we'll be the first to go if we have sex in a haunted castle?"

"What in the world convinced you that saying that out loud was a good idea?"

"Think about it, every horror movie ever has the couple dying when they're trying to, you know . . ." He mimicked thrusting and Pen covered her mouth and nose, snorting.

"Listen," she said, still laughing as she smoothed her hands over his face and scraped her nails through his light stubble, "if having sex right here, right now is our downfall, then I'll take it. I can imagine the headlines: *Very Attractive Native Couple Found Dead with Their Pants Around Their Ankles in Haunted Castle. Did They Fuck Each Other to Death, or Was It Foul Play?*"

He laughed and leaned up on his elbows. "Did you just call us a couple?"

"Did not."

"I think you did." His lips skimmed along her chin, and Pen sank into the touch. Her hands slid up his abdomen, skating across his warm skin, and she reached down with a coy smile, unzipping his fleece, then nudging it off him. She pressed her lips to his throat.

"Too many clothes," she said against his skin. His scent was even stronger along his neck, the musky aroma nearly making her dizzy as she reached between them with one hand and gripped the outline pressing against his pants.

"Is this for me?"

"Only . . . for you," he bit out.

Pen tightened her hold on him, squeezing, and Neil gritted his teeth, unable to look at her.

"Maybe we should—"

"Yes," she rasped.

She climbed off him and hurried to her duffel, searching through her things. Pen could feel his eyes on her as she riffled through her bag, producing a condom.

"Do you always carry a condom with you?" he asked.

Laughing, Pen stripped off her pants and sweater. Once she was down to her underwear and her tank top, she gently shoved him down and straddled him once more, the condom held between them. "If you're asking if I brought this knowing you'd be at the castle, the answer is *no*. I keep them on hand. In case."

"In case," he echoed, hands going to her hips. His thumbs drew gentle circles in her skin, squeezing and kneading.

Pen followed the movement with wide eyes. She used to be self-conscious about her body. She'd spent most of her childhood relatively thin until her curves had blossomed practically overnight, filling out her thighs and breasts until she felt like she'd snap in half. She was aware of the slight scarring on her thighs, on her breasts, but the way he gripped her, the way his hands skated across her, his nails digging in, made her feel like the sexiest woman alive. She didn't want to hide in front of Neil.

Leaning up and wrapping one hand in her hair, he pulled her closer, lips hovering over hers. The five seconds it took for him to kiss her was pure agony, and Pen bit down on his lip, eliciting another groan from deep in his chest. Grinning against his lips, Pen slid her fingers below the elastic of his boxers and the waistband of his jeans until he was firm in her hand. He was so impossibly hard for her, and she wondered if today wasn't the first time, if he'd ever thought about her like this before. Or if it was only the castle, the close proximity, the adrenaline rush. What if none of this was real? What if he didn't care about her in the way she was beginning to care about him? She pulled her hand out of his boxers, dipping her face into his neck and hair to hide her embarrassment.

He ran a thumb along her cheek. "Where did you go just now?"

"Have you ever . . . nope, never mind. We are not going there."

"Penelope."

Pen cleared her throat, blinking up at the canopy over the bed. "Is this new? You and me?"

He leaned back. "What do you mean?"

"Have you ever . . . felt this? Like, *felt*? As in . . ." She gestured to their laps, cheeks blazing, and Neil laughed. She tried to move away, but he captured her around the waist and tugged her back, eliciting a matching groan from her.

"I can't even begin to tell you the number of times I found you infuriatingly sexy. I didn't want to, but I did." He nudged her tank top and bra down before he caught one of her nipples between his thumb and index finger, gently rolling it until it hardened. "That time you wore that blue dress to the Shelley Awards? The one with the slit up your thigh, and only one strap?" He blew out a breath exaggeratedly.

"I didn't even win, *you* did. How do you remember what I wore?"

"I didn't give a shit about winning, Penelope. I spent the night drooling over you and the next month fantasizing about what I'd do to you in that dress if I ever saw you again, knowing I would never act on it because you clearly hated my guts." Neil bent and sucked on her nipple, pulling until it popped free. "And last night? When you licked the whiskey from your hand?"

"You got turned on from that?" she croaked.

Neil cupped her chin gently, his expression suddenly serious. "I have spent the last several years treating you like a nuisance instead of the incredibly brilliant and attractive woman that you are because part of me thought you could never feel anything but animosity toward me. You underestimate yourself, Penelope Skinner."

Pen searched his features for any hint of a lie, but she found nothing. Her mouth crashed against his. Suddenly, they were all hands and lips and teeth and tongues, and Pen tightened her hold on him, her body writhing with his, wanting and needing and taking.

Pulling back and holding the condom wrapper in her teeth, she tugged his shirt over his head and stared down at him. He didn't have chiseled abs or a lean physique; in fact, Neil had a bit of a soft belly. Neil Storm spent his days bent over a laptop, thinking and writing, and something about that image only made her ache for him more.

Smiling, Pen reached for his pants. He inched backward until he climbed off the bed and stood at the edge, waiting. Her fingers smoothed down his chest and skimmed the soft skin below the waistband of his pants. He made a deep sound in the back of his throat, his skin hot to the touch under her hands. Pen took her sweet time unbuttoning his jeans and pushing them down along with his boxers, and a fresh wave of heat slid between her already slick thighs at the sight of him.

She wrapped her fingers around him, slowly stroking, her thumb gliding over the tip. He moved against her as she pumped her hand along his length once, then twice, before she pulled the wrapper from between her teeth. Neil shook his head and gently pried the condom from her fingers before setting it aside.

"Not yet," he said.

"What do you mean? What are you doing?"

Grinning mischievously at her, he knelt. Gripping her thighs, he tugged her to the edge of the bed, snapping the elastic of her plain cotton underwear. The slight sting of pain made her gasp, and Pen reached up to squeeze her breast, watching him with a hungry expression. Nudging apart her knees, Neil tentatively slid down her tank top until it bunched just above her hips, his fingers skating across her shoulder and making her ache. She watched, transfixed, as he leaned forward and used his teeth to pull down her other bra strap. He cupped her full breast in his warm hand and sucked on its fullness, teeth clamping down on her nipple as his tongue encircled it. His other hand traveled down her stomach until he crushed the heel of his hand against the space between her legs, just as he'd done in the study.

Arching back, Pen whispered his name, small, slender fingers sliding into his curls as the pressure between her legs built. Pen's other hand tangled in the bedsheets, gripping tighter and tighter as she edged closer to release. But right as she was on the brink, he pulled his hand away. Pen opened her mouth, ready to complain, her hips lifting slightly as though to chase after him, when he kissed the delicate, sensitive skin of her inner thigh.

"You don't have to," she protested shakily.

"Do you trust me?"

"Neil."

"Penelope."

Her lips parted as she stared down at him, at this man with curls that flopped every which way, who had gentle hands and piercing green eyes. Where would they be if she'd just approached him, been honest all those years ago?

They couldn't change the past, but they could change the future if she let him.

"I trust you." She nodded vigorously, her fingers pinching her nipple until the areola tightened and pebbled. She breathed shakily as she laid back, her eyes fluttering closed as Neil nudged aside her underwear, and his fingers brushed the spot where she was so ready for him. "I trust you," she repeated, for herself this time.

And she was glad, because his tongue knew *exactly* what to do. It slid between her folds, tasting and licking, slowly, sensually. Her back arched as one hand tightened in his curls, the other cupping the fullness of her breast. As he sucked and licked, he slipped in one finger, then a second, and finally a third until she felt like she was on the threshold of something *incredible*.

"You are so wet," he groaned, blowing cool air on her.

Pen's only answer was a low moan. She had no words for this, for him. They simply could not live up to this moment, and the sensation of his breath fanning over her clit was enough to silence Pen on the subject forever. His tongue dipped out once more to taste her, tentative and testing, and when her lips parted and another moan clawed its way out of her throat, Neil's tongue slid up her folds, lapping and licking, dipping and savoring. He moaned against her, and the buzzing electric feeling tipped her toward the edge.

"Neil."

He was kissing her, nipping at her, *tasting* her, and she didn't know why it had taken them so long. Why she'd been so goddamn reluctant to admit that she'd wanted him. Another wave of pleasure crashed into her at the sight of him between her legs, and her muscles coiled as the tension reached a crescendo. Pen's voice cracked as she cried out, and when she came, her thighs wrapped around him, his fingers and tongue only slowing when she loosened her hold in his curls. He grinned up at her, nose and lips shining and slick with *her*.

"Thank you," she panted.

"Are you going to be thanking me for every orgasm?"

"They're good orgasms."

Neil pressed a soft kiss to her thighs before he climbed over her, eyes locked on hers. As he settled above her, his hard length swept against the slick, warm space between her legs. Pen wanted him to ravish her; she wanted him to take his time. She was caught between both as his thumb slipped into the space between skin and fabric. Although her legs felt like jelly and her clit was swollen and sensitive, she desperately needed him.

"Please," she whimpered.

Nibbling her shoulder, Neil slid off her tank top, tossing it to some dark corner of the room before his hand traveled down to grip her thigh. His other hand inched up her body, toying with her breast, and she ground against him, wanting, waiting.

"You are so impatient," he said, kissing between her breasts.

She scraped her nails along his jaw to tug him to her mouth, but he shook his head as he sank even lower, his fingers bunching in her soaked underwear as he slid them off, tossing them away.

He kissed his way up her body slowly, eyes glued to hers as he tore open the packet and rolled on the condom before leaning over her, his tip nudging her opening. Smiling, Neil gently tugged off her glasses, depositing them on a nearby nightstand.

"Are you ready?" he asked.

Swallowing, Pen nodded, wrapping her legs around his hips as her hands tightened on his back. "I'm ready."

She was not ready. She was not prepared for the way he felt, how good he felt. He slid in, inch by agonizing inch, devastatingly slow as her walls adjusted around him. Neil squeezed his eyes shut and stayed still and unmoving for a long moment. And when he finally moved, Pen's breath hitched as he pulled out before gliding back in, the long, emptying sensation making her shudder. And then he did it again.

And again.

She guided his hand from her hip to the heat building at her center, and his thumb drew circles over her clit as he thrust steadily.

Her hips crashed in time with his, his tip hitting that small space in the back, a secret little pocket of pleasure that had her hips gyrating. Eyes fluttering closed, she leaned back on the bed, her nails digging into his biceps as he sped up. His breath huffed out, actions becoming quicker, less controlled, and he grunted as he bent and buried his face in her neck, pressing his lips against the sensitive skin just below her ear. She could tell he was close, so so close.

But Pen wasn't done yet.

"Wait, wait!" she called. He stopped immediately, his brow creased as he leaned away and stared down at her. Blushing, Pen cleared her throat. "Can I . . ." Oh god, she couldn't finish the sentence.

"Penelope?"

"Me . . . on top?" Complete sentences were an impossibility right now. Pen was *mortified*.

Neil's hand traveled down her body, over sweat-slick skin, and his fingers dug into the flesh at her hip. "Dear god, please." They flipped until he lay spread out beneath her, his hands going to her hips as she straddled him.

Gripping the bedpost behind him, she lowered herself down on him, eyes locked on his until she'd taken all of him. He felt *so* good, even better than before. She could take so much more of him like this. Hands tightening on the post for support, Pen undulated her hips, her body moving in time with his until she rode him faster, her motions frantic as she squeezed her eyes tight.

Panting, he sat up, one hand gripping her ass, the other slipping between them, guiding her toward the edge. Pen gasped his name as her hands slid from the bedpost, her nails digging into his back as she neared climax. It was *so* good, better than she could have ever imagined. Better than should have been possible for their first. She cried out as her knees went weak, her body spasming, and together they rode out the wave of pleasure, lips crushing together, breath mingling until finally, they slowed, skin glistening with sweat and bodies weak.

They stopped, foreheads pressed together, chests rising and falling as their heartbeats thumped frantically. Neil pulled back and cupped her face in his hands as their bodies finally went still. "Thank you," he panted.

"What for?"

"For the orgasm."

Laughing breathlessly, she smacked his arm.

"Okay, okay," he relented. Neil nuzzled her jaw with his nose, his breath fanning across her sweaty skin and making her shiver. "For giving me a chance. For giving *us* a chance."

Pen smiled. *Us.* She liked that. She liked that very much.

She stood on shaky legs and held out a hand to him. "What say you to a shower?"

"Yes, please."

He took her hand and followed her toward the bathroom. Never in a million years had Pen imagined showering with Neil Storm, let alone having sex with him, but things changed.

People changed. And as she slipped beneath the steady stream of hot water and Neil reached out to lather her hair with shampoo, Pen wondered, *Who'd have thought?*

Because even she did not have the creative genius necessary to have foretold this. Penelope Skinner and Neil Storm together.

Had the world ended?

Chapter 23

NEIL

Neil's fingers worked meticulously, his brows pinched together as he focused on her hair.

"When did you learn to do this?" she asked, squirming under his touch. Her shirt rode higher over her thighs, and Neil stared down at them, remembering how she'd felt under him, over him, *against him.*

He cleared his throat. "My younger sister." Neil paused, picturing Max's face, that scowl twisting her lips, the furrowed brows, and the dark eyes set beneath them. "As the second oldest, I had to watch her a lot when my mom went back to work."

"What does your mom do?"

"Art teacher."

Penelope pouted. "I know so little about you."

Shrugging, Neil tied off her braid, hiding his smile. "It's not like I walk around spouting off private information. I've always kept to myself."

She frowned as she turned and clambered into his lap. Wrapping her arms around his neck, she leaned in close until that intoxicating smell of coconut surrounded him.

"I know, but if I'd known who you truly were—"

"Things wouldn't be different," he interrupted, pulling back.

"You and me . . . Things were always going to pan out this way. We were both too stubborn to talk it out."

"Maybe . . ." She trailed off, frowning.

"It's dangerous to play the 'what if' game, Penelope."

She ground her teeth, looking away. Neil wanted to wipe that look off her face.

"Don't do that," she said.

"Why?"

She looked at him, *really* looked at him. "Are you telling me that you never stopped to wonder what would've happened if we'd just talked? If, instead of me blowing up at Book Con and yelling at you, we could have stepped aside and had a civil conversation?"

Sighing, Neil pinched the bridge of his nose. "Of course I've wondered. Part of me will always wonder, but it doesn't do any good to dwell—"

Something clattered in the hall, and Neil and Penelope froze, eyes going to the door.

"Did you hear that?" she asked. Her hands tightened on him, lips parting as her eyes widened.

Neil gently pried her arms from around his neck and set her aside. Holding up a hand to quiet her, he stood.

"Neil, where are you going?"

"I'm going to look."

He flexed his fingers as he neared the door. Why he kept running toward things in this castle instead of away, he'd never understand. It probably had something to do with the writerly urge to *know*, to experience things in order to write about them. Whatever it was, it was foolish.

Neil reached for the doorknob and turned it slowly, wincing as the hinges squealed. He looked at Penelope as he swung the door open. After hesitating, she nodded, hands clasped tight in her lap.

He peered down the hall.

"Hello?" he called.

There was no one there.

He stepped out into the hall, leaving the door to Penelope's room open wide behind him. This reminded Neil too much of the night before, of the thing slithering through the halls and that wretched, rotting stench filling the space.

Neil heard it again, that same clatter, this time coming from his room.

"Are you fucking kidding me?"

But they'd seen Georgina. They'd seen and heard and smelled so many things since coming to the castle, so what was another door after all the things they'd already experienced? He crossed to open the door to his room but paused, hand on the knob.

"Penelope," he started, turning back to her.

He froze.

Her door was still open, and she was seated on her bed, but a young man stood on the threshold of her room. He couldn't be much older than Neil, his dark hair combed back, face freshly shaven. He was dressed in trousers, his ironed white shirt open at the collar, suspenders hanging down his hips. A black jacket was slung over his arm, as if he'd been on his way to retiring for the night.

He was so young.

He was so dead.

And transparent.

"Neil?"

Penelope stood from the bed, her eyes locked on the young man.

Ghost, she mouthed.

I know, Neil mouthed back.

Yes, Penelope, this is indeed a ghost.

Neil took a step toward the ghost, trying to motion to Penelope with his eyes. She nodded, as if understanding. But understand, she did not. Neil watched in horror as Penelope crept around the bed and picked up her boot from the floor.

No, Neil mouthed, waving his hands wildly.

It was too late. She chucked it at the ghost. Neil wasn't certain what she'd thought or how she came to that conclusion, but there was no turning back time.

He felt his life flash before his eyes. Neil knew all too well that she had a powerful throw and good aim, but alas, ghosts were ghosts. The boot sailed right through the ghost. Neil could have guessed it would happen, but still, he'd hoped it would land, that the man walking from her bedroom would have a corporeal body. As the boot hurtled toward him, the young man disappeared, there one second and gone the next, leaving behind no trace.

But the boot did not stop.

No, the boot continued its trajectory. Neil thought to duck, to do anything to stop it from coming, but he froze, and the heel of Penelope Skinner's boot crashed into his face.

His head snapped back from the impact, sending him stumbling a few steps as his hands flew to his nose.

"Oh god," he whimpered, dropping to the floor.

Something wet and sticky slid down his lips and chin, and he cupped his hands over his face, blood dripping into his palms. Penelope ran, kneeling before him. She hovered her hands over him, uncertain how to help.

"Neil, Neil, oh my god, I'm so sorry!"

He heard a door click open down the hall and someone screamed. Another door opened, and soon Laszlo and Daniela were huddled around them with bleary faces. Someone offered a hand to Neil, and they stood, touch gentle under his elbows as they guided him down the hall. Neil's nose throbbed, a sharp, stinging pain traveling from behind his eyes to his chin.

"Do I want to know what happened?" Laszlo asked.

"It was an accident!"

Neil laughed as they helped him toward the stairs. "She's not lying," he mumbled around his hand.

"Are you okay?" Laszlo asked.

He waved a bloody hand at his friend, stumbling a step before Laszlo caught him.

"I don't think I can answer that honestly," Neil said. His mouth tasted like copper, and his face felt like it was on fire, but Neil was certain about one thing: Penelope Skinner couldn't be trusted around throwable objects.

Which, Neil supposed, was approximately too many things.

"I'm not violent," Penelope promised as Laszlo led them into the kitchen and lowered Neil into a chair.

He groaned as Laszlo returned with a damp cloth and pressed it gently to his nose before using another to wipe his hands. Neil felt like a useless child.

"I thought you two had worked out your . . . differences," Laszlo hissed to her.

"I'm right here," Neil protested, voice muffled by the towel.

"We . . . well, we *did*," Penelope said.

Laszlo looked at Neil suggestively, brows raised, lips puckered in thought. That made Neil blush.

He kicked Laszlo, and the other man grunted. "Don't you dare say a word."

"Wasn't going to." A pause. "What happened?"

"A misunderstanding," he said after a moment.

"Why do I get the feeling you're lying to me?"

Because we are.

Neil wanted to tell his friend the truth. How many years had he and Laszlo been friends? Too long for Laszlo not to suspect something, but Daniela and Laszlo were clearly not experiencing the same castle as Neil and Penelope. Laszlo narrowed his eyes, and Neil mirrored the action, sending a sharp pang down through his nose. Laughing, Laszlo patted his shoulder as Neil winced, and the tall man turned to go.

The castle was still and silent as Laszlo's footsteps disappeared down the hall. Neil squeezed his eyes shut and tilted his head back, sighing.

"Neil?"

He recognized her touch instantly. Penelope's fingers traced his tattoo, skimming over his skin. She hadn't said a word about it, even though she must have known what the tattoo meant to him. Was she that scared of facing things?

"I didn't mean to hurt you," she said. Neil opened his eyes. She smiled warily, and the sight calmed his racing pulse. "I know things between us are still really new, but I promise I wouldn't hurt you on purpose."

Neil lifted the towel away; the blood having finally slowed. He beckoned to her, and Penelope stepped forward, sliding into his lap. She brushed a few stray curls from his forehead, her fingertips gliding over his skin. Neil sighed under her touch.

"I love your hands in my hair."

"Neil," she admonished. "We just saw a ghost."

"What's one more?"

She leaned forward until their foreheads were pressed together. One of his hands went to her hips, and he was pleasantly surprised to discover she still wore only a shirt and underwear.

Neil caught her fingers in his, gently squeezing. He brought their joined hands down to her bare thigh, his hand engulfing hers. Smiling, he tucked the stray wisps of hair behind her ear.

"I suppose we have things to talk about."

"Do we?" she murmured, her breath skating across his lips and sending warmth flooding down to his pants.

"We do." He wove his hand into her braid, his thumb smoothing over her jaw.

"Couldn't we talk about them after we figure out this whole ghost thing?"

"No."

"Why not?"

"Are you avoiding difficult conversations again, Penelope Skinner?"

She cleared her throat and sat back, putting a bit of distance between them. "How about a proposal?"

"I'm listening."

"We head to bed," she murmured, her hand skating up his neck. "We go to sleep," she whispered as she bent close, her lips to the shell of his ear, "and we deal with all of this in the morning."

Neil shivered, leaning back to get a good look at her. One of his hands inched down, his fingers skimming the underside of her breast through her shirt. He could see the outline of her nipples through the thin fabric, and he rolled one between his fingers.

"I think you're using your feminine wiles to quiet me."

She shrugged and opened her mouth to protest, but her lips parted as Neil's other hand dove down to the heat building between her legs. She inhaled sharply as his fingers inched down.

The small, barely audible gasp she made as he brushed two fingers over her wetness had Neil coming undone. He was lengthening and hardening beneath her, and if it weren't for the pain . . .

Neil's other hand snaked around to grip her ass, and Penelope bit down on her lip, gray eyes going to his. How could she of all people do this to him? Not even an hour had passed, and he was ready to sink into her again.

His hand slid from her ass to her spine and up until it cradled the back of her neck, fingers knotting in her braid. Neil tugged her down to him, ignoring the sharp stab of pain when she kissed him and their noses crashed together. Her tongue darted past his parted lips, tangling with his, and she tasted like sex and mint.

Neil's other hand brushed aside her underwear and his fingers nudged her opening.

"You're already soaked," he groaned, slipping in a finger.

Her hips moved against him, riding his hand as he dipped in a second finger, the pain of his nose forgotten. Penelope leaned forward and clamped her teeth on his neck, hiding another moan against his skin. The sensation made him shudder and pick up speed, his cock twitching as her nails dug into his shoulder.

She pulled back with a tremor, her eyes half-lidded with desire. "I hope you weren't planning to sleep tonight," she said.

She lifted her hips, his fingers popping out of her. Grinning mischievously, she pulled his fingers into her mouth, running her tongue over them, tasting.

Wide-eyed, Neil stood, following her as she backed away.

"You know I would much rather stay up all night doing these things with you than sleep in my bed alone."

Penelope laughed as she tugged him up the stairs to the east wing. "Sleep is the last thing on my mind."

They paused in the hall between their rooms.

"Maybe we should sleep in your room," she said, tugging him to his door.

"That's a good idea."

"You know what else is a good idea?" she asked coyly.

"What?"

"*This.*" Smiling, she dragged him toward his bed. He fell backward onto the mattress as she kicked his door closed and straddled him.

Yeah, Neil could get used to this.

Chapter 24

PEN

Pen's arm was asleep, and as she blinked up groggily at the stream of light coming in from the window, she slowly pulled it out from under her, shaking it uselessly in the air above her. Yawning, she ran a hand over her face, brushing the sleep from her eyes.

The night before came back to her in waves, and when she glanced over at the naked man in the bed beside her, she smiled. Their legs were tangled together, his hand thrown over her hip, warm palm pressed to her bare skin.

It was strange to wake up beside someone. How long had it been since she'd felt comfortable enough to fall asleep in someone's arms? Too long, she presumed.

Smiling, Pen pulled on her glasses. She settled back on the pillows, brushing the curls from Neil's forehead. The bed smelled like him, like morning coffee and warm fires, like the beginnings of something that made her toes curl and her lips spread wide into a smile.

Her stomach sank at the sight of his new bruise, though, and the black and blue and purple blotting his nose and eye along the left side of his face. How had she been so ignorant? Ghosts were not corporeal. She should have known better.

"You're awake," he murmured, nuzzling into her neck. Pen pulled away her hand, trying to ignore the guilt that had wormed

its way into her thoughts so early in the morning. His breath
fanned across her skin, making her shiver as he tugged her close,
arms locking tight around her.

"Only just," she said, her voice thick with sleep.

She stretched in his arms, sighing against him as she took in
the room. His room was like hers, the space immaculately deco-
rated with the same four-post bed and the same cracked and aging
leather chairs. Though her room was slightly larger, the memory
of the man on her threshold, of the door leading up to that abandoned turret, had her shivering.

"Cold?" he asked against the shell of her ear.

"No." She turned in his arms, frowning even as his fingers slid
across her skin, reaching down for her hips.

"Then what is it?"

"Just . . . this place. This castle."

"We're going to be okay."

"I sure hope so."

And then they heard it: a soft *tap-tap*.

Pen glanced up at the canopy over the bed, her brows pinched
together.

"Did you hear that?" she asked.

Neil tightened his hold on her. "I wish I could say no."

Slowly, he let go, and they slid out of the bed as one, pausing
as they scanned the space.

Tap-tap.

Neil tugged on his pants, and she tugged on her shirt.

Tap-tap.

Pen and Neil whipped around, eyes wide.

"It's coming from the hall," she whispered as he skirted the
bed and stepped toward the door.

"You stay here."

"Like hell you're leaving me here alone."

He didn't try to stop her as he opened the door and Pen

trudged after him, pausing in the hallway. All the doors were shut tight, no other sounds to be heard so early in the morning. The castle was painted in the silver-blue light of the snow beyond the windows, and the dark gray sky cast a strange, eerie hue over everything as small flurries flitted down to the already white-covered castle grounds.

She snagged Neil's hand, squeezing tight as the floorboards squeaked beneath their shifting weight.

"Maybe we should stop running toward creepy noises," she said. Her round, stormy eyes flitted over the hall, taking in the busts and paintings as if something in them might move at any given moment.

Tap-tap.

"Come on," he urged, tugging her closer.

She settled against his side as they crept on. One step, and then another, their bare feet sinking into the plush carpet.

Tap-tap.

They paused outside the last door on the left, hands clasped tight as they looked from each other to the door.

"What do you think it is?" Pen asked.

Neil shook his head. "I'm not sure. Maybe Georgina? Should we . . . look?"

Pen swallowed as another *tap-tap* sounded in the room beyond. It was Daniela's room. Was there a ghost trapped in each room or section of the castle? How many ghosts were there in this place? Worse yet, if they died here, would they spend eternity haunting these halls too?

She shuddered and squeezed his fingers, motioning to the door.

As quietly as possible, Neil leaned forward and turned the knob, wincing with each click until the door popped open.

"H-hello?" he called, peering in.

"Get out!"

Pen and Neil screamed as they stumbled away, a barrage of pillows and clothes hitting them.

"Go!" Pen screamed, scrambling to stand.

But Neil stood frozen, eyes crinkling as he lifted a pair of lacy black underwear in the air.

"Penelope, I don't think these belong to the ghost, do you?"

Pen turned to the door. She wasn't sure what she'd expected, but a fuming Daniela wrapped in a sheet was *not* it.

"Would you two *please* keep it down?" Daniela hissed as she readjusted the sheet.

"Who's there?" someone called from inside the room.

Pen and Neil peered around the door to see Daniela's laptop open and what appeared to be a large array of sex toys spread out over the bed.

"Zoe couldn't make it to the retreat, and we've sort of been seeing each other. I finally got a patchy signal on my phone, so I tethered it to my laptop and figured we'd try some cam stuff," Daniela said, leaning against the doorframe.

"I thought the internet was down?" Neil asked.

"It was, but the second you two went to sleep, it was working again. Well, it was, but now that you're up, it's misbehaving."

"Dan . . . la? Losing . . ."

Daniela scowled at the laptop, her curls sticking out in every direction. She turned and winked at Pen. "No hard feelings, right? You and I were not a good fit."

"From the looks . . . she . . . moved on," Zoe said from the laptop.

Pen wrapped her arms around her middle, suddenly aware that she wore nothing but a loose T-shirt and underwear. Blushing, she swiveled toward her room. "I'm going to go put on some clothes."

"Probably a good idea," Neil said as his hand settled on her lower back.

"Next time, knock if you want to join!" Daniela called, laughing.

Neil and Pen stopped in the hall between their rooms, both clearly unsure of what to say. Pen swallowed and glanced down the hall, the sight of the shadowy west wing making the pit in her stomach drop as she imagined the woman in white and the man who'd slipped out of the secret passage in her room and toward the hall as if Pen's presence had been no bother.

"I guess we have some research to do today," Pen said finally, rocking back on her heels.

Neil nodded slowly. They stared at each other in the silence, the dread of the coming day tethering them to the space for a moment longer.

"How mad do you think Laszlo will be if we skip today's itinerary?" Pen asked, taking a step toward her room.

"Furious," Neil said, mirroring her action.

"Then we better get a move on."

"See you in a few."

"In a few," she agreed, slipping into her room and closing the door softly behind her.

She leaned against the door and pressed her palms to her heated face. Would she ever get used to this feeling? To this giddy, bubbly burst of excitement she felt in her chest whenever she looked at him? She doubted it.

Sighing, Pen glanced up and surveyed her room. It was a whirlwind of clothes and blankets and pillows. They'd abandoned everything where they'd left it the night before, tossing things carelessly as they scrambled for each other.

Pen felt her face grow hot as she remembered their bodies meeting so perfectly, and the space between her legs began to ache. Even though they'd showered after the first round, she could still feel the weight of his hands on her, *in* her. His lips against her skin, his tongue and his teeth scraping a path toward the slickness between her legs.

Damn it, she was turned on again.

"What is wrong with me?" she muttered as she shoved her dirty clothes in a laundry bag and pulled out fresh ones.

Pen hadn't felt this way in a long while, if ever. Dozens of failed dates, one-night stands, and a few heated, albeit short relationships throughout the years had not prepared her for the fondness she was beginning to feel for Neil Storm.

This new thing between them felt like it would go up in flames at any moment.

Dressed, and with her hair brushed and pulled into a messy braid, Pen opened her door. Neil's door was still shut, and as she leaned out into the hall, she found the silence of the castle loud. The patter of the snow on the windows fell into a rhythm, melding with the ringing in her ears like a distorted ambiance. Pen's palms were clammy, so she wiped them down her thighs before wrapping her arms across her middle.

Before she could think better of it, Pen stepped out into the hallway, peering down the long corridor. Everything was still. There was no *tap-tap*, no whispers or voices floating down the narrow walls.

"Hello?"

No one answered.

She inched farther down the hall, her sock-clad feet quiet on the floorboards as she crept forward, automatically drawn to the west wing. She paused on the landing between the wings, a creeping sensation dripping down her spine.

"Don't do this," she whispered, her hands balling into the fabric of her sweater.

Pen glanced over her shoulder; the door to Neil's room was still shut tight. Though she knew she shouldn't, Pen slipped over the landing and to the edge of the light, hesitating on the dark threshold to this cursed place.

"This is a terrible idea," she said.

And still, she started down the hall.

Something pulled her here, and though she knew Neil was coming to terms with his own writing, taking back the power he'd given up all those years ago, she was beginning to think that the answer to all her troubles lay in wait in Georgina Walsh's room. She'd been drawn to it since she arrived, pulled like a part of her was connected to the ghost.

The hall was as she remembered from the day before, the same cracked and torn wallpaper, the same blackened walls, as if this side of the castle had survived a tremendous fire. The floors squeaked beneath her weight, and Pen's eyes were trained on the door Georgina had opened.

Pen stopped, clasping and unclasping her sweaty palms. She could still turn around, still return to the east wing and its sconces casting everything in a warm glow. She would be safe. But . . . surely someone would come find her, if only she yelled?

She stepped forward. Pen didn't want to be rescued; she wanted to *know*. It was clear Neil felt it, too, albeit on a lower level. It was that urge to see, to uncover. Pen had never been so close to the answers, and all she had to do was fling open that door and look.

She puffed out her cheeks and reached for the door, her hand outstretched for the copper knob. The tips of her fingers brushed the cool metal, and she clasped it in her hand, fingers itching to turn it. Her gut roiled as she worked up the courage, her nerves buzzing at the bite of the handle in her palm.

A hand clamped down on her shoulder, and Pen screamed, flailing her arms as she stumbled back a step and into—

"Neil?" Pen panted, her hands gripping his arms as she stared up at him. "What are you doing here?"

He frowned down at her.

"I could ask you the same thing. I thought you were going to wait for me?"

Pen whirled around, eyes going to the doorknob she'd been gripping. Swallowing, she and Neil hurried out of the hall and to the landing. Pen shivered, instantly relieved to be in the light.

She shook her head, squinting into the darkness. "I don't know. I couldn't help myself." Pen let out a shaky breath. "It's like I couldn't stop, almost as if something was tugging me to the door." There had been some strange magnetic force pulling her down the hall to the things that waited for her beyond, and it wasn't the first time she'd felt it.

Neil ran a hand anxiously through his hair, pulling on curls.

"This isn't good. None of this can be any good." He grabbed her hand and started for the staircase. "Come on, we have some work to do."

She struggled in his grip, her eyes returning to the hall. "Neil, I was so close."

"This isn't the way, Penelope. There are safer ways to go about this. Just . . . please." His eyes were wide, lips pressed into a thin line as he stared at her, silently pleading.

"Please," he begged, again.

This time, his words reached her.

Reluctantly, Pen followed him down the stairs, but she looked back at the shadows over her shoulder, feet tripping on the stairs as they retreated toward the kitchen. She hated to think it, hated to even imagine it, but she could have sworn she saw the edge of a white dress drifting out from the corner.

Where she and Neil had been only moments ago.

Shivering, Pen tightened her hold on Neil's hands and hurried after him, that awful sensation of being watched making her hands shake and the hair on her neck stand on end.

They were not alone.

In this castle, no one ever was.

Chapter 25

NEIL

Downstairs and in the warm light of the kitchen, Neil felt a strange sort of relief. She'd gone into the wing alone, reaching for that door like it held all the answers. Was she that desperate for the truth? Neil couldn't stop thinking of the woman in white, of the rotting stench that filled his nostrils and made everything in his mouth turn to ash.

They weren't safe here. None of them were safe.

Penelope grabbed the journal, flipping quickly through the pages.

"There has to be something here." Her eyes scanned rapidly over large, swooping handwriting. "This!"

She turned the journal to him, fingers pointing to a charcoal sketch. Neil frowned as he angled the journal closer, peering down at the sketch of a man.

Neil's hands tightened on the edges of the table until his knuckles were white and his joints ached. He wanted to rip the page out of the journal and tear it into shreds. It was the man they'd seen at Penelope's door, the man with the black jacket slung over his arm, seemingly out of place.

The drawing was delicate and yet somehow dark, the lines swift and sharp, shaded and smeared like Georgina had sketched it without looking down. It was beautifully done, Neil had to admit.

Her fingers had left perfectly placed smudges, shadows in all the right places, slinking along the man's jaw and nose, the eyes sharp and distinct as they stared out at Neil from the page.

"But look," Penelope whispered, leaning closer.

Beneath the sketch was a single name in the same, swooping script of the journal and the letters.

"*Archie,*" they said in unison.

So, *this* was Archie. The owner of the name he'd heard whispered in the study.

"Archibald Skinner," Neil said, tapping it. He shivered, imagining the name carved into stone on a grave, abandoned to the elements. They were probably being watched, even now. The thought sent another shiver down his spine, and he slapped the back of his neck like that would convince the ghosts to go away.

"You okay?" Penelope asked, touching his arm.

"Yeah, yeah, I'm fine." He waved a hand in dismissal. "Sorry, what were you going to say?"

She watched him quietly before turning back to the table and running her fingers over the letters.

Neil wished he were those letters.

"Well, we're missing something." He was snapped back to reality by Penelope's voice. "Why is she haunting the castle? Why is this called Skinner Castle when it once belonged to Georgina's family? Archie is probably her lover, right? Maybe a soldier sent off to war?"

Neil frowned as he searched through the letters, eyes flicking over paragraphs and sentences. They were love letters, long, intricate entries to Archie from Georgina. Her words were desperate and aching, the sort of letters he'd seen in movies and read about in books. It sounded as if the world would end if these two were not together. He glanced sidelong at Penelope, and Neil thought, alarmingly, that he knew what that felt like.

"Wait! I read something yesterday . . ." She trailed off as she searched through them, stopping on a letter. *"I do not know what to do without you. I feel it growing inside of me, and there is nothing I can do to stop it. Please, do not abandon me."*

Neil sifted through the letters as she read. He carefully peeled back one of the pages to reveal the familiar cursive, scrunching up his nose in thought.

"What's the date on that letter?" he asked slowly.

"This one is marked May of 1815, why?"

He ran a hand down his face, trying to remember why the date sounded so familiar. "Waterloo . . ." Neil turned to Penelope, laughing. "I should have known. Laszlo fell into a bit of a Napoleon rabbit hole after the release of some big biopic, and I had to listen to him rant about all the ways the film let him down for hours. Anyways, when these letters were written, British forces were under the command of Wellington. This would have been right after he returned—rather, escaped—from exile on the island Elba, marking the beginning of the Hundred Days. Maybe Archie had to go to war and died there? Maybe the legends are true, and Georgina has spent the rest of her time trapped in this castle, seeking revenge for her fallen lover and Archie is the . . . I don't know, protector ghost?"

"But if he went away, how is he here now? And what does that have to do with . . ." Her eyes went to the first letter. Penelope ran her finger over it, her nail dragging along as she reread it to be certain. "She was . . . she was pregnant, wasn't she?" Penelope picked up the journal, reading aloud from it. *"I feel it growing inside of me."* She folded the letter and set it aside, frowning.

Neil scratched his jaw, fingers raking over the beginnings of stubble as he thought. "Maybe . . . maybe she got pregnant, and her dad found out, and then he sent Archie away to Waterloo? Waterloo lasted, what, a day? That was in June of 1815, this passage where it sounds like he was sent away is marked May of 1815, and then the last letter to him is from November of 1815. Her journal entries go further, and the one about feeling abandoned is from . . ."

"December of 1815. That tracks," Penelope said. "Nine months. Maybe it took him longer to return home, perhaps he'd been injured and delayed."

"And he returned by winter after the baby was born."

"But why haunt the castle?" she asked. "Why is she still here, and why is he still here, and how the hell did the castle get passed down to Archie? If he was off at war, then he would have died somewhere else and should be haunting that place instead, right? Unless we have the physics of ghosts completely incorrect and we're going about this the wrong way."

He snapped his fingers. "Maybe it wasn't Archie, maybe it was their kid."

"Her kid is wandering around the castle as a young ghost? Unlikely."

"No, the gravestone. Maybe their kid inherited the castle."

Penelope frowned. "I don't know, we must be missing something else. It just doesn't feel right."

"Sorry, I'm not exactly a ghost investigator, now, am I?"

Penelope ran her fingers over the worn red leather of the journal. Her brows were pinched together, her gaze distant as she stared down at the blank cover.

"Where's the last letter?" Neil asked.

Still frowning, she searched through the pile with him, lifting a slim one from the stack. It was marked November of 1815. Neil took it, carefully unfolding the parchment. Penelope leaned over the table as they read the letter.

> *Father has sent for you, but we have received no word of whether or not you even live. Though I continue to send letters in hopes of a response, I have heard nothing, Archie. There are rumors of others*

returning from war, broken, but still, no such sign of you. Where are you?

I fear you have left us here to rot.

"Us?" Penelope asked, eyes wide. "Her and the baby, right? He'd abandoned *them*."

Neil frowned in thought. She was right, they were missing something, something integral to Georgina and Archie's romance. Maybe he'd been sent away, maybe he needed the money to marry her, to prove he was more than just the groundskeeper's son.

He sifted through the letters, scattering them over the wooden surface. Squinting, he began to unfold them, peering at the dates.

"Help me organize these chronologically?"

Penelope nodded. Bending over the table, they began to sort the letters, swapping the stationery back and forth, watching as the story began to take form. "Me" quickly turned to "you," and then "we," and finally "us." Georgina grew desperate and scared, her letters messier in the autumn months, ink splotching in the corners as if she'd written them in the dark when no one watched.

Georgina was clinging to a fairy tale, and her prince had been sent to his death.

"Neil," Penelope whispered. "Look at this one."

She held out a letter to him, this one marked October of 1815, and he took the delicate paper in his hand, squinting down at the words.

I promised myself to you in the dark of the crypt beneath the glow of a full moon. In turn, you promised to be mine. Pray, tell me, were you lying? Have you deceived me from the beginning, all to take something with which I can give only once? Do you not care about us? It is nearly time, and there is still no word from you.

Archie, do not leave me, do not leave us. Please.

"What are you doing?"

Neil and Penelope let out a loud screech.

"Would you two please stop screaming?" Laszlo hissed, crossing to them.

To Neil's left, Penelope pressed a hand to her chest, coughing. "You scared the living shit out of me."

Neil dropped the letter on the table and Penelope swiveled toward their tall friend, hiding the stack behind her as he stepped into the kitchen, frowning.

Laszlo shook his head. "God, between the loud sex, the throwing of the boot, and you two walking in on Daniela—"

"Now, *that* was a complete accident," Neil said, holding up a finger. "We thought it was . . ." He trailed off, meeting Penelope's pointed stare.

"As for . . . the *other* thing," Penelope went on, blushing, "I didn't realize we were being so loud."

Laszlo stared between them. "I'm unfortunately a light sleeper. I can't help but hear everything. Although I suppose I shouldn't be surprised you two finally got together. I figured it would happen eventually, just didn't think I'd be privy to *the details*."

"Sorry," Neil gasped, pressing a fist to his mouth to keep from laughing.

"Did you bet against us?" Penelope asked.

"I bet *for* you. I always bet for you, Pen."

Silence fell between them, and Laszlo crossed his arms, watching them. Waiting. He knew something was up, Neil could tell, but what was the point when there was no way in hell Laszlo would believe them?

"Laszlo," Penelope ventured, "have you truly not seen *anything*?"

"Like ghosts?" She nodded. "Can't say that I have." He looked between Penelope and Neil. "Why, have you?"

Neil shook his head. "No, no, we haven't."

"It is creepy, though, you know? I have this weird feeling, and it makes me want to run, as odd as that sounds. Not that I believe this castle is haunted, but every time I close my eyes, I think of those stories Fanny told us, of the woman in black and the protector in the cellar. But they're not real, right? I haven't seen or heard anything, neither have any of you. Besides, the van won't start, we're snowed in, and we have no signal. We're already here, and there's no harm in a creepy place, you know?"

"Totally," Penelope squeaked.

"Absolutely," Neil agreed.

"I'm gonna shower and change." Laszlo raised a brow and pointed between them. "See you down here in a bit for today's activities? We'll be reading some work and giving feedback."

"Yeah, for sure," Neil lied.

He tried not to think about how he'd written approximately one sentence since he'd come to the castle. The whole point of the retreat was to work on his book, and instead he'd stumbled into a ghost story with the most unlikely of companions.

Nodding, Laszlo disappeared down the hall, leaving Penelope and Neil alone.

"I haven't written anything," he admitted as soon as Laszlo was gone. "I came here to write my book, and instead we're chasing after ghosts and kissing—"

"Oh, I'm sorry, have I been *distracting* you?"

"I'm not saying I don't like the kisses and the *other* things, only . . ." He tugged on his hair, teeth grinding. He was fucking this up already. "This isn't what we should be doing."

"Yeah, well, I didn't come to this retreat to be haunted by murdery ghosts either. But writing a book is kind of the last of our worries. What if these ghosts can hurt us, Neil? What if this is just the beginning?"

Neil frowned, brushing off his pants as he straightened. "I don't know what we're supposed to do," he admitted.

The closer they got to the truth, to who the ghosts were, and why they were here, the more dangerous it became. He didn't want to put his friends in harm's way, put Penelope in harm's way. But the more they delved into the past, the closer the woman in white seemed to inch toward the east wing. Neil didn't mind the idea of ghosts, didn't mind the mystery they were unraveling, but put the two of them together?

No, thank you.

"We need to finish this," Penelope said quietly.

"How do you propose we do that?"

She didn't look at him as she muttered, "You're not going to like it."

Chapter 26

PEN

Pen and Neil stopped on the landing, and Pen pointed shakily down the hall to the door.

The door.

Her hand trembled as she dropped it to her side. She curled her fingers into a fist, trying to slow her pulse as Neil sidled up beside her, waiting.

"I have been drawn to this hall, to Georgina's room in particular, and unless we go in there, we're not going to know the truth. Every time you stopped me, every time you pulled me out of that trancelike state, I was about to open the door."

"Even on the first night?"

"Even on the first night," she agreed. "I could have sworn I'd seen a hand there."

"And you wanted to open the door?"

"I wish I could explain it, but there's this pull, like a string is attached to the middle of my chest and is propelling me toward it, toward her. This sounds ridiculous, but it feels like the solution to all my problems is in that room."

He reached out and squeezed her hand. "It's not ridiculous."

Pen leaned back on her heels. "I didn't really think the rest of this through. Are we just going to barge in there and demand answers?"

"What do you propose we do?"

She chewed on her lip as she glanced around at the darkened hall. Taking a deep breath, she tightened her hold on him as she stepped forward, dragging Neil with her.

"Before you came here," she started slowly, "did you believe in ghosts?"

"No, I never had reason to."

"That's the problem with us writers. We're artists. We craft these wild stories and characters and worlds, but when it comes to things like ghosts, we think of them in terms of logic. Does it make sense that ghosts exist? How would it even be possible? How can you believe in ghosts if you don't believe in God?"

"You're trying to distract me."

"Maybe." Pen shivered, squeezing his hand to ground her.

"So, I took a philosophy class back in college and the professor had us discuss the differences between being spiritual and being religious. I've grown up surrounded by sage and ceremonies and prayers to the Great Spirit."

"Unetlanvhi," Pen said.

"What does that mean?"

"It's one of the few Cherokee words I know. It means 'God' or 'Great Spirit.' My dad used it a lot when I was growing up."

"U," he tried.

"Oo. Oo-net-lah-nuh-hee."

Neil repeated it and she smiled, nodding. He continued, "Though I don't believe in any entity myself, I asked one of the other students if they would consider that spiritual or religious."

"And what did they say?" Pen asked as they passed the first door.

"Neither. When I told them that a lot of tribes believe in a Great Spirit, a creator, they said it's not the same. And I wondered if they believed that simply because people outside of the community know so little about the actual practices of specific tribes.

When people talk about religion, they don't consider Indigenous practices. Natives and Indigenous people across the globe are left out of this conversation because we don't have something . . . tangible, if that makes sense?"

"It does," she said softly. If Pen closed her eyes, she could smell her father's workshop, smell the old "death box" he'd had her paint as a kid, filled with feathers and skulls and deer hide. She could smell the sage-dense smoke and hear the soft language she didn't fully understand.

"But what's strange is, I never believed in those things, in the ceremonies of the spirits my father prayed to, but in this castle with these people, I've seen the unbelievable." Neil smiled down at her as they passed the second door.

Pen's stomach did little flips, but she tried to focus on his words, on him and only him, blocking everything else out.

"Does seeing the ghosts change your view of religion?"

"No, no, I don't think it does. Ghosts are weird. They're memories of people caught in this place in the center of everything, so close to death and yet, so close to life." Neil cleared his throat, a laugh caught in his chest. "I met this woman once."

"Wait, oh my god, please tell me you spoke to a clairvoyant."

"Oh, I did. I was new!" he exclaimed as Pen bent at the waist to laugh, tugging them both to a stop a few feet from the door. "I'd never spoken to one, you know? And I decided, well, I know nothing about ghosts, so maybe if I speak to a clairvoyant, she can help me better understand them for my book."

"And?" Pen asked, turning to him and taking his other hand in hers.

"And she was a total phony. To be fair, I found her on Craigslist, so I'm not sure what I expected. There were probably better clairvoyants out there. But I did learn quite a bit about the lore around ghosts. She said that ghosts are tied to the place where they die. And that if we see a ghost floating or levitating, they're not levitating, they're haunting the original spaces. Supposedly."

"Ghosts don't seem to live . . . or rather, *haunt* by the rules." Pen sighed. "So, I wish I could pretend we haven't reached the door, but . . ." She motioned behind him. "We're here."

"Huzzah," he said, deadpanning.

"You know, at the very least, I know what book I'm writing next. Something about her, about how this castle has healed the thing that's been broken in me these last five years, filled the well that's been empty for so long. I wish I could explain it, but . . ."

Neil smiled. "Penelope, that's amazing, seriously. Congratulations."

She tried to smile back, but her nerves were a mess. Pen stared at the door, imagining the woman in white floating through it, the way she'd flickered in and out, whole and decaying, back and forth and back and forth. She struggled to see the girl the letters and journal entries had captured, to bridge the connection between a horrifying ghost and a scared mother-to-be. Pen's stomach roiled at the memory of the last time they'd seen Georgina in this hall as she reached out, her hand clutching the cool metal as she paused and closed her eyes.

"We could make a run for it," Neil said. "Tear off one of the van doors as a makeshift sled and slide our way to town for help."

"You'll do anything if it means not going in there again, huh?"

He squeezed her fingers. "Wouldn't you?"

She inhaled deeply, smelling that sickeningly sweet scent of decay heavy on the air. It was nearly suffocating. But the hall and the room beyond were completely silent. Sucking in a sharp breath and forging on before she could change her mind, Pen twisted and pushed, letting the door scream open.

She and Neil blinked against the image before them of a young woman seated at a desk by the window.

Georgina.

Pen took a hesitant step into the room. It was as if they'd leaped back in time, all traces of decay and abandonment gone not only on *her* but in the room. The wallpaper was a vibrant canary yellow with branches streaming up vertically, a forest gathering on her walls. The bed was large, draped in a similarly soft yellow, the edges of the canopy dripping with cream-colored lace.

Georgina sat at a table against the farthest window, a small, narrow desk that reminded Pen of her own. It looked out over the castle grounds, the view disappearing into the tree line, the wilderness far greater than it was in the present day. Her long, lace-trimmed sleeves had been pushed up, and she had a quill in one hand, her other holding open a familiar red journal.

Neil took a hesitant step toward the young woman, and Pen followed, her footfall light and silent. He leaned over Georgina's shoulder, glancing down at the journal entry as Pen looked out the window, spotting a small, square building in the snow beyond the graves.

Neil, Pen mouthed, waving her hand and pointing toward the window. *Mausoleum.*

Georgina glanced up at Neil, silver eyes narrowing.

"Impostor," she gasped, standing. *"Get out of my room."*

She pounded against his chest, and Neil pitched backward, searching for the door. Pen stood frozen as the two stumbled toward the entry. Georgina's image flashed, soft, full colors turning to monochrome and decay. Plump, pink skin turned ashen and gray with death, drooping and collapsed to her bones.

As Georgina's hands found purchase on Neil's shirt, her skin oozed, decay sinking into the flesh and rotting it from the outside in, showing the bones where muscle and skin should have been. Pen pressed her hands to her mouth at the sight and dry-heaved as Neil tried to fight the ghost off. His hands tugged at her, his nails and fingers plunging into rot.

Pen gagged, the smell hitting her anew, and she fell against the small desk as Neil slipped backward. He crashed to the hall floor, knocking his head.

"Neil!" Pen screamed, stepping forward.

But Georgina turned on her, Neil forgotten as he held his head in his hands and struggled to sit up. The door slammed shut, locking Pen in and Neil out as the ghost surged forward, toward her.

Pen closed her eyes, trying desperately not to look. Something oozed over her hand on the desk, and though she shivered, though she could taste bile in her throat, she stood as still as possible.

Something brushed her foot, and Pen knew instantly that it was Georgina's dress. She could feel the sway of the torn, ragged fabric, smell her stench, but still, Pen refused to look.

Cool breath kissed her cheek, and Pen whimpered, eyes still clamped shut.

"You saw it, yes?" Georgina asked, leaning close, her voice a rasp. *"You saw the mausoleum. Go to the church, Penelope. Go to the church and follow it to the mausoleum. You'll find what you seek."*

Pen wanted to ask her what she meant. She wanted to ask the woman how she knew her name, but when Pen opened her eyes, she was alone. She stood frozen for a long moment, taking in the room. It was decrepit, gray, empty. There was no recollection of the beautiful space it had once been.

Neil.

Crying out, Pen ran across the room and threw open the door. "Neil?!"

Hissing, he sat up fully, prodding along his skull. Pen knelt at his side, and he groaned as she reached out to help him.

"Are you okay?" she asked.

Neil shook his head, wincing at the movement. "No, no, I'm really not." He squinted up at her. "I'm sorry, there was nothing I could do." Neil ran a hand along her cheek, leaving behind a smear of grime. "How about you? Are you okay? The door . . ."

"I'm okay," she lied. She could think of nothing but Georgina's words, of the mausoleum hidden in the snow beyond the window. But he was hurt, and the mausoleum could wait for a minute longer. "I need you to walk." Grunting from the effort, she helped haul him to his feet before wrapping an arm around his waist.

He looked dizzy, his eyes not quite focusing on anything as he stood and meandered toward the landing. He leaned against the banister, lips parted as he glanced at the darkness they left behind. In this spot, in the light, it felt safer. They could take a moment to breathe before he attempted the stairs.

Pen reached up on her tiptoes and pressed the back of her hand to his forehead. His skin was ashen and clammy. How badly had he hit his head?

"Neil, I need you to look at me."

He did, spinning away from the shadowy hallway. Pen could feel her pulse pounding, feel her hands go numb as he stared at her. She tried to swallow down the panic, but the way he was looking at her . . .

Something was wrong.

"I need . . ." he said, trailing off and leaning forward.

"Neil?"

"I just . . ."

And then he fell.

Chapter 27

PEN

Neil tumbled right over the stairs. Pen looked out and wondered, *Could I have stopped this?* But down and down he went, short, melodic *thump-thump*s as his body crashed into the stairs, head and arms and legs at awkward angles.

It all happened so quickly and was over just as soon. His limbs were limp when he rolled to a stop, landing with a soft *thump* a few stairs from the bottom of the staircase.

"Neil? Neil!" She rushed down the stairs, falling to her knees and cupping his face in her hands.

His eyes moved rapidly behind his eyelids, a low groan at the back of his throat, but he did not wake. Pen searched the area frantically, and within seconds, the others were there. Laszlo was quick to stoop down and help lift him toward the couch in the study after checking that nothing seemed broken. Daniela was not far behind.

Grunting with the effort, they dumped him on the leather. He sort of flopped onto it, moaning as Pen carefully cradled his head, slipping a pillow beneath and propping him up. She knelt beside the couch and smoothed a hand over his curls, stomach churning. They should have been more careful. They knew about the danger, and even still they'd wandered into that room without a plan or any precautions. Sighing, she stood and backed away, arms crossed tight over her chest as she glanced around the study.

She felt useless.

"What happened?" Laszlo asked, taking the ice Daniela offered and settling the cloth-wrapped bundle atop Neil's head.

Pen's lips parted as she fought for an answer. Should she tell them the truth? Would they even believe her? Being pushed by a ghost sounded suddenly ridiculous.

"We were in the west wing," she started slowly. "He . . . sort of tripped backward and hit his head pretty hard in the hall. I was trying to help him down the stairs when he lost his balance and fell."

"Why were you two in the west wing?" Laszlo narrowed his eyes. "Did you not listen to Fanny on the tour? The west wing is strictly off-limits for our own safety. *Clearly.*"

Pen flinched. She understood more than ever why Fanny had warned them against it, but it only made Pen more curious. She simply couldn't refuse the temptation. Like the sign taunting her at the castle ruins.

"They were probably trying to do it in every room before the end of the week," Daniela said. "Not that I blame them. I would, too, if Zoe were here."

"The images ingrained in my brain," Laszlo groaned.

Daniela shrugged and fished out her wallet before she slapped a bill into Laszlo's hand. "You win this round."

Pen opened her mouth to retort, but the fight was drained out of her. She shook her head, grinding her teeth as she motioned to Neil. "Do you think he'll be okay? It looked really bad."

Laszlo scratched his neck, standing. "It's hard to know. None of us are doctors, and he tumbled down the staircase. I don't think anything is broken, but . . ." He shrugged. "We won't know until he wakes up. Maybe we should get ahold of Fanny and call it quits." He gripped her shoulder gently as he moved past her. "In the meantime, keep an eye on him, okay?"

Pen nodded, sinking into the chair beside the couch.

With her hands in her lap, Pen watched them go. When Laszlo and Daniela had disappeared around the corner, Pen leaned forward, head in her hands. She tugged on her hair, trying to keep the tears at bay. Everything was a mess. Why they were still keeping the ghosts a secret, she couldn't really say. They weren't safe, and if they weren't safe, then Laszlo and Daniela weren't safe. Georgina could touch them, *hurt* them. If there was any reason to believe they were in danger, what happened to Neil was proof enough.

And Pen needed Neil now more than ever.

Sighing, she sat up and wiped at her eyes, focusing on him. She concentrated on the way his hair had been pushed up from his forehead, exposing that silver scar across his brow. She swept her thumb over it, the skin just barely raised beneath her finger.

"I'm sorry," she whispered. "For not believing in you, and for refusing to understand where you were coming from sooner." She licked her lips, blinking back more tears. "It's kind of funny. I'm not even sure why I'm crying or why this hurts so much, but I want you to know that, for all those years, I looked up to you. I wanted to be like you and write the books that you were writing. I absolutely loathe telling you this, but . . . I was *jealous*."

She laughed, short and brisk. "I hated you because I would never be as good as you are, so when you wrote *For What Savages May Be,* I was devastated. And I guess also relieved? This Native horror author, one of the only other recognized Indigenous authors in our genre, had sunken to do the biddings of the publishing industry. I was heartbroken and elated. For me and all the other Indigenous authors and readers around the world who looked up to you. I think part of me was also happy because I thought it meant I finally had a chance to become someone, to make something of myself.

"But I was so wrong, Neil. Everyone loved that book. They thought you were some *genius* for it. And me? I was just a grumpy, washed-up wannabe with nothing to her name."

It hurt to say aloud, but even if it was only to herself, it brought a bit of peace. Because it was true. She should have been supporting him, being a friend, raving about his books, quietly approaching him before he ruined his own career, but instead she'd been sulking, waiting for him to fail so she could take up the reins.

In the end, it all blew up in her face. Which she deserved. God, she was terrible. Pen made to pull away, but his hand caught hers, holding it to his cheek.

"You're awake," she accused. She should be happy to hear that he wasn't in a coma or something altogether terrible, but he'd heard every word, hadn't he? "How much did you hear?"

"Hmm," he whispered, eyes still closed. "Enough."

"You're a little shit, you know that?"

"Quite possibly." He shifted slightly, groaning. "It's nice of you to say, though. I didn't think anyone looked up to me." He smiled crookedly. "Can you imagine? Me, *a hero*."

"Of course people look up to you!" She pulled her hand free, holding it in her lap as if he'd burned her. "You're Neil Storm. Like you said, you're a household name. People know your books. They're the first thing you see when you walk into Barnes and Noble. They're on the ads in Target, celebrated in every single place that sells books. You have turned yourself into a legend."

He peeled open his eyes, angling his head to look at her. "And so have you."

She snorted. "Yeah, for throwing a book at your head."

Grunting, he used his arm to prop himself up, curls falling haphazardly over his eyes. "No." He shook his head and groaned, running a hand through his hair. "For telling the truth. So often, we look at other BIPOC artists and praise them for doing good. And yes, rep is important, but when we let go of what is most important to us and start writing for people other than ourselves, when we start compromising our art, what's the point? And you didn't, Penelope. Never once did you compromise what you stand for, and look at you."

"You're the only one who thinks any of this." She pressed a hand to her chest, fingers curling into her sweater. "You're the only one who cares about my writing."

He glanced up at her from beneath his curls. "I know we're told not to look ourselves up on the internet. I know we're told to keep away, but you need to see this."

Neil searched his pockets for his phone. There was a long crack across the screen, but he waved his hand dismissively as he tapped, scrolled down, tapped again, and then handed it over. Pen took it with a frown, scanning the screen. Her heart thudded. The thread read *Penelope Skinner, Hero of the Book World*.

He motioned for her to flick through them, and she swiped to the left, breath catching. There were dozens of screenshots, as if he'd collected them for her over the last four months. Pictures and videos and GIFs. People posted photos of themselves with her book, with her, and at her events. And not even one of them hated her. No one said that she was in the wrong. Some joked that maybe she shouldn't have thrown a book, but they didn't blame her for it in the least.

"All these people." Her heart was in her throat, her vision blurring with tears as she met those emerald eyes. "I thought they hated me."

"You'd be surprised how many people are rooting for you to make a comeback."

Pen couldn't help it; hope surged in her. She wasn't alone. She'd assumed the world had made her into a villain, but she never stopped to think that a group of people might have sided with her.

Handing his phone back, Pen glanced to the hall, to what she could see of the painting of Georgina from where she was sitting. Courageous, that's what Neil kept calling her. Penelope Skinner was courageous. She didn't back down from a fight. And though it terrified her, she suddenly knew what she was meant to do. What she was always meant to do. She stood, her fingers tapping against her thigh as she smiled and shook her head. She pictured the young woman by the window upstairs, the hint of pain in those silver eyes. The girl she'd been, in love and desperate.

"I'm sorry, I have to go," Pen said as she bent down and kissed his cheek.

Neil grazed her hand with his. "Where are you going?" he called, swinging his legs over the couch with a grimace.

Pen paused in the hall and glanced back at him. She remembered the way Georgina had leaned close. The ghost had steered Neil out of the room long enough to tell *her*. This was always the way it was meant to be. This was how she got it all back.

This was how she got her story, how she'd climb her way out of the hole she'd dug for herself and prove everyone in publishing wrong. This was how she'd make it out on top for the first time in her life.

This was how Pen redeemed herself.

Pen smiled as something settled inside her. She shivered pleasantly, her hand tightening on the doorframe. Sighing, she knocked against the wood and turned to go.

"I'm going to be the hero."

Chapter 28

NEIL

"Hero?"

Neil struggled to stand as Penelope disappeared around the corner. He took a shaky step forward and teetered, his hand reaching out for the wall to steady him.

"Penelope," he started, blinking dots from his vision as a headache throbbed behind his eyes. "Penelope, please! What the hell does that even mean? Where are you going?"

She was moving faster than he was, too fast for him to stop her. Penelope's steps were sure, her hands fisted at her sides as she strode down the corridor and past the kitchen, toward the side door.

"Penelope, wait!"

"I have to do this!" she called, not turning back. "Georgina pushed you out of the room, not me. She wanted to tell me about the mausoleum. Me, not you. For the first time in my life, I was chosen over you, and if that's how this story ends, then so be it."

"Mausoleum?" Neil winced, trying to recall the room, the word on Penelope's lips before Georgina had forced him out. "What do you mean? We can do this together. Whatever it is, we can do it together."

"Neil." She sighed. "You're hurt. You need to lie down and wait for me, okay? I have this handled. I can do this, and then I'll be back, and everything will be okay."

"Please, don't do anything rash. Don't do this alone. She can hurt you! You don't have to do anything alone, not anymore."

But Penelope didn't stop. She hurried down the hall, past the kitchen where the others waited, and into the mudroom. She said nothing as she tugged on her boots and buttoned up her coat. Neil paused in the hall outside the kitchen, the hushed whispers from Laszlo and Daniela dying down when they saw him.

They stared blankly up at him, their expressions a mix of fear, confusion, and concern. He swiveled away, taking a step toward the mudroom right as the side door was flung open. The slap of cold air made Neil wrap his arms around himself, and he heard the soft crunch of the snow under her feet, until those disappeared altogether.

"Penelope! Penelope, come back!" But she didn't. "Is no one going after her?" he demanded, pressing a hand to his head. He was seeing stars. Hell, he probably shouldn't have stood at all, but was he supposed to let her roam alone in the snow to where a ghost had told her to go? A ghost who could apparently hurt people?

"Just give her some time," Laszlo said softly. "You, on the other hand, need to sit down. I'm trying to get ahold of Fanny so we can take you to the hospital."

Neither Laszlo nor Daniela seemed alarmed or worried, despite Penelope wandering off into the snow without any real explanation, leaving the door wide open behind her.

Hero.

Goddamn it, why was she running around, spouting nonsense about being a hero when she already was one? What the hell was she going to do, fight a ghost? What did she think going out there alone in the snow would do to turn her into a hero?

"She'll be fine," Daniela echoed with a sigh. "I'm sure Pen knows what she's doing."

Neil had had enough of this bullshit. Grunting, he stalked

toward the side door, stumbling against the wall as he tugged on his boots.

"What are you doing?" Laszlo demanded. "You might have a concussion!"

"I'm going to stop Penelope from making some foolish, heroic mistake because no one should be alone right now." Venom leaked into his tone, but Neil couldn't help it. What was wrong with these people? They were supposed to be her *friends*.

"You shouldn't be standing," Laszlo chided.

"Let them go off and do their thing," Daniela said, leaning against the wall. "If they want to run out into the snow and fuck, who are we to stop them?"

"Do you even hear yourselves?" Neil yelled, turning on them. "She's out there trying to save your goddamn lives, and you're in here telling me to go lie down?" Neil shook his head, wincing at the stabbing pain behind his eyes.

"Saving *our* lives?" Daniela sputtered. "What are you talking about?"

Neil scowled. Right. Ghosts. Not like they'd believe him, anyways. Shivering, Neil pulled on his scarf and jacket before buttoning it up with trembling fingers.

"Please don't die!" Laszlo called.

Neil clenched his teeth and closed the door behind him. He turned in place, hands balled in his pockets as he searched the snow for her. He squinted, but she was nowhere to be seen. Finally, he glanced down.

Her tracks were still fresh.

He trudged after them, teeth chattering from the cold. The low temperatures did not seem to help the head injury, but he was the only one willing to go after her, and damn it, Penelope, why did she have to go be a hero?

"Penelope!" he called, cupping his hands around his mouth.

His calls were met with silence.

Trembling from the frigid temperatures, he wrapped his arms around his middle and trudged on, his feet dragging as the ache of his fall set in. Nothing was broken, and no serious damage was done, but he felt on the verge of collapse as he struggled through the snow. The trees were frozen solid, and icicles hung off the castle like translucent daggers.

Neil paused, spotting something in the distance. A building, perhaps, though difficult to see from here. He picked up the pace, slogging through the knee-deep snow. His hands had gone numb with the cold; his face was no better off from the exposure. He dug his hands into his coat, trying to bring back some feeling into his fingers.

He came to a stop before a rectangular stone building. From the outer design, it was a church. A simple one, likely built on the castle's property for the tenants to attend. The heavy wooden door had been closed, and he pried it open, grunting with the effort, his unfeeling fingers fumbling.

It swung open, and with a sigh, he stepped inside, blowing warm air into his hands. He glanced around as he rubbed his hands together, eyes skimming stone and candles and wooden pews. It was practically empty, and given the disarray, it'd been unused for several decades. It was built of the same stone as the other buildings on the castle grounds, and Neil could see its age in the grime and the single large tomb in the center of the stone floor that read "Ewan Walsh, Third Duke of Walsh Castle."

Walsh. *Walsh.* And then he remembered.

"Georgina," he said softly. He crossed to it and knelt, running his fingers over the letters. Her father. It had to be. If Archibald Skinner had been buried as the fourth duke, then that was the only way.

"Penelope?" He stood and brushed his hands against his pants. While it was warmer inside the church, it was still freezing. Clenching his teeth to keep from chattering, he walked down the center of the aisle, his boots making a soft *clack* against the floor as he searched for any sign of Penelope.

The pews were empty, and the wood was broken through and splintered on most of them. The candles hadn't been lit in some time, the wax spilling over the candelabras. Cobwebs covered much of the furniture and corners of the room, and the stillness was deafening.

"Somehow, this is creepier than the west wing." He stopped at the front of the room. A tattered old chair was discarded to the left, a dust-covered rug across the floor under his feet. If Penelope wasn't here, where on earth could she have gone?

As he made to leave, the floor squeaked beneath him. Chewing on his lip, he stepped off the rug. There was a set of fingerprints along the edge, as if someone had been there not too long ago. He ran a finger over them before carefully peeling the rug back.

Neil wasn't certain what he'd expected to lie hidden underneath, but a trapdoor was not one of them. It wasn't large, but it was big enough to fit a person. A terrifying thought.

"Don't do this," he said, hands on his hips. It was a *terrible* idea. *Who climbs down into random trapdoors? Who does that?*

"Apparently, I do," he said before flinging back the lid.

It was dark, pitch-black with no end in sight. Pulling his phone from his pocket, he turned on the flashlight and shone the light down. Ignoring the urge to run back to the safety of the castle, he sat on the edge of the hole, then dropped in.

He swayed, catching himself on the walls.

"The walls." He shone the light around him. Stone walls built of the same materials as the castle and the church surrounded him. He had to bend down slightly; the tunnel was built for someone shorter.

A quaint Penelope size. The thought made Neil smile.

Phone raised up to light his way and a hand pressed to the wall to keep his balance, Neil strode on, head ducked.

"A goddamn hero," he muttered, eyes flicking around the darkness.

Why did people feel the need to run off and be heroes? It never did anyone any good.

He heard nothing but his own breath, the *brush-brush* of his jacket as he leaned against the wall for support. His head pounded, still, and his eyes struggled to focus on the dim light ahead.

And then he heard it: the soft *swish-swish* of someone walking near him, almost close enough to touch. Neil's imagination went wild. What was it? A cloak brushing the walls, or long skirts trailing in the dirt? Whatever it was, there was *someone* not far behind him.

Neil froze, phone gripped tight in his hand. He could turn around and shine the light on the thing following him in the darkness. Or he could pretend. He could hurry on as fast as his weary limbs and pounding head would let him and simply ignore the sound. It was a test of his patience, his will.

But Neil was stubborn, and though the curiosity wanted to win, he clamped it down and started humming, the wavering tone enough to cover the sound of the thing following him. Because Penelope was somewhere down here, and he'd be damned if he abandoned her.

The stone walls were slick with grime under his fingers, and he tried not to think about what he was touching, about what crawled beneath his fingernails. He attempted desperately to focus on how, somewhere beyond the excruciatingly narrow tunnel, Penelope was being a goddamn hero.

Neil's voice grew hoarse, the hummed tunes repeating until it was too much. He rocked back and forth on his legs, shuffling through the dirt until his feet were aching and the heat of the confined tunnel trailed sweaty fingers down his back. He unbuttoned his coat and wiped at his forehead, his mop of curls absorbing the sweat.

His arm ached from holding his phone up to illuminate, and his hand shook from the effort. Neil didn't know how long he had been down there—fifteen minutes, an hour, perhaps. It was warm and dark and creepy, and in the end, all that mattered was finding Penelope.

He clicked on his phone screen warily, the red battery blinking back at him. Fifteen percent, his phone was down to 15 percent battery.

Neil tilted his head back, that *swish-swish* of the thing in the dark still close. When he stopped, it stopped. When he moved, it moved. Shivering, he picked up the pace, biting the inside of his cheek to suppress the ache traveling down his body.

"Penelope?" he called out.

He'd hoped to avoid drawing the attention of anything creepy, but with it trailing him, well, there was no point in staying quiet.

"Penelope!"

His voice rang off the stone, disappearing in the distance, dampened by the dirt. Neil's heart was hammering, the worry sinking further. Where the hell had she gone? Out of the castle, down into the tunnel, and *nothing*. No sign of her to be found.

Neil wanted to turn back, but there was a *something* following him, and he didn't want to know what it was. If he'd learned anything on the retreat, it was better to leave some things a mystery.

He swiped up on his phone. Eight percent.

"Oh god," he whispered, panic rising in his voice.

He needed out, back to daylight. But there was Penelope to think about, all alone down here. He could turn around; run the way he'd come—

But 8 percent. He only had 8 percent battery left.

He stared down at the screen. Make it 6 percent.

"Penelope!"

The *swish-swish* of the thing behind him was closer. Maybe

it was a rat. Maybe it was nothing but the air being sucked out through the narrow entrance he'd left open through the church.

Or maybe it was the woman in white—Georgina Walsh.

He shuddered and checked his phone again. Two percent.

"Penelope," he called out, his voice more of a whimper.

God, she was always going to be the hero. Neil was such a coward compared to Penelope. She didn't need to prove herself, *he* did. Neil was the one who fucked up. Neil was the one who took up the space someone with Penelope's skill deserved. He was the one who had been too afraid to face his past mistakes. In the last four months, he'd been crushed by doubt, and now that Penelope had made him face it and dig out a little corner of his heart for herself, she had to run off into danger.

His phone slipped from his grasp, landing with the light shining up, setting a large, cavernous room aglow.

"Fuck," he cursed, pressing a hand to the back of his head as he tripped toward it, missing a step leading from the tunnel into the large space, and landing in the dirt with a *thud*. He groaned, scraping against the dirt to sit up. Blinking, he glanced around, taking in the open slots in the walls, and the . . .

"Oh, fuck no."

A tomb. He was in a fucking tomb.

He scrambled to stand, nearly slipping again. A tomb. *A tomb.* He shouldn't have come out here, should have returned to the castle to start a search party for her with the others, but *nooooo*. No, he had to run off like Indiana Jones and get himself in this mess.

He crossed to his phone, tilting the cracked screen toward him in the dark.

One percent.

His battery had one percent left, and he was in a tomb. Underground.

Probably surrounded by the dead.

Because that's what tombs were, everlasting homes for the

dead. He'd never wished to enter one, never wished to stay in a haunted castle, and still, he found himself belowground in a massive hollowed tomb surrounded by skeletons.

What had he done to deserve such an end?

Neil searched frantically for an exit. His phone would shut off at any moment, and he needed to get *out*. Out before the thing that followed him made its appearance. Out before he found something worse down there among the dirt and decay.

And then he saw it: a set of stairs leading off to the left.

He ran for them, dirt flying behind him as he raced against the dying battery. Right as he reached the stone steps, the flashlight on his phone flicked out, and he was plunged into darkness.

"Shit," he cursed as he clambered for the steps just as a hand clamped down on his shoulder.

Chapter 29

PEN

Pen pressed a hand over his mouth, biting back a gasp.

"Neil!" she said, the sound of her voice echoing around them. "Neil, it's me. Penelope."

She pulled her hand away, blinking against the darkness. Pen hadn't heard or seen him; she'd been too focused on what was down here, waiting for her in the dark.

When she'd climbed down into the tunnel from the church, a lit torch had been waiting for her, illuminating the space with a warm glow as if she'd always been the one meant to find it. It was odd, she knew, that there was a lit torch waiting for her, let alone that there was a *freaking torch* at all, but she tried not to let it bother her.

Neil flinched as the torch in her hand burst into flames once more, and they both blinked against the sudden light.

"Was that . . ."

"Just ignore the strange magical torch in my hand," she said, motioning to him. "Let me show you something."

Shaking himself, Neil followed her, shuffling across the dirt floor. She eyed him sidelong as he peered around the tomb, taking in the stone caskets that lined the walls, and the packed dirt under their feet. This place was a stone monument to the people who once owned this land, and Pen felt ridiculously out of place. She moved the torch from left to right, motioning to the wall as they stopped before a set of caskets, and Neil bent to read them.

The first casket was not in English, nor was the second. The third, though, had that familiar last name, "Walsh." And so did the fourth, and the fifth. They had stumbled their way into the Walsh family tomb, it seemed.

Pen ran her fingers through the cobwebs, eyes scanning names and dates and words chiseled painstakingly into stone. As she did, she pictured Archie's grave, there among countless other head-stones, sticking grimly out of the snow.

If he was out there, then . . .

"I haven't seen it all," she whispered, turning to Neil. "But I think I know why she sent me here."

"She sent you?"

Pen nodded as they circled the whole room, dirt-caked fingers running over beautiful stone caskets.

"I'm sorry I didn't fully explain before I left, but when she pushed you out of her room, she whispered that I needed to come here. And your speech," she said, glancing at him with a shrug, "it convinced me to come out here myself."

"You're already a hero, you know that?" Pen refused to look at him, her eyes intent on something in the distance. He shuffled toward her and touched her hip softly, his fingers soothing. It sent a zap of electricity straight to her toes, warming her from the inside out. "You don't need to prove yourself to me, Penelope."

She slipped the torch into a mount and turned to him, the flame a scorching heat beside them, casting him in warm yellow light. "But I do, Neil. I know you believe I'm some sort of hero for calling you out or standing my ground or whatever, but I don't see it that way. But this? This is how I redeem myself."

"You don't need to prove anything or redeem yourself, Penelope. I don't need any convincing. I know who you are."

She opened her mouth to reply, but her eyes went past him to a name she recognized all too well.

"Georgina," she whispered.

Neil followed her gaze.

Georgina Walsh's stone resting place was much the same as the others, except for an inscription Pen was surprised to read under her name. She pulled the lingering cobwebs free and smoothed her hands over the lid, brushing away the dust and dirt to get a better look.

"Mother and beloved wife," she read, turning to Neil.

"So, she was pregnant. And married?" He made a face. "But her ghost is so young."

Pen ran her finger over the date of death, tapping it. "1818. She was only twenty-one when she died."

Neil shook his head. "But if she was pregnant in 1815 when he was sent away to Waterloo, could she really have found someone else to marry in that length of time? This crypt doesn't appear to have been used since Georgina passed, so what changed?"

"Or did Archie return from the war? The sketch in her journal is the spitting image of the ghost we saw leaving my room. His clothing fit the era, and although he was young, maybe he didn't die in the war. Maybe he made it back to the castle after the baby was born."

Neil nodded slowly, wincing, and pressed a hand to his temple. Pen reached for him, but he held up a hand, thinking.

"There was that letter about the moon, right? What was it . . . something like, 'promised to be mine'? So, maybe they secretly wed, she got pregnant, and when her father found out, he forced him away? Sent him quietly off to his death?"

Pen made a little excited squeak. "But when Archie returned

and Georgina had given birth to a son, the duke had no choice but to let them wed, making Archie the heir."

"Which is why the castle was renamed after *him*." Neil planted his hands on his hips, grinning. "Oh, we're good. Is this what detectives feel like?"

Pen snorted. "We're more like amateur armchair sleuths than Sherlock Holmes."

They pivoted back to Georgina's sarcophagus. Pen sighed as she patted the lid. Although it wasn't a lot of time, Archie and Georgina had had a life together. Years, maybe, but it was better than nothing, and certainly more time than even she'd imagined.

"But this doesn't explain why the ghosts are still here," Neil said. "Are they the type of ghosts who need to wrap up their unfinished business in order to move on? And if so, what's their unfinished business?"

Pen took up the torch once more, pausing as her eyes slid to another sarcophagus parallel to Georgina's.

"Penelope?"

She shook her head and crossed to it, eyes going wide and heart sinking as she read the inscription.

"It's him," she whispered. "Archibald Skinner, Archie." She brushed her sleeve through the dust, coughing into her arm as she scanned it. "He died ten years later in 1828. 'Beloved husband and son' . . . but his inscription doesn't say duke."

She scooted back for Neil to join her. His hip bumped against hers as he sidled up beside Pen, and he wrapped an arm around her waist to steady her before leaning over the sarcophagus. He read over the inscription several times before stepping away, his bottom lip clamped between his teeth.

"They were both so young," he murmured.

Pen sighed but said nothing. Neil held out a hand and she stared down at it, at his waiting fingers. Fingers that belonged to a familiar hand that belonged to a familiar man. They were filthy, covered in grime, and dirt was stuck beneath his fingernails, but they were his. Sniffling, she entwined her fingers with his.

They climbed out of the tomb, and she stamped out the torch in the snow, watching as the flames sizzled out. Quietly, they fought their way through the snow and stopped before the grave, the one he'd shown her what felt like a lifetime ago.

They knelt in the snow side by side, sitting back on their heels. The cold leached in through her jeans as she reached out and tugged off the ivy wrapped around the stone, brushing away the dirt and grime from the engraved dates.

"Born December seventeenth, 1815." Pen glanced sidelong at Neil. "Their son. By mid-March, she was already pregnant with him, and Archie was sent away in April. He fought in Waterloo, and for whatever reason, wasn't able to return home until the baby was born."

"Hold on." He leaned past her, ripping the last of the ivy from the headstone to reveal a set of Roman numerals after the name. Archibald Skinner II.

"That would have saved us a lot of time," Pen murmured.

"Would've, could've, should've."

They sat in front of the grave for a while. Pen's heart felt enormously heavy. She'd hoped for a happily ever after, and she supposed Georgina and Archie had had one, but it wasn't some fairy-tale ending. Pen leaned her head on Neil's shoulder and stared blankly at the gravestone until her hands were cold and she'd lost feeling in her thighs. Finally, after minutes or hours, she couldn't be sure, they stood, and Pen wrapped her arms around Neil, pulling him close. When she leaned up on her tiptoes to kiss him, he tasted like coffee and snow, smelled of the tomb and the macabre things in the ground beneath them. But his hands and his lips were comforting, something she never thought she'd come to know.

When they finally pulled apart, Neil looked dazed, his hands on either side of her face as he bent down and pressed his forehead against hers. He sighed, and she could feel the sound all the way down to her toes.

"As fun as this was," he breathed, "I'm so ready to get the hell out of this castle."

"I concur." She pulled back and brushed a few stray curls from his eyes. "We still have some things to do. Like taking you to the hospital."

"Is that really necessary?"

She raised a brow in answer as they pivoted toward the castle to glance up at the window. Georgina stood as she had the day before, half turned toward them, eyes cast down. But there was something different about her, about the softness around her mouth and the glimmer in her eyes.

Was this it, the closure to her story? Could Georgina and Archie and all the spirits in Skinner Castle finally rest? Or was there more? There was only one way to find out.

"Let's go."

They trudged back through the snow, but Pen did not feel the cold. Neil's hand was warm in hers, and she tried to focus on that instead of what was to come.

When they arrived at the side door to the castle, Neil tugged her to a stop, bottom lip trapped between his teeth.

"Are you sure you want to do this?" he asked, voice low.

Pen looked at the door.

This was it. Once they walked into that castle, there was no turning back. But Georgina and Archie deserved the closure, whatever it was. That's why ghosts lingered, right? They lingered because they had unfinished business, and Georgina had been ripped away from her family at such a young age. Wasn't that traumatic enough?

"I'm sure."

Neil kissed the top of her head. "Okay."

Clearing her throat, she opened the door. Silently, they

shucked off their boots and coats, and when they rounded the corner, Laszlo and Daniela were leaning over the kitchen table, eyes wide as their heads snapped up to take them in.

"We need to get Neil to a hospital," Daniela said, rounding the table.

"What about the snow? We still haven't heard back from Fanny," Laszlo said, scratching his neck as he turned to Pen and Neil.

"I'm okay for now, really," Neil insisted.

"You're not okay," Pen said.

"Well, I can't drive those roads with the ice. And the car won't start; I already tried. I don't know how icy it is, or if we can get someone out here—"

"Keep trying Fanny," Pen said. "I think Neil has a concussion, and he shouldn't have followed me out into the snow."

"I'm fine."

"On it," Laszlo said.

Neil grabbed Pen's hands, ignoring her protests. Scrunching up his nose, he pulled Pen with him through the kitchen and down the corridor, pace quickening as he hurried toward the foyer.

"Where are you going?" Laszlo called after them.

"To figure this out!" Neil responded.

"Neil," Pen said as she tugged him to a stop at the base of the stairs. "Neil, I'm not joking. You're injured. And we don't know what we're doing. These are *ghosts*. We don't even know how any of this works!"

"Georgina won't leave us alone. She pushed me and I hit my head. No, don't look at me like that. Okay, fine, whatever. I'll get it looked at later. Ghosts, whether they can physically touch us or not, can make you see things, make you think things, and make you *do* things. We have to help Georgina and Archie do . . . whatever it is they need to do before it's too late for us all."

Pen's eyes caught on something over his shoulder, and her pulse faltered at the horrific sight behind him.

"Neil."

"Come on, we don't have a lot of time."

"*Neil.*"

She grabbed his shoulders and turned him toward the portrait of Georgina. Black gunk seeped out of the canvas, dripping down and splattering to the floor. The woman in the portrait was practically unrecognizable. The black liquid bled from her eyes and mouth, trailing over the material, staining it.

"Oh, I do not like that," Pen said. "Now this is *really* some real Dorian Gray shit, and I am not comfortable with the level of creeps that portrait is giving me."

"If Daniela and Laszlo don't see this, I'm gonna be pissed."

Georgina was not going to stop. Things were only escalating, and sooner rather than later, somebody was going to get seriously hurt. Pen threaded her fingers with Neil's, squeezing.

"Okay, if we do this, if we go up there to Georgina's room, can you promise me something? Promise me you'll be careful."

He looked at her for a dreadfully long moment. "I promise."

"Okay, then up to our deaths we go."

Neil blanched. "No need to be so dark about it."

He started up the steps, her hand still clasped tight in his.

It shouldn't have been possible; none of it should have been possible. The ghosts, the castle, even she and Neil. Pen sprinted up the stairs behind him, her heart thundering.

She was quickly learning nothing was impossible here.

Chapter 30

NEIL

Neil knew the way well, his feet following a familiar path to the door. If there was one place Georgina would be, it was in there.

He and Penelope stopped outside the door. Though he knew what was needed of him, it was something else to confront a ghost willingly. All this time, he'd tried to find the clues, creeping around the castle when he saw things and heard things. But now he was voluntarily entering a room that he knew was haunted. Again. After the concussion and the black eye he could feel setting in, he should have known better, but it seemed he hadn't learned anything at all.

"So," Penelope started, motioning toward the door. "More ghost encounters on your wish list?"

"Not particularly."

"Do we go in together? Or just you?"

"Together. We need to do this together."

She must have liked the sound of that, because she smiled up at him before nodding. "Okay, together."

Neil squeezed her fingers. He breathed in deeply through his nose, then let the breath out slowly. This was it, the end. The finale. He'd waited days for this, days of sleepless nights and heart-wrenching truths. He squinted down at Penelope, at the dark hair tucked behind her ear, at the set of her jaw as she stared ahead.

There was no way their story would end here, outside this room. They still had so much to do together, so many things to say.

Their firsts had only just begun.

"Are we going in?" she asked, peering up at him.

With a sigh, he turned the knob and pushed.

The room was not as he'd seen it before. Life had been bled out of the space, light replaced with dark, joy replaced with shadows. Black, syrupy liquid seeped from the corners and the floorboards, oozing from every crack and crevice. It reeked of death, stale and sweet and terribly wrong.

The door slammed shut behind them, making Neil and Penelope jump. He laughed it off, running his free hand through his hair to hide how nervous he was. Okay, terrified. Neil Storm was *terrified*. Which, in all frankness, he had every right to be.

"It's fine, we're fine," he said, tightening his grip on Penelope's hand.

"Your grip tells me otherwise," she gasped, flexing her hand in his.

"Sorry," he said, loosening his hold.

The bed was bare, just an empty canopy bed with shreds of old fabric dripping from the top. The doors from the wardrobe on the farthest wall had been chopped into pieces at one point or another, and the markings looked strikingly like those of an axe.

The mirror on the wall adjacent to the bed was cracked, hanging crookedly. Neil tried desperately not to focus on their reflections. He'd seen enough horror movies and read enough horror stories to know that was never a good idea.

Aside from the furniture, the room was empty but for the littered leaves and torn, blackened fabric clinging to the sticky substance that seemed to bubble up from the floor with each step.

Gripping Penelope's fingers, Neil carefully pulled her across the room, tiptoeing around the black liquid. They crossed to the small writing desk he'd seen Georgina stationed at. It was not a beautiful thing, simply a useful thing, the wood weathered and worn from years of abandonment.

Neil ran a finger along it. He held his finger up to examine—no dust to be found—and frowned.

"That's weird," he said.

"This is where she wrote all those letters," she mused. Penelope closed her eyes, leaning into the desk. Despite everything in Neil telling him to run, he could watch her all day. "I can picture her seated here, looking out over the grounds, thinking of Archie."

So, Penelope Skinner was a romantic. Neil should have known. He had the strange urge to reach out and wrap his arms around her, to capture her mouth with his. Something about her made him come alive, particularly in a room so devoid of life.

Neil skimmed a hand up her arm, his fingers brushing her elbow. Penelope pivoted to smile up at him but froze, her eyes going to the bed frame behind him. It reminded him of those moments in the hall, hands clasped over Penelope's eyes as the door creaked open and Georgina floated out.

Penelope opened her mouth to scream, her voice not quite working as she let out a raspy squeak and staggered back a step, pointing past him.

"She's behind me, isn't she?" he asked, resigned.

"N-no. She—she's *under* you."

If there were words worse than he'd imagined, those were them.

Neil hadn't wanted to look down. Hell, if he had the choice, he would have much rather stood there with the knowledge that a ghost crept beneath him than train his eyes on the thing. But his curiosity strained, and even knowing what lay beneath, he couldn't stop his eyes from straying.

He felt the chill first, then the bite of a clammy hand wrapping around his ankle. As he met Georgina's eyes, sunken into a face filled with death and despair and anger, his legs gave out beneath him. His breath *whooshed* from his chest as he fell, and he gasped for air, momentarily stunned.

Neil slammed against the floor, head cracking against the wood. He saw stars as the woman yanked hard, and Neil scrabbled for purchase as Georgina tugged, pulling him under the bed. It was a cliché, but in any other moment, he might have laughed because the monster *did* live under the bed. There was nothing remotely human about Georgina Walsh now, and the sight of her, the *feel* of her against his leg was terrifying.

"Penelope!" he screamed, one hand gripping the edge of the writing desk, the other waving in the air over him. Penelope's hands wrapped around his free one, tugging with all her might. But she wasn't nearly strong enough, and Georgina wasn't human anymore.

She growled from somewhere behind him, and Neil screeched, his heartbeat thundering as she jerked him back with inhuman strength.

"I'm not letting you go!" Penelope promised. Her hands were sweaty, her grip slipping, but still, she struggled, standing her ground. As she always had.

And then the pulling stopped.

Neil blinked in surprise, narrowing his eyes at the darkness under the bed and the not-woman lurking there. Beady eyes stared back at him, gleaming from the shadows like glowing orbs. The thing Penelope had seen in the cellar . . . it *was* Georgina. This would have terrified him then, too. It certainly terrified him now.

"Penelope!" Neil screamed, scrambling back.

Penelope yanked with all her might, and Neil kicked free, both fumbling backward. They tripped, and his arms clamped around her as they turned and watched in horror as two skeletal hands appeared from beneath the bed, the thing freeing itself of the shadows. Georgina stood, bones clambering to right themselves, one leg straightening into position and then the other. She stalked toward them, ratty white dress trailing in her wake. Neil spread his arms before them, blocking Penelope from Georgina, whatever good that did them.

"Georgina!" Penelope yelled, squeezing her eyes tight and clenching her hands into fists. The ghost didn't stop. "Georgina Walsh!" Penelope screeched.

The ghost froze, her eyes going distant.

"*Skinner.*"

Penelope eyed Neil sidelong. "Um, right, Georgina Skinner." Neil and Penelope watched in surprise as parts of Georgina turned more human, her gross, corpse-like state melting away, layer by layer.

"Georgina Skinner?" Penelope said slowly. "Georgina, we know what happened to you."

Penelope took a step toward the ghost, but Neil reached out as if on instinct, his hands tightening around her wrist.

She shook her head. "No, I'm okay. We're safe." He let go as Penelope moved past him, stopping a few feet away from the woman. She held out a hand to Georgina as if calming a feral animal. "You've been looking for your Archie, haven't you? That's why you've stayed all this time?"

Georgina's lips parted. *"Archie,"* she echoed.

Before them, Georgina began to change. Her flesh and bone filled out, no longer skeletal. Her skin turned pink and plump, her cheeks full, life blown back into her. Her eyes met Penelope's, expression pained.

"Archie," she repeated, voice strained.

"He returned to you, but you had so little time together," Neil started, glancing at Penelope.

The ghost moved to her desk, running a slender finger over its surface. And then she smiled, a soft, pretty thing. "He loved me, my Archie. When he was sent away, he wrote me every week. The servants slipped the letters to me, careful of my father, but Archie's responses stopped coming in late May, and I believed I was left alone. Father would not leave for business, insistent that he could not abandon me, fearful I would go in search of Archie and risk the baby."

She focused on Penelope. "Archie and I married before my father sent him away, though my father would not allow it. Archie was but the mere son of our groundskeeper, and I a future duchess. After Archie asked my father for my hand, my father forbade us from seeing one another. And then he caught us in the garden, secretly wed. In his anger, he sent Archie away to war."

"But you were pregnant," Penelope said softly.

"Yes," she answered after a moment. The sound of her voice still grated against him, and Neil shivered, wrapping his arms around his middle as she continued, "I knew by April when my father sent Archie away that I was with child. But I was only a child myself, and when I grew sick that autumn and Father feared what would become of our home and his line, he sent for Archie, only to receive no word back of his whereabouts. When we were certain Archie would not return, he made our son the heir to this castle."

"But Archie did return?"

"Yes, in April of the following year. He'd been injured, an infection in his leg, and he recovered in a hospital in Brussels. It was a miracle he returned home safely at all."

Neil's arms slackened, his chest squeezing tight. All those months she thought he was dead. And even then, they only had three years together before Georgina passed away.

"And you were happy, weren't you?" Penelope ventured. "You and Archie and your son had a life together."

"For a while, yes. We were a family until my sickness returned. When the doctor said there was nothing they could do, I promised Archie I would watch after them always. And I did, until Archie passed, then my father, and when our son built his own family, and they too passed, I knew I would be trapped here to watch every single person in my line wither and die." She reached out to touch the canopy bed, but her finger disappeared into the wood. "I have seen even this castle fall apart because of me."

"Which is why you're still here," Neil whispered.

"I had begun to forget who I was and why I was here. No one has spoken my name in some time," she said wistfully. "No one remembers me, yet I have spent two hundred years making up for the mistakes of my life." Georgina looked between Penelope and Neil. "Do not make the same mistakes as us."

To their left, the door screeched open, and the man from before appeared, his jacket still slung over his arm. Now that Neil could see him more clearly, he saw the slight lines around his mouth, the beginning of age in the crow's feet sprouting from the corners of his eyes, and the slight limp in his walk. Archie smiled at Georgina, a look of pure adoration, of love.

"Are you going to leave now?" Penelope asked quietly, glancing between the two. "Now that you remember?"

Georgina smiled, turning back to Archie. "I believe we have some unfinished business, first."

"And then you'll . . ." Penelope mimed floating away, and Neil caught her hands, pressing them to her sides.

"That might be a sensitive topic," he said.

"I don't know how these things work," she shot back as they inched quietly out of the room. "Where's that clairvoyant from Craigslist when you need her?"

Ghost Archie reached for Ghost Georgina, their hands tangling. Neil thought it was almost sweet. That was until they tugged themselves together, hands and lips reaching for one another, ghostly breaths mingling as they opened their mouths wide for a passionate kiss.

"I did not know that was even possible," Penelope said.

Neil coughed as the room heated up. "I think we better get going," he said, nudging Penelope toward the door.

"Did it get hot in there?" she asked as Georgina flicked her wrist and the door slammed shut behind them.

"I guess ghosts can change temperatures in both directions."

They stopped on the landing, and Penelope gripped the banister, staring down at the large portrait of Georgina, and Neil followed her gaze. Already, it had changed. There were no tears on the canvas, and Georgina's features had softened into that of a kind young woman. The black, ink-like substance was gone, vanished, as if nothing had ever been wrong. Neil's gaze slid from the painting to Penelope. Her braid had come undone some time ago, her messy waves cascading around her face as she peered down at the foyer, and Neil caught a strand between his fingers.

"I want to love someone so much that I'm willing to fuck them in front of some weird, nosy humans," she said, turning to grin up at Neil.

He cleared his throat and pressed a hand to his chest, his heartbeat speeding up as he met those familiar stormy eyes.

"I mean, I *could* make that happen, but that sounds like some messy business."

She inched closer, gripping his shirt in her fists. "I mean, *sex* is a messy business."

"It doesn't have to be," he said as he bent closer.

Penelope snorted, gently guiding him down, her kiss light.

"Should we tell the others?" she whispered against his lips.

"Let's make them suffer for a minute longer," he said, turning to press her against the wall, his most favorite spot in the whole castle.

Penelope's lips curved up into a coy smile. "I have a better idea."

Chapter 31

PEN

Practically shaking, Pen took the stairs two at a time, breath coming out in great, wheezing gasps. She hopped down the last few steps, rolling on her ankle. Excruciating pain shot up her leg, and she half jogged, half hopped toward the kitchen, crashing into the side wall as she tried to steady herself.

Daniela was seated at the kitchen table, gesturing to her phone with sharp, angry movements. "I have no signal!" she yelled.

Pen stopped in the hall, watching Daniela silently for a moment. She opened her mouth to speak, but Laszlo rushed in past her, nearly sending her spinning. Pen caught herself on the entry, teeth grinding.

Laszlo stopped in the kitchen, hands on his hips as he looked between them with wide, worried eyes. "The van won't start," he panted. "Neil was right, we're going *nowhere*." His voice was laced with panic. "And Fanny won't come in. She refuses to enter the castle again. Silly woman thinks there's something cursed about this place. Superstitious, if you ask me."

"I can hear ye!" Fanny said from the mudroom. "And the castle is haunted, nay, cursed! Did ye even listen to my opening tour?"

"Not really!" Laszlo admitted.

Daniela stood and turned to Laszlo, curls whipping around

her face and phone held tightly in her fingers as she pushed past Pen. "We still don't have cell service either. How do people live like this? I haven't checked my socials *in a day*."

"You should be more worried about calling for emergency services than having enough internet to check your socials," Laszlo said. Pen agreed silently.

"Hey," Pen started, raising a hand. This was not going as planned. She hopped on her good leg, biting the inside of her cheek as pain dragged icy-hot fingers up through her hip.

"What are we going to do?" Laszlo cried out.

Pen pointed behind her, voice wavering. "There's a . . ." she said, trailing off. She did not have their attention in the least. They were all scattered.

Grunting, Pen turned and hopped back down the hall. Squeezing her eyes shut, she counted to ten before she nodded to herself and ran toward the kitchen once more.

"Help!" she screamed as she rounded the corner.

"Pen?" Laszlo asked.

This is it.

"Why are ye yelling?" Fanny called.

"There's a—I saw the—" Pen shook her head, waving down the hallway.

Laszlo crossed to her, drawing her into his side. His grip was firm, reassuring, and it took the weight off her ankle, an instant relief.

"Pen," he said, voice tight, "tell me what you saw."

"The ghost," she said, looking to Daniela. She lowered her voice. "The woman in white."

"I thought it was the woman in black?" Laszlo asked.

"Ye saw her, then?" Fanny asked, suddenly behind them.

"Come on," Daniela said with a laugh. "We all know ghosts aren't real."

"They're real! If you'll come with me, I'll show you." Laszlo,

Daniela, and Fanny all shared a silent look. Pen knew Laszlo and Daniela didn't believe her, but if they would just trust her, follow her up those stairs. *"Please,"* she begged. "Neil needs our help."

With a sigh, Laszlo nodded. "For your man."

"He's not my man," she muttered under her breath, blushing as he helped her down the hallway. Although, she still wasn't entirely sure *what* he was to her. She liked him, no doubt, but there was a question lingering in the space between them, and she wasn't quite ready for what *that* meant.

Up the stairs the lot of them went, steps creaking under their weight. Pen stared down at the painting of Georgina hanging in the foyer, and she could swear those painted lips curved up into a knowing smirk, her silver eyes following them until they were out of sight.

"Where?" Laszlo asked on the landing.

Pen pointed shakily to the west wing. "Down there."

"Ye were not supposed to go there," Fanny chided.

"We had no choice," Pen insisted.

Laszlo shared a final look with the others. This was it, their last chance to turn around. Laszlo moved first, hauling Pen down the darkened hall, practically hiding behind her as they approached the door.

Though she knew the story, though she'd been down here several times in a matter of days, Pen couldn't help the shiver that traveled down her spine or the chill that left her shaking. The west wing was daunting as ever, shadows leaking from the corners, movement skittering under the doors like critters, and ghosts lying in wait.

Daniela blew out a string of warm air somewhere behind her, and someone was humming quietly under their breath, voice ragged with fear. They were nervous and terrified, and they had every right to be.

"Neil's in here," Pen said, voice trembling.

She motioned to the door—*Georgina's door*—and Laszlo glanced down at her, lips curved into a frown. "Why does this feel like a terrible idea?"

"Because it probably is," Daniela whispered.

"I'm not sure about this, Pen," Laszlo said.

"Please," Pen begged. She was a broken record, and they had no intention of fixing it. "Neil needs us."

And maybe they finally believed her, because with a surprising amount of resilience, Fanny pushed her way to the door and threw it open.

What they saw there was nothing short of a nightmare.

"Help me!" Neil cried, half-hidden by what was left of the bed. The room was macabre, everything dark and drab, the scent vomit-inducing. It was worse than it had been before, muskier, and darker.

Someone screamed, Fanny or Daniela or perhaps Laszlo, Pen couldn't be sure. She hobbled into the room, hands wrapping around Neil's. The weight on her ankle made her gasp in pain, but she fought through it.

"I've got you!" she yelled.

Although she wasn't certain why she was yelling. The silence from the others was thunderous.

"Quick, someone grab rope!" she said, turning to the others. She angled toward the doorway, hand outstretched for help. Fanny stood frozen in the entry, eyes wide in horror as she took it in. Daniela cowered behind her, mouth open in surprise, arms wrapped around Fanny like a shield as they froze in place.

"*Ohmygodohmygodohmyfuckinggod,*" Daniela was chanting.

Laszlo, to no surprise, had already fled.

Pen turned back to Neil, her grip weak on his wrists as she tugged. "Penelope, please!" he begged, winking.

"I'm trying!" she called. She clamped her lips together as she pretended to pull on him.

And then, he laughed.

The sound split through the desperate silence of the room, and Pen couldn't stop it; she laughed too. Her grip slackened on him, giggles bubbling in her chest. The laughter had taken hold of her. His hands slipped from hers as he fell to the floor, face planting against the floorboards, body shaking with laughter.

Everything seemed to freeze around them, multiple sets of eyes tracking them.

"Um, are you two okay?" Daniela asked from the doorway.

Pen helped Neil stand, shuffling on her good leg. "Sorry," Pen wheezed. "I couldn't keep a straight face."

"Wait," Neil said, wiping at his eyes. He watched her movements, eyes tracking the angle of her foot as she hobbled. "Did you actually hurt yourself?"

"I rolled my ankle on the stairs. I should be fine though."

"Would ye two mind explaining what the bloody hell is going on?" Fanny demanded.

Neil and Pen turned to each other, smiling.

"We have some explaining to do," Pen said. "But first, that was payback for making us suffer all the hauntings on our own."

"Where is the ghost?" Daniela asked shakily.

"All in due time," Neil said, sweeping his arm out the door.

Pen glanced over her shoulder as the others disappeared back down the hall. She stopped to inspect a glob of sticky white stuff, the only thing Georgina and Archie had left in their wake to . . . well, wherever ghosts disappeared to.

"I wouldn't touch that," Neil warned.

"Why, what do you think it is?"

He coughed, turning away as he blushed. "Well, it's white . . . and sticky . . . and when we left them, they'd been about to—"

"*Ohmygodno.*" Pen covered her ears. "Don't you *dare* finish that sentence." She shook her head, trying to forget the image of Ghost Archie doing . . . well, *that*. "Do you think the Ghostbusters ever had to deal with this? No, you know what, don't answer that either."

Neil snorted as he tried to scoop her up in his arms. He teetered sideways, and Pen wrapped an arm around his waist, catching their joined weight against the banister.

"I don't think you're well enough to be carrying me, Neil."

"And you're not well enough to be walking."

She grinned at him. "Then we'll have to make do."

They started down the staircase, albeit slowly, and Neil turned back to her. "Why ask so many questions if you don't want to know?"

"There are some things in this world I'd rather stay ignorant of. Like whether or not a ghost comes, and what said come looks like."

"You're thinking about it. *Ghost jizz.*"

"Only reluctantly!"

They struggled to keep up with the others, Neil wobbling down the steps, gripping the banister with a white-knuckled hand, and Pen limping and leaning into him.

He tapped his chin. "I don't think we can ever watch *Ghostbusters.*"

Pen punched his shoulder. "I would have been fine if you had just stayed *quiet.* You've ruined it for me now too."

"You're welcome."

They stumbled to a stop at the base of the stairs as their friends turned to them.

"Well?" Daniela asked as she crossed her arms and stared daggers at them. "Aren't you going to tell us what all that was about?"

Pen turned to Neil, but he motioned to her. "Why don't you tell them, Penelope? You figured it out, and Georgina wanted you to find the mausoleum, not me."

"Mausoleum?" Laszlo asked, glancing over his shoulder as if Georgina was there.

With Neil's help, Pen hopped through to the study and sank into one of the large leather chairs. Neil propped up her bad ankle and iced it as the others settled in the open seats. He held out the letters and journal for her, and Pen ran her hands over them, something settling in her gut.

She licked her lips, looking around at their eager faces.

"Let me tell you a story."

Chapter 32

PEN

After she told them everything, Neil helped Pen to the kitchen.

The others lingered in the study, voices low and urgent, eyes trailing after them like they suspected more. It was wild to think that Pen and Neil hadn't imagined it all. And though it had been a hectic few days, hunting ghosts, running from ghosts, and kissing someone who Pen had previously thought was her enemy, there was something comforting in knowing the others believed them.

Maybe it had been rude to drag Laszlo, Daniela, and Fanny along and reenact the moments in Georgina's room, but Pen and Neil had spent days haunted and alone in the castle. It seemed only fair.

"I really didn't expect to hurt myself." Pen grunted as Neil set her in a seat at the end of the table. She hissed as he gently propped her foot on another seat, probing what looked to be a rather large bump and a blackening bruise on her ankle.

He laughed as he wrapped some fresh ice in a towel before handing it to her. "You were incredibly moving in your performance."

She chuckled, settling in her seat. With a sigh, she reached out and ran her fingers through his hair, enjoying the stark contrast against her pale skin. A few stray curls flopped into his eyes, and his lips were upturned in the smallest of smiles. It sent a fresh wave of warmth down to her belly.

"I'm thinking of cutting it," he said.

"But I like it."

"But," he said, pulling her hand free, "it's a mess. I'd like to go to bed knowing it wouldn't be a tangled mop in the morning. My mother would be appalled to know I've let my curls run amok."

"That's adorable."

Pen ran a finger down his cheek, her nail scratching at stubble. He caught her fingers with his and pressed a kiss to her knuckles, the touch sending a wave of goose bumps over her arms.

"You know, I hated you once," she admitted softly.

"I know."

"I told myself that you were the reason my life had fallen apart."

"I'm sure."

"But now . . ." she said, trailing off. "You might be the best thing that's happened to me. I know," she said, holding up her hands, "it's cheesy, but maybe it was all for a reason. I'd spent years trying to write before the Incident. Maybe the universe needed to intercede to make certain this is what I wanted."

Neil smirked, his smile soft, not harsh like his usual ones. "I never took you for someone who believed in signs from the universe."

"I never thought I'd be one."

"This is gross," Daniela said from the hall. Pen and Neil glanced at her, laughing. She rolled her eyes, scowling and pointing in the direction of the front door. "Laszlo and Fanny were able to clear a path down the road and get the van started. We're thinking of skipping out early and spending a few days in Edinburgh. You two in?"

Pen met Neil's eyes, mirth dancing in those emerald orbs. She thought of all the things they'd seen and learned in the castle, all the hurdles they'd overcome, the truths they'd admitted.

And then she thought of the letters. She thought of Georgina and Archie and a love that, to all who'd seen it, had been tampered with from the very beginning. Pen had come to the castle to find a story, to find her way back to writing, and in the end, isn't that what she'd done?

"That would be really nice," she admitted, tilting her head.

Neil nodded. "Could we make a pit stop or two?"

"Like the hospital?" Pen urged.

"I was thinking more like Midhope Castle."

Pen raised a brow. "Color me intrigued, but are you referring to a certain castle used in a certain historical romance series?"

Neil shrugged, but Pen didn't miss the way his face reddened. "What can I say, I've got a secret love of *Outlander*."

"It's not a secret! Neil loves *Outlander*," Laszlo bellowed.

"I'm a romantic," Neil said, leaning back with a smile. And Pen thought fleetingly that she could feel herself falling a little more for him.

Daniela began to leave, but Pen leaned forward and caught her wrist. "Daniela? Something's been bothering me."

"What?"

"When Neil and I got to the tower, there were all these pillows. It looked a bit . . . romantic. Was that you?"

Daniela shook her head. "Wasn't me. Maybe your little ghost friend realized you were destined or some romantic bullshit like that."

"You're a romantic too!" Laszlo called.

Cursing, Daniela disappeared around the corner.

"So, do you think it was Georgina?" Neil asked.

"Difficult to say, but I wouldn't put it past her."

Chuckling, Neil helped Pen stand, slipping an arm around her waist.

"Can you believe Daniela and I hooked up once?" Pen asked, not looking at him, scared of what she'd find there.

"Well, that explains what she said this morning." He made a face.

Pen chortled. "What? Is she out of my league?"

Neil nodded solemnly and she punched him. Laughing, he said, "The opposite. You're out of her league." He paused, huffing. "You're heavier than I remember."

She shot him a glare. "Maybe you're not as strong as you thought you were."

"Already back to fighting, are we?"

"Not fighting, bickering."

"There's a difference?" he asked, tone flat.

"Yes, there's a difference. Fighting is intentionally disagreeing, and bickering is much more playful."

"If you say so."

"I do," she affirmed with a nod.

Pen's eyes dragged along the portrait of Georgina as they passed it. The black dress, the thick lashes, the watchful eyes. She found it difficult to believe what they'd gone through to get here, even more difficult to understand the hardships that Georgina and Archie had pulled through. Love rejected by her father, pregnancy and secret marriage, war, death, and loss. So much loss.

"It's okay to be sad," Neil said as he helped her sit at the top of the stairs. "It's not exactly a happy ending to a happy love story."

Pen watched him quietly. She wondered why it felt so easy with him, why, after so many years of hating him, it had turned into something else in a matter of days. With a chuckle, she recalled the day at the castle ruins, how they were annoyed and huffy, both trying so desperately to find inspiration among the stones.

"What?" Neil asked, tilting his head.

Pen stood and leaned against the banister, looking out over the foyer. "I wonder if the only reason I ever hated you was because I didn't think I was enough. By tearing you down, it made me feel . . ." She trailed off, struggling to find the right word.

"Stronger?"

She nodded. "It's silly, isn't it, that tearing down another Native author made me feel whole?"

"No, not that surprising. By limiting the number of Native books being published, we've been pitted against each other since the beginning."

"Fuck the colonizers."

"Fuck the colonizers," he echoed.

Neil leaned against the railing beside her, arms slung out before him, the quill tattoo peeking out from beneath his sleeve. His eyes followed hers, the corners of his lips lifting.

"When did you get that?" Pen asked.

He sighed and pushed up his sleeve, turning his forearm toward her. "Do you remember that moment in *The Lies They Told Us* when Winter used her grandfather's quill to carve the phrase 'I will speak only truth' into her arm?"

"I mean, of course I do, I wrote the damn thing."

"Well, it stuck with me so much I got this tattoo." He smiled down at it. "I reached out to the cover artist for *The Lies They Told Us* and got permission to get it inked."

Pen opened her mouth and closed it. She didn't know what to say. A man she'd reportedly hated for years had liked her book, hell, a *single moment* in her book enough to get it tattooed on his arm. She traced the quill, understanding more than ever why she'd always felt so drawn to it.

"I can't believe I never noticed," she said. She sniffed, blinking away tears.

"I should have told you what your book meant to me," he said, leaning forward to catch her tears. "I've read it so many times, just wishing I had as much talent and courage as you. And I was such an asshole to you. I shouldn't have fought with you like that, and I should have stood up for you after."

"God, you really were an asshole," she agreed, laughing.

Eyes crinkling at the corners, he kissed her slowly, lips lingering before he pulled away and disappeared down the hall. She sat and waited on the stairs as Neil grabbed their bags, packing away their meager belongings. She stopped in the foyer on their way out, squinting up at the portrait.

"There's one last thing I need to grab," she said, shuffling toward the study.

"What are you grabbing?" Neil called.

"You'll see!" she called over her shoulder, limping around the corner to the study. She paused in the entryway, her eyes trailing over the study. So many things had changed because of this room. She and Neil had opened that liquor cabinet together. They had played truth or dare. She'd learned about his family and the sweat lodge he'd grown up with because of that fireplace.

And the journal had brought them together.

"I'll always be grateful for you," she whispered, patting the wall fondly.

Pen crossed the room, careful to keep her weight off her ankle. She stopped beside the desk in the back corner where Neil had placed the journal and letters, and Pen gathered them into a pile, her hands skimming over a love story for the ages. She wanted to tell Georgina and Archie's story; she'd never wanted anything more in the world. She scanned the desk until she found the red journal, and she stacked the letters atop it, turning to go.

"It's okay. Ye can take it," Fanny said.

Pen jumped in surprise, pressing the journal and letters to her chest. Fanny was seated at the windows, tucked in with the curtains, the incoming light casting a bluish tint over the woman. Pen hadn't seen the groundskeeper when she'd come in.

Clearing her throat, Pen said, "When you gave us the tour and said you hadn't seen the woman in black, you meant that you'd seen the woman in white, right? Have you always seen the ghosts?"

Fanny tapped the glass on the window, expression wistful as she glanced out across the snowy grounds.

"I've been seeing the ghosts in this castle since I was a wee one and my father was the groundskeeper. I dinnae ken who they were, had always feared them too much to spend any length of time here, and my father always warned me nay to stay past sunset. That's why it's falling apart. This castle has been falling apart because of my and my father's fear." She smiled sadly, meeting Pen's gaze. "I wish I had taken the time to ken who they were and why they were still here. I wish I'd been less of a coward. Ye taught me that."

Pen blushed, tightening her hold on the journal. "Well, you have nothing to fear now. They're gone." *I think.*

Fanny stood and motioned to the journal and letters. "Yer friend told me yer a bunch of writers. Will ye be telling her story, then?"

"If you'll allow me to."

"Aye. I cannae imagine anyone more deserving."

Pen didn't know how to respond, so she nodded her thanks before limping out of the study and back toward the foyer.

Neil raised a brow as she rounded the corner. "Are you allowed to take those?"

"Yes, I have Fanny's permission."

He grunted, and Pen touched his cheek, warmth blooming in her chest as he looked down at her.

"In the last five years," she started, "I've never felt this way about a story. Maybe because it feels like I'm telling a story that was meant to be told. Maybe it's because it'll practically write itself for me, but I feel . . ." She trailed off, shrugging. "I feel at home."

He smiled, the expression not quite reaching his eyes. "That's really great, Penelope."

"So, tell me one thing," she said slowly. "Tell me why you love to write."

Neil frowned at her, scratching his chin. "I feel like I was born to tell stories, that if I don't, I'll lose a part of myself." He paused, searching her face.

"Go on," she urged, hands tightening around the journal and letters.

"There are stories I want to tell, a writer I want to be, but I'm worried that I still haven't found my story, not like you."

"Neil Storm, are you jealous?"

"No? Yes," he conceded with a sigh. "Georgina and Archie's story is . . . it's everything someone could want. It has all the elements of a wonderful book."

"You know, we did figure this all out together, and there are two sides to the story," she said, taking a step closer.

"And?"

"I need an Archie to my Georgina." Pen held out the journal and the letters, taking another step closer to Neil. "I would never ask anyone else. I don't trust anyone else, but I do trust you. Neil Storm, will you write a book with me?"

Excerpt from *The Lies They Told Us* by Penelope Skinner

The house was moving, writhing, and reaching for me. It had always been a living, breathing thing, but it was showing its true colors now, and I had nowhere to run. Once, I might have called this place home, but it had shackled me to its heart, and I had no key.

Tricked, I'd been tricked.

I could hear them rippling down the hallway toward me as I fought through the fog of my mind. Soft footsteps, the clink of airy, inhuman laughter wrapping around me, yanking me back. I struggled, swaying as sweat beaded my brow.

"Where are you going, Winter?"

There he was, coalescing from the darkness. He stood at a wrong angle, his dark eyes growing blacker by the second, ink-stained pupils tracking my movements. I felt the scrape of his glower over my skin like fresh wounds, and the more I tried to back away, the more I felt the house holding me in place.

I tore at the rope, the friction digging into my ankles as I screamed. I needed to get free. I needed to stop him. Crying out, I kicked against him, but he did not mind. He did not budge. He stood his ground, solid and much too real.

He bent before me, lifting my chin and forcing my gaze.

"You were always mine, Winter."

But he was wrong. I had always been my own person. This house that was left to me. The things that haunted its walls did not define me, just as I did not define it. My hands scrabbled hastily over the floor until my fingers brushed the feather of my grandfather's quill.

It heated in my hand, the metal burning me and searing my skin as I angled my hand and pressed the tip of it into my skin.

The razor-sharp edge bit into me.

"What are you doing?" he demanded.

"What I should have done long ago," I spat.

I pressed down hard, clamping my lips tight together against a scream as the point sliced even farther, white-hot pain sending a fresh volley of tears down my cheeks as I wrote "I will speak only truth" into my own skin.

Despite everything my grandfather did to prepare me for this moment, I was only ever here because it had been a gift. That night, I had been handed the key to this haunted place like God herself had gifted me entry to heaven. As I swooped the last of the H, slicing the quill through my skin with finesse, I glanced up at him with a sharp smile.

"I hope you had a plan B."

Epilogue

NEIL

FIFTEEN MONTHS LATER

It took everything in Neil to drag his pants on. His gaze traveled over the room and past Penelope's cat, Apawllo, curled at the edge of the bed to *her*. Nearby, Penelope sashayed into a tight blue dress. Its fabric clung perfectly to her curves as she struggled for the zipper, reaching awkwardly around her.

"Could you?" she asked, glancing at him over her shoulder.

Smiling, Neil crossed the room. His fingers danced over her back, trailing down her shoulder, over her bra, and to the zipper.

"No funny business," she ordered.

Neil bent to press a kiss to her spine, and she shivered under his touch.

"It's not funny business," he said against her shoulder.

He spun her toward him as one of his hands tangled in her hair, tugging her close. Her palms pressed against his chest, her nails digging in as she stood in her heels and kissed him.

He moaned into her mouth and she shoved him toward the bed, making the cat leap off and disappear down the hall. Penelope climbed into his lap, heels and all, her dress inching up her thighs. Neil bunched the fabric in his hands, his fingers dragging closer to the warm space between her legs.

"This color reminds me of the dress you wore to the Shelly Awards."

"We're going to be late," she said as he bent to nibble at her neck.

"I don't want to go," he grunted as his fingers toyed with her lacy underwear.

Penelope moaned as he rubbed a finger along her clit. Fuck, she was already so wet. Had she already been turned on?

"It's not fair," she whimpered, hands tangling in what was left of his curls. She tugged his mouth back up to her and kissed him hard, her tongue parting his lips. Penelope tasted like summer wine and afternoons in the sun, and he groaned against her, rocking his hips. She slid along him, the friction making them both moan.

She made him come undone.

"Neil." Still, she didn't get up or stop, one hand scraping against his scalp, the other reaching down to pull her dress above her hips.

Smiling against her lips, Neil slipped one finger in and hooked it just the way she liked. She rode his hand, gasping as he slid in a second finger, her walls tightening around him. His thumb rubbed small, tight circles over her clit, and though she opened her mouth as though to chastise him, the words died on her tongue.

"*Ohmyfuckinggod,*" she gasped, wrapping her arms around his neck and clamping her teeth down just below his ear.

"I could stop . . ." He trailed off, pulling one finger out of her.

One of her hands reached down and tightened on his wrist, stopping him. "*Don't you fucking dare.*"

Her hands scrambled for his pants as he laughed, working his fingers in and out as she struggled to focus. Slipping aside her underwear, she positioned his hard length against her opening.

"Let me grab a condom," he gasped, eyes squeezing shut as she gripped him tighter, the tip nudging and sliding against her. "*Fuck,*" he groaned, hands clamping on her ass.

"You better hurry up," she rasped.

Neil reluctantly lifted her off his lap and scrambled for a condom, ripping the foil and rolling it on. Penelope was there in an instant, straddling his lap and guiding him. She always took him slowly, one inch at a time, but today she took all of him with a gasp.

He closed his eyes, picturing old dogs, abandoned dark halls, *anything* to make him last as she rocked her hips slowly. She gripped him, her insides squeezing tight as her nails raked across his skin and her lips parted.

"What did I ever do to deserve you?" he asked, kissing her jaw. God, she felt *so good*.

"Good . . . question." Penelope bit down on her lip and moaned, arching her back as he reached up with one hand to grip her hip, the other slipping into the space between them.

He moved faster, lying back on the bed and thrusting into her as they sped up as one, hips meeting, hands scrabbling at one another. It only lasted a moment longer, both already so close to the edge. He finished with a grunt, followed by a sigh. Her eyes flitted open with disappointment, but he held up a finger as he came back to himself before he pulled out and knelt at the edge of the bed.

Humming, he bent between her, his knees weak beneath him as he tasted her, the combination of his fingers and tongue tugging her over the cliff and into the chasm. She'd shown him, dragging him to each spot over the last year until he knew her body inside and out, and even still, he found it no less attractive when she adjusted his fingers, positioning him just right.

When she was done, she kissed the corner of his mouth, lingering as her body settled and her legs clamped together. "I love you."

His breath hitched as he whispered, "I love you too."

It had taken them nearly a year to say the words, and he was no more used to them now than he was a month ago. She shivered as she pulled off her underwear and tossed it aside, disappearing into the ensuite.

"You'd think we would've had enough of each other," she said breathily.

"Never."

He watched lazily as Penelope pulled on a fresh pair of plain cotton underwear before brushing her hair and pinning it back. Her phone buzzed and she glanced down at it.

"*Shit.* Neil, we're going to be late."

She threw on her jacket and grabbed her bag, motioning to him.

Neil groaned as he tugged his pants back on and buttoned up his shirt, his fingers stumbling in their haste. "I don't see why this is necessary, Penelope."

Penelope laughed as she shoved him out the door toward the bookstore a few blocks down. She responded to a DM on one of her socials before closing the app and pocketing her phone, grinning.

"Come on," she drawled, "you wrote a blurb, and Daniela dedicated this book to us. It's kind of expected that we'd come."

Neil muttered to himself as she pulled him into the bookstore. Penelope had only moved to New York six months earlier with her grumpy cat Apawllo, but already she knew the city better than he. After nine months of traveling coast to coast to see each other, she'd taken the plunge, ever the courageous one, and moved into his apartment.

The upper story of the store had been cleared for lines of black plastic chairs, and two microphones stood before two stools at the front.

"Are you sure we can't stay for a few minutes and leave?" Neil whispered as Penelope practically dragged him to the front.

"It's an early reading," she said, maneuvering them through the throng of attendees. "We don't even have proofs yet."

Neil's left eye twitched. He'd rather be anywhere but here.

Daniela had known exactly how to manipulate him. And he'd blurbed, *oh*, he'd blurbed. She'd personally sent over an early manuscript, and he'd read it. Worse, it was good. Neil had even found himself enjoying it, not that he'd ever admit as much to her face.

Zoe waved to them from the front, motioning to two chairs to her right. Neil was thankful to have met her in person. Their first meeting via Daniela's webcam had been embarrassing enough.

"You made it!" she exclaimed, hugging Penelope.

"Wouldn't miss it for the world," Penelope said, pulling off her jacket.

Neil met Zoe's warm amber eyes. Her curls haloed her heart-shaped face, her dark, glowing skin catching the warm, dim lights overhead as she rolled up the sleeves of her sweater.

"Neil," she said with a nod. She surveyed them, eyes narrowing. If she suspected they were late because they'd had incredible sex before heading over, she said nothing.

"Zoe." He nodded in turn before sitting on the other side of Penelope.

"Isn't it a bit unusual to do a public reading before it's published?" Penelope asked, leaning toward Zoe. "I thought it was several months out, still."

Zoe laughed. "I told her as much, but you know Daniela. She likes to make a show of it. She said she wanted to try something new, get people whispering about it." Zoe shook her head. "I guess we'll see if it gets people talking before it's published."

This is ridiculous, Neil thought.

Penelope and Zoe spoke quietly. The chairs filled quickly, the narrow space packed to the brim. Neil knew Daniela was a popular author. She was charismatic and likable, but damn if she didn't know just how to get on his nerves.

Grumbling to himself, he pulled out his phone, scanning over the email with copy edits for *On the Backs of My Ancestors*. Tabitha had nearly murdered him for asking to yank it from publication and do a massive rewrite, but after some coaxing, he and his editor had sat down and talked through the edits, agreeing in the end that his original vision for the story was far better than the one that had nearly been printed.

"No Laszlo?" Penelope was asking.

Neil pocketed his phone and leaned back, wrapping an arm around Penelope's chair. Zoe sighed. "No, Laszlo is off in Budapest, looking for inspiration."

Penelope snorted. "You'd think a haunted castle would be enough for him."

"Certainly was for us," Neil said with a look.

"How is the editing going?" Zoe asked.

"Good," he said with a nod. "Better than we could have imagined."

Zoe stared at them blankly. "The truth."

Neil and Penelope shared a look.

"He's a perfectionist," she admitted.

"And she's a pantser, so that explains itself."

"It's adorable, you know," Zoe drawled. "You're the sweethearts of the book world, right now."

"I know," Neil fumed.

Penelope laughed, her hand going to his knee. The touch was comforting, calming the annoyance roiling in him.

"He's a little touchy about it," Penelope said.

He was right to be. Daniela hadn't stopped posting about the retreat when they'd returned to the real world. She'd shared a string of photos and videos of them over social media while they were in Edinburgh before roping them into visiting a few stores for some last-minute signings.

Although Neil was grateful Penelope had been welcomed back into the book world after Daniela had announced they'd inspired her next book, he would never hear the end of it.

Penelope leaned toward Neil as if to say something, but Zoe tapped her hand.

"Hey," Zoe started, "I keep forgetting to ask. Did you ever find out if you're related to the owners of the castle? Daniela told me so much about the trip, but she never did mention if you'd found out."

Penelope caught Neil's eye, something passing silently between them.

"Unfortunately, I don't think I'll ever know for sure. I'm assuming not, but you never know."

The lights dimmed, and with a sigh, Penelope swiveled to the front. "You know," she whispered, leaning in toward Neil, "you could be happy for me. Because of Daniela, I've been welcomed back with open arms after everything that happened."

"You could have done it on your own. Besides, they could leave me out of it," he said as a bookseller took up a microphone.

"That's difficult considering you are one half of the equation."

Neil opened his mouth to respond, but already Daniela had taken her seat and began to speak. "Thank you so much for having me," she said into the mic. "I am so honored to be here, and to give you an early sneak peek of my romance debut, *Fight You*."

It's a ridiculous name, Neil thought.

"I found inspiration for this novel from two friends on a writing retreat." Her eyes met Neil's, a smirk curling at her lips.

Oh no.

"After seeing them struggle to come to terms with their feelings, I felt it best to rewrite their story a bit, to tell it the way it was meant to go."

Neil covered his face. He wouldn't make it through.

"I think we all want to hear it," the bookseller urged her.

Neil peeked through his fingers as Daniela's gaze locked on his. She lifted a bound manuscript, cleared her throat, and began.

Acknowledgments

First of all, I just want to thank past me for dropping out of grad school. If you hadn't done that, poor lost twenty-four-year-old me, I wouldn't have come back to writing.

Thank you to my agent, Rebecca Podos. Becca, your vision, your love of these characters and this book, and your absolute belief in me are just astounding. THANK YOU.

To my editor, Vicki Lame. Your enthusiasm for my book and my stories is still unbelievable. It is an honor to work with you. To Vanessa Aguirre, for being an amazing assistant editor and answering my many many emails, thank you!

Thank you to my team at St. Martin's Press (Anne Marie Tallberg, Chrisinda Lynch, Susannah Noel, Janna Dokos, Michelle Li, Omar Chapa, Erica Martirano, Brant Janeway, Kejana Ayala, Alyssa Gammello, and Hannah Tarro) for all the work, for supporting this book and believing in it!

Big thank-you to Senior Art Director Kerri Resnick for all her work, and Jenifer Prince for illustrating the purple cover of my dreams!!! I seriously cannot get over how absolutely rich and vibrant and spooky and hot it is!!!!! IT'S PERFECT.

Magic Discord. I started our group in August of 2022, and I truly don't know where I'd be without all of y'all. Thank you especially to Jordan, DeAndra, Faith, Bella, Irene, Yuva, and

Kayla for being there every step of the way. I love all of you so much!

Of course, to Audrey, my nerdy critique partner and friend who dove into my DMs on that random day on Twitter and said we were now friends. Sometimes, I truly do wonder if we're the same person. Thank you for taking the initiative and being willing to read all of my weird little books! Cheers, Co-Captain!

Jamie Pacton and Rachel Lynn Solomon, who looked over my query package, and Jamie, who walked me through what to ask on my agent call, thank you. And all of the wonderful authors I've met online or in person over the years who gave me advice somewhere along the way! Especially Rosiee Thor, Alex Brown, Shelly Page, Helena Greer, Rachel Griffin, Alicia Thompson, Rachel Runya Katz, Emily Thiede, and all the other wonderful authors who supported me, helped me, and answered my many many questions.

2024 Debuts, particularly the friends I made through the romance channel, you were such a huge support, and some of you I am lucky enough to call friends! We had a heck of an *interesting* debut experience, but I made some truly magnificent friends because of it!

Thank you to my parents for encouraging my intense love of reading when I was younger, for buying me my first laptop for my sixteenth birthday so I could write my own stories, and for believing in me even when I dropped out of grad school and told everyone I had no fucking clue what I was going to do with my life. And to my brother, who congratulated me and listened to my rants at every step along the way and read all the weird books I sent to him.

To Mrs. Long, my high school English and creative writing teacher who advocated for me every step along the way, who made her classroom a safe space and encouraged my weird writing. And who challenged me to try writing romance—and look at me now!

To all the people who thought I wouldn't get far, thank you for fueling my perseverance with just a taste of spite.

To Colby Dockery, who I sent the pitch for IISHY to back in October of 2021 and asked what you thought. Your screeching in my DMs during this whole process has always made my day a little brighter. I'm so glad you followed me when V shared that (admittedly) embarrassing story of me sobbing after reading an ARC of *The Invisible Life of Addie LaRue*.

To you, reader, and to all the booksellers and librarians and every person who picked this up and recommended it, a massive thank-you. Bookstagram and all the wonderful people I've met while I was a bookstagrammer, I wouldn't be here without your massive love and support! And the lovely group who joined my street team, I can't begin to describe how thankful I am to have you rooting for me and these little weirdos!

To my two cats, Kaylee and Rey. Thank you for managing me, making sure I did my work, watching me creepily from the corners, and taking over both my desk and chair on several occasions. If there are any typos in my book, let's just go ahead and blame it on them. If I forgot anyone in these acknowledgments, let's just blame it on them, too.

And finally, to my partner, Alexander. When we met over nine years ago, I don't think I ever imagined what our life would become. Thank you for believing in me and my abilities, for supporting me, for helping me reach my dreams and seeing the world with me. I genuinely could not have done this without you.

About the Author

Colby Wilkens

Colby Wilkens is a queer white and Choctaw-Cherokee author with a heart for adventure. When she's not traveling, she can be found in the Pacific Northwest on unceded traditional land of the Coast Salish Peoples with her partner, two cats, and a vast collection of books and candles.